Winner Takes All

◉

Other books by Christopher Pierce

Author
Rogue:Slave (Rogue Sequence 1)
Rogue:Hunted (Rogue Sequence 2)
*Kidnapped by a Sex Maniac:
The Erotic Fiction of Christopher Pierce*
(all Starbooks Press)

Editor
I Like to Watch: Gay Erotic Stories (Cleis Press)
Biker Boys: Gay Erotic Stories (Cleis)
*Men at Noon, Monsters at Midnight:
Erotic Stories of Shapeshifters, Demon Lovers and
Creatures of the Night* (Starbooks Press)
SexTime: Erotic Stories of Time Travel (Starbooks)
*Taken by Force: Erotic Stories of Abduction
and Captivity* (Starbooks)
Men on the Edge: Dangerous Erotica (Starbooks)

Winner Takes All

Master/slave fantasies by
Christopher Pierce

Perfectbound Press
New York City

Winner Takes All is erotic fantasy not intended as a guide to real-life Master/slave relationships. In real life, please use caution, discretion, and safer-sex protection. All of the stories are fictional, and any resemblance to real persons or events is purely coincidental. The words "boy" and "kid" do not indicate minors; all characters are at least 18 years of age.

All text copyright © 2011 by Christopher Pierce except "Foreword" © 2011 by M. Christian and "Editor's Note" © 2011 by David Stein; cover illustrations © 2011 by Thom Magister; all rights reserved. No part of this publication may be reproduced, stored in a retrieval system, or transmitted in any form or by any means — electronic, mechanical, photocopying, recording, or otherwise — without the prior written permission of the copyright holder or publisher, except for brief quotations used in a review.

Cover design by Thom Magister, interior design by David Stein.
Winner Takes All is set in ITC Stone Serif, ITC Stone Sans, and Gill Sans.

Earlier versions of all stories except "Winner Takes All," Parts 4 and 5, appeared as follows: "Collared at the Dogpound" in *Eagle* magazine, Sept.–Oct. 1996; "The Executioner's Boy" (as "Dungeon Dickmeat" in two parts), *Manscape* magazine, Dec. 1995, Jan. 1996; "First-Time Slave" in *The Care and Training of the Male Slave V* (Jan. 1997); "Five Bucks a Swat" in *Naughty Spanking Stories from A to Z, Vol. II*, ed. Rachel Kramer Bussel (Pretty Things Press, Oct. 2006) and *Slave to Love*, ed. Alison Tyler (Cleis Press, Mar. 2006); "Fucked by a Stranger" (as "Slave for a Stranger") in *Honcho* magazine, Jan. 2002; "Fucking Master's Lover" in *Power Play* magazine, Dec. 1997; "Goodnight, My Slaveboys" in *Honcho*, Feb. 2002, and *Friction 6*, ed. Jesse Grant and Austin Foxxe (Alyson, Feb. 2003); "Hard Day's Reward" in *The Care and Training of the Male Slave VII* (1998); "Home-Made Lube" in *Honcho*, Dec. 2001; "The Horny Houseguest" (as "DogBoy Chews Stranger's Meat") in *Bound & Gagged* magazine, Jan. 2002, and *Friction 6*; "Isle of Chains" (as "Isle of Bondage") in *Manscape*, Jan. 1995; "Master's New Toy" in *Eagle*, Nov.–Dec. 1996; "The Piss Mummy" in *International Leatherman* magazine, Feb. 1999; "Scent Slave" in *The Care and Training of the Male Slave V* (Jan. 1997); "Two-Slaveboy Wrap-Up" (as "Slaveboy Wrap-Up") in *Bound & Gagged Online* (Apr. 2002) and *Ultimate Gay Erotica 2005*, ed. Jesse Grant (Alyson, Dec. 2004); "Sold to the Highest Bidder" in *Cuir* magazine, Jun. 1994, and *Rough Trade*, ed. Todd Gregory (Bold Strokes Books, Aug. 2009); "Winner Takes All," Parts 1 to 3 (as "Won for the Weekend") in *Eagle*, Jan.–Feb., May–Jun., and Nov.–Dec. 1997.

ISBN 978-0-9823693-3-3
LCCN 2011910484

Published by Perfectbound Press, New York, NY.
www.perfectboundpress.com

First edition, July 2011
Version 1.0
Printed in the U.S.A.

*This book is for
all the Masters who trained me,
all the slaveboys who served me, and
Master Matt, as is everything.*

Foreword
Talkin' 'bout Power

LET'S TALK ABOUT POWER. While it comes in various flavors, only two kinds matter here. The power component in erotic "power exchange" is the first.

Power exchange is, in many ways, the ultimate sex — because it is more than sex. Sure, sex can be good, grand, special, earth-shattering, and more, but when it involves literally exchanging power it can move into a whole new realm where "good" can become staggering, "grand" transforms into ecstasy, "special" evolves into life-changing, and "earth-shattering" develops into . . . well, something even more earth-shattering.

That's because power exchange is about *control*: When you exchange power with your partner, you give up control of what happens to you. You can become property, an object, a toy to be used, if only for a while. And when you accept that kind of power in a relationship, you become the Master, able to control your partner in any way you desire and to keep him in line by dishing out whatever devious punishments your mind conceives.

But you already know that, don't you? You know that kind of power — the kind you feel when your eyes meet those of an adoring slave and your body responds with a deep bass chord of desire to use, to control, to dominate, or when the touch of your Master's hand feels like you're tongue-kissing an electrical socket.

Rest assured, then, that in buying *Winner Takes All* you have chosen wisely. Which leads me to the second kind of power I want to talk about, the power of words — the power of writing, of language, of storytelling. That's the power Christopher Pierce wields here.

Writing about power exchange is one thing — believe

me, I know — but to do it the way Chris does it is a rare, beautiful, magnificent thing. In these pages you'll find lots of sex between Masters with firm hands and slaves with firm other parts, but there is also more — a "more" that takes these stories to a whole new level of beautiful language, touching characterization, poignant plotting, and a full-bodied eroticism that will bring a heart-beating roar of desire to even the most jaded porn addict.

Pick a story — any story — here, and you'll see what I mean. Chris doesn't just know how to write, as the incredible fluidity of his prose proves; and he doesn't just know how to tell a great story, as the breath you take at the end will demonstrate; and he doesn't just know how to create living characters, as the way his people walk off the page and into our minds and fantasies reveals. More important than all of these, he understands the essence of sex — and its transcendent potential when one surrenders and the other takes control in a real power exchange.

I'm sure you'll do as I did when I finished reading the collection: after the sigh of satisfaction, after the grin of admiration, after the moan of pleasure, you'll put the book down and give the author a round of applause for showing us the nature of both power exchange and, especially, the written word.

— *M. Christian*, author, editor, and bon vivant

Editor's Note
Value-Added Porn

PORNOGRAPHY of the written variety comprises stories whose sole, or at least main, purpose is to help you, the reader, get off — that is, have an orgasm — by stimulating your libido through your imagination. And there's nothing wrong with that, however much some folks insist there is.

Granted, most porn is formulaic and poorly written, but there's no reason it can't be as inventive, engaging, and well written as more respectable literature — or, rather, no reason except the genre's reviled and ill-paid status. (Yes, "ill-paid": no porn *writer* ever got rich from his work, only porn publishers and the producers of visual porn.) There's simply no external incentive for porn writers to labor over their work, making the characters more complex and engaging, the plots and settings more believable, nor is there much incentive for editors and publishers to demand this or to help writers achieve it.

Yet some do it anyway, and that's when we talk about "erotica" rather than mere porn. To my mind, there's no sharp distinction; erotica is simply porn-plus, porn that has more on its mind than provoking an orgasm. (Note: "more," but not less! Erotica that doesn't at least get you hot and bothered is sailing under a false flag.) The writer may wish to make you think as well as feel, or to feel more deeply, or to feel other emotions besides lust and its satisfaction. Or the author may be so personally engaged in the sexual fetish or fantasy the story explores that he or she can't leave it alone, rewriting and polishing the words until they give off the light of unquestionable truth.

The stories in *Winner Takes All* were written and, except for part of the title story, previously published as porn.

No one, including the author, expected more from them than to help the reader get off. And yet, because the theme of male-male erotic slavery is so close to the author's heart, each contained something more.

Readers treasured these stories, revisiting them over and over in dog-eared magazines and book collections, wondering whether reality could ever resemble the sexy fantasies told so convincingly by Christopher Pierce. And because I'm one of those devoted readers, I wanted to make these Master/slave fantasies available to a new generation of gay men and others who would appreciate them. Moreover, I encouraged Chris to take the time and make the effort to pull these tales up to the next level.

Every story here has been extensively revised — not to make it any less arousing, but to make it more than *just* arousing. They are still fantasies, full of perfect bodies and idealized action, not slices of life, though only a few contain outright magical, supernatural, or other-worldly elements. These "fantastic" tales, however, include some of the most powerful in the collection: "The Executioner's Boy," set in medieval times; "Isle of Chains," set on another world; and "Scent Slave," which gives a scientific twist to sex magic.

Other highlights include "Collared at the Dog Pound," the ultimate lost-pup-finds-a-Master story; "Hard Day's Reward" and "Fucking Master's Lover," which remind us that slaves can also be fearsome dominants; and the amazing title piece, the five-part novella "Winner Takes All," a saga of bonding through pain and respect. Hell, I love all these stories, or they wouldn't be here!

Welcome to the world of Christopher Pierce, where men are Men and boys are toys! While it would be foolish to take these stories as depictions of how consensual slavery among men actually works, they *can* raise questions that will help you explore real-life issues. Besides aiding our arousal (whose value should never be discounted), can we ask erotic fiction to do more than that?

— *David Stein*, publisher and editor

Acknowledgements

HEARTFELT THANKS to my editor, David Stein, whose technical skill and emotional generosity helped my stories achieve effects they had only aspired to in their previous versions.

SPECIAL THANKS as well to Thom Magister for his stunning cover images; to my friends and greatest fans, Bob, Daniel, and Tom; to my friends in Los Angeles, Gregg, Bruce, Chris & Mark, Tim, and Master Vincent; and to my friends in Florida, Mina and Raziel.

EXTRA-SPECIAL THANKS to all the magazine editors who took a chance on a new and untested writer and published these stories in their first incarnations; to Guy Baldwin, who told me what my next step should be; and to Jordan, who started this whole thing by putting handcuffs on me back in 1992. — *Christopher Pierce*

Table of Contents

Collared at the Dog Pound | **15**
Hard Day's Reward | **31**
Goodnight, My Slaveboys | **47**
First-Time Slave | **55**
The Piss Mummy | **69**
Five Bucks a Swat | **77**
The Executioner's Boy | **85**
Fucking Master's Lover | **115**
Home-Made Lube | **123**
The Horny Houseguest | **129**
Isle of Chains | **143**
Fucked by a Stranger | **163**
Two-Slaveboy Wrap-Up | **169**
Sold to the Highest Bidder | **175**
Master's New Toy | **187**
Scent Slave | **203**
Winner Takes All | **215**
About the Author | **291**

Collared at the Dog Pound

I DIDN'T EXPECT to be claimed and collared by a Master that night, but I was. I certainly didn't expect to get pumped full of cum and piss in a back room, but that's exactly what happened. And I *never* thought I'd be carried out of a bar by the hottest man there, but I was that night.

Everyone knows lots of boys are collared and claimed at The Dog Pound, our city's most popular leather bar. I just never thought I'd be lucky enough to have it happen to me. The Dog Pound is always packed full of the hottest men you could ask for. Every night you can feast your eyes on an incredible assortment of male flesh.

That night the place was bursting at the seams with enough sights, smells, and tastes to enrich my dreams for months at a time. Thick clouds of tobacco smoke, laced with the odors of beer and sweat. Shiny black boots that made me want to drop to my knees and worship them right then and there. Muscles stretching the fabric of T-shirts till they ripped. Crotches plump and full, the delicious hardness beneath enough to drive me mad with desire. And everywhere, everywhere was leather: leather chaps revealing perfect round ass cheeks; leather vests with stains so dark you wonder if they're sweat, cum, or blood; leather collars encircling the necks of lucky slaves already claimed as property.

I went to The Dog Pound fairly often, always thrilling to the sight of Masters choosing boys to claim and keep. Lots of men just came to The Dog Pound to cruise and soak up the atmosphere. But the real crowd, the crowd the place was famous for, was the hard-core leather Master/slave crowd. These were men who took the life seriously, who saw leather as a state of mind, not just something to wear on Saturday nights.

I could always tell a hard-core Master from the dress-ups. It was hard to explain, but it was like an attitude, a way of carrying himself, that tipped me off. It was in the way a biker cap was tilted back on a head, the way a pair of eyes smoked when they saw a choice piece of meat, the way a hand thoughtfully stroked a mustache or goatee. Whatever it was, it kept me up night after night, dreaming and hoping and longing for a day when I would be ready to be claimed by a real man and taken home as his property.

The boys who thought they were hot enough to be claimed were also easy to tell from the others. An unwritten law decreed that boys who wanted to be claimed wore plain black armbands on their right arms to signal to the Masters that they thought they made the grade. Whether they did or not, of course, was up to the Masters.

That was the terrifying part. I had seen many boys who thought they were ready for real slavery humiliated in front of the entire crowd, scorned and spat upon and sent home alone when they were found unsuitable. As much as I wanted to be owned, the fear of being disgraced like that was even more powerful. Boys deemed unworthy never showed their butts or faces in the Dog Pound again.

The nightly drama went on and on, as savage and primitive in its own way as the spectacles of the ancient Greeks and Romans. There was something mystical and powerful in it, like an age-old rite enacted over and over again.

The Masters searched and hunted, their focus of attention always the same: the corner of the room designated for those who wanted to be claimed. There, under a sign that read "LOST DOGS," the boys stood. Some were frightened, others proud and arrogant. Sometimes they were as far away from each other as they could be, other times huddled together like the pack of scared puppies they were. Other, braver boys preened and strutted in front of the Masters like wild birds showing off exotic plumage, each one's mind burning with the desire to catch a Master's fancy and be taken to the back room of the bar.

That was where the Masters determined if boys were truly ready or not. That was where the testing happened. Few men knew for sure what was back there, and I didn't know what to believe. There were rumors that the room was a horrific dungeon filled with devices of unspeakable torture. Fear of the testing kept many boys from even entering the Lost Dogs corner.

What actually happened was not discussed. No boy who had ever gone through testing would talk about it, and the Masters were distant and unapproachable. Whatever it was that went on in the shadowy dark of the back room at The Dog Pound, it was a private thing.

The results, though, were very public. Boys who failed the testing were considered lower than dog shit. To present yourself as ready when you were not was the worst crime a boy at The Dog Pound could commit, and anyone who did that was never allowed to enter the back room again. Many of these either gave up the quest altogether or tried different bars.

The few boys who passed were the envy of all the others. Pleasing a Master and being claimed by him was the goal of every one of them, but there was some secret to the testing that most boys failed to grasp.

The ultimate dream, of course, beyond being claimed, was to have your new Master buy something for you at the tiny store in a corner of the bar. It sold everything a Master could want for his new dog: collars, leashes, dog bowls, bondage equipment . . . . The happiest boys in the world were the ones who were claimed and then taken to the store to shop. When their Masters led them out, on leashes, and headed for the exit, they were practically barking for joy. The other boys would howl and whine in sympathy, then go back to trying to find a Master of their own.

I never dreamed that I would experience any of this. Morbidly shy, I was a loner who kept to myself. I had been trained as a slave by a very wise Master, a friend of a friend. While he had been happy to give me the training, he already had a stable of slaves and couldn't keep me.

I knew I needed to be owned by a man, a real Master, but something prevented me from looking in the usual places. No computer bulletin boards or personal ads for me. It had to be in person, had to be physical. A few years before I had had the tarot cards read for me, and the reader said that, without a doubt, the man I was going to spend my life with would come to me, not the other way around.

So I kept a low profile at The Dog Pound, trying to blend in as much as possible. I hung out at the back wall, as far away from the Lost Dogs corner and the Masters perusing it as possible. Watching in silence, I thought I was invisible, telling myself that when I was ready the right man would find me. And one night he did.

"You."

Despite the raucous noise of the bar, the voice was clear as a bell, and so deep that it seemed to rumble the floorboards. I wondered who on earth was lucky enough, or unfortunate enough, to be called by that voice.

That was when the crowd parted. I couldn't believe my eyes as I watched the men in front of me back away until a corridor opened up. At one end was me. At the other was a man, unmistakably the owner of that voice.

"You," he said again, and the crowd quieted down, their eyes moving back and forth between him and me.

I stared at the man in disbelief. He was tall, over six feet. His face was strong, masculine. His body was sturdy and heavy, mostly muscle. In contrast to the elaborate costumes most of the men were wearing, he simply wore a black leather jacket, a white T-shirt, blue jeans, and work boots. His hair was brown, cut short like his beard.

Though far from the best looking of the Masters, he was definitely the most striking. Something about him demanded respect — and got it from Masters and slaves alike. And now he was talking to *me*.

Collared at the Dog Pound

Pain in my crotch snapped me out of my trance. My cock had hardened up in my snugly fitting underwear and was now painfully bent. I adjusted myself, feeling my ears turn red at the playful laughter of the crowd.

Is he really looking at me? I wondered. *Could my close-cropped blond hair, okay face, and decent body really have drawn his attention?* I knew I wasn't a troll, but I was nothing compared with the show dogs, who even now were glaring unhappily at me, thief of their spotlight, or the Lost Dogs cowering in their corner.

"You got a voice, boy?" he asked, more loudly this time. "I'm not going to say it again."

Watching unnoticed was no longer an option. Etiquette and manners slammed back into me all at once.

"Yes, Sir!" I said, bowing my head. "I'm sorry, Sir."

"That's better. Come here."

As if in a dream, I walked along the corridor between us. Keeping my eyes on the floor, I could feel a hundred eyes probing me. But I had the luxury of having no choice except obedience. My cock demanded attention, but there was no time for that. I stood before the man, my head still bowed.

"What d' they call you, boy?" he asked, more softly. Close up, his voice took on even more power, a bass rumble that seemed to enter my body and make it tremble from within.

"Billy, Sir," I said.

"I'm Kirk, but you'll call me Sir. Is that clear?"

"Sir, yes, Sir!"

"No boy calls me Master unless he earns it."

"Yes, Sir, I understand, Sir."

In his presence my cock firmed up even more, blood rushing into it as if the man's mere proximity was causing chemical changes in my body. This was without a doubt the most powerful Master I had ever seen, much less been addressed by.

"Are you presently owned by anyone, Billy?"

"Sir, no, Sir. But Sir . . ."

"Yes, boy?"

— 19 —

"Why me? There are so many hot boys in here dying to get claimed...." He interrupted me.

"I don't want a dog that would parade around in that manner. It's behavior unbecoming of a slaveboy."

"Then why come here, Sir?" I asked. "This place is famous for...." Again he cut me off.

"I know what it's famous for, boy. I come here hoping to find a boy who's right for me. A boy who's interested in serving and belonging to a man, not strutting up and down like a goddamn belle of the ball."

He looked at me hard, as if trying to decide if he had made a mistake picking me. I lowered my head even more, trying to show him I was not belligerent, just curious.

"You got a problem with that?" he asked suddenly.

"Sir, no, Sir!" I said instantly.

"Glad to hear it. Now, let's not waste any more time. You might be the dog I've been looking for, Billy. I'm interested in finding out. Are you?"

I couldn't believe my ears — but wasn't stupid enough to say so.

"Oh, yes, thank you, Sir!"

Kirk smiled and put one hand on the back of my neck. To have him actually touch me, to have him take me into his control, was intoxicating. His hand was firm and steady on my neck. I worked to keep my balance as he guided me from the brightly lit main area to the door that led to the back room, the place of testing.

The crowd murmured in approval and awe as we walked through the door and out of sight. We followed several twists and turns in the dark hallway until we came to a large empty room. The only light was from a few candles.

"Surprised, boy?" Kirk said.

"A little, Sir." Telling him anything but the truth never occurred to me.

"You were expecting a dungeon, right? A big playroom with lots of slings and cages and bondage equipment."

"I guess so, Sir."

"Are you disappointed that it's not?"

"No, Sir," I said firmly and turned to look up at him for the first time. He smiled again and my heart soared.

"Good boy," he said. "Toys and dungeons are all well and good, but if a Master can't dominate a boy without props, then he's no Master. Do you know why so few boys are claimed, Billy?"

"Why, Sir?"

"Because they expect this room to be the dungeon of their dreams, and when they're brought here, they're disappointed and show themselves unworthy."

"Unworthy, Sir?"

In the flickering light of the candles he looked eerie and magical, like a sorcerer sharing secret knowledge with an apprentice.

"Yes. Their disappointment shows that what they're after is a hot scene, not just to be an owned piece of property. They want to get worked over with lots of toys and equipment, not to serve a man however he wants to be served."

He looked at me sternly.

"They're not real slaves, Billy. They're selfish bottoms unfit to be claimed. . . . But I think you are a real slave."

"Thank you, Sir!"

"We're very much alike, Billy. Look at how we dress: in plain, functional clothes to cover our bodies and keep us warm. Look at how we act: off to the side, away from the spotlight, not drawing attention to ourselves."

"I've never seen you here before, Sir."

He laughed and said, "I've been here every night since The Dog Pound opened, boy. But few see me. I don't like a lot of attention. I only show myself if I think there's a chance I've found a real slave, which happens very rarely."

I dropped to my knees and bowed my head, my cock a jutting spike in my pants.

"Oh please, Sir, how can I prove it to you? What test can I take to show you I'm a true slave?"

I heard the clinking of his belt being unfastened and

knew that the moment of truth had come at last. It looked like it was not going to be the test that the boys whispered and wondered about. It would not be a test of endurance, to see how much torture I could take. It would be nothing so obvious and vulgar, simply a test whether I could serve and please this man well enough for him to want to claim me.

His dick came out from his jeans' fly, and it was beautiful: big, uncut, veiny, hard as a rock. I lunged forward with animal violence, taking it into my mouth like a starving man who has finally found food. It was right at home inside me, leaking precum as I stroked and caressed it with my tongue. Kirk grunted in satisfaction and put his hands on my head to anchor me in place. He started fucking my face, plunging his boner into my mouth and out again.

"Yeah, boy," he said. "You're here to be used. I'm going to use both your holes the same way . . . your mouth, your ass. They're all the same to me, just holes to fuck."

My own dick was begging for attention, and I could almost feel the stain of precum that was no doubt seeping through the crotch of my jeans. But I knew that my hands belonged behind my back, that to do anything other than what he ordered would be a monumental mistake.

Without any warning, totally unexpected, my time had come. My test was now, and I was going to do everything I could to pass.

Kirk was pounding me so hard that I almost couldn't breathe. The blood-engorged club in my mouth slammed against the back of my throat over and over again.

"That's it," he said. "Take it boy, that's what you're here for, to take my dick wherever I want to put it. You're here to serve and please me — that's what you're good for."

Bile was rising in my gut. I gagged and choked, trying to signal Kirk that I was having trouble.

"I don't care if you're going to throw up, slave. It feels good on my dick. If you throw up, you'll get down and lick it back up until the floor is nice and clean again, like it was when you came in here."

Collared at the Dog Pound

I knew there was no use trying to resist him. Once I resigned myself to letting whatever happened occur without fighting, my mind relaxed. Miraculously, my stomach calmed down and the puking feeling disappeared. I was there just to serve, to take his cock and make him feel good.

Then he pushed in as far as he could go. His boner filled my whole mouth. My nostrils flared to take in the oxygen I needed. But his hand clamped down on my nose, pinching it and cutting off all air. I was plugged up completely, and panic exploded in my brain.

"You'll breathe when I let you, boy." Kirk said.

Fear tried to get a foothold in me, but I fought it down. My hands wanted to push him away, but I controlled myself and kept them behind my back. I tried to stay calm as Kirk started counting slowly:

"One . . . two . . . three . . . four . . . five . . . six . . . seven . . . eight . . . nine . . . ten." He released me then, letting my nose go and pulling out of my mouth. I sucked in as much air as I could, gasping and panting.

"Good boy," he said. "Now get on your hands and knees like the dog you are."

Still trying to recover from the breath control, I maneuvered onto my hands and knees with my butt in the air. He knelt down behind me, his hands snaking around my waist to unfasten my pants and yank them down. He seized my underwear and ripped it off me, tearing it to shreds. My cock sprang out into the air, released at last. Its head shimmered with precum in the candlelight.

Kirk's enormous weight settled on me from behind. I didn't know how I could support him and take his cock up my ass at the same time, but I'd do it somehow. I had to pass this test no matter what!

"Do you want to be my dog, Billy?"

"Oh, yes, yes, Sir!"

His cock was nosing around my butt hole. I heard the sound of plastic and latex and knew he was sliding a condom over his big meat. He hocked up some spit and let it fall, then used to it to slime up his cock and get it ready for entry.

My muscles were tense with nervousness and excitement. I tried to relax so that it wouldn't be too painful, but it was too late. Kirk plunged his huge dick into my asshole, breaking through the sphincter ring like it was nothing. I screamed like a virgin getting his cherry popped.

"Yeah, howl like a good dog boy, howl for me..."

White-hot fire was burning my ass as I forced myself to stand still. I longed to crawl forward, to force him out of me, but I locked my arms and legs and stood my ground. How could I back out now when he seemed to be pleased with me? I didn't know how it was possible to be in such pain and such pleasure at the same time.

But there I was, on my hands and knees getting my ass plowed on the floor of The Dog Pound's back room. It was the last thing in the world I expected to happen, yet my chance had come to be claimed once and for all by a real Master — if I could prove I was a real slave. I pushed my ass backward, engulfing Kirk's cock even further inside me.

He exhaled loudly and groaned in pleasure. "Yeah, push back, dog, push your slave ass back on my big dick..."

"Yes, Sir!" I gasped.

It felt like my spine was going to snap under the strain of the huge man lying on top of me. The fire in my ass burned hotter as he started pile-driving me. In and out of me his cock surged, its forward-backward motion as precise and insistent as an oil well's pump.

I tried to concentrate, hard as it was. My knees were getting scraped raw through my jeans on the rough floor. Somehow I found a secret place in my mind, a place where everything was calm, a place of utter submission where all my needs and desires fell away to leave one and one alone: the desire to serve.

My job, my purpose, my whole reason for being crystalized in that moment: *I am here to serve this man. That is all. There is room for nothing else in my existence. Just to serve.*

"Yeah, dog boy, your ass is so fucking hot.... I'm going to come!"

He thrust into me harder than ever before, seeming to force his cock up past my rectum into my guts. He reamed me wide open, making it feel like my whole body was splitting in two.

I screamed again, and this time my cry was joined by that of the man above me. His cock jerked like a machine-gun, shooting off blast after blast inside me. His whole body shook, quivering and trembling as if from an internal earthquake.

"Good dog...," he murmured in my ear. "Good dog..."

Despite the pain in my arms, legs, and ass, I felt elation at his approval. *I'm pleasing him! Maybe I'll pass the test!*

But it wasn't over yet.

Kirk pulled out of me, and it felt like he was taking my insides with him. With his cock gone, I felt empty and naked. But there was no time to dwell on that, because he walked around to stand in front of me again.

He was holding the condom in his hand, its end full and plump with his jizz. Suddenly he dumped it out onto me, the cum splashing onto my head and dripping down onto my face. His big hands came forward, rubbing it into me, into my skin. Its warm stickiness felt magical on my body, like some kind of enchanted potion or salve.

"Thank you, Sir...," I moaned.

"What do you want, dog boy?"

"Just to serve you, Sir. Just to serve you."

He stood over me, the candlelight making his shadow flicker and sway on the walls. The man above me could have been an ancient caveman, a Roman gladiator, a warrior from the future, it didn't matter. All that mattered, more than anything else in the world, was that I serve and please him and pass his test.

"Open your mouth, dog slave." Obediently, I did so. "Clean my dick," he said as he stepped forward.

Its delicious softness felt wonderful in my mouth. My

tongue caressed and massaged it like a priceless porcelain objet d'art, savoring the warm, salty semen left on the cock head.

"Now," Kirk said. "Jerk yourself off."

Disbelief and joy flooded my brain. My hand grabbed my cock and started pumping it up and down. Jacking myself had never felt so sweet. I wanted to thank him, but my mouth was stuffed so full of cock there was no chance. The intensity of all that had happened was like a wave washing over me, filling me with an ecstasy I had never known before. All I wanted was to serve this man. And right then I served him by jerking myself off.

"What a good boy," I heard him say. "What a good dog," and a flood of piss surged out of his flaccid cock into my mouth and down my gullet. I coughed and slobbered, trying not to let any of the precious fluid hit the floor. It was amazing to be filled by his warmth, to take something of him directly from his body into my own.

I was a total boy, a total dog . . . a total dog slave.

"Come for me, dog slave!" Kirk said, and I did. Spunk splattered out of my cock and hit my chin. The pleasure that blossomed inside me, while hotter than I'd ever felt before, was eclipsed by surprise at my own vigor. I had never shot this hard or this far.

The orgasm roared through me as Kirk continued pissing down my throat. My brain almost exploded with the overwhelming sensations flooding through me . . . the feel of his cock in my mouth, the bitter warmth of his piss, the white-hot charge of my hand around my own cock, the rainbow firestorm of my own coming . . . . Once the last drops of his piss dribbled out of his cock, he backed away. I fell forward onto the floor, prostrate at his feet.

"Thank you, Sir . . . ," I moaned with my last strength. "Thank you for the privilege of serving you." Exhausted, I would have passed out except that what Kirk said next demanded alertness.

"You've served me well, Billy," he said. "I was right about

you. You're not like those other boys out there. You don't want to primp and preen in front of a bunch of wannabe Masters. You want to serve a man with your whole body, mind, and soul, and to be his property forever."

"Yes, Sir," I whispered.

"I've been waiting a long time for this moment."

I hoped he was going to say that I passed the test, but he didn't. Glancing up, I saw that he had knelt down and was just looking at me, a tiny smile on his face.

"If you've been here every night since the bar opened, it's been a very long time, Sir," I said, desperate to fill the yawning silence of his stare.

"Yes, it has," he said. "But trying to find a boy of my own isn't the only reason I'm here so much. I also need to keep an eye on the place, make sure it's running well, that the customers are happy." That went right past me.

"I . . . don't understand, Sir," I said, staring at him in confusion.

"I own The Dog Pound, Billy," he said simply.

"But . . . but if you own it, Sir, why do you let all those men parade around? Why the Lost Dogs corner? You said you hated all that stuff, Sir . . ."

"I do, but it's good for business. It brings people in. I figured if I set the bait, the Masters and the boys would come. If I made this the hottest leather bar in town, eventually the boy I wanted would come . . . and then I would go to him, and test him, and make him mine."

"And then I would go to him . . . ," I thought. *Just like the tarot cards said would happen. I didn't go to him, he came to me, singling me out from all the other boys . . .*

"Please, Sir," I said, trying to fit his revelation with everything else he'd said and done, "you mean you opened The Dog Pound just to find a slave for yourself?"

"Yes, Billy. Now, don't get me wrong — it's fun owning a bar and everything, but I don't need to. I've got more money than I know what to do with. I knew the boy I wanted couldn't be bought."

I lowered my head dejectedly, saying, "I'm sure he'll be a very lucky boy, Sir."

Kirk threw back his head and started laughing, great peals of mirth, so loud I was sure that the men out in the bar could hear. It made me angry to be made fun of, especially after I had tried so hard to please him. I was about to ask him to stop when he spoke again.

"It's you, Billy."

"What did you say, Sir?" I couldn't believe I'd heard him right.

He rose to his feet and pulled me up with him. Automatically, I pulled my jeans up and fastened them as, staring into Kirk's eyes, I tried desperately to understand.

"It's you," he said again. "You're the boy I've been looking for all these years. You're the one."

"Did I . . . ," I started, but the words wouldn't come out.

"Yes," he said, nodding. "You passed the test."

The smile that lit up my face must have been bright enough to fill the whole room, and I started babbling like an idiot.

"Oh, thank you, Sir! It was so hard sometimes, but I just kept focusing on serving and pleasing you and not thinking about anything else . . ."

He put his hand over my mouth, and my monologue trailed off.

"That wasn't the test," he said. "You had passed the test before I even fucked your face."

I stared at him dumbly. Once again, he'd told me something I couldn't make sense of without help. But he waited until I asked.

"Please explain, Sir . . ."

"When we first came in this room, and you weren't disappointed that it was just a room, not a dungeon, I knew everything I needed to know about you."

Kirk could see that I still didn't understand.

"You're the first who's ever said he wasn't disappointed," he added. "I knew then that you were there to serve, not to be a pushy boy who wanted to top from the bottom. I knew you were a true slave, a real dog slave."

Filled with an overflowing joy, not thinking about anything else, I reached out and hugged him.

"Thank you, Sir, oh, thank you, Sir!" I cried, leaning my head on his chest. His arms came around me, and I was flying. Then I felt him get something out of his pocket. I started to kneel at his feet again when he showed me a leather collar, but he motioned me upright. He buckled it around my neck, then locked it in place.

"Thank you, Sir," I said, my voice choked with emotion.

"Let's get out of here," he said.

I felt I was walking on air as I followed him through the twisting hallway back to the bar. The light of the main room blinded me as we stepped through the door, but I heard a gasp of delight when the crowd saw the collar around my neck. Then a hush fell over the room as Kirk put his hand on my shoulder and pushed me to my knees. Everyone seemed to be holding his breath.

"Billy," Kirk said in that booming voice that had shaken me to my core.

"Yes, Sir?" The room was silent, our voices clear.

"From now on you will call me 'Master.'"

"Yes, Master. Thank you, Master."

The crowd cheered, roaring like fans of a winning team. All around us men offered congratulations, clinking their beer bottles together in tribute, clapping Kirk on the back or shaking his hand, bending down and petting me . . .

After just a few minutes of this, I got very tired and started to sway back and forth on my bent knees. Overwhelmed by what had happened to me, dying of happiness at being claimed at last, I couldn't deal with much more. Sensing this, my Master got me to my feet and then, without a moment's hesitation, scooped me up in his arms and hoisted me over his shoulder.

"C'mon, dog boy," he said. "Time to take you to your new home."

The crowd went wild again and eagerly watched Master Kirk carry me to the bar store, where he spoke to the boy behind the counter. Grinning at the sight of this incredibly hot man with a boy slung over his shoulder, the salesclerk went to get what my Master asked for.

Carrying me like I was no more of a burden than a jacket thrown over his shoulder, Kirk took what the boy gave him with the hand that wasn't holding me in place, then let it drop to his side — where I could see that he'd bought a brand-new shiny, black dog bowl.

I was floating on a cloud as my new Master waved goodbye to his friends and employees and took me, his new property, out the door. Fresh night air greeted us as he carried me out into the parking lot, where his truck was waiting. ◉

Hard Day's Reward

MAN, THERE'S NOTHING like fucking some sweet, tight boy butt to blow off steam! But that's getting ahead of my story. It had been a bitch of a day for me at work, and I was in no mood for any more shit to be handed my way.

As I drove into my building's parking lot, I couldn't wait to get inside, take my clothes off, get down on my knees, and serve my Master. He usually got home before me and was all ready with his clothes off and a nice big boner between his muscular legs, just waiting for me to take it into my greedy mouth and suck it off real good.

Still, serving a Master can be frustrating, especially when you're owned by one who takes delight in not letting you come for weeks on end. It drove me crazy sometimes, the length of time he'd make me hold it.

It wasn't as if he just neglected me sexually for a few days at a time. No way, that would be too easy. He liked to torture me. He'd fuck the shit out of me, work my cock in his hand, sometimes even take my fat pecker into his mouth, just to drive me to the brink of orgasm and then pull back, not letting me shoot no matter how badly I needed to. No matter how much I cried, begged, or moaned, he'd just laugh and pat me on the head.

"Not yet, slave," he'd say in that deep voice of his. "You haven't earned it yet."

And I'd die where I stood, not knowing how much longer I could take it before I snapped or went off the deep end for good. The times he'd let me come were getting fewer and fewer, with much longer gaps in between.

I didn't dare take matters into my own hands. Even if I could find it in my heart to be dishonest with him, he'd know if I shot off a load without his permission. He knew the rhythms and cycles of my body better than I did and could work me like a musical instrument.

Sometimes in my crazed state I'd find myself thinking of things that hadn't crossed my mind in months, maybe years. I'd start remembering all the ways I used to come before I was claimed. Don't get me wrong — I love being Master's slave, and I adore him more than anything else on the face of the earth.

But I had been a top before I was claimed. Can you appreciate what that means?

Most slaves start out as bottoms, so all they have are memories of serving other men and being submissive to them. When they're denied the privilege of coming, they just fixate on their Masters and hope and pray for the day they'll get some relief.

It was worse for me because I not only have my Master to obsess about, but also a whole previous life where I had been a hunter in my own right. One where I'd get those fresh boys, new to the leather scene, take them home, and teach them what it meant to be a real man.

As total as my devotion was to my Master and slavery at his hands, it hadn't obliterated my top self. That side of me lived on, burning for the time when it might get to express itself once again. But sometimes I'd wonder if I'd ever get to *come* again, much less have a chance to be a top. Day and night I would toss and turn in bed, mad with desire and my head filled with images and memories not only of serving my Master, but of dominating boys and making them my whimpering sex slaves.

I would fight to control myself, to be disciplined, to be the good slave I knew I could be. But it was damned hard, especially when weeks would go by without relief, my testicles a sack of blazing desire between my legs, my cock stiff and dripping all the time.

I pulled my car into my parking space, turned off the ignition, and got out. Tossing my bag over my shoulder, I headed up to our apartment. I was looking forward to what I knew would happen when I went in: My Master would take me, make me serve him for hours on end, let me loose long enough to cook us some dinner, then go to work on me, torturing and tormenting me until I cried and begged and finally passed out from exhaustion, my balls still full and bursting.

Turning my key in the lock, I took a deep breath and opened the door. It was dark inside. *That's weird*, I thought. I like the dark, but Master usually has all the lights on when he's home. I saw his truck in the space next to mine, so he had to be home. *What's up?* I wondered as I advanced into the living room.

"Slave?" his voice called from the bedroom.

"Yes, Master," I answered immediately, my cock growing full and hard as always.

"Stay where you are and strip down."

"Yes, Sir." Right away, I started taking off my clothes. It felt good to loosen my tie and yank it off, to unbutton my shirt and let it fall to the floor. I stepped out of my formal dress shoes and let my slacks and underwear drop down, too. My socks followed seconds later. I fucking hate dressing up, but my high-profile corporate job requires it.

Naked and hard, I stood there, my hands clasped behind my back, waiting for my Master's orders. "Surprised" hardly begins to describe what I felt next.

My Master walked out from the bedroom into the living room. Tall, over six feet, chiseled muscle, strong bearded face, he looked hot as ever, but it's what he was carrying that made my jaw drop to the floor with my clothes.

It was a naked boy. And not just any boy, but an award-winning boy, the kind you see on the covers of the hot gay magazines: beautiful dimpled face, short blond hair, slim and lean, toned and hard, with a butt made up of two gorgeous melon globes of firmness that sang out to be grabbed and slapped, and fucked. He was a treasure.

Master had him slung over his shoulders like he was a

fireman rescuing a victim — or, more appropriately, like a caveman bringing home fresh meat from the hunt.

"Sir, what's this?" I asked, so stunned I forgot the rule about not speaking unless spoken to. The boy hung on Master's shoulders as if he belonged there, a smile of contentment on his luscious face. Master grinned, splitting his beard to reveal shiny white teeth behind.

"He's for you, boy."

"What, Sir?" I couldn't have heard him right.

"He's for you. You've been working real hard lately, being a real good boy, taking care of your Master's every need . . . and I know you've been having a rough time at work."

"Yes, Master . . ."

"So I figured I'd get you a reward for being such a good slave."

My eyes drank in the vision in front of me. The boy was almost my opposite, his body so pale next to my own dark skin, his face immaculately shaved instead of my black goatee, his muscles lean and long, mine stocky and bulging. *And he's . . . for me?*

"Mine, Master?" I asked aloud.

"Yes, slave, he's yours for the night. I won't turn him loose until tomorrow morning. Until then, he's yours to do whatever you please. He's under orders to obey you without question, or he'll have to answer to me — and you don't want to do that, do you, boy?" He shook the burden he was holding.

"No, Sir," the boy whispered. I was surprised at his low soft voice. He had hardly seemed awake, much less listening to us. Blissful to be carried by Master, he looked like he was off in his own world.

But now he was in my world, and I was going to make good use of him. Master gently lowered him off his back to the ground, where he knelt obediently in front of me.

One thought stuck in my mind.

"Master?" I asked hesitantly.

"Yes, slave, you can come tonight."

I breathed a great sigh of relief, thinking, *This is going to be a wonderful night!*

"To let you have your way with this piece of meat but not let you come would be too cruel," Master said. "I'm not that much of a sadist."

"Thank you, Master!" I said, laughing. "Oh, thank you!"

And then I focused my full attention on the creature on the floor in front of me. He was exquisite, to be sure, yet ... there was something in his manner that bothered me. Something in his face, his tiny smile — was I mistaken, or did the boy have a hint of sarcasm or mockery in his expression? Was he daring to be amused by this situation? To be arrogant?

He can't be, I thought, but there it was as I looked at him, taking in the graceful curves of his figure. Now I could see it in the tilt of his head, the way his hair fell down over his forehead: he was being obedient, yes, but at some level he was holding back, keeping something in reserve.

And there were few things I had hated more in my top days than a boy who thought he was above it all, that it was all a game and he had choices in the matter. I fucking hated it. Well, I knew how to deal with boys like this, and I'd done so many times before. *Looks like I'm going to do it again tonight*, I vowed.

"Stay, boy," I said.

"Yes, Sir," he answered immediately.

I walked back to my room, where Master lets me keep a small stash of my leather gear from before I knew him. I grabbed it and was back out in a moment. Master was sitting in his big chair, cracking open a beer and watching me. Without a word I fastened a leather collar around the boy's neck, loudly locking it in place with a padlock.

"Thank you, Sir," he whispered.

Then I fastened my leash to the collar, letting the long silver chain dangle down so he could see it. I wondered if he was aware of how hot he was, how alluring and seductive he looked sitting there.

"Down on all fours, boy."

He complied languidly, sticking that gorgeous ass of his up in the air, the tiny smile on his lips.

Oh, he knows what he's doing all right, I realized as I felt my dick get even harder. A tiny drop of moisture appeared at the tip. *Well, I'll wipe that smile off his face soon enough. It isn't fitting for a slaveboy to be so self-satisfied. This piece of meat needs a lesson in humility. And I'm just the man to give it to him.* But first, I turned to face my Master.

"Sir?"

"Yeah, slave?"

"Permission to enjoy my reward in your bedroom, Sir?"

"Go ahead, boy," he said with a big smile on his face. "You've earned it. Have a good time."

"Thank you, Sir," I said and gave my boy a little slap on his ass. "Let's go, boy!"

He trotted forward, and I led him on all fours into Master's bedroom, that place of my torture I would now get to use myself for the first time as the top.

"Sit."

He gathered his legs under him and knelt in place, looking up at me, his smile changing to a smirk. He obviously didn't think he'd get much of a workout as the boy toy of another slave, and he clearly preferred the company of the Master of the house. But things were about to change. I shut the door of the room and turned to face him.

"Now listen, you snot-nosed little punk." His eyebrows raised in surprise, but he was smart enough not to say anything. "You think because you're fucking beautiful you're king of the world, don't you? You've always gotten everything you ever wanted, haven't you? Stuck-up little prick."

He pressed his lips together. He was getting angry and wanted to say something, but he knew it wasn't a good idea.

"Well, have I got news for you, boy," I said, walking closer to him. "You don't impress me one bit. And you know why you're in here with me and not out there with my Master? Because you're not good enough, that's why."

He was definitely angry now.

"You didn't even deserve the privilege of being carried by him, you worthless piece of shit. I'm going to teach you your place in the world tonight, boy. And it ain't to wave your ass in the air with a smirk on your face. It's to serve the slaves of Masters you aren't worthy of."

He couldn't hold back any longer.

"Who the hell do you think . . . ," he started, but before he could finish I slapped him across the face, nice and hard and loud. It stopped him cold mid-sentence.

He started to get to his feet, fire in his eyes.

"You want to take a poke at me?" I said. "Go ahead. But I'd better warn you — I could take you in my sleep, boy. My brothers were gang members and taught me everything they knew. You want to take me on? Just try it."

He got back down on his knees, shivering with anger.

"Who do I think I am? Is that what you were going to ask?" I put my hand on top of his head, ruffling his beautiful blond hair in the most condescending way I could. "I'm the slave who's going to use you tonight, use you like you need to get used, teach you a few lessons."

He glared up at me, but I could see grudging admiration in his eyes. His own dick, which had been soft all this time, was starting to get hard. *Just as I thought — he needs somebody to take charge of him and not let him pull any shit.*

"Or were you going to ask who *you* are? Is that the question you were going to ask? I'll tell you. You're the worthless piece of boymeat my Master's given me as a reward tonight. You belong to me as my property to use any way I see fit. So the sooner you accept that the easier this'll be for you."

He looked down at the floor. I slapped him again.

"I didn't hear you."

"Yes, Sir," he said softly.

"Louder, boymeat!"

"Yes, Sir!"

His dick was fully hard now, a trickle of precum starting to appear. That was it — I couldn't hold back any longer. I stepped forward, leading with my boner. The boy's succulent mouth opened to receive it, taking it all in. He immediately started sucking it, stroking and caressing it with his lips and tongue.

"Mmm, you're a good little cocksucker, ain't'cha, boy?" I grabbed his head and forced him further onto me. "Yeah, a good little whore boy that's mine for the night."

He wanted to suck me, controlling the speed and depth of my dick in his mouth, but I wouldn't let him. I whacked the side of his head again.

"Don't forget who's in charge," I said as I started face-fucking him hard, screwing his mouth just like it was an asshole. "Mmm, that's good, boy, your mouth's real nice . . ."

As before, he reacted well to the harshness, becoming compliant and obedient. I forced my club-like dick in and out of his mouth at my own pace.

"That's right, boymeat," I whispered as he gagged and choked. "I'm doing you how I want to. . . . I don't give a shit what *you* want, or even if you can breathe or not. You're here for me, and that's all you're good for."

I could see his hands quivering, and I knew what he was dying to do. Liking the feeling of power I was experiencing, I knew I just had to wait. I kept my eyes on his hand as I drilled the boy's mouth, waiting for what I knew was coming . . . and it did.

Getting face-fucked by me was too damn hot. He couldn't keep his hand off his own fully erect dick. I let him wrap his fist around it before I smacked him upside the head again, much harder than before.

"Get your fucking hand off that thing, whore!" I snarled down at him as I grabbed a handful of his hair. "That little dog dick of yours ain't yours to touch anymore, you got that?"

"Yes, Sir," he mumbled around my dick.

"Now keep your damn hands off it from now on. As a matter of fact, keep those fuckers behind your back unless I tell you different. You got that?"

"Yes, Sir," he mumbled as he obeyed me. His dick was harder than ever now.

"What are you?"

"I'm your property, Sir. . . ." He was struggling to talk as I pumped him more and more violently.

"What else?"

"I'm your boymeat, Sir . . ."

I was nearly ready to shoot, just needing to hear those magic words from his arrogant little mouth.

"What else?"

"I'm your whore boy, Sir!"

Aaah! That's it! The orgasm filled me, covered me like a shadow of pleasure. I shot off, my hot sticky spunk filling his mouth. Holding his head tight against me, I ignored his snorting and sputtering.

"Better swallow it down, boymeat, if you want to breathe again." He had the nerve to struggle, trying to get away from me, grunting and moaning in discomfort and fear. "You know I'm at least twice as strong as you, dog whore, so why are you fighting me? Swallow it down or this'll be the last fucking night of your life."

My softening dick felt the luxury of his throat flexing, taking it in, filling his gullet with my jizz, taking my essence inside. Only when his mouth was empty did I pull out. He collapsed onto his back, gasping and choking for air. I watched him for a minute as he caught his breath.

"What a drama queen," I said.

He shot a glare my way but, lucky for him, didn't say anything. Now it was my turn to smirk.

"You think you're in some soap opera, huh? You think you're a silent movie star? Who do you think is watching this little melodrama? No one, that's who. I'm not impressed, so you can stop trying."

He rolled over on his side, still glaring at me. His dick was rock hard, and he hated me for that, I knew.

"I don't want a queen, I want a whore."

"I said I was your whore boy, Sir," he ventured as he

knelt upright again, the tiniest trace of hurt feelings in his voice. I had broken through his armor without even trying. But I wasn't surprised. Breaking arrogant boys' pride used to be my favorite sport.

"That's just it, boymeat," I said as I took his chin in one hand and looked into his eyes. "You *said* you were my whore boy. But you didn't *feel* it. You're an actor, like all pretty boys your age. You can pretend to feel everything, but you don't *really* feel anything."

"What the hell are you talking about?"

This time I hauled off and punched him. No dainty slaps anymore, not for this one. He let out a yelp of pain and shuffled backward, but I was on him in an instant, locking my hand behind his head and forcing his face down onto my bare feet, mashing his nose to my toes.

"I'm talking about you, boy," I growled at him. "I'm talking about this. Breathe deep, boymeat. Take in that smell, the smell of my sweaty feet. That's the scent you need in your nostrils, not some fancy cologne that costs more than you're worth. Breathe it in, breathe in the smell of a hard day's sweat, and know what you're good for."

He obeyed, inhaling deeply.

"What do you say, boy?"

"Thank you, Sir."

I snatched his leash up off the floor.

"For what?" I asked.

"Thank you for the privilege of smelling your feet, Sir."

"Good boy. You're not as dumb as I thought. Now kiss my feet, and get them nice and clean." He hesitated an instant too long, and I slapped him again.

"Do it!" I snapped, and he was there, his soft tongue lapping at my stinking feet, slurping between my toes, absorbing all the sweat and lint and whatever else was on them.

"Good boy, good dog boy," I said. "Now, you need some obedience training."

"Yes, Sir," he said between licks. "Thank you for the privilege of cleaning your feet, Sir."

I yanked on his leash, pulling him around so that he was kneeling next to me like a dog in obedience class.

"Now, walk with me."

Stepping forward, I started walking to the other side of the room. The boy kept pace with me, walking on all fours like a good dog. When I stopped, he did too, sitting down on his haunches smartly.

"Good boy," I said as I scratched behind his ears. He responded well to it, raising his head to give my fingers more access. "Now it's time you got fucked like the dog whore you are," I said. "Up on all fours, boymeat!"

He obeyed instantly, readying himself for what he thought was coming. But I dropped his leash on the floor and sat down on the bed. The boy looked back at me, a confused and uncertain expression on his face. No trace of his earlier arrogance remained. He was being humbled, slowly but surely.

I picked up a magazine and started leafing through it. The boy started whining softly, a pleading, desperate sound.

"What're you whining for, boy?" I asked without looking at him.

"You said it was time for me to get fucked, Sir."

"Yeah, that's what I said."

"Well, aren't you going to fuck me, Sir?"

I looked at him then.

"I said it was time for you to get fucked. I didn't say I was going to fuck you."

The confusion on his pretty face deepened.

"I don't understand, Sir."

"I'm not going to fuck you unless I get some proof," I said, my attention going back to the magazine.

"Proof of what, Sir?"

"Proof that you're no longer the proud, smirking, spoiled brat who walked through that door earlier."

Out of the corner of my eye I saw him look down at the floor, his face getting red with embarrassment. I knew he was fighting a battle with himself. But when the brain goes up against the dick, it never wins.

"How can I prove it to you, Sir?" he asked a second later, and I looked him in the eyes.

"Beg me, slaveboy," I said. "Beg me to fuck you, and maybe I will."

"Please fuck me, Sir."

I laughed.

"You call that begging, boymeat? You think you're so fucking hot? Well, this magazine is more interesting than you. Beg me like you mean it, or keep your damn mouth shut."

There was another pause, and when he spoke again, his voice was higher and more anxious.

"Please, Sir, I'm begging you, Sir . . ."

"Yeah?" I answered in an uninterested tone, raising my knee to block his view of my dick, which was getting hard again.

"I need you to fuck me, Sir! I don't just want it, I need it!"

I turned to look at him, and his eyes were closed, his head jerking passionately. Between his legs his dripping dick jutted forward, parallel to the floor. I silently opened the bedside-table drawer and pulled out a condom. Carefully unrolling it, I made sure every inch of my dick was covered with the tight latex.

"Please fuck me, Sir! I want to be your whore boy, Sir! Please let me be your whore boy!"

I reached for the bottle of lube Master always keeps on the table and squeezed some into my palm. As I listened to the boy whimper and moan, I started stroking my dick, getting it stiffer every minute.

"I need to be your whore boy, Sir! Please let me be your whore boy! I've learned my lesson, Sir. I'm sorry for the way I acted, and I won't do it again. My asshole is aching for you, Sir. Please, Sir, *please* fuck your whore boy, Sir!"

Quietly, I sat up and got off the edge of the bed. The boy's eyes were still closed, his hips flexing forward and backward in the air, his butt hole dying for attention, dying to be filled.

"I know I'm not worthy to serve your Master, Sir," he went on, not aware I was kneeling behind him. "I know I'm not worthy to serve you. I'm lower than a dog, just a dog whore, but please show me mercy, Sir!"

My dick was inches from his asshole now, quivering with anticipation. Suddenly he was yelling, "OH, GOD, SIR, PLEASE FUCK ME NOW!"

I pushed my hips forward, my dick spiking his asshole and cleanly pushing into it. He gasped, almost losing his balance and toppling to the floor. I grabbed him around the waist with my left arm, holding him tight, and took another handful of his beautiful hair in my right hand. Pulling his head back, I exposed his neck, forcing it into a sublime curve, an image of total submission.

This boy is mine, I gloated silently.

It felt fantastic being inside him, as it always did to fuck a newly humbled boy. Being Master's slave is wonderful, but this was glorious. All my conquests as a top returned at once to my mind, flooding it with memories of pleasures real and imagined.

I plugged him in and out, stuffing his hole with my manrammer before pulling it nearly all the way out. My dog whore panted and whined, taking it like the slut he was. His tongue lolled out of his mouth, leaking slobber on the floor.

Loud slapping noises were heard each time I plunged into him, my thighs and hips sticky with lube. Little yelps and gasps started coming out of him with every thrust. Pretty soon I got tired of listening and reached for the rest of my leather gear. My grasping fingers found my cock gag, and I shoved it into the boy's mouth, muffling his noise.

"I don't want to listen to you anymore, boymeat. Keep quiet now."

Remembering when Master had this piece of boyflesh slung over his shoulders, when he first got down on his knees like a dog, I gloated to myself. *I changed him. I broke him from the little prick he'd been when Master brought him home. Now he's the whore we both know he is. And he's mine. Even if it's for only one night, he's mine.* It would be a night he'd never forget, because in some way, no matter what else he does in his life, he'll always be my dog whore.

I was so grateful to my Master for giving him to me. He knew how much I love cocky little boys like this. He knew I hate those passive wimps with no fire, no spark. I like breaking a boy down, no matter how short or long it takes, no matter what I have to do.

Oh, it was awesome to stuff that boy butt with my dick, to pump in and out until the pleasure got too intense and I just had to . . .

"Come, boy!" I yelled. "Grab your dick and shoot off with me. You've got ten seconds!"

Instantly the boy gripped his dick and started pumping. His body jerked and convulsed as I rammed him harder and harder. I was hitting him so hard that if I hadn't still been holding him around the waist, I'd've pushed him off me.

"I'm gonna come boy, I'm gonna let it out!" I yelled into his ear. He arched backward, rearing up like a dog standing on its hind legs.

Then it happened, and there was no stopping it. Like a countdown to a blastoff, a fuse had been lit inside me. The fire burned through me and then out of me, racing down the length of my dick like a lightning bolt and igniting it. I shot off, feeling my milky cum spurting out of my dick head in a burst of ecstasy. Animal howls came out of me as my body rocked and shook with the orgasm.

My boymeat shot then, too, his dog dick squirting his load all over his hand and the floor. He shuddered, then let go of his dick and grabbed onto me. Standing up, I pulled him up with me, and together we fell onto the bed. Withdrawing slowly, I pulled my dick out of him. When I had the condom off, I admired the impressive load of jizz I'd dumped into it, then tied it off and tossed it in the wastebasket.

Hard Day's Reward

The boy snuggled into me, squeezing me like I was his big brother during a scary thunderstorm. His breathing deepened and then leveled out — he fell asleep. All evidence of his attitude before was gone. He was a changed boy, and I had changed him. I had my arms around him and held him as if he *was* my little brother.

God, it was great getting to top a boy again, I said to myself. *I need to thank my Master* . . . . And there he was, standing in the open doorway with a big smile on his face.

"Well, slave," he said quietly, not wanting to disturb the sleeping treasure in my arms. "Did you enjoy your reward?"

"Oh, yes, Master, thank you! It was fucking fantastic!"

"I figured he'd be a good one for you, what with that attitude and all."

"You . . . shopped around, Sir?"

"Yes, slave. I wanted to get you just the kind of boy you like so much to break. I trust you've humbled his proud little soul by now."

"Oh, yes, Sir," I said, smiling. "He's a perfect little dog whore now, just like he should be."

"You've done well," Master said as he stepped backward out the door. "I'll sleep on the bed in the den, maybe join you later. Just think what you could do to him by morning."

"Morning, Sir?"

"It's still early, slave. There are many hours until tomorrow. He's yours until then. And . . . ." He was almost out of sight behind the closing door.

"Sir?"

". . . if you keep on being as good as you have been," I heard him say, "who knows what might happen? I just might have to get him for you permanently." ◉

Goodnight, My Slaveboys

IT WAS 11:00 P.M. Time for all good slaveboys to go to sleep. At least all of *my* good slaveboys — yes, *slaveboys* plural. I have five currently. Yes, *five*. I'll tell you, I'm not very popular in certain circles of the leather community — mostly with Masters who can't train and keep even *one* slaveboy, much less more than one. I'm not aware of any special touch or "magic" that I have. Slaveboys just seem to come to me, and if they're still around after my (admittedly tough) training sessions, I claim them as my property. Five isn't all that many considering the number of boys who've come to me over the years to be trained.

But back to what I was saying: Sitting in my office in my underwear, surfing the Web to prepare for my next big project at work, I'd been so engrossed in my research that I hadn't noticed the time. When I had looked at the clock earlier it read 9:30, and now it was already 11:00.

My slaveboys are trained to help each other get ready for bed when the time comes — almost all the way. I make my rounds at 11:00 p.m., checking to make sure everyone is safely restrained the way I like. Then I tuck them in — finish them off, so to speak. Now another day was over, and it was time for bed again.

First, to the living room.

There was Jeremy, all nicely tucked away in his sleepsack on the couch. The leather bag completely encased his body, leaving only his head and his cock and balls sticking out. I stood there a moment and admired his long floppy auburn hair and handsome face. His eyes were closed. The sack hid most of his 5'10" body, but I knew what the leather concealed: a well-toned 170 pounds. The sack had been laced up and strapped tight by his slavebrothers, and his exposed cock was hard, as usual.

When I knelt down next to him, he opened his eyes.

"Master...," he whispered.

"I'm here, Jeremy," I answered softly. "Master's here..."

Gently, I took his cock in my hand and started stroking it. With my other hand I carefully brushed away some hair that had fallen down over his eyes. He murmured with pleasure as I jerked him harder, now using my free hand to caress his balls. With a soft yelp of bliss, Jeremy came, shooting a nice big burst of semen onto my hand and making his whole body quiver inside its bondage. I brought my hand to his mouth and fed him his own cum, which he licked up happily. Within seconds he was asleep. I tucked his soft cock and drained balls back inside the sack and zipped it up.

One down, four to go. Next stop, the "dungeon." We'd converted the second bedroom of the house into a playroom of sorts. Painted black, it held most of my large bondage equipment and furniture. This included the large metal puppy cage in which I found my next slaveboy.

"Jake!" I said excitedly. He was awake, on his hands and knees, his tongue hanging out and his naked butt waving back and forth, just like a real dog greeting his Master.

"Woof! Woof!" he said, as always delighted to see me. He's small and cute, like a puppy (or human pup) should be, 5'6" and a nicely muscled 140 pounds, with bright blue eyes and short brown hair.

There was enough room in the cage for him to be up on his hands and knees or to lie down comfortably, but not enough to stand up or turn around. I stuck my hand into the cage. Jake licked my fingers happily, then pushed the top of his head into my hand so I could pet him and scratch behind his ears.

"Have you been a good dog, Jake?" I asked with mock seriousness.

Goodnight, My Slaveboys

"Ruff! Ruff!" was the answer.

"Good dog, good dog, you're my good dog," I said.

"Ruff."

"I know what my puppy boy wants," I said, reaching into my shorts and pulling my cock out. "He wants his nightly feeding!"

"WOOF!" Jake barked, going absolutely crazy in his cage, banging against the walls and wagging his butt so hard it looked like he actually *had* a tail. I got down on my knees and moved closer to the metal so my stiff cock went between the bars and into the cage.

Jake excitedly licked it a few times, then started sucking. It was wonderful to feel my pup suckling me as if my fluids were his life's blood. As he'd been trained to do, Jake started jerking himself off without taking his eyes from me or his mouth from my cock. In less than a minute he whined and moaned with such desperation that I laughed and said, "Good dog, go ahead."

His eyes lit up, and seconds later a big healthy dose of puppy cum squirted into his hand. Jake moaned and groaned in such loud ecstasy that I had to put my finger to my lips to caution him.

"Good dog," I said softly as I pulled my cock out of his mouth. "Go ahead, lick it up." He licked his own fingers as hungrily as he had mine earlier until he swallowed all of the cum he had shot. "You're my good dog. . . . Settle down now, good dog, settle down . . . ."

I softened my voice until it was just a whisper. I petted him, the strokes becoming more gentle, just like my voice. As always when I did this, Jake became sleepy and finally curled up on his side and closed his eyes.

"Good puppy boy," I said. If he had had a tail it would've wagged one last time, and then my puppyboy was asleep. I turned off the light in the dungeon and closed the door behind me as I walked out, then down the hallway to the master bedroom.

The way into the bedroom was blocked by a small mountain of muscle and steel lying across the doorway — my slave Jeff. Yes, all my slaves have names starting with "J." It's no coincidence.

When I train a boy and he makes the grade, I give him a slave name, and because I like the sound of names starting with "J," that's what they get. Their real names are still on all their paperwork and legal documents. The slave names are just what I call them.

"Jeff," I said. "Assume the position."

"Yes, Sir!" he said, standing up. And up and up. Jeff is 6'4" (4 inches taller than me) and a prize-winning bodybuilder — as I said, a mountain of muscle and steel. The steel included the wide, custom-made collar around his neck, marking him as my slave, and the long, heavy chain attached to it, his leash, which at the moment was locked to a ring on the wall.

He was naked, like Jake in his cage and Jeremy in his sleepsack. I keep them that way inside the house. It reminds them that they're owned property, slavemeat that belongs to me. Not that there's ever any doubt. But with a house full of red-blooded American men, all brought up to prize their self-determination, it's important to remind them that they're mine. Literally.

That's why this enormous bodybuilder obeyed me and assumed the position he had been trained to take in my presence: feet apart, shoulders back, hands clasped behind him, head bowed respectfully, his enormous cock erect.

"How long have you been my slave, Jeff?" I asked.

"Two and a half years, Sir."

"How long would you like to remain my possession?"

"For the rest of my life, Sir!" He seemed shocked that I'd even ask.

"And how would you rate your performance as my slave so far?"

"Uh . . . ," he started, clearly not expecting this question either. "Satisfactory, Sir?"

"Wrong!" I said, and his face fell, *What have I done poor-*

ly? showing in his eyes. As amusing as this was, I didn't want to torture him for too long.

"Your performance has not been satisfactory," I said, and he closed his eyes in anticipation of the coming blow. "Your performance has been *exemplary*."

After a second of confusion, he understood that I had been teasing him and got a big grin on his face as he let out a relieved sigh.

"Thank you, Sir."

"I love you very much, Jeff."

"Thank you, Sir. I love you, too."

"Now show me what a good boy you are, and come in ten seconds."

I took his dick in one hand and started jerking him. As always he thrilled to my touch, his eyes rolling back as he closed them.

"One . . . Two . . . Three . . . . You're my slaveboy, Jeff — you belong to me. Remember that — always!"

The bodybuilder moaned with passion as I jerked him.

"Four . . . Five . . . Six . . . Seven . . ."

Sweat broke out on his forehead as he concentrated.

"Eight . . . ." I put my other hand up, ready to catch his seed when it spurted. "Nine . . . . Come for me, boy. Ten! Come for your Master!"

Jeff groaned as I pumped him one last time, and a surge of cum shot out of his cock and into my waiting hand.

"Good boy!"

"Thank you, Master . . . ," he said breathlessly. I put my hand up to his lips, and he sucked the cum off, slurping like a kid with an ice-cream cone until it was all gone.

"Now go to sleep," I said, reaching up to tousle his hair playfully.

He obeyed, dropping back down to his favorite place — guarding the door to my bedroom. He stretched out on the thick rug I leave there for him, looking like a lion on the savanna. He's a powerful boy, and I had tamed him. I'd harnessed his tremendous strength into a tool that I could use at will. The clinking of his chain stopped when he found a comfortable position and settled in for the night. I looked down at him lovingly. He was mine, all mine. They all were.

I stepped over Jeff and headed into my sanctuary, my bedroom, the place of my most intimate moments. Two more slaveboys were waiting on my bed, rounding out my stable of five. I call them my "bed boys" because they're the ones I actually sleep with most of the time. The other boys each get to share my bed once in a while, but they're happy where they are. Indeed, they'd be happy wherever I put them.

Jason, a bleach-blond skater I'd found on the beach, was lying on the left side of the bed, nicely tied up and gagged. He made a handsome and humpy piece of property. I know how valuable he is, because I own him! He's 5'11", lanky and yet graceful. His hands were bound together in front of his chest, his feet tied at the ankles. A padlocked chain was around his neck.

Joel was reclining on the other side of the bed, waiting for me with a big, wide smile on his good-looking, clean-cut, wholesome face. He's an all-American boy next door — one who's also an owned and trained piece of slavemeat. He's beautiful in his simplicity. All his needs and wants are clear to me, with no hidden agendas of any kind. His emotions are all right there on the surface, in his face and body language. He was naked, of course, with a custom-made leather collar around his neck. No chain was attached to his collar. His bond to me is invisible, but strong as steel.

Three down, two to go.

"Get on your hands and knees and give your brother some attention," I said to Joel.

"Yes, Sir," he said obediently, straddling Jason and taking his slavebrother's hard cock into his mouth. Jason shuddered as the pleasure rippled through him. Joel gently sucked his brother's dick as I looked on.

But as enticing as this was to watch, I had something else to do. Joel's delicious naked butt was right in front of me, and I could never resist that ass. Among all my slaveboys, he has the most delicious ass.

I put my face between his butt cheeks and rimmed him, stimulating and caressing his asshole with my lips and tongue. Joel moaned with joy as he continued to suck his slavebrother's cock.

"I'm going to come, Master . . . ," Jason said, his words distorted by the gag.

"That's good, boy," I said reassuringly. "Go ahead, whenever you're ready. Your brother's right here, and he'll drink it all down. Just go ahead."

Jason yelped in ecstasy, and I knew he was shooting his load down Joel's throat, the perfect place for it. Joel swallowed a few times, gulping it all down, before letting his brother's cock slide out of his mouth. He started to back up, as if to get off Jason, but I said, "No. Stay right where you are, Joel. I like you there."

"Yes, Master," he said, staying straddled on his hands and knees over Jason.

I stepped out of my shorts and slipped a condom over my cock, then spat into my hand and used the moisture to lubricate myself. I grabbed Joel's hips, one in each hand, and pulled him closer to the edge of the bed. He stuck his butt out, wiggling it a little, as if to show me how badly he wanted it. I nosed my cock up between his ass cheeks, prodding his butt hole with my hard, stiff tool. Then I started to push it in, slowly and gently at first, then harder as my cockhead slid inside him all the way. The fucking began.

As always, fucking one of my slaveboys was spectacular. To screw another man is dominant and possessive already, but when you add in that the man being fucked, being penetrated, is a slaveboy, a man who has turned his will and his life over to another man — to *me* — the effect is stronger than the most potent aphrodisiac in the world.

With thoughts like those running through my mind, it didn't take long for me to come. I shot my load into the condom deep in Joel's guts, and I heard and felt him sigh in bliss as he jerked himself to orgasm. As he had been trained to do, he ate his own cum off his hand when he was done while I stayed inside him, my cock slowly softening.

It was over.

I pulled out and threw away the condom, then helped Joel get Jason under the covers. Jason loves sleeping in bondage, so I just left him tied up. Joel and I got under the covers, and I pulled my two bed boys close. My arms were around just the two of them, but the grasp of my love and Mastery extended over all the boys throughout my home. Our home.

"Goodnight, my slaveboys," I whispered, and turned off the light. ⊙

First-Time Slave

I HAD ALWAYS BEEN CURIOUS about Master/slave relationships, but the first time I experienced real bondage and submission was more intense than anything I had imagined. Being handcuffed a couple of times by a guy I was dating was hot, but I knew I needed heavier action, and I found it. Did I ever!

I was about 22 then, just out of college, and I felt my life was missing something big. So when I saw the name "Master Steve" come up on my computer screen while I was on a local gay bulletin board, I had to talk to him.

He turned out to be a real Master all right. He had a lover, Robert, who was his slave, and they were looking for another man who would be a slave to both of them. My dick was rock hard and stayed that way the whole time we chatted over the computer, talking about our mutual expectations if I were to offer myself to them as a slave.

I had a lot of reservations, but the idea of being a bondage slave was too exciting to let go. Here, it seemed, were the more intense experiences I wanted! At 5'9" and 160 pounds, with a boyish face and a muscular body from years of wrestling and skiing, I figured I'd be a decent piece of property for a Master to own. So I decided to try it out.

Master Steve said the first thing that had to happen was for me to come to his house for an inspection. I was instructed to arrive at 3:00 p.m. sharp that same day. With trembling hands I wrote down the address and typed, "Thank you, Sir." After stripping off the underwear under my shorts and throwing on an old T-shirt and the Greek fisherman's cap I liked to wear, I got in my car and headed off for what became the defining experience in my life.

I was running late and knew I wouldn't get to Steve and

Robert's house until 3:15 or so. I didn't think much of this at the time, but I would sure regret it later.

Finding the place easily enough, I knocked on the door, where I got a first look at my potential Master. Steve was tall, 5'11" or so, weighing around 250 pounds, beard and mustache, in his late 30s and pretty hot looking. His stern face made me hope I wouldn't disappoint him. I got the sense he didn't take no for an answer from anyone.

Master Steve looked at me with appraising eyes and then invited me in, telling me Robert was at work and that he always conducted the preliminary inspection alone. He invited me to sit down. When we were seated, he said he was pleased with my looks, but not to expect a lot of compliments or praise about that after today. I was quivering and shaking, too terrified to try to escape and too excited to want to.

He showed me a slave contract that he had printed out from his computer. I read it, and it scared the shit out of me. It talked about giving up my will to my Master, giving all my money to him, and stuff like that. Steve told me to relax, that he wouldn't expect me to sign anything like it for a while, and even then only if he, Robert, and I all wanted it to happen.

We decided to try a day and night as Master and slave and see how it went. Then we negotiated terms for the trial: that I would obey commands without question, that he would ensure my safety, that I would be put in bondage if there were no tasks for me to perform, and that I would be available sexually anytime they wanted.

My cock, which had been flaccid with fear, started getting hard. Steve ordered me to stand up and strip. I unbuttoned my shorts and stepped out of them. Feeling kind of embarrassed about my hard-on, I tried to concentrate on what I was doing. I took off my cap and my shirt and stood at attention in front of my new Master.

My eyes closed as I felt his hand touch me. It moved over my pecs and abs, down to hold the fullness of my balls

First-Time Slave

for a moment, then curled around behind me to pinch my firm, round butt. His hand stroked my clean-shaven cheek and ran up through my short brown hair. Every stroke sent shivers through me. I had never been touched this way before. He was treating me like property to be inspected and evaluated, like a piece of art or a rare breed of animal. It was electrifying.

He slipped a smooth band of leather around my throat and locked it in place. I opened my eyes in time to see him pull a pair of handcuffs from the end-table drawer. Knowing what cuffs were like, I didn't get too scared. Master Steve pulled my arms behind my back and encircled my wrists with the cuffs, binding them together. Now I couldn't use my hands or my arms. My cock was fully erect now and oozing precum.

The next thing he pulled out from the drawer made me want to run. It was a piece of leather shaped like a head — a bondage hood. I had never been hooded before and was very frightened, but my cock didn't go soft. It got harder.

Master Steve stood behind me and slipped the hood over my head. It was lined with smooth leather. The eye flaps were snapped on, so I couldn't see anything. As the cool leather slid down over my face, I felt the beginnings of panic — my gut churned. The hood felt like nothing I'd ever experienced. My ears were covered and sounds were muffled, as if from far away.

My first thought was, *This must be what being buried alive is like.* But I realized I could still breathe — my mouth and nose were free. Having my whole head enclosed was terrifying, but the terror was exciting.

I felt Master Steve begin to lace up the cord that would tighten the hood and mold it to my head. My whole body was shaking. I could feel myself withdrawing inside my head space, yet at the same time my active senses were becoming more acute every second. I had never felt so helpless and vulnerable. There I was, being put into bondage in the house of a man I had only spoken to online. My hands were cuffed behind my back, and I was robbed of sight and hearing. Raised in a culture and environment where the rights of the individual are strongly protected, I had never had any of my faculties out of my control.

No one knew I was there. Master Steve could do anything with me. That thought almost made me panic. I worried I might throw up but controlled myself. Fighting the fear down, I tried to open my mind to the new experience. After all, this was what I'd been so curious about for so long.

At least I can still scream if I have to, I thought. But not for long. Something large and firm was being shoved in my mouth. I must have made a sound of protest and tensed my body, because I heard his voice saying, "Relax. Don't fight me, boy. It'll be a lot easier on you if you don't fight me." I knew I couldn't hold my own against this man even if I wasn't bound, so I went limp.

He worked the gag into my mouth and snapped it in place on the front of the hood. I couldn't see, could barely hear, and now couldn't speak. All that was left uncontrolled was my nose, which I prayed he would not cover.

My cock, which was still hard, suddenly flared back into the foreground of my attention. Master Steve had taken it in his hand and was stroking it gently, almost lovingly. I had been jerked off by guys before, but having my cock completely in the power of this man felt incredible beyond anything I had ever dreamed. His thumb rubbed my piss slit, spreading slimey precum over the head of my cock.

"Stand up, slave."

With a little help, I stumbled up to my feet and was led forward into another room. Trying to walk while hooded was bizarre, like swimming through a sea of black leather.

"On your knees."

I knelt down and heard the big man hunker down next to me. His heavy, masculine scent filled my nostrils, and I inhaled deeply. The next sound I heard made my blood run cold and my cock get even harder. It was the clinking of metal on metal — *chains*.

First-Time Slave

Something heavy was attached to my handcuffs, making them heavier. Cold shackles were placed around my ankles. Something else was fastened to my collar. I tried to move and found I had only a few inches of slack. Master Steve had chained me to the floor. This was so far beyond my few handcuff experiments that it almost blew my mind. Now there was no turning back. I was a prisoner, a captive unable to move unless my Master allowed it.

"Stay here, boy. I'll be back for you."

I heard footsteps moving away from me, and then a door close. Alone and in bondage, I tried moving again to see if there was some degree of freedom I had missed. But there was none, and every move I made caused the chains to clank loud enough for the whole house to hear.

Satisfied that I had no option but to await my Master's bidding, I settled down on my haunches. Time seemed to have no meaning now that I was a hooded slave, so I have no idea how long I was there. I do know that I was hard the whole time.

At some point I heard the front door open and muffled conversation from the front room. I guessed it was slave Robert coming home from work because the door to whatever room I was in was held open for a few silent minutes, then closed again. I figured Master Steve was showing Robert his latest slave candidate.

Being on display totally bound, and gagged, for the eyes of other men was another new experience for me. *I hope they appreciate the sight*, I told myself, and I basked in that thought for a few minutes. I figured I looked pretty damn hot all chained up like a captive in a dungeon. When the door closed and I heard them walking further into the house, I felt left behind and neglected.

But as a slave, how I felt didn't matter. My job was to serve in obedience. After a while my arms got really sore, and my knees ached from kneeling so long.

Sometime later the door opened.

"Get your ass in the air, slave," Master Steve said.

Glad to finally have a new order to carry out, I scrambled to obey, leaning forward as best I could with my hands cuffed behind me. When my ass was up as high as it would go, I felt something flat and rough being rubbed against it. I didn't know what it was at first, only that it was wide and hard ... but then I realized. The gag muffled my moan of fear.

"You were instructed to arrive here at 3:00 p.m., boy. You arrived 15 minutes after that time. Since I received no phone call telling me you got lost or were in a car accident, my conclusion can only be that you were late out of negligence and disrespect."

I tried to shake my head. He was right, of course, but I was terrified of what he was about to do. I have never been a pain pig. My trip is being a slave, being dominated and controlled and owned by another man as a piece of property — not being hurt. I have never found that magical place where pain is transformed into pleasure. Consequently, I am a ridiculously easy slave to keep in line, as Master Steve was about to discover.

"Because this is your first time," he said, "I'm not going to give you as many strokes as I will after you become a full-time slave, but the strokes are going to be as hard as the ones a full-timer gets."

I was whining into the gag by this time. The first stroke on my ass came out of nowhere, pounding me so hard I was surprised I didn't fly forward and bang my head on the floor. The pain was intense, but it was the sheer impact that astounded me. I couldn't believe how hard he had hit me. *I guess he really wants me to learn my lesson*, I thought as the second stroke landed. I could feel my butt turning red and yelped like a dog.

The third one was the killer. Somehow my balls had worked between my legs and were exposed to the wrath of the paddle. The blow fell and I screamed. It felt like my ballsac had been broken open and my testicles were spilling out.

Mercifully, that was the end. Master Steve's hand was the

next thing I felt, gently rubbing my throbbing ass cheeks. I whimpered like a little puppy grateful for some affection. Then his hands were behind me, unfastening the locks that bound me to the floor. The chains noisily fell away.

I didn't know what I expected next, but it certainly wasn't to have my hands uncuffed and the hood removed. It felt like losing my top layer of skin, I had become so used to it. Even though my aching arms were glad to have their freedom restored, I amazed myself by missing my bondage. The light of the room, which I saw was the kitchen, was so bright I had to squint when the hood finally came off. With the gag out, my mouth felt empty, as if it needed to be stuffed full of something to be whole. The collar stayed locked around my neck.

As soon as I was completely free, I hugged Master Steve tightly. In a clearer frame of mind I probably wouldn't have even asked for that privilege, but right then the need to touch the man who had punished me was too strong to resist. He surprised me by putting his arms around me and hugging me back.

"It's okay, boy, it's okay," he whispered. "You're never going to be late again, are you?"

I shook my head violently, burying my face in his chest. "No, Sir!"

"Good slave, good slave . . . ," he murmured, and I was filled with joy at his approval.

Then Master Steve went to another room to get something. Left alone, I had my first look at what had held me down. It was a mass of chains attached to rings that had been bolted into the floor. There were so many chains it looked like a pile of metal snakes. The chains were thick and very heavy, so there was no way I could have escaped even one of them, much less the several holding me down.

Master Steve returned and ordered me to stand at attention again. I stood there with a hard-on as he put new fetters around my ankles, joined by a chain. This chain was lighter, so I could walk, but certainly nothing I could get out of on my own. He then attached a pair of metal tit clamps to my nipples. I winced at the pain as they bit into my pecs but soon got used to it and almost forgot they were there — until Master Steve slapped them and bolts of pain shot through my chest.

"To remind you of your place in the household," he said.

"Yes, Sir," I said, breathlessly.

Then he gave me a list of tasks: vacuuming the floor, washing the windows, scrubbing the bathroom, and other household stuff. Excited about having some freedom of movement while still in bondage, I got to it right away.

I am no stranger to hard work and enjoyed the chores. I was even able to savor the extra challenge of performing with my ankles chained together and tit clamps digging into my nipples. The house was nice, and I entertained myself by imagining what it would be like if I was accepted as a permanent slave. The idea pleased me — I could picture myself living in this place. It sure beat the hell out of my tiny studio apartment!

I didn't see Robert anywhere around but knew better than to ask to meet him. I knew I should not speak without being spoken to. That much I had figured out from the one-handed fiction I'd read. My Master hadn't given me very many rules, so I figured he was testing me. I knew I had better be on my best behavior if I wanted to become a "permanent" slave.

My cock remained hard through it all, which amazed me because I usually needed a cock ring to maintain an erection this long. I was trailing precum everywhere I went now, so I just started cleaning it up as I went along. I wondered briefly if Master Steve would let me come, then thought, *Don't hold your breath.* Despite my churning balls, I tried to put coming out of my mind. Being denied the pleasure of shooting off was yet another new experience for me, and I was determined to get the most out of every part of this overnught trial.

Even with the enjoyment I was feeling, I became pretty tired after a while. I was working my ass off to do a good job, and I had already had a long day before reporting for duty. When I finished everything on the list, I found Master Steve in the den working on a computer. I knelt on the floor with my head bowed and my hands behind my back.

"Your orders have been completed, Sir," I said after a few moments.

"Robert's asleep in our bedroom," he replied, barely looking up. "Go snuggle next to him. He'll like that."

"May I have permission to go to sleep, Sir?"

"Yes, boy, go ahead. I'll come get you when I need you again."

"Thank you, Sir."

The bedroom was done all in black, with a nice big bed that could comfortably sleep three, although I doubted I'd have the privilege of sleeping with Master Steve and Robert very often. Robert was asleep on the bed, lying on top of the covers. I slid down next to him as quietly as I could, not wanting to disturb him. The chain connecting my leg cuffs clanked a little but didn't wake him up.

Lying there, I got my first good look at him. He was attractive, more pretty than butch, with long eyelashes and high cheekbones. His body was well shaped, slender and lithe, without my bulky muscles.

I decided the best way to get comfortable was to lie with my back to his chest so my tit clamps had the least chance of getting disturbed. *God, I'm tired.* I couldn't wait to rest my head on a pillow and go off to dreamland.

No sooner had I gotten into a good position when I felt Robert's arms wrap around me from behind. He'd been awake the whole time. It felt so good I snuggled closer to him. His cock stirred as my ass rubbed against it gently.

"You're very hot," he whispered in a voice still mostly asleep.

"Thank you," I said. "You're beautiful yourself."

He murmured in appreciation and squeezed me tight. It felt wonderful, and I started slipping into sleep.

"Welcome to our home," Robert said.
"Thanks," I answered, and was out.

BRIGHT, KNIFE-LIKE PAIN in my chest woke me up. My nipples were screaming in pain. Opening my eyes, I saw Master Steve kneeling on the bed straddling me with a big smile on his face, the tit clamps hanging from his fist. I howled as blood rushed back into my nipples, shocking the now ultra-sensitive nerve endings. Robert was gone, and my hands were tied above my head, this time with rope.

I bucked and struggled against my bonds as the pain in my nips tore at my chest, desperate to touch my pecs to try to soothe the fire. But the rope was securely tied off on the headboard where I couldn't reach it.

"Settle down, boy," Master Steve said. "It's time to serve your Master."

I hadn't noticed that his pants were open, but a second later he leaned forward and his cock was in my mouth, huge and hard and dripping. Grateful for any distraction from the agony, let alone one as sweet as this, I sucked greedily. I slobbered all over my Master's cock, moving my head forward and back to give him pleasure. The head hit the back of my throat over and over, his precum dripping down my gullet.

The pain still throbbed in my pecs, but now there was something else to concentrate on. His cock was so large that I thought I'd never take it all the way, but Master Steve soon took over, holding my head and thrusting deeper and deeper into my throat. His mocking grin changed to a smile of ecstasy. He pushed in so far I gagged, and that did it for him.

"I'm going to come, boy," he said urgently. "I'm going to pull out and shoot on your chest and mark you as my property." After he pulled out, he jerked himself a couple of times with his hand and then came with a shout.

The only thing I can compare it to is torpedoes being shot out of submarines in old war movies. The hot jism spurted out of his cock and hit my chest hard enough to splash, then again and again. When Master Steve was finished shooting, he rubbed his cum into my pecs, which felt amazing.

"Good boy," he murmured. "Good slave..."

My Master's words filled me with pleasure, and any remaining pain faded away. Nothing else mattered. All that was important was that he was happy, that he had been served well. I felt so great about it that when he gave my cock a few quick strokes I almost came myself.

"That was for making Robert feel good," he said with a grin.

"Thank you, Sir...," I said as he started to untie me.

"Now get up and make us dinner. We're hungry."

We had talked about this online. I'm no Wolfgang Puck, but I had learned enough to put together a decent meal. Still with my feet shackled together, I made dinner for my Master and his other slave while they watched TV and talked about their days. I was allowed to sit on the floor and eat next to them while they had their meal. Loving every minute of it, I even curled up like a dog at their feet when they'd finished and were relaxing. After a while, though, I was sent back to clean up the kitchen.

Once I had everything there squared away, Master Steve chained me to the floor again. Even though I had prepared myself for it, I was still a little disappointed that I wouldn't get to sleep in the bedroom with him and Robert. But I was a slave, and I was grateful just to be allowed to spend the night on my first visit.

"Goodnight, boy," Master Steve said.

I twisted my head around so I could see him. He was standing in the doorway, the light from the hallway almost making him a silhouette.

"Goodnight... Master," I said, the first time I'd addressed him that way.

He smiled and then was gone. The door closed and the hall light snapped off. Happy that I had made him smile, I twisted and turned to find a comfortable resting position. It was strange to think I could sleep with my neck, hands, and feet chained to the floor. But as soon as my exhausted body settled onto the carpet and I felt the cool summer breeze blowing in through the window, I was asleep with a grin on my face.

THE NEXT THING I KNEW, sunshine was coming through the windows and I was getting yanked up onto my knees. The now-familiar scent of Master Steve filled my nose, which should have clued me.

"Wha'...?" I started to protest.

That was when the hood was jammed down over my head, much more forcefully than the day before. I got scared and tried to squirm away before remembering that I was chained in place.

"You're not going anywhere, slave," Master Steve said. "So shut up and take it."

He's going to fuck me, I realized suddenly. Now *that* scared me. Having come out after the AIDS crisis began, I had zealously guarded my negative status since Day One. But now I was tied up on my knees with my butt in the air about to get screwed by someone whose cock I couldn't even *see*, much less tell if it had a condom on it.

I must have started whimpering in fear again, because Master Steve grabbed my bound hands and pulled them down between my legs. He jammed my probing fingers against his hard-as-rock fuckstick, and I felt the latex covering it.

Thank God.

Never having been nailed in so awkward and uncomfortable a position, I braced myself for a brutal ass fucking. Master Steve stuck a few lube-covered fingers up my butt hole to get it slimy enough for him to fit in something much bigger. The pain of his huge cock being pushed inside me was almost as bad as the paddling he'd given me earlier. I yelped and whimpered pitifully.

First-Time Slave

"I don't want to listen to you, boy," Master Steve snarled as he shoved the gag part of the hood into my mouth and snapped it in place. "Now you can scream all you want, and no one'll hear."

And scream I did, especially when he started thrusting, crushing me downward into the floor with his sheer force. It was lucky I was on carpet, even tough industrial carpet — anything harder, and he'd have broken my arms or my neck. But amid the terror I realized something extraordinary: *There's nowhere else I'd rather be. This is what it is to be a slave, and I fucking love it!*

My cock was so hard it felt like a steel rod between my chained-down legs. I was getting fucked by a man who hadn't asked if I wanted it, who hadn't asked if I was okay, who didn't care how I felt. He was using me like the piece of bound and gagged property I was.

This is what's been missing from my life for so long, I said to myself, and in that moment I knew I was born to be a slave. When Master Steve reached under and grabbed hold of my cock and started jerking it, the bliss was so total and sublime that I couldn't hold back for even a second.

I screamed into the gag at the top of my voice as every muscle in my body flexed harder than it ever had before. I shot off like a geyser, spurting out glob after glob of cum. My asshole tightened like a clenching fist, and I heard Master Steve groan with delight.

"Oh, yeah, slaveboy, squeeze my dick. Your Master's gonna come... *now!*"

And those torpedo bursts started going off inside me. He bucked and roared against me, pressing me into the floor so hard I could feel carpet burns on my face.

Then he collapsed on top of me and lay there for a couple of minutes before pulling out. My muscles groaned in relief when he got off me and I could relax. I felt him unlocking my restraints. He took off the hood, and a few minutes later I was free, sitting naked on the floor looking up at him with a goofy grin on my face.

In one hand he was holding the condom, its end plump and full with his captured cum. It swung gently in his grip, shining in the morning light.

"Good morning, slave," he said. "You've done real well. Time for you to go home and get to work."

I didn't want to leave, but I knew I had to. Reluctantly, I pulled on my clothes, disliking how they felt on my skin. The leather and metal that had bound me felt much more natural. I put my cap on, wishing it was the hood instead.

Hugging and kissing both Master Steve and Robert before I went on my way, I thanked them from the bottom of my heart. As I got in my car and started the ignition, I reflected that I had reached a turning point. Everything in my life from now on would be either "before" my first slave experience or "after" it. I had found my true nature, and in it real satisfaction. Having arrived at Steve and Robert's an uncertain and curious man, I left a happy and fulfilled slave. I was on my way.

Although I never did become a full-time slave to Master Steve and Robert, I had many more intense and exciting bondage-slave sessions with them. But those were nothing compared with the amazing journey that led me to my current situation as a full-time bondage slave to the best Master a boy could hope for. ◉

The Piss Mummy

"**D**O YOU UNDERSTAND your instructions, boy?" I said into the phone before taking another swig of bottled water.

"Yes, Sir," the young, breathless voice answered back.

"And you understand the use to which you will be put?"

"Completely, Sir."

"Then get your ass over here. You have the address."

"Yes, Sir! Thank you, Sir!"

I set the phone down and went to get the things I'd need. A little while later, there was a hesitant knock on the door. I hoped, for his own sake, that the boy wasn't having second thoughts. There was no turning back now. Whether he was willing or not, I was going through with what we had discussed.

Opening the door, I finally saw P.J., the young man I'd been talking with on the phone for the past few hours. I drank some more water as I sized him up.

He was pretty small, only about 5'6" or so, good-looking, 23 or 24, with one of those compact muscular bodies that I find so hot. His hair was dark blond, and he had a cute dimple in his chin. He had followed instructions, wearing nothing but a tank top, shorts, and tennis shoes. He would do for what I had in mind.

"Reporting as ordered, Sir," he said.

"Good boy, P.J.," I answered, putting my hand on his shoulder and pulling him inside. "You've been very obedient so far. I hope you plan on continuing to be so."

"Yes, Sir, I do, Sir," he said as he stepped over the threshold and entered my apartment.

"You understand that your purpose here is to be used by me, to get wrapped up and used as a piss hole?"

I saw his shorts tent at the description. He breathlessly whispered, "Yes, Sir..."

"Then get going," I said and shoved him toward the hallway. He stumbled forward, entering the corridor and turning the corner into the bedroom.

Joining him there, I had him assume wrapping position, standing straight as a rail with his hands at his sides. Satisfied that he was going to be obedient, I began my process. First, I blindfolded the boy, to better focus his concentration. I didn't want him thinking about anything other than the reason he was here. I placed small pillows between his knees and between his arms and torso so that he'd be comfortable.

Then I started wrapping him. Unspooling a huge roll of plastic wrap from the warehouse store, I encased the boy in a clear layer of bondage. Its surface shimmered with light reflections. P.J. let out little moans of submission as I wrapped the plastic around him tighter and tighter, pinning his arms to his sides and his legs together.

Soon enough he was done, a crystal mummy constricted head to foot with clear "bandages." His blindfolded eyes were underneath the wrapping, but I left his nose and mouth uncovered. His mind could wander, but he could still breathe easily. The only other parts of him still exposed to the air, hanging out over the plastic, were his uncut cock and his balls.

I took another swig of water and gripped his balls in one hand, liking the way the sudden touch made him shiver. His cum sack felt nice and warm, soft and hairy in my palm. With a few gentle pulls on his shaft, his cock hardened nicely. He was obviously a grower, not a shower, as his meat stretched out much farther than I had expected.

I was pleased.

Now it was time to get him into the bathroom. Gently, I lifted P.J.'s body off the ground and put him over my shoulder. I love carrying boys because it robs them of something they take for granted, their ability to walk. By mummifying P.J. and then picking him up, I was demonstrating without a doubt that I was in charge. He was my boy to use as I saw fit.

I carried him into the bathroom and carefully laid him in the bathtub, resting his head on the folded towel I'd placed at one end of it. My bladder was full, but I got my bottled water and drank some more. I'd need plenty of piss to make my plan work.

P.J. looked so hot lying there, his strong little body totally wrapped up in plastic, his hot cock and balls sticking up out of it. He was still hard, so the little fucker must have gotten off on being carried.

Well, if he thought that *was hot,* I told myself, *what was about to happen will blow him away.*

Slowly, so he'd hear every little sound, I unhooked my belt. The heavy buckle clinked as it was loosened, and I saw the boy below me tense at the sound.

I unzipped my pants, letting out my own sizable tubesteak. Uncut, my cock head was uncovered as it poked out of my pants. I took it in my palm and aimed it carefully down into the tub, at P.J.

I relaxed, willing my body to relinquish control after a long time of holding back. A few seconds later, the first stream began. It was a bright yellow, probably from the soda I'd drunk earlier. The stream of piss arced through the air and landed with a splat on the wrapped-up body in the tub.

P.J. wriggled in pleasure, groaning ecstatically as I continued to piss on him, bathing his chest with my water. The warm liquid trickled down both sides of his body. I'd been holding it for a long time, so I was really gushing with no end in sight. I started moving the stream, aiming lower and lower until I was spraying his cock and balls.

The cock flexed in response, precum oozing out of the piss slit. I bathed his cock with my urine as I up-ended my bottled water and drank deep.

There was plenty left in my bladder, but I halted the flow, slowing it to a trickle. I didn't want to give it all to him at once. I wanted to savor this. I hadn't had a piss mummy for a long time, and I was determined to enjoy him to the fullest.

P.J. moaned, desperate for more piss, needing it like he needed air. He was truly a piss pig, a hungry whore for piss that I had in my power to use and "abuse" as I saw fit.

"Are you my piss mummy, boy?" I asked loudly.

"Yes, Sir!" P.J. answered instantly.

"Are you my piss hole?"

"Yes, Sir!"

"Do you want it?"

"Desperately, Sir!"

"Do you *need* it?"

"More than anything, Sir!"

"Then open your fucking mouth and keep it open," I said as I released my bladder and let fly with another volley of recycled water. The nearly clear liquid splattered all over his encased chest, but this time the stream started moving the other way, toward his mouth.

The boy's whole body was twitching, quivering in anticipation. I couldn't hold back anymore and aimed for his open mouth, the stream filling the cavity in seconds.

"Mmmmmmm," the piss mummy gurgled.

"Keep that mouth open, boy," I warned. "Don't swallow unless I tell you to."

With his throat sealed off, the piss boy's mouth started overflowing, my water running down both sides of his head to gather beneath. I knew he badly wanted to swallow, that every second I made him hold back was sweet, sweet agony. I pinched off my cock again, halting the flow of piss into his hole.

"Okay, swallow," I said, and the mummy's throat flexed as he gulped down the piss that filled his mouth. When it had all disappeared down his gullet, he smiled a huge happy smile.

"Thank you, Sir! Thank you, Sir!" he said.

As I drank more water, I imagined it moving through

me, from the bottle to my body, out my cock and into the boy lying at my feet, worshipping me and my piss with his whole body, mind, and soul. Then I pulled my pocket knife out of my pocket and knelt down next to the tub. What I was going to do next required concentration.

With extreme care, I slit the plastic at the boy's side with the knife and slipped the blade inside. Turning it gently, I cut a gash in the wrapping and left a large air pocket behind. P.J. let out little whimpers. He didn't know what I was doing and was probably scared.

"It's okay, boy...," I murmured to him as I started cutting another gash. "It's okay. You're my boy, you're my piss mummy, nothing bad's gonna happen to you. Just relax...." My voice seemed to soothe him, and he calmed down. But his cock stayed hard the whole time.

I continued the process until P.J.'s mummified body was covered with holes, his pink skin exposed to the air. I stood back up, turned my load loose again, and watched the piss stream splash out onto my boy. Aiming my cock at the various holes, I was able to fill them with piss. The mummy started writhing in pleasure as my water began seeping downward, between his skin and the plastic holding him.

His hands were jerking at his sides, and I knew he wanted to get them free so he could jerk off. But no such luck — I wasn't letting him get off that easily. If he was going to shoot off, it would be at *my* hand, not his own. And besides, tops first. I squeezed out the last of my piss and started jerking the hefty cock in my fist. It felt good, the lingering drops of piss providing lubrication.

The jacking quickly got me hard, and I stared down at my piss mummy as I worked my cock in and out of my hand. He looked so hot ... that compact muscular body all wrapped up in the plastic, unable to move ... the piss all over him and gathering in pockets where I'd cut the holes ... the memory of how P.J. felt over my shoulder ... his nice cock hard and raging ...

"Oh, yeah!" I yelled as I came, my load bursting out of my cock head to hit the mummified body below me. The sticky, milky spunk hit the plastic and mixed with the piss, creating a liquid that the boy would've loved to pour down his throat. But another time. It was late, and since my load was shot, I wanted to get this over with.

Taking my last swig of bottled water, I knelt down next to the tub and took the boy's cock in my hand. He tensed at the sensation, his whole body flexing with desire.

"You want to come, boy?" I asked.

"Yes, Sir. Oh, yes, Sir!"

"Just think about my piss, boy . . . . It's all over you, and even next to your skin, between your skin and the plastic . . ."

"Oh, yeah . . . thank you, Sir!"

"My cum's on you too. My big cock shot out a load all over your piss-covered chest. Did you feel it? Did you feel the force of my cum when I shot on you?"

"Yes, Sir, oh . . ."

His cock was getting harder and harder in my hand. I knew he wasn't far from the moment of truth.

It was time to go in for the kill.

"You're my little piss slave, aren't you, P.J.?"

"Yes, Sir! I'm your piss slave, Sir!"

"My piss whore, my piss pig, my piss mummy!"

"Yes, Sir! I worship you, Sir! I worship your piss!"

"Then take this . . . ," I started as I let my last load of piss go, aiming right for his mouth, ". . . and *come!*"

"Oh, thank you, Sir!" he gurgled with passion as his back arched and spooge sprayed out of his cock. It was beautiful to watch his cum splatter all over him and mix with my piss and cum. P.J. thrashed around in the excitement of being totally covered and filled and owned by piss.

After a few minutes his orgasm faded, and his cock returned to its softer state. At my command, P.J. let his own bladder loose, and his saved-up piss flooded out of him into the tub.

"That's my good boy," I said.

The Piss Mummy

Then I helped him stand up and pulled my knife again. The boy whined and complained, wanting to stay as he was all night, but I was firm. There was no way I would sleep with a boy covered in piss and cum.

No way.

So I cut him out of his plastic bondage. He was one tired boy. Although he'd been immobile almost since he got to my place, he'd exhausted himself being my piss mummy. He could barely shower. I had to wash him, cleaning the sweat, piss, and cum off his beautiful body.

After I got him out of the shower and toweled him off, his eyelids were drooping. I didn't want to go through the hassle of dragging him to the bedroom, so I just picked him up. Gratefully, he wrapped his arms around my neck as I cradled his body. I carried him to my bedroom and gently laid him down. After I'd tucked him under the covers, I stripped down myself. Surprisingly, I felt tired, too. But I guess that's normal — creating a piss mummy is almost as tiring as being one.

I slid under the covers with P.J., and his body cuddled next to mine like we'd been sleeping together for years. With the boy in my arms, I relaxed. And as sleep softly came, I still had a big smile on my face. ◉

Five Bucks a Swat
For Master Vincent / Love, Chris

THERE WAS SOMETHING different in the air that night, something that said it was going to be special. Tony hadn't said anything out of the ordinary as we dressed to go out, but as the sub in a dominant/submissive relationship, I'm used to being told only what I absolutely need to know. There had been plenty of surprises in the six months Tony and I had been seeing each other.

And that night *was* special.

Tony had told me to wear what he calls my "jailhouse shorts," a pair of too-tight workout briefs striped in black and white. They clearly show the twin globes of hard flesh that make up my bubble butt. Tony loves my butt, describing it as "perfect" on more than one occasion.

He has many uses for my ass — burying his face in it, fucking it with dildos or his fingers, and his favorite, spanking it. I love it when Tony spanks me, and he loves doing it. It's our favorite thing to do aside from him fucking the shit out of me.

I finished dressing myself with a white tank top that showed off my lean chest and flat stomach. Tony came up behind me and buckled a leather collar encircled with short, blunt spikes around my slender neck. It's a show collar, so we were probably going to be around other people.

He came around front to admire his boy toy, and I saw he was dressed in a plain T-shirt, jeans, boots, and leather jacket. He never likes to draw attention to himself when I'm with him — he wants people to be looking at me. He enjoys showing me off.

After locking the collar with a small padlock, he had me put on my combat boots and follow him out of his condo to where his new truck was parked. When we got in, Tony tied a blindfold over my eyes and adjusted my seat so it was leaning way back, making it hard for other drivers to see that I was blindfolded. Then we were off.

Without sight, I couldn't tell where he was taking us. We drove for about 20 minutes, but that didn't tell me anything — we could've been anywhere in the city. I felt him slow the truck down, stop, and parallel park. He got out and came around to my side. Opening my door, he helped me out of the truck but didn't take off the blindfold.

"Do you trust me?" he asked.

"Yes, Sir." I was a little scared, but also excited.

"Everything will be okay."

"I believe you, Sir."

"Come on," he said, putting his hands on my shoulders. As he guided me away from the truck, I heard him close the door and activate the vehicle's alarm. We walked along the street and then turned into a driveway. I heard muffled sounds of music and multiple voices. My anticipation increased.

Tony led me up some stairs and through a door. Now the sounds were joined by smells — beer, smoke, and men. Lots of men. I heard some jeers and laughter as I was guided through what must have been a large crowd. An amplified voice rang out, drowning out the other sounds.

"Here we go, guys," said the Master of Ceremonies. "Give it up for Master Tony Gardner, who has graciously provided us with the first subject for tonight's event!"

Subject? Event? What's going on here? I wondered. But there was no pause for explanations. Tony pushed me up a short flight of stairs onto what must have been a stage, because the voice of the M.C. was louder and closer.

"What's happening?" I whispered.

"Trust me," Tony said in my ear, and then other hands took me. I was bent over something wooden, probably a table, my arms stretched out in front of me and my wrists bound with leather cuffs. I struggled, but the cuffs were secured to something solid. My shorts were yanked down, exposing my naked butt to the room and leaving my cock and balls to hang free off the edge of the table. Finally, my legs were spread wide and my ankles restrained in that position. As the crowd of men whooped and hollered, I blushed in excitement and embarrassment.

"Step right up, men!" the M.C. said. "Be the first to lay your hands on this beautiful butt!"

Huh?

"What's this boy's name, Master Tony?"

"He answers to the name of Spanky," I heard Tony say, prompting a roar of laughter from the crowd.

"Five bucks a swat, guys, five bucks a swat!" the M.C. continued. "And it's for a wonderful cause — the Gay Center's Youth Task Force, which provides food and shelter to homeless gay kids. Who's going to be first to spank this ass for charity?"

Goosebumps rose on every inch of my body as I processed what I'd just heard. *Spanked for charity?* This was bizarre, yet undeniably hot. *But it doesn't matter what I think*, I realized. *I'm in no position to object!*

The M.C.'s voice boomed through the air.

"You, sir. Come on up here! You'll be the first to spank Spanky's ass tonight. How much are you donating to our worthy cause?"

"$30," a new voice said. "I'd do more, but it's all I have on me."

"Fantastic! $30 — that's six swats on this magnificent ass!"

The man's hand on my butt cheek felt good as he rubbed it a little. My cock was getting hard in anticipation. *This is all so incredible*, I thought. *Is it a dream?*

Any doubts about its reality were banished when the first swat hit my left ass cheek with a loud smacking sound. It hurt like hell, but it made my cock flex. The second and third swats were even harder, and the crowd rumbled its approval as the remaining blows fell.

"Well done, sir!" the M.C. boomed. "Just the warm-up we needed! Who's next?"

I wondered where Tony was. I resisted the urge to be scared — Tony had asked me to trust him, and I had said I would.

"You there! With all the tattoos. How much are you going to give to help those kids?"

"Fifty bucks!" a deep voice answered.

"Come on up. Ten swats, gentlemen, ten swats on this choice piece of boymeat!"

The men cheered.

Tattoo-man alternated his spanking — first one cheek, then the other. But all his swats were hard. The M.C.'s running commentary pounded in my ears. After eight swats, I heard him say, "We've got some good color coming out there, guys. Look at Spanky's ass cheeks turning nice and pink!"

Smack! on my left cheek (No. 9).

Smack! on my right cheek (No. 10).

"And that's ten swats! Thank you, sir, for helping our worthy cause!"

"I'm next!" a voice bellowed.

"Yes, you — get on up here!"

I heard the stairs creak as my latest tormentor walked up to the stage. *He must be a big guy,* I thought with a hint of panic. *He's probably got a hell of a swat.* I found myself tensing up, my knees locking and my butt clenching. I knew it was a stupid thing to do. I'd learned from experience that it doesn't help and can sometimes make it worse to tense up when you're getting spanked. But I couldn't avoid it — I was scared.

"How many swats are you buying, sir?" the M.C. asked.

"Only have money for three," the loud voice said, "so I'm gonna make 'em count." I didn't want to know what that meant, but I was about to find out.

The big guy's first swat was like a thunderbolt, his hand connecting with my ass so hard that I cried out in pain.

Five Bucks a Swat

He didn't do one cheek at a time like the other guys had but aimed right for my butt crack and got both sides at the same time. He must've had a really big hand. Before I could catch my breath, the second swat came, exploding against me with enough force to bring tears to my eyes and force another yelp of agony out of me.

The assembled men groaned sympathetically — my ass had to be bright red by then. I was ready for big guy's third swat, but it didn't make it any less painful. I bit back a third scream, not wanting to hear it myself, maybe afraid to hear it myself.

The crowd roared in approval.

"Three unforgettable swats!" the M.C. said. "Thank you for your $15, sir. It's going to help a lot of people."

No more, I thought, *please no more.* But somehow, through all of this, my cock had stayed hard. Maybe I didn't want it to end as much as I thought I did.

"All right, gentlemen, we're ready for another volunteer. Yes, sir, would you like to go next? Is that a $100 bill in your hand?"

I tried not to freak out. *Twenty swats — how can I take that? How can I take any of this?* It was more intense than anything I'd experienced before. *Think of Tony,* I told myself. *Think of his warm, caring eyes; think of his low, soothing voice; think of how good it feels when he puts his hands on me...*

But instead of my lover's reassuring touch, what I felt next was a hard smack on my butt from the big spender. It was painful, but at least not as bad as the beating I'd gotten from the big guy. I endured the pain as best I could, gritting my teeth as sweat began to drip down my face. I was starting to get sore from being bound in one place for so long, but there was nothing I could do. I didn't want to embarrass Tony or myself by calling for help, so I just lay there and took it like a man.

The big spender had his own style of spanking. The first five swats were hard and painful, but the next five were soft and gentle, more pats than swats. My punished flesh was grateful for even a short break from the pain, but the third five were once again painful strikes. My ass must've been beyond cherry red by then, and it felt like raw hamburger. I hardly felt the final soft five — my butt was going numb.

After the big spender was done I lost track. The M.C. kept talking and the swats kept coming, but I was in a haze of pain, fear, fatigue, and sexual desire.

Just as I felt that I couldn't possibly take any more, the M.C.'s voice penetrated my confusion: "Okay, I think Spanky's had enough for one night. We've raised almost $700, so let's give him a hand. Come on, men, give it up for the boy!"

Loud applause and cheers followed. Then there was a long pause — for the first time that night, something had made the M.C. speechless.

Finally, his voice came again: "Master Tony? You want to pay to spank your own boy?"

"It's worth paying for," I heard Tony say.

My heart leapt at his voice. I didn't realize how much I had missed him. I'd almost forgotten he was there, I'd felt so alone in my private hell of pain. Then his voice was in my ear.

"Everything's going to be okay," he whispered.

"I believe you, Sir," I said, echoing my earlier statement.

"Twenty-five dollars from Master Tony!" the M.C. said. "Watch the last five swats for Spanky!"

Tony rested one hand on the small of my back, the other on my flaming ass. Then he raised his hand.

I closed my eyes behind the blindfold.

Smack!

"One!" roared the M.C.

The pain was like an explosion in my butt cheek.

Smack!

"Two!" The crowd joined the M.C. in the count.

But what's happening? Tony reached between my legs and took my softened cock in his hand. I was immediately rock hard again.

Five Bucks a Swat

Smack!

"Three!"

He was jerking me off with one hand and spanking me with the other! The pain in my ass and the pleasure in my crotch mixed, hurting and confusing me, but taking me so high that I felt I was floating above my body, observing what he was doing.

Smack!

"Four!"

I couldn't take much more of this — I was in total sensory overload. My butt was blazing, matched by the inferno of ecstasy between my legs.

Smack!

"Five!"

As Tony's last swat hit me I came, squirting my sperm onto the floor beneath the table where I was bound. The crowd went wild, cheering and clapping like they'd just seen the winning touchdown at a football game. At the same instant something broke inside me. The wild mix of feelings over the last hour overflowed, and I started to cry. Tears squeezed out from my tightly closed eyelids and dripped down my face.

I hardly felt it when my wrists were released from the restraints. My ankles were freed next, and I almost fell to the floor of the stage, I was so exhausted and disoriented. The blindfold was removed, and I squinted at the bright lights that were hitting the stage. Someone pulled my shorts back up, my butt still stinging under the fabric. Turning around, I recognized the place as the city's leather bar, with a hot crowd of men in their best cruising gear. But mostly I saw Tony, standing onstage in front of me, grinning.

"You did good," he said.

"Thank you, Sir," I said, and began to collapse again.

Tony caught me before I fell and hoisted me gently up and over his shoulder. He adjusted me for maximum comfort and secured my legs in place with one arm. To the cheering of the crowd, he carried me down the stairs. I was too tired to do anything but hang limply over his shoulder, happy that it was all over and I was safe in his arms.

As he carried me out of the bar I heard the M.C. start the whole thing over again: "Okay, guys, the next spankboy is being provided by Master Richard..."

The quiet and the fresh air of the street were most welcome. Tony carried me over his shoulder for the whole walk back to his truck. When he set me down next to it, I grinned at him.

"Five bucks a swat, huh?"

"You're worth much more, but I figured it was all they could afford." ⊙

The Executioner's Boy

I AM THE EXECUTIONER'S BOY. It was only after the man in the black hood kept me in his dungeon for more than a month that I realized he will never let me go, that I am his prisoner for good.

Because everyone thinks I am dead — just one more executed criminal — no one will ever know that I am still alive. Terrified, beaten, and raped, but still alive. No one will ever know that instead of killing me, the executioner took me to his deepest dungeon and locked me in a cage, hidden from all eyes but his own. No one will ever know that I was claimed by the executioner as his personal slave, and that he intends for me to serve him there for the rest of my life.

No one.

I was just a farm boy from a little village about five miles from the royal city. Every time I went there to visit the marketplace, I would stop if I saw an execution going on. Many people seem to be fascinated by the degradation, suffering, and ruin of others, but I am not one of them. I did not stop by the enclosed courtyard where the dreadful events took place in order to watch other human beings die horribly.

No, I stopped to watch the executioner. Ever since the first time I saw the man in the black hood, when I was very young, I had been utterly entranced by him. I never gave a name to what I felt. All I knew was that once I looked at him I couldn't take my eyes away.

I marveled at the tensing and flexing of his huge muscles as he lifted the ax, the sweat flying off his enormous chest as he brought the hideous weapon down on the victim's neck. How many times did I long to reach out and feel the thick furry hair of his body, to caress the black fabric of the hood that concealed his face from view, to fling myself at his feet and offer myself to him?

The aura of power that surrounded him was so strong I felt I could touch it. There was something else there, too: fear. The fear that walked with him was more intense than any other feeling he inspired. Maybe that is why I never saw anyone else watching him as I did. Everyone else just watched the condemned criminals, watched them writhing in despair and agony until finally they stopped moving altogether.

Many of my fellows were so afraid of Satan that they refused to speak his name aloud, for fear of calling attention to themselves and bringing his wrath upon them. So it was with the executioner. Hardly anyone looked at him, and none were foolish enough to catch his eyes, blazing out from holes in his hood.

Hardly anyone, that is, except me. I stared at the executioner, every time I stared, for hours it seemed, waiting for ... what? I never knew. Being so young and naive, I knew little of the world, much less of the darkness that lies just beneath its surface. So I sought out his eyes, vainly trying to lock his gaze into my own.

But it never happened. Years and years went by, and I was 16, then 18, then 21. He never looked at me, not even once. For all I could tell, he never looked at anyone. He seemed to exist in a separate place, as if his massive body lived here but his mind was somewhere far, far away.

I soon despaired of ever catching his eye. I felt myself invisible, so ignored was I by him. But I was foolish, a stupid farm boy. I should have realized that as time went on, the executioner couldn't help but notice me — a young man with hair the color of straw, tanned and muscled from 24 years of hard work in the sun.

All my thoughts of other worlds and separate places were ridiculous. He was a flesh-and-blood man, just like me, and he could not help but notice me as I stood in the front of the crowd at every execution. I was coming to every one he did, not merely every time I came to town — I would schedule special trips into the city just to see him. My parents, forever tending to my plague-sickened brother, noticed how often I was going to the city.

"Keal," my father would say, "why are you going again? You were there the day before yesterday!" My mother, always on my side, put her hand gently on his.

"Leave him be," she said softly. "He's a man now. He's done all the work that needs to be done around here. Let him go."

My father would grumble and mumble about the lack of discipline in the house, but he would never directly challenge my mother. Then my brother moaned in his sleep, and their attention was on him instantly, kneeling over his prone body as if he were already dead.

My own feelings for my brother had died long ago. I knew that he was doomed, and so I closed up my heart to him. I wished to know no suffering when he finally did die. I had felt so close to him when we were younger, yet now I let him go and said goodbye to him in my heart. Now I longed for another masculine presence, not that of my father but someone else. Power attracted me strongly, and my father was powerless. My brother had been strong until the plague struck him down.

Perhaps that was another reason I was so drawn to the executioner: He was the very embodiment of power — he could take someone's life.

Curiously, my feelings for my parents were starting to die as surely as those for my brother had already done. I loved them and all, but I had begun to feel more and more disconnected from them as I grew older. They were always taking care of my brother and had little time for me. I felt both invisible and in the way. I was alone, all my friends having gone off to fight in the Crusades several years before. None had yet returned, and I had given up hope of ever seeing them again — at least alive.

The only thing that seemed to matter to me anymore

was the executioner. My almost daily visits to the city to see him occupied more and more of my thoughts until they became the focus of my whole existence.

I'll never forget the day when everything changed. My eyes had been searching his body, crawling up and down his expansive chest, rock-solid stomach, and tree-trunk legs. I had done this thousands of times, covering every inch of his body with my gaze, taking it all in, trying to absorb every shape, every contour, committing them to memory as if they weren't already burned into my brain.

On this day my eyes were rolling up the man's legs to his codpiece, that full pouch that hung from his belt. But this time, the familiar shape was changing. My eyes stopped in their ascent and watched as the pouch elongated, growing, whatever was underneath stretching the fabric nearly to the breaking point.

The unthinkable was happening: he was getting hard! In all my months of watching him I had never seen this before. What could possibly make him get hard? I tore my eyes off his bulging codpiece and looked up at his face. I came very close to losing control and pissing down my leg.

The executioner was staring at me. His eyes, burning through the holes in his hood, were trained on me where I stood at the front of the crowd. The bolt of electricity that passed between us seemed so real, I was amazed the people around us didn't notice it. I felt my own crotch stir and my cock grow as hot blood surged into it.

But there was no power or strength in my own reaction, only in his gaze. I felt as if the mere power of his eyes was ripping aside the layers of my being, all the barriers I had put up, flinging them aside as if they were nothing and tossing them to the wind to be carried away like dandelion seeds.

I couldn't move. I felt absolutely rooted to the spot, and nothing else mattered. I didn't know what to do, who I was, where I was. Anything and everything about myself was lost in that apocalyptic instant.

The Executioner's Boy

Paralyzing fear coursed through me, filling me like ice water. I felt utterly naked and alone in his eyes, isolated from the world and reduced to a tiny insect, writhing and crawling in agony. I felt that this man could completely destroy me with the slightest effort. But somewhere within the fear was that first feeling, that galvanizing pleasure and excitement to be caught up by him and held ever so tightly by his smoldering eyes.

Then it was over. His gaze flickered onto something else, and I felt as if I'd been dropped off a roof. I longed for his gaze again, forgetting the terror that had filled me a second before. More than anything I wanted to be held in the grip of his eyes again, to feel them burning into me from above even as the stench of the death he had caused wafted down to defile the air.

The crowd began dispersing. The royal servants assigned to clean up after executions moved in and began their grisly work. The executioner, without so much as a second glance my way, came down from the scaffold and moved out into the city toward the castle. Before I could think to follow, he was swallowed up by the throng of people.

It was over, and I was devastated. Of course, if I had used what little brain I have, I would have realized that it was just beginning.

I went home and slumped into bed, falling asleep almost instantly. The daily walk from my home to the city and back was building up my body even more than it already was, but it made me dog tired every night.

I dreamed of the moon and of a dark cloud covering it . . . a cloud that allowed only two shiny beams of light through a pair of slits. I startled myself awake when I realized that the cloud was the executioner's hood and the two slits were the eyes that had held me so very tightly that day. I fell asleep again, and this time there was only darkness. Darkness, and a strange sound, like a pack of wild animals screeching in the night, miles and miles away.

The next day I was awakened by my father. A shocking

piece of news was circulating through the kingdom. Someone had stolen a precious jewel from the royal treasury! The heralds screamed it day and night.

I waited at my brother's bedside with my parents for news of the criminal's being caught. Surely death was the only sentence for such a heinous crime. I sat on my brother's bed as I stared out the window, lost in thought. All I could think was, *Another execution is going to happen. Another reason to go to the city and watch the man in the black hood.* I was excited by the thought of seeing him again, although I didn't think things could get more exciting than they had the day before when he looked at me. Had I but known what was about to happen!

I could not have been more surprised when royal guards appeared at the door of our home and declared me under arrest for the theft of the jewel. Astonished, my parents cried out for mercy, saying that there was no way such an accusation could be true — their son was honest, forthright, upstanding in every way.

Stunned into silence, I could do nothing but kiss my brother's damp forehead and say farewell to my parents. I dumbly gave myself to the guards and went with them. My parents had to be restrained from running after me.

That very day I appeared in the royal court before an honorable judge to answer the charge of stealing from the royal family. Maintaining the placidity that had sustained me this long and prevented me from panicking, I calmly declared my innocence of any such crime. I was certain that if I was honest, logical, and reasonable, the error would be exposed and I would be set free.

But the prosecution raised point after point to support their claim, a veritable mountain of evidence against me. With astonishment I listened to the testimonies of at least a dozen citizens who swore that they had seen me on the night of the thievery creeping around near the lower entrance of the castle — one even said she saw me break the door and enter the treasury.

The Executioner's Boy

My boots were examined, and the tread was shown to match footprints taken in and around the trove the night of the theft. The alibis and arguments I had so carefully prepared fell on deaf ears. The evidence against me was impossible to ignore.

With my mouth hanging open I listened to the verdict — I was found guilty, and the sentence was death. I was deemed so low and vile that my execution would not even be performed in public but in the darkest depths of the castle's dungeon.

My reserve broke, and I shrieked in terror. I leaped up from my seat and tried to escape the court chamber. The guards caught me before I took two steps.

I was no match for them, of course, but I put up a good struggle. They finally had to tie my hands behind my back. When my screams grew tiresome they gagged me, and when I made it clear I would not cooperate with them at all, I was knocked over the head with a sword handle. The last thing I remember before I sank into unconsciousness was being slung over a guard's shoulder.

WHEN I WOKE UP, I was in some dark place. I tried to stand up and reeled in pain as I struck cold, hard metal above and around me. *What is going on?* I asked myself. I reached my hand out into the terrifying blackness and felt the metal carefully. It was not solid. I could put my hands through it in some places. *A cage! I'm in a cage!*

The fear that gripped me was so total, I'm amazed that I could control myself. I think the only thing that prevented me from pounding on the bars was the memory of the pain I had just felt. If I did flail about, the only thing that would happen was more pain. I suddenly noticed that the chill air was pebbling my skin — I was naked, my cock and balls hanging helpless and vulnerable.

What am I going to do?

"Help!" I shouted. "Where am I?"

After a moment, a figure appeared. I couldn't tell if my

ability to see had improved or there was more light near the cage, because the figure seemed to materialize from the darkness itself, as if it was blacker than the blackness. (Later, after my eyes adjusted, I saw that torches mounted here and there on the walls — one right behind the cage — provided the flickery illumination, their smoke escaping through ceiling vents.)

I didn't have to see the dark figure clearly to know who it was: the man in the black hood. The executioner himself was standing over me, staring down at me in the cage.

Seeing him filled me with dread, but somewhere there was excitement, too. At least he was a familiar image amid the unknown surroundings. I suddenly remembered the judge's sentence and reeled in terror. *The executioner is here!* I thought in a panic. *I am to be his next victim!*

But no, that cannot be possible! Not after what has passed between us. There must be a mistake — he is going to tell me they discovered at the last minute that I am innocent, and he is here to set me free.

"What's happened?" I asked him. "Please, tell me . . ."

He said nothing.

"Talk to me!" I yelled, angry now. "Tell me what's going on!" Still he stared without speaking. Rage and panic were fighting for dominance inside me.

"Help me!" I screamed. "Someone! Help me please!"

I kept screaming, certain that someone else would hear — someone, anyone but this ghastly creature that stood over me like the grim reaper himself. My screaming continued until I could no longer hear myself.

Then the man in the black hood stepped closer to the cage, into the light. I wasn't really watching what he was doing until I felt a stream of hot liquid hit my chest. The rank odor assailed my nostrils, and I cried out in disgust. The executioner was pissing on me!

I was disgusted but momentarily distracted by the sight of the man's huge cock. It looked as thick around as my wrist, yet it was not even hard. It lay in the executioner's hand like a limp sausage, the yellow piss spewing out as if from a fountain. I wondered what that cock would look like fully erect. I was getting absorbed in staring at the thick veins that coursed across the shaft when I remembered what was happening. *He's pissing on me!* I shouted in my head.

I tried to pull away from this grotesque indignity, but there was nowhere to go; the metal bars surrounded me on all sides. I turned so that the piss hit my back and dripped down onto the thin bed of straw lining the cage. I had never known such humiliation, such degradation.

"Please stop! Why are you doing this?" I cried out. There was no response besides the liquid sound and the sickening warmth bathing my back.

After what seemed like several more minutes, the stream began to thin and finally stopped. Warily, I turned around. The executioner was shaking the last drops of piss out of the folds of his foreskin. I couldn't help but be fascinated by this sight despite what I had just been put through.

His eyes were utterly calm and uninterested, as if there was nothing odd or unusual in what he had just done. He pulled his cock back into his codpiece and walked away into the dark, leaving me alone once more.

I struggled to make sense of what had happened. I could understand the *what*, but not the *why*. My cry came back to me, *Why are you doing this?* and I remembered what had been going on just before he pulled his cock out. I'd been screaming for help. *So? So what? Why had he done it?* The silence around me was oppressive.

Silence. . . . It came to me suddenly. *He wanted me to be quiet, so he pissed on me. Now I* am *quiet. But why didn't he speak to me? Why hadn't he told me not to scream?*

I was in the legendary dungeons beneath the castle. The full impact of my situation hit me, and I was again seized with terror. I had been sentenced to be executed within the dungeons! Again I began yelling and screaming for someone to let me out, that there had been a mistake, that I was innocent!

The man with the black hood appeared out of the dark again. This time he had some rope coiled over his shoulder.

"This is a mistake!" I yelled. "I'm not guilty! I didn't do it, I swear!"

All the elements of the situation came together in my mind — the horrible injustice of the accusation, the trial, the verdict. All the evidence had been so well designed and presented that there was no way I could possibly defend myself. It was almost as though someone had *wanted* me to be found guilty. And suddenly I thought I'd figured out what had happened.

"I was framed!" I said. "Someone set me up!"

The realization was blinding, shocking — I was elated with my discovery even as the fear continued to freeze my blood. *But why and how would someone do this to me?* I desperately asked myself. *And who?*

The executioner took some keys off his belt and unlocked the cage. Before the door was halfway open I was jumping out, gratefully stretching my sore muscles. I turned to the executioner, now sure that I could convince him this was a mistake.

"I was framed . . . ," I said breathlessly. "Please believe me . . ."

"I do . . . ," the man in the black hood said, his voice rich and full and resonant. The assuredness with which he spoke chilled my blood as he finished the first sentence I had ever heard him speak: ". . . because I'm the one who framed you. I wanted you, and now you're mine."

My eyes went wide and the scream of horror that was about to fly out was blocked by the leather gag that he suddenly shoved in my mouth. I struggled wildly, but the executioner grabbed me and squeezed with all his strength.

Once again I had a strange mix of emotions. The horror of what had happened was threatening to make me lose all control. But I was also reeling with excitement at being close to him. His rich scent, musky and sweaty, almost made me swoon. Even as I squirmed in his grip I was overwhelmed by the pure tactile pleasure of being near him, of feeling his rough skin rubbing against mine. It was fantasy plus nightmare. My bones seemed close to snapping in his vise-like grip, and I moaned through the gag. He released me, and I fell to the floor in pain.

THE MAN IN THE BLACK HOOD knelt down next to me and slowly and deliberately tied me up. I couldn't resist, I was so stunned from the prior squeezing. Powerless and terrified to move against him, I felt him loop the coils of rope around my arms and legs and pull them tight, knotting them securely until they dug into my flesh. When my arms were secured to the sides of my body and my legs firmly tied together, he lifted me up to a standing position.

Lightheaded, I stared at him as he looked me over. Then, without warning, he hit me across the face so hard that I fell back down. My ass and back hit the hard stone floor, and I whimpered in pain.

The sound of it seemed to incense him, and he started beating me. My tears started flowing with the second punch to my stomach. I couldn't hold in my crying no matter how hard I tried. What was happening to me was so unthinkable that I didn't know what to do, so I just withdrew into myself, reverting back into the scared little boy I had been when I was younger . . . and the further I withdrew, the harder he beat me.

His open palms slapped me across the face, his club-like fists punched me in the stomach, and his heavy studded boots stomped on my chest, my back, and my balls, abusing them so harshly that I was sure the ballsac had been slashed open and everything inside was spilling out onto the floor.

After a while I stopped crying and just let it happen. My world had become a mostly dark void shot through with horrible streaks of red and silver, agonizing shards of orange and purple.

Eventually he was satisfied. He stopped and stood over

me, sweat from his monolithic body dripping onto me and mixing with my blood. Then he reached down and yanked me off the ground as he would a misbehaving dog, as if I weighed no more than a sack of grain. He was so strong he carried me with only one arm.

He brought me back over to my cage and tossed me inside. I whimpered in pain as I struck the ground, though I took some meager comfort because at least my cage was a familiar place. The executioner locked the cage door and disappeared into the blackness. Something stuck in my mind: *"My cage."* When had that *happened? When did I start to think of this hideous little prison as "mine"?*

Perhaps it was because I knew that the man in the black hood could inflict less pain on me inside the cage than when I was out in the open. In some strange way, it protected as well as imprisoned me. But it was not even these disturbing thoughts that frightened me almost as much as the beating I had just received. No. It was the *way* I had thought them, passive and resigned, as if . . .

I almost couldn't think it, couldn't feel it. But there it was . . . as if I had already accepted the fate that had befallen me, as if I had even begun to embrace it.

I am never leaving here, I realized suddenly. The executioner had decided that he wanted me, so he framed me, got a private execution ordered, and now had me down where he alone ruled. *No one will ever suspect that I am still alive.* The fear that gripped me was paralyzing. My mind was spinning frantically, formulating plots and plans, trying to think of some way, any way to escape this place.

But it is foolish to think of escape, I concluded. *There's no sense in trying to resist the man in the black hood. Such thoughts are madness, and surely the path of defiance can only lead to death.*

Then something changed in me. The feelings of horror and terror still mingled in my gut, but from somewhere there was another feeling — one of calm.

Calm? From what source am I drawing calm? I wondered.

The Executioner's Boy

Maybe it was born of the knowledge that this new existence, as terrifying as it was, might actually be somehow better *than the one I had been plucked from? But isn't that as mad as wanting to fight him?*

Or is it? What did I have to look forward to? A lifetime of work on the farm? An endless, uneventful existence growing up, being locked into a marriage of obligation to a woman I don't love, taking on a family of my own, and growing old and dying?

I shuddered. *Down here, my life will undoubtedly be shorter, but at least I will be serving a purpose. And I am, after all, in love with this man.*

These thoughts so entranced me that I hardly noticed the throbbing pain of my wounds. Soon enough the sharp pain ebbed away and was replaced by a dull ache all over. I fell asleep, and when I woke up, my wounds had been cleaned and dressed, and I was unbound. The wounds still hurt, but I realized there was nothing broken, and hopefully nothing had been permanently damaged.

Of course not, I thought suddenly. *He wouldn't have gone to all this trouble just to kill me. He wants me submissive, but alive.* Just the same, I would try not to anger him.

That's when I felt the skeletal gnawing of hunger in my stomach. *How long has it been since I last ate? Hours, days, weeks?*

I looked into the gloom of the dungeon, but nothing moved. I waited and waited, but no food was forthcoming. Finally I had to start calling for the man in the black hood, even though I was still covered with bruises from the result of my last call. After a few minutes he appeared out of the darkness again.

"I'm sorry to bother you, Sir," I said meekly. "But I am very hungry and thirsty. Can you please give me something to eat and drink?"

He stared at me for a long time, as if considering. Then once again he pulled down his pants. His cock was hard again. I backed away, not knowing what to expect, but his hand snaked between the bars and grabbed the back of my neck, forcing me forward. I tried to keep my mouth closed but his cock shoved itself inside. I thought about biting him but didn't want to face the punishment for that.

The executioner had to work his cock against my mouth and throat for a long time before it was in far enough to please him. I gagged and tried to escape, but there was nowhere to go. I coughed, and phlegm filled my mouth, lubricating it a little. I guess that pleased him, for he let out little grunts of pleasure whenever I gagged.

When his cock was inside my mouth far enough, the executioner fucked my face for a while. It hurt. He was doing it too hard, slamming his enormous organ further and further into me. The tender flesh at the back of my throat was getting rubbed raw, and my jaws ached from being forced open so long.

I felt lightheaded, like I was going to faint, and I was gagging so much that spit and phlegm was leaking out of my mouth onto the floor. But somehow I must have enjoyed it, because my own cock was getting hard.

"Feeding time, boy," he suddenly said. "Eat."

Oh God, I thought, *he can't mean it!* But in the next instant he was pumping his cum into my mouth. The sticky mass of jism dripped down my throat, and I felt my stomach cramp and seize up. I gagged even harder than before and tried to push him away, but he held me tight.

"It's this or nothing, boy. It doesn't matter to me."

I relaxed and let the last of it jet toward my gut. I opened my mouth wide to let him remove his cock, but he didn't. He just let it rest on my tongue and get soft. When it was totally soft I tried to pull away from him, but he held my head in place. *What is he doing?* Once again I guessed too late what was about to happen.

"Drink, boy," he said. "Here comes your slave water."

I felt movement in his dick and knew what was coming. In a second the horrible acid taste flooded my mouth, and I almost vomited.

The executioner was making me drink his piss. As much

as I fought and twisted, he held me in place and pissed until the last drop was out. Then he let me go, and I moaned a little at the sudden pain. He had been holding me so tight against the bars that the metal had begun to dig into my flesh. I fell backward onto the floor of the cage as he left me once again. My cock hung between my legs, gone soft thanks to the repulsive experience I had just had.

I felt so angry, so violated, and so disgusted that I came very close to making myself vomit it all up right then and there. But after a moment's consideration I decided not to. I knew it would do me no good. And if it was all I was going to get to eat, I didn't want to lose it. Even though I had woken up only minutes before, I tried to go back to sleep. It was all I could think of to do.

SEVERAL HOURS LATER, I guess, after dozing in fits and starts, I came to and realized my cock was hard. I hadn't come in what seemed like years. My hands were unbound, so I did what any man would do. I started to jerk myself off, spitting on my hand to make it slicker. I figured at least this was something I could do to ease the immense boredom of being locked in a cage like an animal.

I closed my eyes and leaned back, my mind searching for something to think about, something to take me away from the living nightmare that had engulfed me, something to make me come. I was surprised when the image that flowed to the surface was that of myself getting face fucked and then pissed into by the executioner. I tried to fight it for a second, but then gave up. I was tired of fighting.

I thought about the feel of that huge cock in my mouth, about the sensation of the liquids pouring down my throat. What had moments before sent my cock flopping downward was now making it pulse with arousal. My hand worked faster and faster as precum started dripping out of it. I reveled in the sensations, the first real pleasure I'd felt since I'd been brought down to this hellhole.

A searing impact left what felt like a trail of fire on my

chest. I screamed and doubled over, trying to shield myself. A second pain exploded on my back, which felt like it had been rent open by a jagged blade.

"Please!" I yelled. "Please stop!"

It happened a third time, this time on my legs. I crumbled onto my side and started shaking uncontrollably. The man in the black hood loomed over me, a riding crop in his hand. I was surprised to see that it wasn't dripping with blood.

"Never, boy," he said. I didn't understand.

"What? What did I do, Sir?" I asked meekly. He pointed at my limp cock.

"That is not yours to touch. Don't ever touch it again, or I'll hack it off."

Fear and revulsion swam from my chest down into my groin. If my cock hadn't already gone soft, his threat would've wilted it in a second.

"Yes, Sir," I whispered, looking up at him with the eyes of a rabbit talking to a wolf.

It took me a long time to get back to sleep. When I woke again, I guessed that he didn't trust me to do as I'd promised. My hands were tied behind my back, and my cock was encased in a leather chastity belt padlocked shut.

The soreness from the crop would take longer to fade away than the soreness from the beating. I knew that time was passing, although my sense of it had become completely dulled. I swam in and out of delirium. I never remembered eating or drinking, yet I had lots of memories of sucking the executioner's cock and getting fluids pumped into me. Somehow I managed to stay alive.

I was never let out of the cage. It was my home now. Eventually my hands were released, and I was free to move them around. I didn't even try to unlock my chastity belt, and not just because I knew it would only result in losing the use of my hands again. I had grown used to it and somehow found the rough leather against my skin comforting.

In the same way, I no longer had thoughts of escaping.

The dungeon had become my whole world, and the little lighted chamber my cage was in was my neighborhood. The executioner brought weights into the chamber and once in a while let me out to use them. He said he didn't want a slave that wasn't in good shape, so I had to keep myself up for him. All the times I used the weights, I never even thought of trying to explore the nearby chambers and hallways.

I'm where I'm supposed to be, doing the job I was born to do. Where and how this realization came to me I never really knew. I think it happened very slowly over time as I became used to my strange surroundings.

The man in the black hood became the focus of my existence. He was my captor, my kidnapper, my king, my god, and my family all at once — the one human being I had contact with and therefore the one on which I lavished all my emotions. I hated him, despised him . . . yet loved him, too. After all, he was keeping me alive. He hadn't executed me or let me starve like he could have. I was living a life that would have been unthinkable to me before, yet now I had trouble imagining any other life.

Little by little, day by day, the executioner was making me totally and absolutely dependent on him, not just physically, but emotionally, sexually, spiritually — every way a human being *can* depend on another. I spent so many hours locked in my cage with nothing to do that I longed for him constantly. He was my only connection to any kind of human reality, the only break in what was otherwise aimless mental roaming.

ALL THROUGH THIS TIME, he never again spoke to me, and I never saw the features that lay eternally concealed behind the black hood. I gave up wondering and imagining what his face might look like and almost came to think of the hood *as* his face, its only organs the eyes that glared down at me like a hawk's.

I had become like a domestic animal. I was so docile

and obedient that he soon saw fit to leave me unbound in my cage, with no rope, cuffs, blindfold, or gag to keep me in line. I had gotten to the point where I thought I would do anything for him. Little did I know how far from that point I still was. But I realized it one day when he came to my cage and said that it was time for me to be marked. I didn't know what he meant, but I kept my mouth shut as he unlocked the cage and let me out. I knelt before him.

"I live to serve you, Sir," I said. He looked down at me, eyes gleaming.

"I hope you mean that, boy," he said. "Because I'm about to find out if you do."

Before I could even get scared, he pulled out what he had been holding behind his back. In one hand he held something that was shaped like a letter "T," with a metal ring forming each point and two lengths of chain forming the bars. In the other hand he held a long needle.

Terror exploded in my brain as all of the mind-numbing experiences of the last few weeks (*months? years?*) disappeared. I was fully rational again, and I could not allow what he was planning to happen.

"I'm going to pierce your nipples and your cockhead, boy," he said, "and connect them all together. That way you'll always know you are an owned slave, that you belong to me and only me."

He started toward me, and I bolted away from him toward one of the doors to the outer chambers. In a second he was blocking my way.

"No!" I screamed at him. "You can't do that to me!"

He tried to grab me, but I punched him and struggled away. Seeming not to feel my blow, the man in the black hood fell upon me again and wrapped his arms around me. I twisted and struggled against him, but it did no good.

I felt something smooth sliding down my face and knew that the executioner was hooding me. Even though there were holes for my eyes and nose, my mouth was covered, and I couldn't have been more terrified if he had blindfolded and gagged me. I fought down blind panic, because now I realized what was happening. *He's going to execute me after all!*

He lifted me off the ground and tossed me over his shoulder. I tried to squirm away, but he was holding me too tight. I rained blows down on his back, but they didn't make any difference. He was even taller than I thought — I seemed to be seven feet above the ground moving beneath me. Even in my fear I felt excitement — he was taking me somewhere. Since coming to the dungeons, I had never been outside of the chamber my cage was in.

"I should've known you weren't ready, boy," the executioner said as he carried me deeper and deeper into his dungeon. "I've been collecting boys for a long time, looking for just the right one. But every time they failed me. You want to fail me, too, I know, but I'm not going to let you. You're going to be mine forever."

I began to hear a terrible sound — like a pack of wild animals screaming and howling. I gave up struggling and hung over the man's shoulder, trembling with terror.

"I'm going to break you whether you like it or not, boy. I don't want to have to kill you, but I will if I have to. I won't have you end up like the others. You're either going to be mine, or you're not going to live. It's that simple."

I had no idea what he was talking about. With a sick feeling in my stomach, I realized that whatever he had in store for me was going to be infinitely worse than being marked or executed. But it was too late for resistance, too late for anything — except terror.

We passed through chamber after chamber, hallway after hallway, and all the while the noise of the animals got louder and louder. As always, his nearness made me swoon, his scent filling every cell of my body with longing and desire. My stomach began to cramp where his shoulder was digging into it, but that didn't matter. Nothing mattered but him.

Then the executioner stopped, and I realized that the

howling was coming from very nearby. He turned around and pulled the hood off my head. The light around us was dim, and below me yawned a pit of darkness. It was from this that the animal screams were coming. I tried to wiggle my way out of the executioner's grip, but he held me tight so I couldn't move.

"What you hear are the wildboys," he said. "The boys that I brought down here one at a time to be mine, but that failed to serve me properly. They were driven mad and are now no better than animals."

"What are you going to do, Sir?" I asked, trembling.

"I'm going to give you to the wildboys."

"No, Sir, please, Sir!"

"Be quiet, boy," he said, and I was, though tears were running down my cheeks. "I'm going to give you to the wildboys," he continued. "Not forever, but long enough for you to live like them for a while. There are three steps to breaking a boy. The first is what you've been through these past few months.

"The second is what I'm about to do now, to show you what's in store if you don't agree to be mine absolutely. The third is what happens when I pull you out of that hole and ask if you're ready to give yourself to me. You'll either agree to be mine, now and forever, or I'll kill you."

"I'll be yours, Sir!" I pleaded. "Please let me be yours!" I shifted on his shoulder while he laughed.

"It's too late, boy," he said. "You're just saying what you think I want to hear. You have to mean it with all your body, mind, and soul. And you will, after the wildboys are done with you." He paused. "Don't worry, they won't kill you . . . only I get to kill boys. Remember me when you're down there, boy. . . . You have only two choices left: you'll be mine, or you'll die."

"Sir, please . . . ," I started, but it was too late. I tried to slip out of his grip, but the man in the black hood threw me off his shoulder and I was falling, tumbling into the black pit that opened beneath me like a gaping mouth.

The Executioner's Boy

The screaming of the wildboys filled my ears as I fell. The sound seemed to be all around me, echoing and re-echoing off the stone walls of the pit, filling up the empty space I was falling through. The last thing I saw before the darkness enclosed me was the gleam of the executioner's eyes, staring down at me.

I knew the wildboys wouldn't get me, because there was no way I could survive the fall. *It's over at last,* I thought with surprising calm. I curled into a ball, preparing for the impact I knew was coming, the impact that would break every bone in my body and smash my head open like a melon.

It never came. What did come was a shuddering impact, an impact that made me cry out in pain, but not one that killed me. Within seconds, I was sorry it hadn't, because I realized that the screaming of the wildboys was no longer far away, or even close, but *all around me.*

What felt like dozens of *hands* had caught me, and now they were dropping me down to the floor of the pit. Hundreds of little blossoms of pain sprouted all over my body as their mouths seized me — biting my nipples, kissing my lips, tearing at my skin, pulling my hair, ripping at my legs.

The total blackness around me caused my terror to double, triple, to increase with every passing second. I tried to scream, but the wildboys covered my mouth with their filthy palms. Their horrible stench of years-old sweat filled my nostrils as I strained for air.

Their insane gibbering seemed to get more and more maniacal as they invaded every inch of my body. Even though every one of them was moving on his own, they seemed to be joined somehow, as if they shared a single mind. The enormous group of men/animals acted like a flock of birds that turns all at once in midair. *How can I possibly survive this violation?*

I panicked and tried to wrench myself out of their grip. Some of the grasping hands clutched me tighter, while others curled into cruel bony fists that slammed into me, punching me in the gut and knocking my wind out. I collapsed onto the unseen floor. The hands that covered my mouth were removed.

I tried to scream again, but as soon as my mouth opened a cock shoved itself inside. I began to bite down but another mouth sank its teeth into my balls, and I shrieked in pain. The hands invaded me further — pinching, rubbing, punching. The erect cock pushed itself further inside, into the back of my throat. Other cocks started pressing against my lips. I heard snarling as the wildboys fought over which would get to fuck my face.

I don't remember how many cocks got inside my mouth — I think it was four at most, but at that point I was so delirious with pain and panic that I didn't even notice I'd vomited until later. Then I felt a cock against my ass, and I clenched my cheeks tight. I had never been fucked before, not even by the executioner. I certainly didn't want the first time to be like this.

But the wildboys had other ideas. They shoved me onto the ground and leaped on top of me. They punched me hard in the back. I started crying again and tried to call for help, but cocks kept going in and out of my mouth and I could barely breathe.

I realized there was no point in resisting. I was in the deepest hole in the deepest chamber of a dungeon several hundred feet below the ground. There was no way in hell anyone who might help me could hear me.

I let my ass relax and instantly a cock was there, shoving itself inside me. I bucked against the incredible pain and was forced back down onto my back again. The wildboy pushed his cock further and further into me until a brilliant light exploded in front of my eyes and I passed out.

After that I remember only little pieces of things. I remember being beaten . . . getting raped dozens of times . . . sucking dozens of cocks . . . getting cum and piss as my only nourishment beside the occasional crusts of bread and flagons of water that were lowered into the pit by the executioner and forced into my mouth by my violators.

The Executioner's Boy

The wildboys were truly animals, their communication with each other limited to grunts, moans, and cries. Their guttural sounds still haunt my nightmares. Screaming and cackling, screeching and moaning, those horrible noises pushed me to the brink of madness and may have shoved me over it.

I WAS IN THE PIT for what may have been days, weeks, or months for all I knew. There were so many wildboys that I could do nothing against them. The second I made a move to protect myself, I was punished for hours with merciless torture by their mouths, fists, and feet.

Finally, I just gave myself over to them and started praying to the man in the black hood. I longed for Him, dreamed of Him, vowed that I'd do anything for Him and be His slave forever if only He would come and take me out of this hell of pain and darkness.

One day it happened. I was dozing on top of a pile of wildboys when I felt something smooth and cool gently fall on me from above. Like a whisper from a dream, the executioner's voice came to my ears, "Slip into it." The sound was as soft and light as a feather, but it was unmistakable. *What is this?* I wondered as I felt it in the darkness. Finally I realized that it was a leather harness tied to a long rope, which I hoped ran up out of the pit.

In that moment I understood. The wildboys would never let me leave this pit alive, so the man in the black hood was going to take me by stealth.

Trying not to tremble, I slowly slid my arms into the harness, then tugged on the rope to let him know I was ready. Instantly I was moving upwards. Gently, carefully, but definitely up and away from the torture of the pit. I felt my legs slowly slide out from beneath the tangled limbs of the wildboys, who always entwined me in their grasp while sleeping to prevent my escape. I heard a grumble, then another, followed by a gasp.

"No!" I screamed as the entire pit came to life in a chorus of shrieks and calls. From above I felt a yank on the rope, and suddenly I was moving faster, sailing upward at unbelievable speed toward the dim circle of light that had become visible at the top of the pit.

The wildboys screamed in anger and leaped up, trying to reach me, but it was too late. The prize was already out of their grasp. They disappeared beneath me, leaving only their howls and cries. They howled in rage and loss as I was taken from them once and for all, away from the horror I had been subjected to for so long.

As fresher air flowed over me, I felt an emotion I had thought I would never know again: elation! For as I traveled farther and farther away from the hell of the pit, I was traveling closer and closer to the man in the black hood. Surely whatever he had in store for me would be better than what I had been experiencing.

The circle of light above me got brighter and brighter as I neared the top. Finally I had to shield my eyes as I scraped against the edge of the pit, then was pulled up and over the edge. I stared at the executioner, who was not even breathing hard from the exertion of pulling me all that distance with no assistance, mechanical or otherwise. He unfastened the harness, and I crumbled to the ground at his feet.

"Thank you, Sir, thank you, Sir," I said over and over as I polished his boots with my mouth and tongue.

Very gently the huge man leaned down, gathered me in his arms, and lifted me off the ground. Before he had carried me over his shoulder like a sheep to be slaughtered — now he cradled me in his arms as tenderly as he would his own son. Or slave.

We moved off at a fast pace, and at several chambers' distance from the pit he set me down without a word, laying me on my stomach on a hard, rough surface raised above the floor. I lay there with my eyes closed, feeling safe and cared for. He looped rope around my wrists and ankles and stretched me taut. I remained calm, and then I heard a creaking sound.

The Executioner's Boy

Excruciating pain shot through my body. My eyes flew open, and in horror I saw that I was in a torture chamber and he had tied me to a rack! He was slowly turning a winch, and with each turn my bound arms and legs were pulled further apart. The pain was killing me, and I knew he could rip my body clean apart if he wanted to.

I tried to speak but couldn't inflate my lungs against the relentless pressure. After the man in the black hood had me in enough pain for his satisfaction, he stopped turning the winch. I was stretched so taut, I was no longer touching the slab of wood beneath me, held in midair by the bondage.

A flogger whooshed through the air and landed hard on my back. *Crack!* Somehow my lungs found air, and I howled in pain. I hardly noticed how much like a wildboy I sounded. *Crack! Crack!* The pain in my body doubled, tripled. . . . I didn't know it was possible for a human being to hurt so much and still be conscious.

The pain of the rack receded to a dull burning ache as blow after searing blow landed on my back, shoulders, ass, legs, feet. It felt as if hours and hours went by. The executioner's sweat landed on my lacerated body as he lashed me over and over. Finally I could stand no more and somehow found the breath to scream.

"ENOUGH, SIR! I'VE MADE UP MY MIND, SIR! I WANT TO SERVE YOU! I NEED YOU TO OWN ME! THERE'S NOTHING I WON'T DO FOR YOU, SIR!"

At last he stopped. I lay there quivering, with no breath or tears left. The man in the black hood turned the winch the other way, and I was able to relax my arms and legs. I moaned in pain and release as I settled onto the hard surface. Then I felt my limbs being untied.

I lay there like a piece of raw meat. I was utterly spent. Absolutely every last shred of dignity and resistance had been taken from me. I had nothing left to give. Then the executioner climbed onto the rack with me. I could feel his weight shake the structure as he settled into position.

"Thank you, Sir," I whispered, knowing it was the only thing to say to my new Master.

I heard the sound of his pants being jerked down, and I knew what was coming — he was pushing his enormous cock into my asshole. Even countless rapes by the wildboys couldn't have prepared me for the enormous spike that was impaling me. It hurt so bad I wanted to scream, but I knew it would do no good. He had no intention of stopping, and my comfort was not important to him. And there was no one else to hear me.

HE FUCKED ME FOR HOURS, thrusting and pumping as if he would never tire. I swam in and out of delirium, even falling asleep at one point. Every time I woke up he was still fucking me, so what difference did it make? Never in my life had I been so utterly vulnerable and submissive.

He felt different from the wildboys. Getting fucked by them had been like being attacked by wild animals, but getting fucked by the man in the black hood felt like... I don't know, the way things should be? It was as painful and terrifying as being impaled by a hot poker, but it felt right, like I was doing exactly what I *should* be doing, serving the purpose for which I was designed.

It was as if everything that had happened since the first time we looked at each other had all been leading to this one moment. In that moment I saw my entire life, in all its various stages and times, and experienced again all its emotions.

In that moment I was at a gateway, a crossroads. I sensed that I could go forward or go back, but if I went back only madness and death awaited me. In that moment, going *through* the gateway meant understanding and accepting something that had been unthinkable before.

In that moment there was no choice. In that moment I knew I would not be driven mad like so many boys before me. I would not become a wildboy, no better than a simple animal. *I will survive this*, I told myself with perfect certainty. I stepped through the gateway. And in that moment I realized that I had been broken: *I am this man's property, and I would die without him. I am owned and can never look back.*

As if sensing my breakthrough, the man in the black hood lifted me up and turned me around. I swiveled on his cock. It was so big and in so deep, there was no chance of its coming out while he did this. He set me down on my back so I could see him. He was staring into my eyes through his hood as he fucked me, harder and harder.

He suddenly grabbed my cock. Untouched for so long by anyone, it leaped to life in his grip. I had not come once since being taken down here, and it immediately started oozing. The executioner scooped up all of the precum and rubbed it on my face. Then he started jerking me off, all the while thrusting in and out faster and faster.

When I was seconds away from coming, I knew what had to be done. I remembered my earlier mistake, the one that sent me into the pit of the wildboys, and knew it could not happen again.

I am not going to disappoint him, I vowed to myself. *I am not going to fail him. I am going to be his or die.*

"PLEASE MARK ME, SIR!" I screamed. "I BEG YOU TO MAKE ME YOURS, SIR!"

And instantly he had the needle in one hand and the piece of ringed chain in the other. I felt sublime pain rush through my body as he pierced first my left nipple, then my right one, and finally the dripping head of my cock. He inserted the rings into the holes, and the chain fell across my skin, so cold and harsh it seemed to burn.

The executioner pushed himself into me further than anyone ever had. It seemed that the shadows on the walls of the chamber came to life, joining together in a single mass that surrounded me. Even as it happened I knew this was no illusion brought on by fatigue or fear — this was real. The dark forces wrapped me in their cold embrace, and I felt the already enormous cock inside me start to expand. As impossible as it was, the executioner's cock was growing, straining inside my guts as if trying to get out.

The pain was so intense it seemed to paralyze every muscle in my body. I wanted to cry out, but the huge cock had already squeezed the air out of my lungs. I was going to explode. Impossible pain and impossible pleasure coursed through me like a tidal wave, mixing, overlapping, becoming one and the same.

Then, when I thought I was about to die, the most incredible experience of my life climaxed. I felt the executioner shoot his load inside me, and it was so hot it was like the breath of a dragon inside my body. To my utter astonishment, my own jism spouted out of me, and it was so cold that vapor rose from it as it shot upward in a fountain of white. Rainbows of color sailed through the air around me, and I knew nothing would ever be the same.

The gateway had closed behind me.

SOMETIME LATER, I woke up in my cage. I was happy. There was nowhere I'd rather have been. I lived to serve the executioner and would do anything for him.

There were two new things in my cage. One was a key. Instinctively, I knew that it would unlock my cage and that I would be free to go. I have never touched that key and never will. The other was a small leatherbound book with a pen — a diary. I knew what I was then. I had not disappointed him. I had not failed him.

I ran my hands over my pierced, ringed, and chained body and felt a shiver of pleasure and happiness like nothing I'd ever felt before. After a short lifetime of wondering where the meaning and purpose of my life could be found, I had finally found him. And after many years of searching for the one boy who could go further than any other had ever done, he had finally found me.

In my time in the dungeon, I had seldom thought of my family, but I did then for a moment. I was sure that, their grief at my death long since healed, my family was now at peace. I felt in my heart that my brother would recover from his illness and go on to a long and happy life.

The Executioner's Boy

I did not know much about the man in the black hood, but I had seen and felt enough to know that he could not be an ordinary man. His darkness was so complete that it could not be anything human. It was as if a black spirit, which had been searching these many years for an innocent soul to enslave and keep as its own forever, had finally been satisfied, and the scourge of disease and despair that had tortured the land would now be lifted.

I was the last in a line of young men that may have seemed endless at one time, for each and every one failed to pass the tests. Until me. Whatever it was in me, whatever steel or fire or water, it had allowed me to look at the gateway without fear and walk through it. And if my former self had had to be burned away to reveal a new being on the other side, so be it.

My whole life is now the executioner. I live to serve him and for nothing else. I am his, and I love him. And I know that in his own strange and dark way, he loves me, too.

I opened the diary and began to write.

"I am Keal . . . ," I wrote, amazed at myself. My name, so long unused, had been lurking in the back of my mind all along. *But now it is meaningless. Everything that was Keal no longer exists. I have been changed, reborn, awakened.*

And I could feel that name disappear from my mind even as I thought it. A second later I looked back at the page, wondering what the strange word meant and what had made me write it. I crossed it out and started over.

"I am the executioner's boy . . ." ◉

Fucking Master's Lover

FUCKING MY MASTER'S 21-year-old lover hadn't been on my mind that night when I laid down to sleep. But he looked at me with those big hazel eyes, his pretty face desperate with desire, his body so ripe and hot that I'd hardly be a man if I hadn't taken him the way I did...

Better start at the beginning: Being an owned slave was what I wanted more than anything else in the world, but I didn't realize at first how difficult it would be. Don't get me wrong — I'm no wimp. I can take pretty much anything that Master dishes out. I've got endurance and self-discipline to match. *That's* not the hard part.

What *is* tough to deal with, much tougher than I had imagined, is that Master owns my sex drive, so I can only come when he says I can. And that isn't often.

Like a lot of bottom men, I've got a top side, too, an urge to sometimes throw a guy down and plow his butt with everything I've got. But as a slave, I can't give in to that urge. My hot mancream collects in my ballsac, waiting for a release that might not come for a long time.

It drives me crazy, but Master gets off on seeing me uncomfortable. He doesn't even let me touch my cock, much less jerk off without permission. If so much pressure hadn't built up in my balls, I might have been able to resist Will — Master's lover — when he came to me that night.

He's hot in a quiet sort of way, with a handsome face, slim body, dark hair, and pretty olive skin. There's something about him, an energy or aura that says he's primed for fucking. It's easy to see why Master took him as a lover.

Master is a tough customer with a strong sex drive.

That's why he has both a lover and a slave. In any case, my standing orders are to obey Will — in the hierarchy of the household, he's above me. But I'm forbidden to touch him, much less have sex with him.

Will knows this, and he certainly doesn't want to get Master angry at him. So why, before that night we fucked, did I so often catch him watching me? Why did he linger longer than necessary when he talked to me, his eyes drinking me in like a parched plant absorbing water?

Every night before Master retires to his bedroom with Will, I am put down on my own "bed." Chained to the floor in a little passageway between the kitchen and the living room, I sleep on a mat like an animal. The heavy chains that bind me are attached to my collar and steel cuffs around my wrists and ankles. I am never released until the next morning, after the sun breaks the horizon to shine through the eastern windows and the house wakes up.

Then that night came, that special night...

It had been a very difficult day and evening. Master likes to fuck me, then jerk me off, but not let me come. He'd done it twice that day, delighting in the pained expression that crossed my face when the pressure built up in me went unrelieved.

My cock was stiff and raging the rest of that evening, and it took all of my discipline not to touch myself. It was like a war inside me, with my urge to obey and my urge to come battling head to head. But there was nothing I could do. I had no outlet for my passion and just had to deal with it. That was the way of things.

After Master chained me down for the night, it took me a long time to relax. I had an intense impulse to rub my cock on the mat beneath me, to hump the floor like a dog. Finally I conquered it and dropped off to sleep.

I was sleeping soundly when I was awakened suddenly by the telltale sound of my fetters being unlocked. Blinking stupidly, I tried to rouse myself. *Master's releasing me*, I thought. *It must be morning...*

Fucking Master's Lover

But it was still dark aside from the nightlight in the passageway. And it wasn't Master unlocking me — it was Will. I watched as he put a towel on the floor in front of me. Our eyes met, and I knew in an instant, like a flash of foresight, everything that was about to happen. Or maybe I just knew myself — and human nature — too well.

It's forbidden! We can't do this! I frantically told myself. As a slave loyal to my Master, I had to protest, to put up a fight. But I knew very well that, like any other man, I am first and foremost a slave to what is between my legs and the terrible desire that burns there.

I hoped and prayed it was something else that brought Master's lover to me in the middle of the night, some other reason than the one written on his face.

No such luck, I realized. Will badly needed to get fucked. Master had been neglecting him, screwing me so often that he had nothing left for his lover. Apparently Will had been driven beyond endurance, beyond obedience.

I didn't *want* to be there in that place with him. But I was. My legs and arms were now free, and that beautiful man, the living temptation I had resisted so long, was right there in front of me, as desperate and horny as I was.

This is impossible, but it's happening! I screamed silently. It was unfolding in front of me like a play I was watching, no more able to alter its course than the audience in a theater. The thin, delicate hand that held the keys to my restraints moved up to my collar. Will inserted the key into the padlock on the chain that connected me to the floor and turned it gently. With a soft click, the lock released and I was free. He caught the chain as it fell and noiselessly piled it on the floor with the rest.

I was free, unchained, in a most dangerous condition. I felt like a lion in the zoo that had been released by accident into a crowd of people. I hoped Will knew what he was doing, because I sure didn't.

We can't do this! I told myself. *If Master finds out....* My mind raced as I imagined the disastrous consequences.

"What are you doing?" I finally whispered to Will.

"Sshh!" he hissed urgently, putting a finger to my lips. The contact with him was intoxicating, an instant rush. I suddenly caught his scent, a warm husky smell that energized my cock and made it harder that it already was. I shook my head, begging him silently: *Please don't do this, please, please* ...

Will leaned close, his lips almost touching my ear. It took everything I had to stay still, to not move. I felt like a man who's just roused a cobra: he knows that his slightest move could mean death, yet he's powerless against his own instinct to run.

"Please fuck me ... ," Will whispered, his voice tortured.

That's it. I'm lost. My standing order to obey Master's lover is what did it. The only thing holding me back had been his order not to have sex with Will, but now my desire broke that dam like a raging flood. Passion flowed through me, infusing every muscle with power and determination.

"Damn you!" I whispered back as my hands shot out like tentacles to encircle him, to capture him, to make him mine. I had never felt this way before. My desire was more ferocious, intense, and dangerous than anything I'd ever experienced. Rearing up on my knees, I shoved Will down toward my crotch. His hungry mouth opened, engulfing my dripping cock all the way to its base. I bit my tongue to keep a moan of pleasure from escaping my lips.

Fucking his throat was exquisite. Such delicious submission had never been given to me before. This man was utterly in my power, a prisoner of his craving to be fucked. Mercilessly, I plunged my cock in and out of his mouth, holding him in place by locking my strong legs around him and guiding his head with my hands. I could have shot my load then and there, but I wasn't done with him. Not by a long shot.

My cock was happy to be inside a hot little cocksucker's mouth, but I needed to truly possess him to reach nirvana. I had to get deeper inside him, to force my rock-hard tool between his luscious butt cheeks, to defile and deflower the hole that to my knowledge had only been taken by our Master. Soon it would be mine, too. That was my intention, and nothing could stop me now. Will was lucky he wanted this, because even if he changed his mind, he wasn't getting out of it.

I yanked my cock out of his mouth. Strands of his spit trailed after it, and he started to whine for more. I slapped his face, hard.

"Shut up!" I hissed at him. "Shut the fuck up! If Master wakes up we're both dead! You know that! I'm not gonna lose my nuts because a little slut-boy needs his butt plowed. You keep your mouth shut, understand?"

Will nodded quickly, wide eyed. Terror and passion mingled in their warm, hazel depths. I rearranged my body on top of his, forcing him to lie on his stomach. I slid down his back, my cock leaving a snail trail of precum, until I found the beautiful hollow between his ass cheeks. Wet with his spit and stiff from my excitement, my cock was ready to enter him. Grabbing his shoulder with one hand to steady him, and covering his mouth with the other, I lined up with my target and pushed my way in.

He tried to squeal and wiggle away from me, but I'm at least twice as strong and outweigh him, too. I tightened my grip on his shoulder and smashed my hand against his mouth as he struggled helplessly beneath me, unable to escape. His feelings didn't matter anymore. All that mattered was the ecstasy building in me, the blinding pleasure of being inside this man, of holding him hostage and violating him in the most intimate way possible.

I was mounting Will like a dog in heat, fucking him like there was no tomorrow — and I knew there might not be. The game we were playing was the most dangerous either of us had ever played. The man who possesses us is not someone you'd want to upset. We had both been targets of his anger, and now we were tempting fate like never before.

There I was, fucking Master's lover despite express orders not to touch him, reveling in my disobedience, fascinated and enthralled with my own daring. I almost laughed out loud, I was so excited by what I was doing. Thrills shot through my body, bouncing around inside as if it were a pinball machine, with each ricochet of the ball triggering more lights and sounds than the last.

Will cried and struggled beneath me, but I knew he was enjoying the fuck. His little whore's ass was forcing its way up, higher and higher, as he tried to pull more of me inside him. I saw his hand slip between his legs to jerk himself off.

When I felt him shuddering, I knew his climax was imminent. Mine, too. That was a good thing, because as much as we were enjoying this coupling, if it didn't end soon we could be caught. This was stolen pleasure, rape and pillage, get what you can when you can.

I pulled my "victim" up off the floor. He rose willingly, and both of us reared upright on our knees. Now I was impaling him, holding him tight against me, my cock forcing its way deeper and deeper as if it could bore a hole through his body. His jerking hand became frantic, and my thrusting matched his rhythm until the pressure building up in me was ready to explode. Gritting my teeth to hold in my roar of release, I let the climax smash through me. It was as if everything in me shot into my cock, then into Will, as if gallons of jizz poured from me into the man I'd taken.

Will's orgasm immediately followed mine, his cum bursting out of his cock to splash harmlessly on the towel beneath us. He shuddered again in my arms, quivering and trembling like a child. Slowly we sank back down to the floor. Only when he stopped shaking did I release my grip on him and take my hand away from his mouth.

It was over, and at last my nuts had some relief. Will's too. Soon he got up and without a word began to chain me down again. Utterly spent, I allowed him to lock the cuffs around my wrists and ankles and to reattach the chain between my collar and the floor. Curling up on my mat like the animal I was, I was ready to go back to sleep.

Fucking Master's Lover

I was safe. We'd gotten away with it. We both knew that neither of us could tell without incurring punishment himself. It was our joint secret, one we would have to keep for life.

Will gathered up the towel and, after wiping the evidence of the fuck from my cockhead, left the passageway without another look at me. *I hope he'll manage to wash that before Master notices the cum stains,* I said to myself. *But it's out of my hands, and I have to stop thinking about it. Will is no longer the little slut-boy I raped on the floor. He's Master's lover again, a man I'm under orders to obey.... Well, I obeyed him all right,* I thought with a smile as I drifted to sleep.

The next morning everything seemed normal, with Master unaware that anything unusual had happened the night before — though he did give me a few strange looks. Come to think of it, he gave Will a few of those looks, too. It could have been just my guilty imagination. Or maybe not. But no matter what would happen next, I knew one thing for sure.

It was totally worth it! ◉

Home-Made Lube

"**W**HERE THE FUCK'S THE LUBE?" Master Troy yelled, hurting my ears. I was in a good position to hear him, as he was standing over me. But that wasn't the only thing I was in a good position for. I was tied spreadeagle to his bed, my arms outstretched and roped to the headboard, my legs elevated and bound to the bedposts so that my butt hole was right there with a "How d' you do?" smile for the world to see. Or maybe it was a wink.

In any case, with a sock shoved in my mouth I couldn't say anything. And whether his question hurt my ears was utterly unimportant, at least to him. He wanted to fuck me, and fuck me now! All that mattered was that he needed something and didn't know where it was.

I was on loan to him. My Master was on a business trip for the weekend and had decided it'd be better if I didn't go with him. So he asked his friend Master Troy to look after me. What that meant, of course, by the solemn unspoken rules of behavior Masters followed, was that Master Troy could use me in any way he wished over the weekend as long as there was no permanent damage. Then he would return me to my Master in the same condition in which he had received me — healthy and well used.

My feelings on the matter were, as I said before, unimportant. I hated being away from my Master, but I had bound myself to him and his wishes. For better or for worse, what he wanted is what I did.

The weekend wasn't going to be so bad. It's not as if Master Troy isn't hot. He is — very. Probably 5'9" or so and 200 pounds or more, he's built like a football player with huge, broad shoulders. With his black mustache and hairy arms, he looks like a high school sports coach. His cock is nice and big, nine inches or more, and his low-hanging balls beg to be sucked.

But as hot and sexy as he is, I still missed my own Master, and I wished someone had asked me how I was doing or something.... I mean, the second I arrived at Master Troy's door, I was yanked inside, forcibly stripped, and hustled into the bedroom to get trussed up like a Thanksgiving turkey, without the stuffing.

But not for long. He was getting ready to stuff me good, to shove his thick sausage right into me, filling me up and getting me ready to eat.

And that wasn't the only hole to get stuffed. As soon as I tried to speak, the sock I mentioned before was shoved in my mouth. My purpose was clear, and it wasn't conversation. I was, at least right now, only there to provide Master Troy with a nice juicy slave ass to fuck. And ream, and ram, and pork, and bone, and pummel... you get the idea. But he was missing something, something he needed.

"I SAID, WHERE THE FUCK'S THE LUBE?"

I wished my hands were free so I could cover my ears if he did that again. Just then Blaine, Master Troy's live-in slave, ran into the room. He's a thin, slender man, about 5'11" and 160 pounds. His eyes and face are beautiful, and he has pale skin and no body hair — not only his pubes are shaved but everything below his eyebrows. He's kept naked in the house at all times, except for the chain locked around his neck to remind him and anyone else that he's Master Troy's property.

"I'm sorry, Sir!" Blaine said, panting for breath. He must have run through the whole house looking for lubricant. "We don't have any. I looked everywhere, in all the usual places. There's none. We used it all, Sir."

"AND YOU DIDN'T BOTHER TO GET ANY MORE?" Master Troy roared.

"Not yet, Sir. I'm sorry," was the answer.

"Remind me to whip your ass when I'm done with our

guest," he said, gesturing at me. At least he was finally using a normal tone of voice. "I don't want us to run out of lube. Ever. Do you know why?"

"Yes, Sir," Blaine said, hanging his head in shame.

"Why?"

"Because Master hates fucking dry. Master always has to have lube nearby because you never know when the chance to fuck will come up."

"That's right, slave," Master Troy said, his voice softening a little. "So now you're going to help us."

Help us? I wondered. *What's he talking about?*

"Sir?" Blaine asked.

"We're gonna make me some home-made lube so I can plow this pup!"

"Yes, Sir!"

Master Troy jumped up onto the bed and straddled my head with his body. I looked up and saw the inviting darkness between his butt cheeks and his low-hanging ballsac, full of cum he wanted to shoot (into a condom) inside me.

"You know what to do, slave?" he asked Blaine.

To answer, Blaine licked his hand and grabbed hold of my cock. I sucked in air as the shock of his grip melted into the pleasure of being touched that way. My fellow slave wasted no time, starting to jack my cock vigorously.

"That's it . . . ," Master Troy breathed as he yanked the sock out of my mouth and started lowering himself down on me. At either side of my peripheral vision I saw the man's powerful legs bending down, carefully controlling the descent of his body. Before I knew it all light was blocked off as my face was engulfed by Master Troy's butt. I didn't need any order now. I knew what was expected of me, and I welcomed it — even though I still didn't know what "home-made lube" was.

I stuck my tongue out and up, tasting the salty flesh of Master Troy's asshole. Blaine kept jerking me, and I started writhing around on the bed as the sensations flowed through me. Rimming Master Troy and at the same time being jerked off by Blaine felt so good, I almost lost control of myself. I was thrashing so hard it was lucky I was lashed to the bed, or I might've fallen off.

"Yeah . . . yeah, slave . . . ," Master Troy purred above me, like a tiger baring its fangs.

I massaged his butt hole with my lips and tongue, loving his musky scent filling my nostrils. I could barely breathe, but it didn't matter. All that mattered was the asshole I was worshipping and the pleasure from Blaine's handjob.

"Come on," Master Troy whispered. "You can do it . . ."

Within a minute I was ready to shoot, and I moaned under the weight of the Master sitting on my face. Then it was over. I screamed in ecstasy as I came. The force of the orgasm kept moving through me, as inexorable as the tide, as more of my hot spunk splattered on my chest.

"Thank you, Sir . . . ," I sighed as Master Troy got off me and joined his slave between my legs. Then, "Thank you, Sir," in a more normal voice.

"Good slaves," he said, patting my upraised leg and ruffling Blaine's hair. "Good slaves. We're halfway there."

Once again I didn't know what he was talking about, but I was too blissed out to care. I listened to what they were saying down there between my legs as if it had nothing to do with me.

"On your knees!" Master Troy said, and Blaine dropped. Now his mouth was level with his Master's still-hard cock.

"What do you need, slave?"

"To suck your cock, Sir!"

"What do you *really* need?"

"To serve your cock, Sir!"

"Beg me!"

"SIR! PLEASE LET ME WORSHIP YOUR COCK, SIR!"

I heard Blaine gag as Master Troy shoved his big tool between the slave's lips. He moaned and whimpered around the mouthful of cock. Through the frame of my legs I could see Master Troy moving violently back and forth, face-fucking his slave. After a couple of minutes, he pulled out.

HOME-MADE LUBE

"Now, slave, finish yourself off!"

"Yes, Sir," Blaine said, his voice breaking as his breathing speeded up. He stepped up to the bed, leaning against its edge, his cock stretching between my legs.

"Come, man!" Master Troy commanded, and his slave obeyed, shooting a volley of cum right onto my chest to join what I'd already deposited there.

"Good slave!" the Master said as Blaine panted, trying to catch his breath. "That's what I like," he growled, looking at the sticky puddles of man-seed on top of me, "nice home-made lube."

Master Troy grabbed a condom and tore it open with his teeth, spitting the wrapper away and unrolling the elastic shield over his manrammer, which was still drooling at the sight of me tied up and helpless with my butt hole just waiting to get plugged.

With one hand he scooped up some of the spunk from Blaine and me, mixed it with his other hand, and slathered it all over his cock, getting it nice and slick, the better to ram me with. He got himself into position and grabbed my raised legs to steady himself. Then he started pushing at my asshole with his cock, forcing himself into me. It felt good, but also hurt since I had just come.

How I feel isn't important, I reminded myself. *Serving Master Troy is important. I have to make my Master proud.*

In only a few minutes, Master Troy yelled in ecstasy, and I knew he was shooting a huge load into his condom inside of me. When he pulled out, he threw the safe away and grinned down at me.

"You're hot, slave. And just think, it's only Friday!"

I nodded weakly. It was going to be a long weekend. ◉

The Horny Houseguest

WHEN MITCH FIRST came to visit, I knew he'd have me before he left. He's one of my Master's closest friends — they met back when they were both starting businesses in New York. Master later moved to Los Angeles, and when he got the news that his buddy would be in L.A., he insisted that he stay with us.

Having seen photos, I knew Mitch was handsome, but I still wasn't prepared for the hunky stud I saw when Master opened the door. (As his dog slave, I was on all fours at the time, so door opening wasn't my job.) About 5'11", Mitch had gray-blond hair, a clean-shaven face, and bright blue eyes that looked almost silver in the late-afternoon sun. His polo shirt gripped him tightly enough to show off well-shaped pecs and a washboard stomach. Thanks to the big athletic bag over his shoulder, the bulge in his left bicep almost equaled the one in his jeans.

From my vantage point on the floor, Mitch's crotch was right in my line of sight. I must have stared at it too long, because Master thumped my ass with his size-12 boot.

"Get out of the way, boy. Give the man some room."

Snapping out of my trance, I crawled to the side so that Mitch could walk into Master's apartment. Exchanging handshakes and hugs, they smiled and laughed as friends do who haven't seen each other in too long.

"This is my dog slave," Master told him. "Say hello to Mitch, boy."

"Woof!" I barked enthusiastically, wagging my naked butt back and forth like a tail.

Master laughed as Mitch hunkered down on one knee,

put a hand on my head, and scratched me like a dog. I figured he must have known what we're into, because he didn't seem at all surprised that I was naked except for my leather collar.

"How ya' doin', boy?" he asked.

"Great, sir." I'm allowed to speak in English if addressed directly, but otherwise Master prefers dog speak. "I've been looking forward to your staying with us."

Mitch grinned, and the sight of his flashing white teeth got my doggy dick hard. He saw it and reached between my legs, gripping it lightly in his hand. His touch was as strong and masculine as Master's, yet very different.

"He's a horny one, ain't he?" he asked Master.

"Yep," Master said. "He's always ready t' get plowed."

"Is that right, boy?" Mitch asked me.

I let out a horny howl, and they laughed again as he stood up, then walked into the living room with Master. As they sat down to talk, I padded into the kitchen and got beers for them, which I had to carry in standing, though I knelt to deliver them. I noticed Mitch watching me, his eyes roaming up and down my body.

"You always keep him that way?" he asked Master.

"Damn right. Naked and collared like a slaveboy ought t' be."

"Amen," Mitch said.

They clinked bottles, as if for a toast, while I crawled back toward the kitchen.

"He's one fine-looking boy," I heard the visitor say behind me, and the praise brought a blush to my face.

"That he is," Master agreed as I exited the room.

Back in the kitchen, I kept my mind on my work, trying not to be distracted by the scraps of conversation that reached me. When dinner was ready, I served them at the table in the dining alcove before returning to the kitchen for my own meal. As usual, I ate the same food as Master, but out of my dog bowl, no hands.

When Master and his guest finished eating, I served

them coffee, then emptied my water bowl and poured java in it for myself. After they left the table, I cleared it off and did the dishes.

Once the kitchen was set to rights, I was allowed to curl up on the carpet at Master's feet while he and Mitch smoked cigars and reminisced. It was very satisfying to lie there as the owned property of my Master. When he scratched me behind the ears and told me how proud of me he was, I was a very happy boy, so content lying at his feet that I dozed through most of the evening.

It was pretty late when Master woke me, saying it was time he went to bed. Mitch said he was going to stay up and watch some TV before going to sleep.

Master ordered me to double check the guest room and report back to him — that morning he'd had me clean the room thoroughly and put clean linens on the bed. I quickly confirmed that everything was up to his standard.

When I reported to Master in his bedroom, he was already nearly asleep. I sat obediently at the side of his bed, sniffing his arm like the curious dog I am. He reached out to scratch behind my ears. I love it when he does that, and his affectionate touch made my puppy dick hard.

"Boy," he said, "Mitch doesn't have a slave of his own right now, and he's really aching to work over a hot piece of meat. I want you to go out there and offer yourself to him. He's a good man, and I trust him." Master gestured to a drawstring sack on the floor next to the bed. "Take that to him, and tell him I said he can use anything in it."

I stared at the sack, wondering what kind of gear he'd selected for the guest to use on me. Master gently took my chin in his hand and brought my focus back to him.

"As for you," he said, "serve him like you do me."

"Woof!" I responded, wagging my butt in enthusiasm.

"Good dog," Master said, settling back against the pillows. I leaned over and picked up the sack with my mouth. It wasn't very heavy — probably there were only a few items in it. I padded out of the room on all fours, taking care to quietly pull Master's bedroom door shut on the way out. The apartment was dark except for the glow of the TV in the living room.

Squaring my shoulders, I crawled down the hallway toward the light, toward Mitch. As the TV came into view, I saw that it was no late-night talk show our houseguest was watching. Two gorgeous stud pups filled the screen, kissing each other and stroking each other's dicks. Mitch had discovered Master's collection of porn DVDs.

Coming around the edge of the couch, I saw that the guest was far from asleep. Mitch's eyes were wide open, and he had pulled his dick out of his pants and was jerking it off. He had a beautiful cut tool, not especially long but wide and firm, the foreskin's absence revealing the powerful head. In the strange light from the TV, his erect dick seemed like a glowing talisman.

He glanced over at me with a surprised look on his face. "Hey, boy," he said. "You scared me for a second. C'mere."

I dropped the sack and crawled over to him, rubbing my head against his leg.

"I thought everyone was asleep. What did you bring me?" he asked, gesturing at the sack with one hand while petting me with the other.

"Master told me to offer myself to you, Sir," I said, looking up at him. Out of the corner of my eye, I could see his dick flex at the words. A big smile bloomed on his handsome face.

"Is that right?"

"Yes, Sir."

I reached back and pulled the sack close, picking it up in my mouth and holding it out to him. He took it and set it on his lap.

"Master said to tell you that that I'm yours for the night and that you can use anything in that sack on me. I'm to serve you as I do him."

"Well, now," he said. "That's what I call hospitality. Let's see what we've got here." He opened the sack, perused its contents, then set it aside. His cock jutted up, and just the sight of it made me salivate. "You can start by serving my cock, puppy boy."

"Woof!" I barked, then said, "Thank you, Sir."

I maneuvered myself between his legs, my mouth enveloping his gorgeous dick head. I planned to savor it, to stay there on the head and just enjoy how it felt, stroking it with my tongue. And it seemed to come alive in my mouth, growing and pulsing with his pleasure and excitement.

"Mmmmm . . . ," Mitch murmured, putting his hands behind his head in a gesture of utter satisfaction and contentment. Precum started to ooze out of his piss slit, and I slurped it up eagerly. My doggy dick was standing straight out, rock hard from serving this gorgeous man.

I couldn't hold back anymore and slid my mouth down his shaft until the head hit the back of my throat. His dick was a throbbing hot iron in me, except it burned only with passion.

Mitch reached down and grabbed a fistful of my hair, using it to guide my head up and down on his dick just the way he wanted — not too fast, not too slow. I followed the rhythm so smoothly that he soon let go of me and put his hands behind his head again.

I sucked his dick deliberately, cherishing each stroke down to his crotch and back up to the head. I felt full and complete being used by this totally hot stud, used like the dog slave I am, used to bring him pleasure. I wondered what could possibly be more fulfilling . . .

As I continued sucking him, Mitch pulled off his polo shirt, letting it fall to the couch. What I could see of his torso made my heart pound. My evaluation of him earlier had understated the case: revealing as it was, the shirt had covered up a physique that would do credit to a Renaissance statue.

He reached into the sack and pulled out something that I couldn't identify in the flickering light. I struggled to keep his dick moving in my mouth as he leaned forward, reached down, and wrapped a strong, powerful hand around my balls. I felt trapped, completely in his power. He could crush my nuts in a heartbeat if I didn't serve him however he wished. And I would. I had my orders.

But even if I hadn't been under orders, serving a man like Mitch is second nature to me. Worshipping men like him and my Master is why I was born.

Then both of his hands were in my crotch, pulling something around the base of my extended ballsac. I soon realized that it was a leather thong binding me. He wrapped it tightly around and around before knotting it, pushing my balls out from my body. In response, my dick filled out even more. I yelped in pleasure when Mitch's thumb brushed precum from its tip and smeared it across my lips.

Having left himself a long trailing end of the thong, he sat back on the couch. Now he had me by the balls and could pull on them at his whim, using the thong as a leash. One yank of that thong, and I would drown in a sea of pain. As always, I was intoxicated because another man had this kind of power over me, because I was helpless in his hands.

"Oh, yeah...," Mitch moaned as I sucked his dick harder, the pain in my crotch as he pulled on the thong arousing me more and more.

Suddenly he was sliding forward, and he dropped off the couch onto his knees beside me. Even though I turned toward him, his dick pulled out of my mouth — a long tentacle of saliva connected us until it snapped apart. Now Mitch's chest was right in front of my face, and his powerfully muscled arms were going around me, squeezing me tight.

"Good boy," he said. "Good dog... you make me feel so good."

I wagged my butt in happiness, and he chuckled. Dropping the thong and taking my head in his hands, he kissed me hard and fast and firm on the mouth. Then he pushed his tongue inside me, probing and searching and dominating me from the inside out. Wanting to be totally open to him, I willed my throat to open even further, to show him that my whole body, my whole soul, was his to explore and use however he saw fit. His kiss was wonderful — forceful yet tender, both rough *and* sensual.

Then his mouth was moving, leaving my lips and traveling down my neck and onto my chest, sucking and biting as it went. He settled on my left nipple. Little yelps of pain/pleasure came out of me as he worked my tits, alternating quickly between biting and caressing. His tongue swirled around the sensitive skin, and then he was chewing me, gnawing the nubs of flesh like tasty treats. His arms squeezed me again.

"Good dog," he crooned into my ear. "Good boy..."

I whimpered in response. Human speech could no longer express how I felt. The funkiness from his day of traveling invaded my brain as much as his touch electrified my body. Then he was moving upward and wriggling out of his jeans and boxers, which he let fall to the carpet. I closed my eyes and put my face forward, connecting to his body with my mouth. My lips and tongue left a trail of saliva on him as he stood up to his full height.

Looking up, I saw that our houseguest's magnificent dick, standing straight out from his body, cast a huge shadow on the wall behind the couch. But the stud pups on-screen had outlived their usefulness, so he picked up the remote and clicked off the TV and DVD player, extinguishing the flickering light.

"Time for bed, boy," Mitch told me, leaning down to pick up Master's sack with one hand. With the other hand he gripped my wrist and pulled me up to my feet. Then he slung me over his shoulder like a sack of laundry and headed for the guest room.

I love being carried by guys — it's so primally possessive. My doggy dick was raging as Mitch carried me into the guest room and shut the door behind us. Then he laid me down on the bed that I had so nicely made.

"I've had my eye on you since I arrived," he said, reaching into the sack and pulling out a leather cock gag. "Don't want to wake your Master," he explained as he slowly, sensually pushed it into my mouth while I stared up into his beautiful eyes. It was intense.

Hope it'll be as good when his dick pushes into my ass, I said to myself. *And hope I won't have a long wait for it, either!*

Mitch tightly fastened the gag straps around my head, then pulled a pair of handcuffs out of the sack. He expertly cuffed my wrists together in front and pushed my hands over my head. With my armpits exposed, I felt even more helpless and vulnerable.

"Keep those hands out of my way, boy."

I mumbled "Yes, Sir" into the gag, which brought a smile to my user's face. What he did next surprised the hell out of me, and somehow that made it even hotter than if I'd known it was coming.

The big stud leaned over, took my hard doggy dick in his mouth, and started sucking me like a pro! The way I was trained, only slaves and bottoms suck dick, and in all the time Master had owned me, I'd never gotten a blow job.

But another rule I'd learned, more important than any other, accounts for my not freaking out when Mitch, a consummate top, starting slurping on my tool. I'm a slave, and slaves are there to serve *however their Masters see fit*. I had been ordered to give myself to this man, and if this was how he wanted to use me, that was his option. Besides, it felt unbelievably good! His mouth was smooth and hot on my desperate dick. The suck job didn't last long — it was more a tease than anything else. But for the seconds that Mitch blew me, I was in pig heaven.

When he pulled his mouth off my dick, he put his hands on me and explored my abs and chest, probing and searching like a blind man whose only way to experience another's body is by touch. His hands moved over every inch of my torso — my erect nipples shivered under them.

"Mmmm...," he sighed contentedly, as if savoring a fine wine. "Haven't had a slave to work over in a long time...." It was like he was talking to himself, but I was overjoyed to be there for him, available for whatever he wanted to do. Then he climbed onto the bed and laid down on top of me. He wasn't as heavy as my Master, but all that solid muscle felt wonderful. Being trapped, held down, restrained . . . all of these disturb or frighten a lot of people, but I got off on them.

Mitch started moving, grinding his big Top dick against my smaller pecker. His mouth was on my face, kissing my eyelids, my cheeks, my lips, his tongue flicking in and out like a reptile's, every touch a lick of fire. The man gripped my cuffed wrists with one hand, pinning them to the bed. *As if I'm going anywhere!* But the added restriction made me even hornier and hungrier for him to use me.

Our hard dicks rubbed each other as he humped me. His panting in my ear told me he was getting more and more excited. Suddenly he was grabbing me by the waist and flipping me onto my stomach.

I immediately stuck my ass in the air, resting my weight on my elbows and knees, to show how much I wanted him, how open I was to his invasion. If I hadn't been gagged, I'd have been begging him to fuck me. But the houseguest had other ideas, as I could see after he reached into the sack again and showed me the coiled flogger he came up with. He shook it out in front of me, the flat leather tails hanging down menacingly.

Climbing back onto the bed, Mitch spread my legs and planted his dick on top of my ass, just over the crack. This, of course, was maddening, and I pushed myself up and back as if I could somehow get him inside me on my own. He chuckled quietly and played with the flogger, dragging the tails across my back and between my shoulder blades. Every touch drove me deeper into sexual hysteria, silently crying out, *Please whip me! Fuck me! Use me!*

His dick was moving slowly back and forth on my ass without entering me. I whined and moaned into the gag. Then the flogger began to hit my back, lightly at first, then harder and harder.

Mitch kept hitting my back with the flogger and torturing my asshole with anticipation. I could feel his body moving rhythmically, but whatever music the stud was following, it was a song for his ears only.

The blows on my back were hitting now like little karate chops, the pain flashing brightly and fading quickly, replaced seconds later by more.

"Y' know what, slaveboy?" Mitch asked suddenly, pausing both the flogging and the motion of his dick on my ass.

I made a questioning noise through the gag.

"I don't think you're ready for this yet," he said and pulled his pulsing dick away from me.

Shaking my head violently, I made desperate pleading noises that I hoped were communicating, *No, please no! I am ready! I AM ready!* It was devastating to feel him pull away from me, and I collapsed on the bed, breathing heavily. Still on my stomach, I couldn't see what Mitch was doing behind me, but I heard him rummaging in Master's sack, then the sound of a lube bottle being squeezed. In moments something new was between my butt cheeks, and I realized it was a dildo. A big one.

"Yeah, this is better," the stud growled.

He worked the dildo up and down my ass crack, teasing me some more, as if I wasn't excited enough already! I wondered what it would take to please this horny houseguest. I moved my ass around, moaning and crying, trying to let him know I was ready, that I needed to be taken, needed to be penetrated!

Mitch yanked at the thong that held my balls in its tight grip, and pain seared through my groin. I must have made too much noise, because the stud on top of me said:

"Shut up, dogboy. Quit whining or you can go down to the floor and think about what you've done while I get some sleep. You can lie there, all open and empty, waiting for a cock that won't come. And you'll have plenty to answer for when I tell your Master how disappointed with you I was. Then you'll be shit out of luck, won't you?"

All I could do was slowly nod my head, trusting that he would notice the gesture.

"Now, you gonna behave? Gonna be my nice hungry *quiet* dogboy?" he asked, yanking the thong again. I swallowed the yelp of pain and just nodded.

"Fine," Mitch said. "Now we can get back to the good stuff." He let go of the thong and resumed probing my butt with the dildo, the thrusts more direct, less teasing.

I flexed my ass muscles, trying to open myself as much as possible to provide the easiest access for my welcome intruder. When Mitch was ready to insert his plastic dick, I would be as prepared as any boy could be.

The dildo's sculpted head nosed its way inside me, easily popping past my ass ring and into my most private places. The houseguest pushed, and the simulated dick moved further into me. He pushed more, and soon I had the whole shaft inside me, with just its base sticking out.

Mitch's low, heavy breathing made it sound like he was getting off on this as much as I was. Trapped between the bed cover and my pubes, my doggy dick was getting its share of action too.

"Turn over, boy," the stud said a few minutes later, after pulling the dildo almost all the way out, then shoving it back in, "but don't lose this thing."

Holding my breath, I clamped my ass muscles around the dildo, then began to turn onto my back. Mitch held the ass toy where it was, so I relaxed my ass and felt the strange pleasure and minor pain of rotating around it. Exposed by my new position, my hard dick dripped pearls of precum onto my abs.

"That's what I like to see," Mitch said as he yanked my dick away from my body and let it snap painfully back. "Now I can see your face, your eyes."

He ran a hand up my arms. My muscles were strained from holding them over my head and my wrists sore from pressing against the hard metal cuffs. His hand also found my nipples, tweaking each one in turn. And all the while he was fucking me with the dildo. This went on for what seemed a long time. Though I loved being used and stimulated like that, I hoped it was only a prelude to a *real* fuck — with his dick.

Finally, Mitch seemed to tire of the game. He pulled the dildo out and laid it aside, wrapped in a black bandana from his jeans, then dipped into the sack again. The shiny square condom package he fished out was unmistakable.

Mitch removed the wrapper and unrolled the condom down the shaft of his big pecker. The whole time, his eyes never left mine. Climbing back on the bed between my legs, the big man grabbed them and tossed them over his shoulders, leaning forward over me.

With a clear shot at my quivering hole, he shoved himself through it. The muscles of my rectum automatically tightened — not to keep his dick out, but to keep it inside me. Finally, he fucked me! Deep and hard. And I loved being used this way by Master's buddy, being there for him to do whatever he wanted. *Just a piece of Master's property that he can lend out*, I mused, *like a power tool or . . .*

Quicker than I expected, I felt Mitch's body tense up and knew that he was shooting off inside me, the condom catching all of his spunk and holding it prisoner, just like he was holding me prisoner.

I'm his, I realized. *Mitch's dog slave . . . Mitch's fuck toy.* Though only for a short time, I *belonged* to this man. For a second, a heartbeat, he completely and utterly owned me. And in that instant, his eyes boring into mine, he grabbed my dick in his fist and jerked it once . . . twice . . . three times . . . and I came! Ecstasy flowed through me as jizz spurted out of my rod, landing thick and milky on my pecs.

The man whose dick was inside me sighed in contented exhaustion, breathed deep, and gently pulled out. Moments later, with the condom and its contents tossed into the wastebasket, he joined me on the bed.

"That was . . . perfect," Mitch said. "Fucking perfect."

He reached between my legs and carefully untied the cord that had pushed down my balls. Initial relief was replaced by prickly pain as fresh blood flowed into them, but

The Horny Houseguest

I kept myself from crying out. Mitch grinned and took the gag out of my mouth.

"You won't be making any more noise tonight, will you, boy?" he asked softly.

"No, Sir," I said just as quietly. "Thank you, Sir."

Smiling, he pulled my hands down to check them. He left the cuffs on, then slid into the circle of my arms. It was great having this hunky stud snuggle with me, but I was fading fast. As I drifted off I heard him whisper, "Go to sleep, boy, go to sleep . . ."

I slept deeply, satisfied that I had performed as ordered.

MITCH LEFT THE NEXT DAY after giving a full report to my owner. Master beamed with pride as he hugged his friend and wished him well.

"Remember that you're welcome here any time!"

"Thanks! You'll see me again," Mitch said as he threw his bag over his shoulder, then looked down and winked at me. "Count on it."

After he was gone, Master leaned down and scratched me behind the ears.

"What a good boy!" he said.

Overjoyed at pleasing him, I barked and gamboled like an excited puppy. Master laughed and knelt, taking me by the shoulders.

"My good boy . . ."

I licked his face, and Master kissed me, long and deep. I was one happy dog slave. ◉

Isle of Chains
For Tim / Love, Chris

MY BEST FRIEND, Lagan, had been gone six months. He is an explorer by nature, but this was a long absence even for him. The archipelago of Gaelund where we lived has ample places to explore, and since we were kids Lagan and I had visited all of them many times. With us both now in our late 20s, I could understand his wanting a new challenge.

But I knew that his destination had to have been the one island we'd never been to, the island that Gaelund's queen had declared forbidden. It lay outside the archipelago by several miles and was spoken of only in whispers. It was said that no one who ventured there had ever returned.

It was called the Isle of Chains.

Understand, I was always a top, and I always got what I wanted. I had never been fucked, never once taken the submissive position. It just wasn't in me. I had to be in control, the one making the decisions. That spilled over into all aspects of my life, and I saw myself as keeper and guardian of everyone around me, especially my friends and family. So I knew I had to find Lagan and save him, perhaps even from himself.

That night, after the whirlbirds had begun calling, I took a boat from the docks and sailed out toward the western edge of the archipelago. The wind was swift, and my boat moved along nicely under the light of the three moons. The mournful calls of the whirlbirds were accompanied by the snapping of the sails in the wind.

Several hours passed uneventfully. I wondered if I'd see any Yemurians. Prominent figures in the story of Gaelund's creation, the beautiful and elusive watermen were rumored to appear more frequently the farther out to sea you went.

Why am I doing this? I asked myself. *Do I love Lagan this much? Has my sense of responsibility for my friend grown so great that I'm risking my own life to find him?* . . . No, I decided. There was something more. Something that scurried out of reach whenever my mind tried to grasp at it. It was something I knew, that I had always known, yet it slipped from my grasp as elusively as the Yemurians themselves.

But I had no more time for musing, for once my boat sliced through a cloud of mist I beheld my destination. The Isle of Chains lay before me, rising from the water like a leviathan. The sandy shoreline soared upward into a cliff towering hundreds of feet high. A few torches were mounted on poles here and there on docks jutting into the water. Otherwise all was dark except for the top of the monstrous cliff, where a great furnace of light was glowing.

I pulled up to the end of one of the docks and secured my boat. I readied my sword, sure I would meet resistance, but I could never have anticipated what I saw as I looked down the pier: half a dozen naked dock boys, in the flush of early manhood, their tan skin glowing in the flickering light of the torches. Each one's head was shaved except for a single long braid of hair at the back. Studded leather collars encircled their necks.

They were in a row on their hands and knees, each one rimming the boy in front of him! The boy in the front of the line was sucking the cock of an older man, perhaps in his late-20s. The man being sucked wore no collar but instead had a band of black leather wrapped high around his left arm. He had a short whip in his right hand, which he tapped idly against his leg as he was pleasured. A gear belt around his waist held a variety of implements that looked capable of inflicting great pain. Seeing me about to step out of my boat, the dock leader started lashing the dock boys with his whip.

"All right," he cried. "Feeding time's over! There's work to do. You've got five seconds to come."

Isle of Chains

He grabbed the head of the boy sucking him and started face-fucking him hard. Without changing position, the others started vigorously jerking their cocks. Sweat soon ran off their bodies as they strained to come within the time limit.

"You won't get to come again for a month unless you shoot *right now!*" the leader yelled as he cracked the whip.

There was a chorus of moans and whimpers as the dock boys came. Several jets of milky jism flew out of each organ and splattered onto the wooden planks. The leader held the head of his boy on his cock, forcing him to eat his cum. I saw the boy's throat flex as he struggled to swallow every drop. When he was finished, the leader pulled his cock out, stood up, and gestured with the whip at the spilled semen.

"Clean that up, boy," he said. The others got to their feet while the dock leader's boy began to eagerly lick up all the cum. Shaking my head in astonishment, I climbed out of my boat. Without missing a beat, the leader asked, "How can we serve you, Sir?"

"Uh . . . I've come to see my friend Lagan."

"Yes, Sir. You will find Lagan at the top of the cliffs, in the Palace of the Master." He gestured beyond the beach to where a stairway climbed up the imposing rockface. At the top stood a gigantic castle from which came all of the light I had seen from the water.

I noticed that some of the dock boys had jumped into the water and were pulling my boat onto the beach.

"Hey!" I yelled. The boys stopped.

"Yes, Sir?" they said together.

"Leave my boat in the water. I won't be here long."

The boys obeyed but gave me skeptical looks. That was when I realized there were no other boats at these docks. Not a single one. A little shaken but still determined, I turned and walked down the dock toward the stairs. The nagging thought at the back of my mind flitted into sight again but faded before I could make it out.

When I reached the stairs, something made me turn

and look back: the dock boys were again pulling my boat onto the beach. They didn't seem to mean any harm, so I shrugged and went on.

I avoided looking at the castle all the way up the stairs, and I almost swooned when I finally faced it. The place was even larger than I had expected. And the light that came from it! The whole building glowed. It was so bright and warm, I felt myself drawn toward the entrance. I had to tear my eyes away from that mesmerizing light, so I focused on the huge, ornate door, which depicted naked males copulating in every possible position.

I had no idea what I was going to do once I got inside. *Lagan must be a prisoner*, I thought. *How am I going to get him out?* I hadn't seen any guards, but I was pretty sure I couldn't just carry a prisoner off the island without a fight.

The name of the place ran around and around in my mind: *The Palace of the Master. What man could claim this whole island as his own?* No matter. I had a job to do, and I was going to do it. I would deal with "the Master" if the time came. I pushed the door open and stepped into the castle.

The light inside made the outside glow seem like a feeble candle flame. It was so bright I had to shield my eyes until they adjusted. Torches, lamps, and candles burned everywhere, but the exquisite light also seemed to come from the floor, the ceiling, even the air itself.

This entry room or foyer, so large it could be called a salon, was all gold, jade, and marble, combining in a display of wealth beyond imagining. My breath was taken away.

And the men! Everywhere I looked there were absolutely gorgeous men, all naked with shaved heads and long braids in back like the dock boys. Some of them wore collars like the dock boys had, others leather arm bands and gear belts like the dock leader had sported. Each man's gear belt was different, with an individual assortment of implements: gags, clips, dildos, whips, paddles, clamps, leashes, blindfolds, butt plugs.

Isle of Chains

The hierarchy was clear: collared men were submissive, arm-banded men were dominant. There was a wide range of ages represented on both sides, though it seemed that the youngest men, say 18 to mid-20s, were all collared. Some were being led around the salon on gold-chain leashes attached to their collars, some upright and some on all fours. Collared men were chained to walls or lying on the floor like animals. There were blindfolded boys, bound boys, gagged boys all around — kneeling in corners, tied into slings, harnessed in groups, hanging from the ceiling.

I saw a banded man carry a collared boy in from another room and set him down on the floor next to some other boys. The man secured the boy with chains fastened to the floor. He snapped his fingers, and the boy obediently got up on hands and knees and pushed his rear end out. The man pulled a huge butt plug off his belt, stuck it into the boy's asshole, and slapped his cheeks. Then the man walked away, and the boy snuggled down to sleep with the other boys around him.

All over the salon I could see similar things happening. My eyes and mind were overloaded by the rush of images: leather, collars, padlocks, whips, chains, arms, legs, butts, cocks . . . and this was just the entry room. I could see doors, hallways, and staircases leading to hundreds of other chambers and rooms. No one seemed to care that I had walked in unannounced. This awesome spectacle stirred something deep within me, something akin to the thought that had been nagging me all along.

A few feet from me a banded man was sitting on a luxurious couch, his feet up and resting on the back of a collared boy on hands and knees in front of him.

"I'm looking for my friend Lagan," I said to him.

"Lagan belongs to Viejo . . . ," the collared boy said to me. Instantly the banded man put his feet down and grabbed the boy by his braid, yanking his head back.

"You're a forgetful boy, aren't you?" the man said.

"Yes, Sir. I'm sorry, Sir," his boy whispered.

"Speak up, boy. What did you forget?"

"I forgot that I may only speak when given permission," the boy said. The man turned the boy so that his backside was facing him.

"Good boy. Don't let it happen again. Did you lube your ass like I told you?"

"Yes, Sir," the boy said as he pulled his ass cheeks apart with his hands. I watched as the man slowly inserted his hand into the boy's asshole. The boy shuddered but received the intruder without complaint. When his hand was inside the boy up to the wrist, the man called over his shoulder.

"Viejo!"

Another banded and belted man, blond and striking, walked over. He looked at me, and the intensity of his look was almost too much to bear. Viejo was very handsome, with a boyishness to his face belied by the predatory way he looked at me. His body was sharply defined, and his healthy-size cock poked out of a nest of crotch hair as light as the hair on his head.

Without a word, he lifted the collared boy's chin and pushed his cock into the boy's mouth. Now being fisted at one end and face fucked at the other, the young man started sweating as he tried to please two dominants at once. The first man watched with a smug expression. Viejo kept his eyes on me as he continued to ram his cock into the submissive's mouth.

I felt paralyzed. I found that somewhere deep down I *liked* what I saw and didn't want it to end. I was enjoying the sight of the boy being used in this way. I watched his muscles strain against the men who impaled him, and I saw that his cock was hard and felt my own stiffen beneath my tunic. Yet I thought, *What kind of a culture is this? How can these men act as if all this is as normal as can be?*

Continuing his assault on the collared boy's mouth, the blond man finally spoke.

"I am Viejo," he said to me. "And you?"

"Conga," I said, surprised at myself for giving my real name so easily. But something about this place made me *want* to tell the truth. There came that thought again, leaping and dancing like Viejo's eyes.

"You have come to find Lagan?" he asked.

"Yes," I said. "How did you know?"

He smiled. "Lagan is one of mine. He knew you'd come. If you follow me, I'll take you to him." Viejo pulled away from the boy, turned, and started walking. After a moment, I followed. As we mounted one of the stairways, something he said nagged at me.

"What did you mean, Lagan is 'one of yours'?" I asked.

"Just what I said. He is mine. I own him."

We reached the top of the stairs and began walking down a long corridor. On both sides of the corridor elaborate candelabras sprouted from the walls, holding hundreds of brightly burning white candles. On each side a row of collared boys knelt on the floor with their hands restrained behind their backs.

"You are shocked by what you see, are you not?" the blond man asked suddenly.

"No . . . well, a little," I managed. Viejo smiled.

"That is the way of things here," he said. "Acolytes serve Mentors."

"Acolytes," I said, "they're the ones wearing collars?"

"Yes," Viejo said. "Mentors wear arm bands and bear tools, and we teach the Acolytes."

"Teach them what?"

"The meaning of submission. Then, when they have learned enough, they can become Mentors themselves or else remain Acolytes if they feel that is their destiny."

"Who decides when they've learned enough?"

Viejo stopped and looked at me as if I'd asked a foolish question. "The Master, of course," he said. "Owner of us all."

"Masters and slaves," I said. "This whole island is a world of Masters and slaves."

"Call it what you will. Everyone knows his place here. Watch."

Viejo stopped in front of a kneeling Acolyte.

"Open your mouth, boy," Viejo said, and stuck his cock into it.

"See?" he asked me. "You try."

"Me?" I said, thinking I hadn't heard him right.

"Yes. Do it."

I hesitated, but the tone in his voice made me reluctant to disappoint him. Looking back, I think what I didn't want to do was *disobey* him. I turned to the wall, where a beautiful red-haired boy knelt before me. I fingered my cock through my trousers and then pulled it free.

"Um, please . . . ," I started. Viejo interrupted me.

"Don't say 'please,' just say what you want."

I looked back down at the red-haired boy. He was looking up at me with utter submission in his eyes. My cock hardened further.

"Open your mouth," I said, and instantly the boy did so.

As if in a dream, I moved forward and felt my cock embraced by the velvet warmth of his mouth. Expertly, the boy took me in and eased me out, caressing me with his tongue until I was on the verge of shooting down his throat.

"Enough!" Viejo's voice pulled me out of my reverie. He had pulled out of his boy and was looking at me as if expecting me to do the same.

Reluctantly I moved backward and tucked my shiny hard cock into my trousers. I followed the blond man as he resumed walking down the corridor, glancing back wistfully at the red-haired boy, who stared back at me.

Now we were moving even deeper into the castle. We went through doorways, down stairs, across hallways, taking so many twists and turns that I was soon lost. This should have worried me, but for some reason it didn't. If I had stopped to consider *why* it didn't, I might have bolted right then and there, struggling blindly to retrace my steps. But I just kept following the exquisitely beautiful man who was leading me into the very depths of the Palace of the Master, whoever that was.

"What else troubles you?" Viejo asked presently.

"What do you mean?"

"Your mind is racing with questions. Why not give yourself some peace and ask them?"

I considered not saying anything, but again the thought of displeasing Viejo was unwelcome, so I answered.

"Why are there no guards anywhere? And why have I seen no weapons?"

Viejo laughed. "Because we have no need for such things, Conga!"

"How can you say that? Surely you must need to defend the security of the Palace..."

"From whom?" he asked. "No one enters this place without the Master's knowledge and approval. There is no crime here, no dissent. There is no reason for guards or weapons."

"Who is the Master?"

"If he decides to grant you an audience, you will know."

Intrigued, I wanted to ask him more but was distracted by what I saw. We were walking through a room where dozens of boys were kneeling over golden bowls. Mentors walked among them, occasionally patting the boys' heads or flogging their backs.

"What is this place?" I asked.

"They're the candlemakers," Viejo said. "All the candles here are made with the boys' precum. It burns much longer than wax alone."

I stepped closer and looked. Sure enough, all the boys' dicks were hard and dribbling precum into the bowls. The men were stimulating them to keep them dripping.

I felt Viejo's hand on my arm.

"Come," he said. "We're almost there."

I followed him, leaving the candlemakers behind. We passed through many more rooms and chambers, more than I could count — rooms filled with men and boys sitting amid thick clouds of incense (Viejo said they were meditating); rooms of men instructing other men how to use whips and properly tie knots; vault-like exercise chambers where hundreds of boys were lifting weights, running, boxing, and wrestling each other; a huge door that was triple-padlocked (the dungeons, Viejo explained); gigantic rooms where cages were stacked floor to ceiling, each one with a man inside (storage chambers); and *everywhere* men serving other men — boys being fisted, fucked, dildoed, spanked, whipped, tortured, being forced to suck off their Masters and provide them pleasure in every possible way.

My head was reeling. My initial shock and disgust had worn off to be replaced with simple disorientation. I was numb and in a daze as I followed Viejo around the last corner and we stopped in front of a door.

I still could not believe all that I had seen, yet I felt a strange emotion, almost like comfort. I was starting to feel at home in this place, as if I'd been here sometime in the past and was returning to a place of fond memories. *But that's insane!* I protested silently. *What is happening to me?* And that strange thought whispered to me yet again from the back of my mind. I smashed it down and returned my attention to the here and now.

"How far have we gone?" I asked. "Surely we must have traversed the entire length of the Palace..."

Viejo laughed as he took a key off his belt and unlocked the door.

"Oh, my dear man," he said. "What you have seen is the merest fraction of the Palace. An entire tour would take several weeks. The route we took was the shortest possible way to get to Lagan."

Badly shaken by *this* piece of news, I could not have been less prepared for what I saw when the blond man swung the door open. This room was much smaller than the other chambers we had seen. Metal rings protruded from the walls on all sides, and a gagged boy was tied to each one. From each ring a length of taut rope extended into the center of the room, where a group of large men were crowded. Viejo gestured me into the room, and the men parted to reveal what was on the ground in front of them.

I gasped: The ropes all came together to bind a single man. They crisscrossed his body, securing him to the floor. He had a nice physique, although nothing special compared with the huge muscle studs standing over him. But despite the leather hood covering his head, I recognized the bound man. It was Lagan. And the men were pissing on him.

I nearly vomited in revulsion. All vague feelings vanished in the sudden glaring light of reason: *I have to save my friend from this.*

"Lagan!" I yelled.

The bound man's head jerked up at the call. Silently, Viejo gave a hand signal to the men around Lagan, and they backed away as he handed me a key. I ran over to my friend and unlocked his hood, pulling it off to reveal the features I knew as well as my own. He smiled at me, his face flushed.

"You've got five minutes, boy," Viejo said.

"Yes, Sir. Thank you, Sir," Lagan said as Viejo left the room. The muscle studs followed him, shaking the last drops of piss out of their big dicks.

"Conga! It's so good to see you! I knew you'd come."

"This is insane. I've got to get you out of here," I said, drawing my sword and starting to hack at the ropes that bound him. He sat up and piss ran off his torso to splash on the floor.

"What are you doing?" Lagan cried.

"Saving you," I said as I cut away the last of his bonds. My friend gave me a strange look. Ignoring this, I looked around at the other boys. They were staring at me with astonished expressions. "We have to get *them* out of here, too. Come on," I said, starting to hack at their bonds with my sword. But when the severed ropes fell to the floor, the boys didn't move. I yelled at them.

"What's wrong with you? Get up. We've got to get out of here. I've got a boat — we can escape tonight!"

No one moved.

I turned to Lagan: "What's going on? *What's happening on this island?*"

"This is the Isle of Chains, Conga," Lagan said. "We all serve the Master."

I gaped at him, unable to believe the calm tone in his voice as he described this lunacy.

"What are you talking about? Why aren't you helping me free these men so we can escape?"

Lagan hugged me close, squeezing me tight and whispering in my ear: "I love you very much, and I know you mean well, but you just don't understand."

I looked at the boys kneeling among the shredded ropes watching us. "Why aren't they moving?" I asked.

"Oh, dear, sweet Conga, they're not moving because they don't *want* to be rescued. And neither do I."

"But . . . ," I started, trailing off.

"Viejo is my Mentor, Conga. I exist to serve him. Not only do I love him, and he loves me, but *he owns me*. I am his property. I've given myself to him, freely."

"You're his *property?*" I asked, horrified. Lagan smiled.

"Yes. And I've never been happier in my life. This is what I've needed since I was born. That's why I came here. To find my true self."

I gestured to the others. "Is that why all of them came here, too?"

"That's why *everyone* comes here, Conga," a voice from the door said. Instantly, Lagan and the kneeling boys bowed their heads.

I whirled around to see an unbelievably stunning man standing in the doorway. He was far bigger even than the muscle studs — huge, bald, and buff, with a braid of hair reaching all the way down to the floor. Instead of a collar or an arm band, he wore an elaborate leather harness that made his chest look even more massive and powerful than it would without it. He was probably eight feet tall, with a proportionately large cock hanging between his legs. Viejo, whimpering like a dog, crawled at the giant's feet. My heart stopped, and a chill surged down my spine. My hand went to my sword hilt. There was no doubt who this was.

"You are the Master," I said.

"Yes," the giant replied, his voice like liquid fire running through my veins. "Master of all that walks and crawls on this island. You have no need of your weapon here."

"I think I do," I said.

"Nonsense. I mean you no harm."

"I cannot believe that. You preside over a world of perversion and depravity."

"Indeed," the Master said.

"I have come to rescue my friend from this island, Sir."

Sir? I thought. *Why did I say "Sir"?* Something about the man made it necessary. Everyone *there* obviously respected him above all others. But I had taken no vow to respect this man or this way of life. What was that whispering in the back of my mind? No matter, the giant was speaking again. And I didn't want to miss a single word spoken in that voice.

"Yes, I understand why you have come — to take Lagan from this place. He told us this, and all about you. But as you can see, he does not want to leave. So come with me now, and we'll discuss the situation privately."

I looked at him warily. It was hard to resist him — trust seemed to surround the man like an aura. I felt Lagan's hand on my arm.

"It's all right, Conga," he said softly. "Go with him."

I debated for a moment and, realizing that there was no alternative, agreed. I walked toward the Master, and he smiled at me. My bladder nearly gave way at the beauty and intensity of that smile. The Master snapped his fingers, and Viejo jumped to his feet.

"Rebind these boys," the Master said.

"Yes, Sir!" Viejo said.

The boys kept their eyes respectfully down as the blond man pulled a lever in one wall and new lengths of rope slid out beside each ring. Viejo's cock was growing, and I could see Lagan's mouth quivering in anticipation of taking it in. My own cock throbbed in my trousers.

No, I thought. *What's happening to me? This is not the time for that — I must resist!* But I could do nothing as the Master led me out of the room and down the corridor. I considered attacking him — we were alone — but instantly discarded the thought. *Surely I cannot hope to conquer this man who has others far stronger than me kneeling at his feet. And I don't want to,* I realized. I wanted to see where he was leading me and to hear what he had to say.

The journey was not so long this time. After we climbed up another long stairway, the huge man led me into an enormous room whose transparent domed ceiling revealed the entire star-filled sky. Its beauty took my breath away. The only illumination was from the stars and the two smaller moons; the third had set. The rest of the room was sparsely decorated, with only a few carvings on the walls and cushions on the floor. The Master walked briskly forward into the room, turning around with a flourish.

"It's lovely, isn't it, boy?"

I nodded. "Yes, Sir, it's . . . ." I stopped. *What am I saying?* "Excuse me, I am not one of your subjects. I would prefer to be called by my name."

The Master favored me with an indulgent smile, as if he was humoring me.

"I'm sorry, Conga," he said. "I was mistaken. I thought you *liked* being called 'boy'."

I do, I suddenly realized. But that didn't change the essential reason I had come to this place.

"I have come here . . . ," I began. The Master interrupted me, his voice seeming to deepen as it got louder.

"You are Conga, the brave warrior who has come to rescue my people," he said mockingly.

"Yes, that is why I have come here," I said angrily. "And I have certainly *not* come to be a figure of your amusement."

"No, that isn't the real reason — and you know it," the Master said.

Fear suddenly coursed through me like ice water in my veins. I reached for my sword, but the Master's eyes held me and I couldn't look away. Something was happening — every sense in my body was screaming, *Danger! Danger! Danger!*

"Everyone comes here for one reason and one reason only, Conga. To learn the meaning of submission. To live their true lives of servitude or, in some cases, dominance. You are no exception."

The giant turned his back to me, looking out at the sumptuous view. His voice filled the room, caressing and soothing me with its intoxicating strength.

"Your whole life you've taken it upon yourself to save the people around you. You're always out saving your family, your friends, people you hardly know. You're a warrior, a crusader, a rescuer. But what you really want, deep down, is to be saved yourself. What you really want is to have someone *else* make the decisions . . ."

Every muscle in my body was tense. Even as I readied myself for battle, I felt that nagging thought that had been plaguing me appear again in the back of my mind, coming forward fast.

"You always get what you want, don't you, Conga?" The Master's soft, mocking voice was driving me mad. "Big topman . . . never been fucked . . . . Ooh, you're such a stud . . . ." He turned around, and what I saw caused a thousand emotions to rise to the surface of my consciousness and fight for dominance.

The Master's enormous cock was erect, as hard as the very foundation of the island itself.

Furious and terrified at the same time, I pulled my sword out of its sheath. With inhuman speed the Master was there in front of me, smacking me across the face with his hand. Pain exploded in my face, and I dropped my weapon. Instantly he was behind me, wrenching my hands behind my back. I struggled against him, but he was a hundred times stronger. Effortlessly, he ripped my tunic and trousers to reveal the bare flesh of my back and ass. I tried to yank myself out of his grip, but he held me tight, my arms pushed high on my back. Suddenly I felt searing pain as he lashed me with a short whip.

"Beg me, boy," he said.

What? I thought. *What is he saying?*

"Beg me to stop whipping you and start fucking you."

No! I thought frantically, but the pain got worse and worse. His voice was burning my mind as surely as the lash was burning my ass and back, and the thought that had eluded me since I set sail was getting closer every second.

"Come on, boy, beg me to give you what you really want, what you came here for...."

I can take this, I said over and over to myself. *I can take this. I won't give in.* But every second was like an eternity, and when the pain was like fiery rain on my back the elusive thought finally crystallized: *I came to this place not to rescue Lagan, but to join him — I came to be claimed as a slave, to learn the meaning of submission.*

That was the truth, as surely as anything else I had ever believed. And it had been there all along, just waiting for the right moment to emerge and stagger me with its obviousness. But there was no time to ponder the revelation, because I couldn't stand the pain any longer.

"Please fuck me, Sir!" I screamed with every ounce of strength I had. "Please give me what I really want!"

Instantly the pain stopped, and the whip fell to the floor. Both of the Master's massive hands grabbed me and held me in place. I felt his hot breath as he put his mouth to my ear, and my cock leaked precum, soiling my trousers.

"What you really want," he whispered, "is to be a *slave* — and that is what you are."

The Master jammed his gigantic cock into my ass with no lube, no spit, no warning. I screamed, and he clamped his hand over my mouth, silencing me. The giant plowed into me effortlessly, his massive cock leaking its own lubrication, sliding up as far as it could go. He wrapped his free arm around me, holding me tight against him as he started fucking me harder than I had ever dreamed was possible. I felt his incredible muscles tense and flex as his cock jammed itself further and further into me.

I started crying, tears flowing down my face and over the hand that covered my mouth. I whimpered as he plowed my ass harder and harder. I had never felt anything like this before. It was the most significant thing that had ever happened to me, both joyous and terrifying.

He fucked me for what seemed like hours. I became delirious, swimming in and out of consciousness. The Master held me easily with his one arm and just kept screwing me.

Then he lifted his head to the ceiling and called out a single word. I didn't know it but could tell it was from one of the old tongues, an ancient dialect. At the sound of the word the walls responded with a single musical tone, bright and piercing. I was amazed by this, but it was nothing compared with the wonder that happened next.

Every pane of glass in the dome changed, turning first opaque, then silvery. For a moment I didn't understand what he'd done, and then the full impact hit me. Every flat surface in the room had changed to a mirror, and the wall carvings now glowed softly. Everywhere I looked, I saw myself locked in this man's arms, being raped. There was nowhere I could escape from the sight of myself being subjugated, forced to take the submissive role.

Even when I closed my eyes the image stayed with me in all its awesome and terrible glory, as if branded on my eyelids by the Master's sorcery. I opened them again and looked at myself. My features twisted into a grimace of joy and pain, every muscle in my body straining, every inch of my skin covered with sweat or tears, my cock straight and full and dripping. I found the sight pleasing. I saw that I was, once and for all, a slave, an Acolyte.

I looked in the mirrors at the huge man behind me and gazed into his eyes for the first time. If Viejo's eyes had been dancing, the Master's were burning. Burning with fire hotter than the core of the planet, hotter than the hearts of the suns themselves, they seared my brain and touched my soul and claimed me then and forever as his property.

As if acknowledging my surrender, the Master uncovered my mouth and let his hand slide down to grasp my own cock, which was still totally erect. He started jerking me off, and the pleasure was so intense that I cried out. Then I felt that steel-hard cock inside me tense. I felt as if I was about to fall off the highest cliff in the world.

"Come, slave," he said. "Come for your Master!"

And as we came together, the twin orgasms rocked me backward and forward and caused me to scream in ecstasy. I writhed in the huge man's arms as I felt my body fill up with his sacred jism, and he squeezed me so tight I couldn't breathe. The Master threw his head back and howled to the heavens in pleasure. I heard the mirrors shiver in the strength of that cry.

The sensations that bathed my body were unlike anything I had ever felt. Being fucked by this man had put me in such an altered state that the walls of my mind came tumbling down. Pain and pleasure overlapped and merged. My own load spurted out of me, splattering onto the floor. Then everything went black as I collapsed into his arms.

WHEN I WOKE UP, I was naked except for a studded leather collar with a leash attached to it, and my head had been shaved so nothing remained except an Acolyte's braid in back. I was lying on a hard marble floor. Lagan sat above me on a luxurious chair, holding the end of my leash. We must have been in one of the many private salons that I had seen when Viejo led me through the Palace — ages ago, it seemed. Lagan's big cock was standing straight up, and he smiled down at me.

"Serve my dick, Acolyte," he said.

"Yes, Sir. Thank you, Sir," I said, and it felt like the most natural thing in the world.

Lagan yanked my leash and pulled me up off the floor.

"You belong to me now, Acolyte. You are my property. I am your Mentor. Do you understand?"

"Yes, Sir!" I said, loving the sound of the words as I said them. "Yes, Sir."

Lagan pushed me down onto his cock, and I took the large, stiff organ into my mouth without resistance. He started pumping hard, and I fought down the urge to gag. I knew that how I felt didn't matter — all that mattered was serving Lagan. And when he threw his head back and his hot cum shot down my throat, I knew it wasn't over even before he locked his hands behind my head to make sure I didn't pull away.

As his cock softened in my mouth, I was more content than I had ever been in my life. I had stopped fighting the destiny that I had always known I was heading toward. I had surrendered to my innermost instincts and found the life I truly wanted.

Lagan's big, soft cock quivered — something was coursing through it. And as my Mentor started to piss and the sour liquid poured down my throat, I knew that I would never leave the Isle of Chains — and that I didn't want to.

In the air above the island, the whirlbirds sang their baleful song. Far out on the green ocean, the Yemurians danced on the waves. And on the beach, the dock boys began to dismantle my boat. ◉

Fucked by a Stranger

I AM A BONDAGE SLAVE owned by a Master. I have completely turned myself over to this man as his property. He can (and does) do anything to me (or with me) that he wants, so I am always ready for the unexpected. A 27-year-old Caucasian male with a good body and a handsome face, I weigh about 185 pounds and stand 5'10".

Yesterday was a very hard day at work. After I got home I threw together some dinner, ate it, and then conked out on the bed my Master allows me to share with him. (He would come home later, so I left his dinner in the refrigerator, ready to warm up in the microwave.) I didn't even have enough energy to get undressed. Taking off my shirt and shoes was all I could handle before I fell asleep lying on my stomach, dead to the world.

I don't know how long I slept, and I wasn't sure at first if I was awake or dreaming when I felt someone pulling off my clothes. Being handled like this immediately got my dick hard. Assuming it was my Master, I stayed where I was with my eyes closed and my mouth shut. If Master wanted me naked for some reason, I wasn't going to make it harder for him by moving around. He'd do whatever he wanted to me whether I liked it or not, so it was better to just lie there and let him do it.

After my pants, underwear, and socks were off, I felt Master sit down on the bed next to me. He's a big guy, and I recognized how the mattress sagged under him. He slipped my left wrist into what at first felt like a noose. Then I realized what it was: a friend of ours had given Master a great set of bondage cuffs made of braided rope, each with a couple feet of rope to secure them somewhere.

After the cuff around my wrist was pulled snug, Master

stretched out my arm and attached it to the top left bedpost. With my left arm securely bound, he did the same to my right. I couldn't have reached the knots even if I'd wanted to untie them. Then he slipped my ankles into the same kind of rope cuffs, pulled and stretched me so I was spreadeagle in the middle of the bed, and tied off the cuffs to the bottom. I wasn't going anywhere.

Next, he tied a blindfold over my eyes and stuffed a black rubber dildo gag in my mouth. I lay there and whimpered like a dog while my sight and speech were taken away. My dick was quite hard by then, though I had no idea what would happen. Master loves surprising me, so he never tells me what he's planned. He could've just had an urge to tie me up so I wouldn't go anywhere, as he'd done in the past. Or maybe he had something else in mind. I wouldn't know until it happened.

This time he did have more in mind. After roping me, he left the bedroom — though I couldn't see anything with the blindfold on, I heard him click off the light. Since he didn't come back right away, there was just me and my bondage, and the soft breeze from the open window.

Getting tied up does weird things to me. It's somehow exciting and relaxing at the same time. I knew I couldn't escape, but there was no reason to panic. So, lying there bound and gagged with a raging hard-on poking into the bed, I fell asleep again. I figured that was just how Master wanted me to spend the night. But I was wrong.

A long time later, I was awakened by the sound of Master opening the door, flipping the light switch, and walking back into the room. I felt something warm and rough rubbing over my asshole. *He's using a wet washcloth!* I realized. It felt really good, and I must have let out a little moan of pleasure as my dick stiffened again, because Master chuckled. I even pushed my butt back a tiny bit, grinding against the washcloth. It was over much too quickly.

Master spoke then, quietly and not in my direction. I heard another voice respond — a man, also talking softly. *There's someone else in the room with us!* I had no way of knowing who it was. Even if it was someone I knew, he was speaking way too softly for me to recognize his voice.

As the stranger walked over to the bed, next to my Master, my hard-on got even stiffer. It was hot to have another man there watching me, seeing me tied up and blindfolded and gagged. I felt like a slave on the auction block as a potential buyer looked me over.

I could practically feel the guy's eyes on me, burning trails down my skin as he examined every inch. Fingers plunged between my ass cheeks and started playing with my hole. I assumed they were Master's. One pushed through the ring of muscle and probed deep inside me. *That feels so good*, I thought, *though it's pretty bizarre to be finger-fucked while a stranger is watching.*

But maybe it isn't Master doing it! I suddenly realized. *I know how my Master's* dick *feels in me, but he doesn't finger my butthole that often. Maybe it* is *the stranger.* That thought made *my* dick even harder, squeezing it painfully between my abs and the bed.

A second finger pushed its way inside me, and my asshole expanded to accommodate it. Things continued like that, slowly, until it seemed all four fingers of the hand were inside me. I'd never been fisted and wondered excitedly if this was going to be my first time. But that wasn't what Master wanted to happen.

When I heard him say, "Looks like he's ready," it confirmed my earlier suspicion. His voice had come from the top end of the bed, around three feet away, while the fingers were still inside my ass. *It is the other guy who's been working me, not my Master!* I got stiff as a steel rod at the thought of Master watching someone else do this to me.

The stranger's fingers pulled out slowly, and the unmistakable sound of a condom package being ripped open told me what Master thought I was ready for. But he thinks a slave who just lies there and takes it is no fun — he likes us to have some fire. So before anything else could happen, I started fighting my bondage, jerking around, moaning loudly, and shouting through my gag about not wanting to get fucked.

Master and his guest laughed. This time the man was closer to me — he'd just taken his fingers out of my butt! — and I heard him clearly, but I still didn't recognize the voice. *Definitely a stranger,* I told myself.

Suddenly something smacked hard on my ass, and I yelled in pained surprise. It felt like Master's long leather paddle, the one he prefers to spank me with. The fucking thing hurts like blazes, but Master gets endless joy out of using it on me, so...

My response to the initial assault was rewarded with more whacks on my backside, and I strove to respond more appreciatively. Unfortunately, the gag reduced whatever I said to gibberish. Master laughed again and said, "He's ready, all right. Go ahead."

"With pleasure," the stranger replied as he climbed up onto the bed. He straddled me, pinning me down with his weight, which was much less than Master's. I figured he wasn't much bigger than me — I might have been able to wrestle him off me if I hadn't been tied up. But I *was* tied up, and I could've been overpowered by a 98-pound weakling. I wasn't going anywhere. I was about to get fucked, and there was nothing I could do about it.

The man put his dick between my cheeks and started rubbing it up and down my ass crack. It felt good, but I kept moving my ass, pretending to resist. The dick pushed into my asshole, its head just sliding past the sphincter ring inside. Oh, man, it felt great! Now that the penetration was underway, it was okay for me to submit. I had been taken, claimed, my masculinity undermined by being entered from behind like a common hustler.

"That's good, man," Master said to the stranger, and I felt his dick enter me further. More and more went in, and I took it easily. It wasn't as thick as Master's, which usually takes a lot of effort to get inside me. But this dick was *long*, definitely longer than Master's.

Fucked by a Stranger

Being used by this other man for the pleasure and amusement of my Master was humiliating, but I loved it! The stranger started fucking me, and I worked with him, pushing my ass back as much as I could in my bondage. The guy started moaning and fucking me faster. Going in and out of my ass at super speed, his dick felt incredible. I was totally turned on, my own pecker grinding and writhing against the bed.

Suddenly my invader pulled out. I heard him rip the condom off with a grunt. Seconds later warm spurts hit my back and a long sigh of release filled my ears. I loved the feel of his spunk on my skin, tangible evidence that I'd done my duty and made him come. Then the two men left the room, leaving me all alone with my bondage and my still raging hard-on. I must have calmed down and fallen asleep again, because the next thing I knew, Master was untying my limbs and gathering me in his arms.

"Good slave . . . ," he was whispering. "What a good slaveboy . . . ." I had no idea if the stranger was still there or not, and I didn't care. All that mattered was that I had pleased my Master.

Leaving the blindfold and gag in place, Master pulled me close, my back to his chest. With one hand he took hold of my hard dick and started jerking it. It felt so good, I knew I was going to shoot any second. I screamed into the gag as my slave cum spurted out of my dick and splashed onto my abdomen and chest and the waves of orgasm surged through me. Coming in my Master's arms was glorious — nothing could possibly feel any better.

After Master took off the blindfold and gag, I asked who the stranger was and if he would ever let him use me again. He wouldn't tell me. I would have to wait and see — or wait and feel, since I might never see the stranger at all.

I sighed in satisfaction at having made it through another episode of the amazing adventure that is life with my Master. Safe and secure in his arms, I fell asleep — this time, for the rest of the night. ◉

Two-Slaveboy Wrap-Up

I WAS WASHING DISHES when my Master called me to join him in the bedroom. Shutting off the water and wiping my hands on a dish towel, I headed there. Like many slaveboys, I'm kept naked at home, with just a leather collar locked around my neck to mark me as property. Luckily, Master lets me keep the thermostat high enough in cold months so I'm not shivering.

Walking down the short hallway, my bare feet trodding silently on the carpet, I was relaxed and free of expectation. But when I reached the bedroom door, I stopped and stared, and my cock snapped up against my abs, showing how much I liked what I was seeing.

Master, still in great shape at 63, was sitting on the end of his bed. A smile brightened his tanned face, deeply etched with character lines and complemented by a dark mustache. His muscular arms were barely contained by a flimsy tank top, and his jeans were tucked inside his favorite boots: tall, black, oil-tanned loggers. He was mummifying my slave-brother, Keith. Yes, Master owns two slaveboys — one isn't enough for him.

Keith, also naked and with a collar matching mine, stood next to Master. His hands were tied together in front of him, and Master was wrapping him with transparent plastic. It already covered his ankles and calves, and Master was applying more by the second, winding the roll around and around Keith's slender body.

Being mummified isn't like anything else — it's completely confining, total bondage with no escape possible. When you're bound with rope, you can usually move your limbs and torso at least a little, and chain bondage typically leaves even more leeway. But when you're mummified you're like a shrink-wrapped product on a store shelf — you can't move except to breathe.

"The dinner dishes aren't done yet, Sir," I dutifully reported, though I figured Master would be as happy as I was to let them sit.

"Shut up," he said, "and get over here. While I was wrapping up this slaveboy, I got an idea that will make it even better."

Walking over to them, I wondered how Master intended to involve me in this production. My brother's handsome ass was still visible, delicious and tempting as always. I'd buried my cock between those cheeks many times, experiencing white-hot pleasure that's better than anything except when Master fucks me or has me suck him off. That's the best sex *ever*, but fucking my slaveboy brother is pretty damn hot, too.

Keith's eyes were shut and his mouth slightly open as he tilted his head back in joy. His uncut cock was standing straight up, with a tiny pearl of precum at its tip.

"You like seeing your brother this way, don't you, Sam?" Master asked me.

"Yes, Sir," I said, though with my own cut 8-inch cock reaching for the ceiling at the sight of Keith in bondage, he didn't need confirmation.

"He's getting all wrapped up and ready to use," Master said. Sweat beaded on his forehead — he always sweats buckets when he's working on a slave. Reaching over to me, he grabbed my balls and pulled me closer. "Yes, I've got an idea to make this even hotter."

Standing up, Master pulled me into position behind my slavebrother, then reached between my legs and fondled my cock and balls. At his touch my erection got even stiffer, aiming toward Keith's asshole as if it had eyes. My slavebrother and I are about the same height, so we lined up well.

"Yeah," Master murmured. "That's good." Grabbing a

square foil package from a small pile of gear on the bed, he ripped it open, took out the condom, and slid it onto me.

"Now your cock is wrapped up like your brother's," he said, "wrapped up nice and tight, huh, Sam?"

"Yes, Sir. It feels great."

"Then you're going to love what I've got planned," Master said as he lubed my wrapped rod and pushed it against Keith's butt crack. My slavebrother moaned with desire when he felt it.

"That's it," Master said. "Yeah, you love your brother's cock, don't you, slaveboy?"

"Yes, Sir!" Keith said. "Especially when it's fucking my tight butt!"

Master and I both laughed.

"Fuck your brother," Master instructed me. "Take that hot rod of yours and stick it up your brother's ass. You'd like that, wouldn't you?"

"Yes, Sir!" we said at the same time, and Master laughed. He must have relaxed Keith's asshole with some finger action earlier, because when I pushed my cock between his butt cheeks it slid right in. My brother moaned with pleasure, and so did I — dominating him felt really good to me. I'm bottom/slave to Master, of course, but I still enjoy topping Keith. I took hold of his waist, one hand on each side, to keep him still while I screwed him.

Under Master's watchful eyes, I reamed my slavebrother's ass. Having Master watch us made the whole thing sexier than it was already. I held Keith's hips tight, not that he'd try to escape even if he could. He started mumbling, and I covered his mouth with one hand to silence him.

I'd gotten into a good fucking rhythm when Master said, "Okay, slaveboys, that's enough for now."

Holding my cock still inside my brother's ass, I dropped the hand gagging him back to his hip and let out a little groan. *Does Master know I haven't come yet? He'll let me climax, won't he? . . . But I'm a slaveboy*, I reminded myself. *It's my job to please Master, not to give myself pleasure.* Sometimes, though, when I'm lucky, what pleases Master is for me to get pleasure from obeying him.

"Hold still," Master said. "I want a two-slaveboy wrap-up here."

What's that mean? I wondered.

A second later, I knew, as Master started wrapping the plastic around both Keith and me, making a double mummy out of us — something I'd never experienced before. The stretchy plastic was cool on my skin as it went around my ankles, my calves, my thighs, binding us tightly together.

My cock was still in Keith's ass. *Should I pull out?* I wondered. I tried moving my hips backward, but the wrapping already in place, though looser there than elsewhere, kept me from gaining more than a few inches of space.

"Don't move, slaveboy," Master growled at me. "You're exactly where I want you. Keep your dick where it belongs — up your brother's ass."

"Yes, Master," I said obediently, and he continued to wind clear plastic film around us. As he worked his way up our bodies, I started to feel relaxed, floaty, but horny all over, as I always did when mummified. My cock, still rock hard, was buried in Keith's butt for the duration. Even if it went soft, which I was sure wouldn't happen, it could never slide all the way out of his juicy ass.

The plastic was up to my elbows now as Master patiently wound it around his slaveboys. It was exciting to feel my hard-toned flesh press up against my humpy brother, who was letting out his own little moans of excitement, but neither of us could do anything about it except stand there and breathe in unison. My arms were completely bound in place by now, my hands still gripping Keith's hips. The plastic was almost up to my neck.

I felt like a statue, frozen in place, yet alive and full of fire, sharing this most intimate bondage with another man. Being wrapped up together with my slavebrother felt incredible. My stiff cock raged, begging for friction from Keith's ass channel. He clamped down on me from time to time, but that wasn't enough, and I was too hard even to flex inside of him.

As Master wound the plastic wrap loosely around our necks, he muttered about his "two-slaveboy wrap-up." My brother was moaning again with passion and need. In my own euphoria, I let my eyes close and my head loll back. Then I felt the plastic wrap around my head, covering my eyes and ears, my forehead and hair, but leaving my nose and mouth free. I figured Master did the same with Keith's head before pushing it against mine and wrapping us tightly together so we wouldn't bang into each other.

Finally, the sound of plastic wrap winding off the roll stopped. Our double mummy was complete: two slaveboys wrapped up together, with one's cock inside the other's ass. I hoped Master was pleased with his handiwork.

"Now let's see what we can do," I heard Master say, his voice a little muffled by the plastic wrap over my ears. Suddenly Keith gasped, and his whole body quivered.

"Oh, Master!" he said breathlessly. "That feels so good!"

For a second I was confused, then realized what must be happening — Master had left my brother's cock exposed and was now jerking him off!

"Yeah, that's it, slaveboy," Master said to Keith. "You love having your brother inside you, the two of you wrapped up like a mummy, don't you?"

"Yes, Sir," my brother answered. "I love being your mummy slave. . . . I love your hand on my dick. . . . Please let me come, Master!"

"No, not yet, slaveboy," Master told him. "And no shooting off without permission."

"Yes, Sir," Keith said obediently, with no complaint.

"Okay, Sam," Master said to me, "you're up next."

"Sir," I asked, "what do you want me to do?"

"Finish what you started, of course. Finish fucking your brother!"

So that's why he left me some slack! It wasn't much, but I could move my groin enough to fuck.

"Yes, Sir!" I said happily and resumed plowing Keith.

"Oh, yeah!" my brother said as he felt my stiff dick start pounding him again.

"Good slaveboys!" Master said to us. "I think I'll let you both come."

"Oh, thank you, Sir!" my brother and I said at the same time.

Master laughed and said, "You fuck 'til you shoot, Sam, and I'll take care of Keith."

"Yes, Master," I answered and shoved my cock forward as far as it would go. My slavebrother gasped again, and I imagined what he must be feeling, jacked off by Master on one side and screwed by me on the other.

Pumping hard, I knew I couldn't hold back my explosion for long. My brother's moaning was continuous. Knowing how hot it is to have Master jerk *me* off, I figured Keith was close, too.

"Come for me, slaveboys!" Master commanded. "Let it out!"

That was all we needed: our orgasms shot through us simultaneously, and each of us screamed with pleasure and release. My cum went into the condom, and I assumed that Master caught my brother's in his hand.

"Thank you Master!" I said breathlessly, echoed by my brother.

"Good boys," Master said, hugging us both together. "My good slaveboys."

Once the ecstasy receded, the desire to stretch my muscles came to the forefront, but of course I was still bound to Keith by the plastic wrap.

"Are you going to cut us loose, Master?" I asked.

"Are you kidding, slaveboy? The night's only begun!" ◉

Sold to the Highest Bidder

ALTHOUGH IT HAD BEEN nearly a year since I was claimed as a slaveboy, I still didn't really believe that my Master owned me. *It's all a game, isn't it?* I thought. *We're role-playing these parts because we get off on it — we pretend to be Master and slave because that's how we like to see our relationship. I love him, but being his slave isn't real.*

I even had the nerve to *say* that to him. Did I have a lesson to learn! I was speaking out of turn, I knew that, but I don't think I fully realized what deep shit I was in until I said it. We were arguing about something, I don't even remember what, and he had gotten me so angry that I finally just said I wasn't going to do it and he didn't own me.

He went dead silent. After 15 minutes of talking and yelling, he just stopped. Somehow this was more frightening than anything that had ever happened between us. He just stared at me with those eyes, eyes so dark and deep they were impossible to read.

I had gone too far, that was clear. But was there still time to save my ass? *No*, I realized when he got up suddenly and I felt a chill go down my spine.

"Assume the position, boy," he said.

The time for belligerence was over. I instantly dropped to my knees and put my hands behind my back. He walked into another room and opened some cabinet doors, then went into the kitchen. With my head bowed, I couldn't see what he was doing, but I felt a cold wave of fear wash over me when I heard the sound of a knife being drawn from the rack.

Oh, God, what is he going to do?

His heavy footsteps filled my ears again and his work boots filled my vision as he stepped in front of me. My Master grabbed the collar of my shirt and yanked it up so there was a gap between my neck and the fabric. I heard a tearing sound and realized he was cutting my shirt off with the knife.

"Hey!" I said. *Now this is going too far*, I thought. "Who the fuck do you think you are?"

The blow that hit the side of my face was more powerful than any I had received before. It sent me sprawling, and all my anger was replaced with fear. I must have let out a whimper, because, "Shut up, you miserable slave!" was the next thing I heard.

He grabbed me by the shoulders and lifted me up, setting me back in the position. I quickly put my hands behind my back again.

"Who am I?" he said. "I'm your Master, you little ass-eating, cocksucking, piss-drinking dog, and after tonight you're never going to forget that!"

He finished cutting my shirt to shreds and yanked it off me, then ordered me to lift my ass off the ground. I wanted to whine in fear but knew better than to make any noise. He slid the knife between my shorts and my ass and sliced through the cloth, cutting them cleanly off and leaving me naked and shivering on the floor.

Then cold steel was on my wrists as he bound my hands together behind my back with those old-style British cuffs, Darbys, that won't cut your wrists even if they're on for days. I smelled leather as he slapped a collar around my neck, fastening it tighter than he ever had before, and padlocked it. My vision went black as he blindfolded me, and I tasted something firm and sour as he stuck a cock gag in my mouth and buckled it tight around my head. I realized that the mouthpiece had been soaked in his piss.

"Get up, boy," he said as he yanked on my wrists.

Even with Darbys, the pain was sharp, and I got to my feet as quickly as I could. His hand on my neck pushed me forward. I stumbled through his house as best I could, trying to go where he wanted me to but making frequent mistakes and getting slapped hard on the ass every time.

Then we entered a place where the air was cold and smelled of gasoline. *The garage,* I thought, just as he kicked my legs out from under me and I tumbled forward into something hard and small. I couldn't see anything with the blindfold, but I could definitely sense the darkness closing in when I heard the sound of a heavy lid slamming shut above me. When I heard a door open, I got what was happening — I was in the trunk of his car, and he was getting ready to drive away somewhere.

Now I was *really* scared. *What is this about? Where is he taking me?* My mind raced with possibilities as the car moved out of the garage and onto the road: *Is he taking me to one of his friends' dungeons to punish me? To a bar to publicly humiliate me? To some faraway place to leave me stranded?* I wouldn't put any of those things past him — I had never seen him so angry before. After a long time the car stopped, and he took me out of the trunk.

"Just walk where I push you, slave," he said. "And don't make a fucking sound if you want that hide of yours to stay so goddamn pretty."

He pushed me roughly forward, and I moved as quickly as I could. We were outside for a minute and then entered some enclosure. There was no noise. *Can't be a bar,* I thought, *or a friends' house* — I would have heard people talking.

We walked for a long time. My arms started to ache from being behind my back so long. We took so many twists and turns that I lost all sense of direction. Finally, my Master yanked my collar backward and I stopped walking.

"Hello, Sir," a young male voice I didn't recognize said. "Is that one for us?"

What are they talking about?

"Yeah, he is," my Master said.

What? They're talking about me! What is this?

"He's a fine-looking boy," the other man said. My Master barked a harsh laugh.

"Yeah, well, he's got an attitude problem I can't deal with anymore."

"Can't deal with anymore"? What's happening?

"We'll be able to get something for him, I promise you," the other voice said, increasing my worry to a fever pitch. I heard the snap of fingers, and suddenly there was someone else in the room. "Let's discuss details . . . ," I heard just as I was lifted off the ground and flung over someone's shoulder. *I'm being carried away!* I realized. The voices were fading, and I started struggling.

"Stop it, boy," an extremely deep voice said above me.

I couldn't help it — I was so scared I struggled even more, trying to escape the firm grip the man had on my legs. He stopped and whacked my ass with something. The pain that roared from my backside all the way to my head was so intense, I screamed into the gag, then went limp on the guy's shoulder, and he started walking again.

"That's better," he said. After walking for about five minutes — *this place must be fucking huge*, I thought — he set me down and uncuffed my wrists. But before I could rub some circulation back into them my hands were grabbed and I was reshackled with my arms stretched above my head.

"Good one," another voice said.

"Grade Triple-A meat, F.D.A. approved." Laughter.

"Where'd he come from?" asked a third voice.

There must be at least four of them, I decided. I got so scared that I must have started moaning, because the guys started laughing again. Rough hands groped my nipples, pinching them hard.

"Don't worry, boy," one of them said. "We're not going to hurt you . . ."

". . . permanently," someone shot in.

"Shut up, asshole," the first guy said. "We leave any marks on his skin, and we're all in deep shit."

For some reason, despite the terror, my cock was rock

hard. The first guy put his lips to my ear, and my knees got weak at his closeness.

"It's okay, boy," he whispered. "We only have you for the night. Tomorrow's the big day, so we won't tire you out too much." *What the fuck does that mean?* I wondered. Soon enough, I found out.

I was like a new toy for a bunch of rowdy kids for what seemed like hours. They pinched me, prodded me, stuck clamps on my nipples, whipped my ass with what felt like a riding crop. Finally one of them took the gag out of my mouth, and I gasped for breath.

"Please . . . ," I started.

"Nope, none of that," one of them said, and I felt my arms get unhooked. I was roughly shoved to my knees, and before I could move or say anything else the same man spoke again.

"I don't want to hear his voice, guys. Can you fill his mouth with something?"

Then I was lost in a mix of terror and pleasure again as a huge cock shoved itself into my mouth and started face-fucking me. The others were holding me down, but I wouldn't have struggled even if I was free.

"I'm going to shoot, boy, and if one single drop of it hits the floor, you're going to be one sorry slave."

I pushed my lips forward, taking the whole pulsing rod in until my lips were buried in his pubic hair. My stomach convulsed as he shot a huge load down my throat. The man pulled out slowly, and I kept my lips tight on him, hoping I was getting every last bit. When he was all the way out I heard applause.

"Good boy!" a voice said.

"Hey guys, it's getting late."

"Yeah, let's finish him, I'm tired."

You're tired? I thought, almost delirious. But at least this meant they were nearly done with me. I had no hope of getting my own rocks off even though my cock was throbbing so hard that I doubted I could sleep even if I got the opportunity. Without warning, I was knocked forward so I was resting on hands and knees, and something huge started pushing into my asshole. When I screamed in pain as it plunged all the way in, I was roughly slapped across the face and hit in the back of the head at the same time.

"Goddamn, you do have an attitude problem, don't you, boy? No wonder your Master brought you here. Gag him again."

I tried to keep my mouth closed, but my mind was so occupied with dealing with the huge cock in my ass that all it took was one slap for me to open up and let the plastic cock slide in again. Then I was fucked at least five times, maybe six. Either there were more guys than I thought, or some of them did it twice. I didn't care. I just wanted it to stop. My knees were killing me, my chest and back were covered with bruises and sweat, my ass felt like it had been reamed with a broom handle, and my arms were about to give out.

After the last guy shot his last load of spunk into me, I was allowed to rest. Exhausted, I collapsed on the floor, then was picked up again and carried to some other room where I was laid down on something soft. I was asleep before they finished chaining my cuffed hands to the bed.

It seemed only seconds later that I was brought to my feet and the cuffs removed from my wrists. I was still half asleep, so even though it was the first time I'd been left unrestrained since this nightmare started, I didn't try to escape.

I was picked up and carried to yet another place, where I was hosed down with warm water and scrubbed clean. As I slowly reached full consciousness, I realized that something was different: Last night I had been treated like a worthless piece of meat, a toy to be used. Now I was being handled with exquisite care, the hands on my body gentle and caressing, as if they were polishing a priceless statue.

They finished soon enough, and I was given something to eat and drink, being fed with the same care with which I had been washed. Although my blindfold had not been removed once, and I was still collared, I felt refreshed and energetic, even somewhat relaxed.

"Is he ready?" a rough voice asked. I recognized it as one of the men from the night before.

"Yes," someone said. "And be careful with him."

I guess I'm never going to get to walk, I thought as I was swung up onto yet another man's shoulder to dangle over his back like a sack of laundry. *Where to now?* I wondered as the man carried me even further into the depths of the place. At the slowly rising sound of many men talking, I felt nervousness creep back into my stomach and start to grow. The sound got louder and louder, and as I was unbound, I figured I might have a chance to escape if I was very quick.

With one fast movement, I twisted out of my carrier's grip and fell to the floor. I stumbled and got to my feet, starting to run. I quickly slammed into something huge and flat, and rebounded backward. Loud, deep, booming laughter told me I'd run into another man.

"This one's got a lot of spirit," he said when he stopped laughing. "That'll come in handy." Big hands locked around my wrists and pulled me into a standing position.

I had had enough of this. I was tired of being touched, of being groped, of being carried, of being treated like a . . . like a slave! Anger flared inside me, and I started fighting, swinging with my fists and kicking with my feet. At least I had the satisfaction of knowing it took more than one guy to subdue me.

"That's enough, boy," someone said, and something hit my cock very hard. I cried out and almost fell.

"As much as I want to whip your pretty ass and brand your fuckin' hide, I got orders to leave that skin of yours clean and smooth. So count yourself lucky, you worthless pig!" And I was struck across the face with such ferocity that I would have fallen this time if I hadn't been held up. The roar of the nearby voices pounded in my ears.

"Prep him," the deep voice said, and suddenly the hands were hard at work. Nipple clamps were stuck on me again, my ankles were shackled together with a length of chain, a leather hood with a gag attached was pulled over my head, and, last but not least, my hands were bound behind my back yet again, but with rope instead of steel.

"It's time," someone said. "Bring him in."

I was carried only a short way, brought through a passageway out into a wide-open space filled with voices. *So many men*, I thought, *it must be a whole fucking crowd.*

There was a murmur of approval from the crowd as they brought me in. Then the handler set me down in a standing position, kicked my legs apart, and whispered gruffly into my ear:

"You only move when ordered to, slave. Do what the auctioneer says. Step out of line, and I'll whip your butt so hard you'll have more than one asshole when I'm through."

Auctioneer? My stomach did cartwheels, and my mind screamed: *Auctioneer?* All the fear and terror of the previous day came back in a rush, so strong I almost vomited.

"Our next boy is 24 years old, 5'11", weighing 160 pounds, in prime physical condition, intelligence above average. His only flaw is an attitude problem — but that can easily be beaten out of him." Laughter from the crowd.

It's true — unthinkable but true: my Master has sold me into slavery, and I'm being auctioned off to the highest bidder.

I wanted to scream and cry at the same time. *This can't be happening!* But it was. My knees started to buckle, and I felt the sting of a whip on my ass and the handler's hiss of warning from behind me.

And the auctioneer hadn't stopped talking: ". . . needs to be broken, but a fine addition to any Master's stable."

"The ass!" someone in the crowd shouted.

"Show us the ass!"

"Turn around, boy," the auctioneer said.

I didn't believe he was talking to me. It took being hit by the whip again to make me turn around. A big swell of appreciative noise was heard as my backside was revealed. The handler grabbed my collar and yanked my head down, exposing my asshole to the room. There were catcalls and more laughter. My Master had abandoned me to be purchased like a piece of livestock. I was returned to the standing position, and the bidding began.

"We'll start at $1,000," the auctioneer said.

"Two thousand," a voice said immediately.

"$2,000!" the auctioneer repeated. "Do I hear $5,000?"

"Five thousand" from another voice.

"$5,000! Ten thousand?" There was a pause. "Surely this fine specimen is worth more than $5,000, gentlemen . . . ," the auctioneer purred.

"Not without seeing his face he ain't!" someone called to a swell of laughter.

"All right, all right," I heard and then felt the scrabbling of the handler's hands unfastening the hood. The leather was pulled off my face and the gag from my mouth. A great roar rose in the room.

"Ten thousand!" someone shouted.

With the blindfold still on, I couldn't see a thing, but I guessed they could see enough of my face to make a judgment. Even ungagged, I didn't think of speaking. I had felt the handler's whip too often already.

Now the bidding went fast and furious. It climbed up higher and higher as the men fought for me. I was poked more, prodded, forced to show my asshole again — once I was even ordered to display my cocksucking technique by sucking the handler's cock for a few minutes, to delighted whispers from the crowd.

Standing under the hot lights, I was getting weary again. I felt like a thousand eyes were burning into me, and all I wanted was just to be left alone for a few minutes. I'd given up all thought of escape. Without my Master, I was nothing. I resigned myself to being a slave to some anonymous man, never to see my Master again.

I realized after a while that the bidding was dwindling down to only a few voices, four or five it sounded like. And soon enough it was down to three, then two. These two men outbid each other for a long time, to the mounting excitement of the crowd. Finally it seemed that one of them had given up and would bid no more.

"I have $40,000 from the gentleman in the second row," the auctioneer said. The room was silent. Everyone, including me, held his breath. "$40,000 . . . ," he murmured. I wondered how much of it the auctioneer would get. ". . . going once, going twice, s–"

"Eighty thousand," a new voice said. The crowd roared with excitement, and the previous bidder swore loudly.

"$80,000! New bidder!" the auctioneer screamed. "Going once, going twice, SOLD! To the man against the far wall!"

As the crowd applauded wildly, the handler grabbed my arms, pulling me backward. The last thing I heard as he tossed me over his shoulder again was, "Payment in full must be made now. The handlers will prepare him for shipment, and he'll be in your possession by this evening . . ."

The handler took me away from the auction room, and as the sound of the crowd faded, my spirit died with it. *It's over. I've been sold. I am a slave for real, and for good now. I have been purchased . . . for eighty fucking thousand dollars.* Then something sweet was brought to my nose, and I started to black out. The last thing I remember is being slid into what felt like a canvas bag and hearing it tied closed.

WHEN I WOKE UP the blindfold was gone. I was standing, naked, facing a wall to which I was shackled with my arms and legs outstretched.

So this is my first day as a true purchased slave, I thought miserably. *I've been bought and sold. But whoever this new man is, he will never truly own me. My last shred of pride will be used to resist calling him "Master." My true Master has given me up, but I will always belong to him and him alone.*

I heard bootsteps behind me, and a note was suddenly shoved in front of my eyes.

"This is your first day as my slave, boy," it read. "I am your Master. Your only purpose is to serve me. You will obey me unquestioningly, or you will be severely punished. You are my property. Nod if you understand."

I quickly nodded my head up and down. Then the man turned my head to the side.

"Look at me," he said.

I raised my eyes, and what I saw was so unbelievable that I lost control and pissed down my leg. It was my Master! I stared at him open mouthed.

"I bought you back for two reasons, slave. First, I wanted you to know how valuable you are to me." He leaned forward and very tenderly kissed me on the lips.

If I hadn't already lost my pee, I would have lost it then. His gentle kiss was so filled with love that it melted my heart. Then he stepped back and pulled a whip from his belt.

"And second . . . ," he said — lashing my back at each pause — "I wanted it . . . to be . . . perfectly clear . . . that I will take . . . no more . . . of this . . . 'I don't belong . . . to you' *shit!*" Then he started raining lashes on me, striking me with the whip again and again.

It was more painful than anything I had felt before in my life. I screamed, throwing my head back and slamming it forward against the wall. But in time my screams of torment changed to screams of pleasure — my cock became hard as steel and ready to explode.

"I bought you, slave. YOU BELONG TO ME!" my Master shouted.

I felt the whip cut my back open, and as my warm blood spilled out, the most incredible orgasm I'd ever had ripped through my body. I shot a gigantic load against the wall.

"I BELONG TO YOU, MASTER," I screamed in turn, and I never doubted it again.

As I sank into unconsciousness, I was dimly aware that the blows had stopped and that my Master had come up behind me and was forcing his hard cock into my asshole. He started fucking me, but there was no more pain, only the ecstasy of belonging.   ◉

Master's New Toy

"SLAVEBOY! STEPHEN! Get in here!" Master yelled from another room. "Yes, Sir!" I yelled back. As always, I thrilled to the sound of his voice, my cock hardening almost painfully fast. Setting down the clean underwear I'd been folding, I jumped to my feet and ran out of the laundry room to join him.

Glancing at a mirror as I passed it in the hallway, I was pleased at my reflection, which left nothing to the imagination. Master keeps me naked at home except for the chain collar that encircles my neck and has never come off since he first put it on me five years ago. I was a top when we met, but his sexual authority was so compelling, and he was so insistent on owning me, that I finally consented.

I've been told that my eyes are my best feature. Big and round like a cartoon character's, they're so revealing of my emotions that I can't play poker without dark glasses. I have a good face and a nice chest. My belly used to be a problem, but Master took care of my fondness for candy bars right away, refocusing me with other kinds of rewards and giving me very effective reminders with his belt when I backslid. Now my stomach is flat and hard, and my torso tapers down to tight thighs and legs made powerful by years of skiing.

They're also good for running, and I think I set a new record as I headed down the hall and into the guest room, which we'd converted into our playroom. Master's trunk of gear is stored there, and it's where he takes "guests" who are kinky enough. Skidding to a stop in front of Master, I assumed the position he'd taught me: legs apart, hands clasped behind my back, head up, and eyes down.

"Reporting as ordered, Sir!" I said a little breathlessly.

"A new recruit is on his way over," Master said, "and I need to get you ready."

With my eyes down, all I could see was his heavy black work boots. Now I knew why he hadn't let me take them off when he got home — he likes to wear these boots when he's training new meat. While Master owns one 24/7 slave, namely me, he continues to train other boys to keep his skills sharp. If he ever finds another one as good as me, he's said, he'll keep him and I'll have a brother slave. I really like the idea!

Master's equipment trunk was laid open, and seeing all the treasures inside — handcuffs, blindfolds, gags, coils of rope and chain, collars, full leather hoods, paddles, and so on — not only made my dick harden again but made me remember what usually happened when he "entertained" another boy. Sometimes Master let me watch him work, or even let me help him. More often, depending on his mood, he would tie or chain me up in another room; if he *really* wanted me quiet and out of the way, he'd gag me, restrain me, stuff me in a sack, and put me in a closet. In those cases, I generally wasn't released until after the new boy had been dismissed.

The times I *was* allowed to watch were amazing: like seeing my own training from the other side — better than any porno video. I was wondering if Master would get me out of the way this time when he pulled my attention back to him by clapping his hands.

"Fall asleep, boy?"

"No, Sir!" I risked a glance up at him. I loved seeing the angular contours of his face with its close-cropped beard and sharp, bright eyes. His large, powerful frame is several inches taller than mine.

Master pointed at a bare wooden chair across the room and growled, "Go bring that over here. Then sit your ass on it."

"Yes, Sir!" I said and hurried to obey. *I'm going to get to watch!*

"Thank you, Sir! Thank you so much!" I babbled as I sat in the chair.

"You're welcome. Now shut the fuck up."

Master shoved a leather cock gag into my mouth and fastened it tightly behind my head. His voice was gruff, but I glimpsed a smile on his face as he leaned down to grab some rope out of the trunk. Yanking my arms behind the chair's back, he expertly bound them in place, then attached cuffs to my ankles and fastened them to the rear chair legs.

He paused to look at me, evaluating his work as if it was a painting or sculpture in progress. Then he got some wooden clothespins and attached them to my nipples. They hurt, a lot, but I knew better than to make a sound. My dick, which likes pain better than I do, stood as straight as a chalkboard pointer, its tip glistening with precum. Master spread a towel on the floor in front of the trunk and headed out the door.

I would have waited patiently, and quietly, for hours, but I didn't have to. Soon I heard the doorbell ring and then muffled voices from the foyer, followed by heavy footsteps away from there and lighter ones toward the guest room. I was delighted by what I saw when the boy entered: probably 22 or 23, he was tall — not as tall as Master but several inches taller than me — with beautiful long, blond hair and a cute dimpled face.

The boy stopped a few feet from me and stared as if he couldn't believe his eyes. He shuffled in place for a couple of minutes like he couldn't decide whether to stay or go, but then seemed to make up his mind.

Apparently following orders given earlier by Master, the boy started stripping off his clothes. The body that was revealed when the jeans and T-shirt fell away was firm and defined from regular gym visits. A large, sausage-like dick flopped between his legs. As I imagined taking that wanker in my mouth and working it hard with my lips and tongue, my own tool flexed in excitement.

I knew I shouldn't get my hopes up. It's a privilege just

to watch Master work on another boy. I had rarely been allowed to touch one — it would be greedy and ungrateful to expect such a treat. This boy, though, seemed as fascinated by me as I was by him. His eyes kept returning to my bound body as he neatly folded his clothes and looked around for a good place to put them. I smiled as he piled them on the floor at the side of the trunk — a last exercise of will before he was stripped of all control. Then he knelt on the towel Master had placed, clasping his hands behind his back and lowering his head in submission.

"I have come to serve you, Sir, in any way you see fit," he said in a strong, masculine voice, though it trembled a little from fear and uncertainty. Then he repeated the formula: "I have come to serve you, Sir, in any way you see fit."

A slight noise alerted me, and I turned my head. Master was standing just inside the room, looking at the boy. He had simply replaced his shirt with a black leather vest above his black Levi's and favorite boots.

He's so fucking hot, I said to myself, meaning my Master. I wanted to wriggle out of my bindings and worship him, covering every inch of his hulking body with my tongue. *But this is not about me — it's about Master and his new toy. I have to remember my place and pay attention, not let my mind wander.* What I was about to see would fuel many a fantasy on many nights to come, but if Master caught me daydreaming during his session, I'd never get to watch him train a boy again. So I settled down and watched intently as Master strode across the room to stand before the boy, who was now visibly trembling.

"Why are you here, boy?" Master asked.

"I have come to serve you, Sir, in any way you see fit," the kid answered instantly. I nodded in approval. *He might be scared, but he's obedient.* Master doesn't much care what boys are feeling as long as they're obedient.

"Kiss my boots, boy," he responded, "and thank me for the privilege of kneeling before me and submitting yourself for training."

"Yes, Sir," the kid said and leaned down, pressing his mouth against the matte-black, oil-tanned leather of Master's boots before settling back on his heels. "Thank you for the privilege of kneeling in front of you, Sir, and for the privilege of submitting myself for training, Sir."

"Good boy," Master said, and I glowed with pleasure. Even though they weren't directed at me this time, I *live* to hear Master speak those words.

"Kneel before my slave, boy," Master rumbled.

I couldn't believe my ears: *Am I going to be part of this? Master must really be pleased with me!*

Crawling toward me, his eyes boring into mine, the boy still looked scared, but there was a little less tension in his limbs. As he knelt before me, his hair hung down over his face.

"Suck my slave's cock, boy."

The boy lunged forward and took my rock-hard dick into his mouth, his lips and tongue stroking and caressing me. I started to swoon in pleasure, my head lolling back, but Master quickly put an end to my bliss.

"That's enough, boy," he said. "I don't want my slave to come yet."

"Yes, Sir," the boy said, crawling back and resuming his position kneeling before Master. "Thank you for the privilege of serving your slave."

This boy is good! I said to myself, trying to remember if I had been as poised and obedient my first time.

"Stand up," Master commanded, and the boy smoothly rose to his feet. On closer inspection, his body was not just nice — it was awesome! While he wasn't bulked up with muscles on top of muscles like some guys, he had his own kind of sexy hardness.

Grabbing handcuffs from the trunk, Master slapped them on the boy's wrists, locking them together in front of him. Then he wrapped a bandanna around his new toy's eyes, cutting off his sight. A tiny moan escaped the boy's lips, but Master took no notice. I took a deep breath when I saw Master draw a flogger out of the trunk.

"Spread your legs, boy!" he barked, startling both the kid and me.

"Yes, Sir!"

"Now . . . ," Master said, circling him like a jungle cat playing with its prey. "You were five minutes late, weren't you, boy?" The boy didn't answer immediately, as if searching his memory. Master smacked the flogger across his butt.

"Yes, Sir!" the boy cried out in a strangled voice. "I'm sorry, Sir!"

"Being sorry isn't enough, Kyle," Master said, using the boy's name for the first time. "You have to *show* me you're sorry and that you won't keep me waiting again."

"How can I show you, Sir?" Kyle asked, biting his lip nervously.

"Just take your punishment like a good slave."

"Yes, Sir . . . ," the kid said in a worried voice.

"Count each stroke, and thank me for the discipline," Master instructed him.

"Yes, Sir . . ."

Master struck him again, much harder. The sound of the flogger's leather tongues smacking Kyle's hard body was very loud.

"One, Sir! Thank you, Sir!" the boy counted.

Again Master hit him, but from another angle.

"Two, Sir! Thank you, Sir!"

Now Master walked around and lashed the boy's chest.

"Three, Sir! Thank you, Sir!" he called out, his voice breaking a little. After Master struck again, harder, deep red streaks marked the flogger's path.

"Four, Sir! Thank you, Sir!"

Circling back behind his prey, Master flogged the boy in the hypersensitive area right below the butt.

"Five, Sir! Thank you, Sir!" Kyle was nearly yelling now as he obediently counted out his punishment.

"Six, Sir! Thank you, Sir!"

Finally came his back — Master reserves his heaviest lashes for this toughest part of a man's body. While the skin would not be cut open by the flogger's wide, flat tails, their strikes would be painful enough.

"Seven, Sir! Thank you, Sir!" Kyle breathlessly counted.

I was torn: thrilling to the sound of leather pounding male flesh, but cringing at my fellow slave's pain. Above all, though, I loved being with my Master as he exerted his will and power over another man.

"Eight, Sir! Thank you, Sir!"

The kid staggered under the force of the ninth blow, almost losing his footing.

"Nine ... Sir! Thank you, Sir!"

I wished I could jump forward, gather him in my arms, and help him stand up. I wanted to hold him and whisper in his ear as Master continued to discipline him, to tell him that it was all right, that I was there, that I knew what he was going through ... that it would be over soon. But I was a bound and gagged slave, as powerless to help as the chair I sat on.

Master pulled his arm back, way back — the last blow would be the hardest of all. The flogger tails flew through the air all in a bunch, with the force of a hurricane, and pounded the boy square between his shoulder blades.

"Ten!" Kyle shrieked and tumbled to his knees. "Sir, thank ... you ... , Sir ... ," he finished in a broken voice.

"Good boy ... ," Master crooned, his words sounding like a benediction. It was over.

"Now come to me, Kyle," he said, "and serve my cock to show me how grateful you are to have been disciplined."

"Yes, Sir," the kid whispered, then turned around and crawled back toward his tormentor's voice. Master loosened his thick black belt and unbuttoned his jeans. His dick flopped out, nearly hard and looking as wide as a firehose.

Kyle reared up onto his knees and, still handcuffed as well as blinded by the bandana over his eyes, moved his head around in search of Master's dick. With Master's guidance, he found it and sucked it into his mouth, slurping and sucking with enthusiasm.

"You're never going to be late again, are you, boy?" Master said, stroking the kid's hair.

"No, Sir," Kyle said around a mouthful of dick.

I couldn't help feeling a twinge of jealousy. *Worshipping Master's dick is a privilege, and this boy better realize that!* Then I laughed at myself for being so willful. *My job is to sit here and watch, not to pass judgments or issue ultimatums.* Kyle did seem to be serving Master well, taking as much of the intruding sausage into his mouth as would fit, even gagging a few times to show he was trying his hardest.

Suddenly Master yanked his dick out and reached back into the trunk. Light glittered on metal in his hand as he pulled out a pair of wicked tit clamps joined by a light chain. Seeing them made me remember when Master put the clothespins on me. My nipples were numb now, but I knew the original pain would be nothing compared with what I'd feel when he removed the pins.

Unable to see, Kyle had no warning, when Master lifted him to his feet, that the clamps were coming. But he sure felt it as Master snapped them in place! His breath came out of him in a whoosh, and he whined and moaned in protest.

"Ssshh . . . ," Master purred. "You can take it, boy, you can take it. . . . You're stronger than you think." Reaching into the trunk yet again, he pulled out a black, dick-shaped butt plug.

I felt shivers of excitement and desire — and the need to be part of what I was seeing. A slave shouldn't want more than his Master grants him, of course, but Kyle was a stunning piece of boymeat, and I worship my Master, so it's no wonder I wanted to be there with them, touching and feeling, taking and receiving. Bound as I was, though, I had no choice but to repress the willful thoughts and concentrate on being an observer.

Having lubed up the butt plug, Master was teasing Kyle with it. Resistance and fear seemed to have left the boy. I saw the glint in Master's eyes and knew what was coming: With one smooth thrust, he plowed the dildo into the boy's ass.

Kyle let out a yelp of pain and jerked forward, trying to escape the intrusion. But Master held him tight as his rectum stretched to accept the thick plastic plug. The kid shivered and moaned softly, nuzzling Master's chest. The movement jostled the tit clamps, but the pain of that had to be nothing compared with what his ass was feeling.

"Good boy . . . good boy," Master said, and for the first time looked over to me.

I straightened up, thrusting out my chest to show how dutiful and attentive I was. Master smiled with that mischievous glint still in his eyes, then grabbed the bandanna on the boy's face and yanked it off. Kyle blinked, slowly and stupidly, like a newborn animal. Even the dim light in the room seemed to dazzle him, and he closed his eyes and nuzzled Master's chest again.

"Kneel down, Kyle," Master said. The boy obeyed, and Master strode over to me, covering the distance in seconds. Despite my desire for more involvement, I could hardly believe it was actually happening.

Master looked me in the eyes. I longed to tell him how painful my bondage had become — both my arms and legs ached — and to beg to be released. But my mouth was dry as a desert, my tongue like a piece of sandpaper under the tight gag. It often seems as if my owner can read my mind, and this time was no exception. Master quickly unfastened the gag and gently removed it.

"Thank you, Master," I said in a low voice.

"You're welcome, slave . . . ," and then, without warning, he grabbed the clothespins on my nipples and yanked them off. Fiery pain shot through my chest as blood rushed back into the flesh they'd been pinching.

I howled in agony, and through the glaze in my eyes I saw Master grinning. He loves to hear me scream — I should have guessed what was coming when he took out the gag.

"Good boy . . . ," Master said to me, and hearing those words from him was worth the pain.

"Thank you, Sir!" I said through gritted teeth. He lightly massaged my nipples, which only increased the pain. I whimpered like a puppy.

"That's my boy," he said softly. Then he was behind me, loosening the ropes and cuffs that bound me to the chair. In seconds they fell away, and at a gesture from him I stood and stretched my aching limbs.

"Thank you, Master," I said, then knelt before him and kissed his boots. I couldn't imagine what he had in mind next, though I knew what I *wanted*.

"You've been a very good boy lately," Master said, "and I think you deserve a big reward."

A reward? Really? I thought, grinning happily. *Score one for the slave team!*

"That boy kneeling over there?" Master said, pointing to Kyle. "He's yours. Do whatever you want with him."

This was *way* more than I'd hoped for! I dove down to lick Master's boots.

"Oh, thank you, Master! Thank you, Master!" I said between slurps at the tough leather.

"Kyle," he said in a louder voice.

I jumped to my feet, my dick throbbing, as Kyle's head jerked up.

"Yes, Sir?"

"I'm giving you to my slave," Master told him. "Obey him as you would me."

"Yes, Sir, thank you, Sir," the kid responded with an eager grin. *Glad the attraction is mutual*, I thought.

I walked over to him, grabbed an arm, and pulled him to his feet. Fishing the handcuff key out of the trunk, I released his hands.

"Let's go, boy," I said. "You're coming with me."

Picking the kid up, I slung him over my shoulder. I *love* carrying guys. Something about the weight of their bodies on me, their submission to me and my will . . . it's totally fucking erotic. And Kyle was obedient, hanging limp over my back without struggling. I even heard him whimper a little as I carried him, and his dick, jutting into my shoulder, was hard again. *Seems he gets off on being over my shoulder as much as I do having him there,* I said to myself.

After bowing my head to Master and once again thanking him, I took the beautiful boy to the master bedroom. I flung him face up on the bed, then jumped up after him and straddled his chest. *He's so hot like this,* I exulted, *so helpless and submissive, ready to serve me however I want.*

Lifting one of the manacles attached to the posts at the head of Master's bed, I locked it around my boy's wrist. After doing the same on the other side, I got off the bed and called for Master. Seconds later, he appeared in the doorway.

"What is it, boy?"

"Permission to beg, Sir?"

"Go ahead."

"Please fuck this recruit with me, Master. Please use him with me, please take total possession of him with me . . ."

"Is that what you really want, slave?"

"Yes, Sir, please. More than anything, Sir!"

Master grinned and walked over to the bed. "Then I will give you that gift, Stephen."

"Thank you, Master!"

He got up onto the bed, straddling Kyle's chest as I had before. While Master made himself comfortable, I leaned over behind him and pulled the butt plug from the boy's squirming ass. After disposing of the plug, I got the lube and slathered some on my pulsing dick, getting it nice and slick, then climbed back up on the bed between Kyle's legs. When I stuck a finger into the boy's butthole, he flexed around it. I followed that finger with another one, then another and another, relaxing his hole before I pulled them all out.

"Master?" Kyle asked suddenly.

"Yes, boy?"

As they were talking, I carefully unrolled a condom over my rock-hard boner.

"Please let me serve your slave, Sir!"

I lifted the kid's legs up into the air as Master laughed.

"You're doing it, Kyle, right now."

Master turned his head and winked at me. I took my cue, shoving my dick into the boy like a hot knife into butter. He let out a little gasp. That was Master's cue, and he pulled Kyle's head onto his big, uncut wanker. Any response the boy might have made was instantly muffled.

"That's it, boy," I said. "Serve your Master and his No. 1 slave..."

Kyle thrashed around, but Master and I are both bulkier and stronger. We had no trouble keeping him in place as I fucked him, sliding in and out of his tender asshole. He might have been a virgin, he was so satin-velvet smooth and tight at the same time. It was exhilarating to have such a hot piece of boymeat enveloping my hard dick while Master fucked his face, using him like the slave he wanted to be.

"You're here to be used, boy," Master even said. "You're nothing but a piece of property to get us off."

The kid's untouched dick jiggled with our every thrust into his mouth or butt, sending drops of precum flying every which way.

"You're our cum hole, boy...," I said as I started stroking his dick in my fist. "Our little hole to fuck anytime we want..."

Kyle was moaning around Master's dick, his voice vibrating with passion. It felt so good to be inside him. *It's like his rectum was molded around my dick, like he's my personal fuck boy, just for me... and Master, of course.* Since I'm his property, anything that's "mine" is really his.

The sight of Master's broad back in front of me, the motions of his pelvis as he pummeled the kid's mouth, Kyle's body shaking under me, my memory of the shocks and pleasures I'd experienced over the last couple of hours, like the feel of the boy slung over my shoulder... it all came together to push me toward a climax.

"Permission to come, Sir?" I asked urgently.

"Only if you can make our fuck hole come at the same time," he said.

"Yes, Sir!"

I felt more than equal to his challenge. Accelerating my thrusts into Kyle's ass, I gripped his dick tightly in my hand and really pounded it. Impaled at both ends and manhandled in the middle, he whimpered and twisted between us like an animal in a trap. My own countdown had started, and there was no turning back. I had to make this boy come with me, or there'd be hell to pay.

"You want to belong to us, Kyle?" I asked, loud enough for him to hear despite Master's bulk between my mouth and his ears.

"Yes, Sir!" he answered as well as he could around the dick in his mouth.

"You want to be our little whore boy all the time?"

"Yes, Sir!"

"You want to be our sole and exclusive property, fucked and plowed by both our dicks every day and night?"

"*Please*, Sir!"

"Then come *NOW!*" I said as I felt my dick throb. My orgasm blasted off like a rocketship. Hot cum shot down the length of my dick as a wave of fucking awesome pleasure roared through me! And then another and another!

Although I was delirious with bliss as my load dumped itself in the reservoir at the end of the condom, I still felt Kyle's dick flex in my hand. Like a geyser erupting, it spurted rope after rope of sticky cum. Master laughed heartily as both of us emitted loud sounds of pure animal release. After fucking boys, his favorite thing is to get us to make a lot of noise.

Once Kyle and I shuddered out the last of our orgasms, I pulled my dick from his asshole. Master retrieved his dick from the kid's mouth, turned himself around, and moved up. While he settled against the pillows at the head of the bed, I stripped off my condom, dumped the creamy goo on the boy's chest, and rubbed it into his pecs.

Kyle had been mumbling something under his breath, too low for me to hear, since he shot. I leaned down next to his mouth and finally understood what it was.

"Thank you, Sirs, thank you, Sirs, thank you, Sirs, thank you, Sirs...."

What a polite, well-spoken lad, I thought. *I should follow his example.*

"Thank you, Master, from both of us," I said out loud, bowing my head so I was staring at his dick. He reached over and scratched behind my ears. I love it when he does that. It makes me feel like Man's Best Friend.

I figured this was the point when Master would release the boy and dismiss him. But after freeing Kyle's wrists, he got off the bed and left us boys alone in his room. I took off the tit clamps and, as soon as the boy stopped hissing and shrieking, gently massaged his aching nipples. We embraced and then lay there in each other's arms, luxuriating in the close contact.

"How're you feeling, boy?" I asked after a few minutes.

"God, I'm so fucking happy," he said, his voice breaking. "He's not going to send me home, Sir, is he?"

"I don't know, Kyle. It's his house, and he's boss. I'm happy too. You're the best boy I've ever played with."

"Thanks, Sir.... You're the best too."

When Master came back into the room, I was expecting him to say, "Get up, boys. Kyle has to go home." But he had an empty black canvas sack over his shoulder, one of those he'd had made to put me in sometimes. Kyle looked questioningly at me as we both got up on our knees. I shrugged my shoulders. Master might be able to read my mind, but I sure can't read his, so I never know what he's planning.

"C'mere, Kyle," Master said once he stood next to the bed. He had a big smile on his face.

Obediently, Kyle crawled over to Master. As soon as he was within reach, Master grabbed the boy and threw him over his shoulder. Opening the bag with one hand, he began guiding Kyle's legs into it with the other.

"It's all right, boy," Master said, patting Kyle's butt reassuringly. "I'm just putting you in here for safekeeping, so I'll know where you are. Okay?"

Master's New Toy

"Okay, Sir," Kyle mumbled happily as he slid the rest of the way into the sack. Master pulled the drawstring closed and tied off the top, then slung the bag onto his shoulder.

"Master . . . ?" I started to ask.

"Yeah, slave. This one's a keeper."

"Fuckin' A! Thank you, Master!"

Master's found another boy he wants to keep! I have a brother slave! I could have hugged myself, or him, I was so pleased at how the evening had turned out.

Master carried the bag with Kyle in it over to a corner of the bedroom and laid it gently on the carpet. He put a pillow under the boy's head, then hurried back to the bed to lie next to me and enfold me in his big, muscular arms.

"Happy, boy?"

"You know it, Sir!"

He nuzzled me and cuddled my head on his shoulder. "You've got a brother slave, now," he said as my heart soared. "And I've got a new toy."

Nothing could be any better, I thought — *except I can't remember Master shooting a load when Kyle and I did.*

"Master?"

He grunted.

"One question?"

"Okay, Stephen, what is it?"

"Why aren't you getting off tonight?"

Master laughed again.

"What makes you think I'm not? I was savin' it up for *you*, my alpha slaveboy!"

He grabbed my wrists and slapped the bed-post cuffs on them, then pulled off his jeans. His dick was hard, dripping, and ready for action — and so was mine again! Wrenching my legs apart, Master aimed his enormous uncut monster at his alpha slave's butt hole. It was then I realized that what I had thought earlier was true after all: *It doesn't get any better than this!* ◉

Scent Slave

JERKING MYSELF OFF, I stared through my apartment's steel-mesh security door. A sweaty, wild-eyed man knelt on the other side, totally naked except for a leather collar around his neck.

"Please let me in, Sir!" he said. "Please let me come in and serve you! Please, Sir!"

I've got him, I thought. *He's mine.*

"What will you do for the privilege of serving me?" I asked as I pumped my dick in my hand.

"Anything, Sir!" he moaned desperately. "I'll do anything for the privilege of serving you!"

All mine...

It had started about two months earlier when he joined my gym. I noticed him right away because he had a sharp look that made him stand out from the other guys. The gym attendant told me his name was Bryan. He was quick-witted and smart, aware of everything that went on around him — so different from the narcissistic haze most gym-rats are in. He always wore black, as if he didn't have time to fuck around with color coordination. His clothes matched his eyes and his hair, which was jet black and glossy, like he was something out of Greek or Roman mythology. Without his early '90s goatee, he could've been mistaken for a faun or a satyr, some mischievous creature from a fantasy world.

His body wasn't huge and bulked out, just sort of quietly buff, as if there was no flesh on him, only bone and muscle, sculpted like a beautiful statue. Every move he made was as graceful as a ballet dancer's.

I knew I wanted him the minute I saw him. It was that simple. I wanted him. And once I made that decision, I would stop at nothing to achieve my goal.

Christopher Pierce: Winner Takes All

How to get this one? I wondered. My usual style was to go for someone directly, and if he wasn't into kink, to take him by force. That method didn't seem right this time. What I had to do was clear: I had to make him want me. I had to make him want me so badly that he'd do *anything* for me. Then he'd be mine for keeps.

I usually jerked off at least once a day. Even when I was dating someone, it was impossible to blow off all the steam I built up without some hand action every day. As soon as I shot a load, I could feel my balls start to fill up with juice again. I had honed beating off to an art and could control my cock like a fine instrument. I could sometimes jerk myself for hours without letting myself come. The power that built up was incredible.

The few times I experimented with holding my cum, something wild had happened. When I didn't let myself come for days at a time, I would get even more attention from guys than I usually did. When I looked in the mirror and saw the muscle-bound man with floppy blond puppy-dog hair and pale blue eyes looking back at me, I knew I was hot. But when I held my cum it was as if I sent out chemicals into the air, pheromones like those that animals release to let potential mates know they're hyped for humping. I didn't think people had any pheromones, but I was wrong.

The sperm would collect day by day in my balls, and my attractiveness would increase and multiply with it. Heads would turn, men would whisper into their friends' ears, and total strangers would walk up to me and start talking. They'd get embarrassed looks in their eyes, as if something beyond rational thought was compelling them to be near me. They wouldn't normally be so direct, but something about me was becoming irresistible. And I would smirk to myself and know that it was the sack of cum in my shorts that was hanging lower and lower every day below my nine-inch cock that was driving them wild.

But usually I didn't have the patience to go through that ordeal. As hot as it was, giving up jerking off every day wasn't something I'd do for just any boy. Bryan was different. I wanted to see him kneeling in front of me naked and begging to be my slave more than I needed to come every day. So I started saving up — saving for the future.

And the boys noticed. Even though I always went to the gym really early or really late to avoid the rush, the men who were there noticed. But all I noticed was Bryan, who always seemed to come in when I was there even though I had no set schedule.

I smiled at the salivating boys, flashing them my killer smile and letting them go with that. My eyes were on Bryan. I stared at him from the minute he walked in with his gym bag over his shoulder to the minute he left.

From the beginning it was clear that he'd be tough to land. As stunning as I was, so was he. It was to be a competition of equals, a challenge of wills, a clash of the titans. It would take everything I had to get him.

Bryan usually glanced away as soon as he saw me looking at him. But one night I caught him and held him with my eyes. We were facing away from each other, me riding a Stairmaster and him on one of the treadmills, but the mirrors that covered every inch of the walls gave us clear views of each other. It was almost closing time. Most other guys were already in the showers and would be gone within minutes. The area we were in had emptied out already.

But we were still hard at work, the sweat rolling off us like we were caught in a rainstorm together. The ever-present dance music pounded through the big speakers mounted in each corner of the room. The bass line rumbled in my ears, and I was moving to the beat. Bryan was, too.

We were moving together, our legs straining and sweating in unison. That was something else I liked about him, his fully developed legs. Unlike most gay boys, who buff up their upper bodies and forget about their legs, Bryan had quadriceps and calves that were full and strong, almost as built as mine.

The glaring fluorescents caught the trickling sweat on

his thighs, causing it to sparkle like rain in summer sunlight. I imagined catching it with my tongue, following it up higher and higher, tracing the broad, rock-hard muscles down toward his groin . . .

My eyes found his in the mirror, and this time he didn't look away. *This is it*, I thought. *There's never going to be a better time than this.* And I locked him with my gaze, giving him such a look of desire that he couldn't turn away even if he'd wanted to. I shifted my position on the machine. Bryan followed the movement and saw that I was rubbing my leg against the side rail. He stared at my leg as if mesmerized. His eyes moved to my crotch.

It was time to throw him the bait and see if he bit. I conjured the image of him tied up and gagged on my bed, and instantly my cock hardened. Bryan's eyes widened in surprise and excitement. The gray fabric of my tight little gym shorts strained from the pressure of the fuckstick underneath, which was getting bigger and bigger.

We were moving in unison. He looked up at me, and I gave him an evil smile that said, *You're going to be mine, man.* He looked back down at my crotch. I hadn't come in a few weeks. I knew a little stain of precum was spreading on my shorts. I flicked my eyes down to my prey's crotch and was happy that even his baggy black sweatpants couldn't hide that his cock was erect and firm.

My workout was done. I jumped off the machine and tossed my towel over my shoulder. Bryan looked surprised, the look on his face saying, *Wait, this can't be over!* It wasn't, but the next move had to be his.

Though I didn't glance back, I knew he was following me. We walked through the rest of the gym, totally empty by then. The attendants had started cleaning up for the night. The scent of my stored-up cum was leading Bryan on like the smell of food would lead a starving animal. I heard his soft footsteps behind me as I trotted down the stairs to the showers. The locker room was empty, too, nothing but blackness showing through the steam-blurred windows.

Knowing he was behind me and watching every move, I stripped off my sweaty shorts and stepped into the big communal shower stall. I flicked on the water, and it sprayed down on me. I cracked one eye open and saw him staring at me. He was slowly taking off his own clothes. The body beneath was hard and healthy.

My hand, as if on its own, starting caressing the light dusting of hair that covered my pecs. Then it slid down between them to the hard washboard of my abs. The hot water filled my vision with steam and electrified every inch of my body. I grabbed my hard cock and slowly began working it back and forth in my hand. I knew I'd get kicked out of the gym if an attendant saw me, but I didn't give a shit. It felt so good — it had been a long time since I'd touched myself that way.

Another shower started running. Bryan was next to me, his hands running over his body like mine had done. I looked at him, my eyes burning. He was gripping his own hard cock, stroking it and caressing it in his palm.

We were less than three feet away from each other, but we weren't touching. It was as if there was an invisible wall between us. The look in Bryan's eyes kept changing, from surprise to pleasure to anger to desire. He wanted to touch me so badly, but the look in my eyes told him not to: *You can look but not touch. I'm in charge.*

I knew I could take him right then. I could throw him against the wall, turn him around, and shove my cock up his butt, and he'd beg me for more. But it wasn't enough. It wouldn't last. After it was over he'd move on to someone else. This was a man I wanted for good. I wanted him as my slave — nothing less would satisfy me. That meant I needed to capture him beyond all hope of escape. He had to be driven almost mad with desire and taken at just the moment when he couldn't stand it any more. Then, and only then, would he be mine for keeps.

As difficult as it was, I tore my hand away from my cock. I turned the water off and grabbed a towel, turning away from Bryan and rubbing it over myself. Nothing more was going to happen there. Dressing quickly, I headed out of the locker room.

Bryan scrambled to follow me. By then, there was nowhere he *wouldn't* follow me. His cock had locked onto the scent of my cum, and nothing his brain could tell him would take him off the trail. He followed me out into the parking lot and then home in his car. He followed me all the way to my apartment. As I unlocked the heavy security door, I saw him behind me out of the corner of my eye. He was dying to follow me inside and go to it once and for all, but it wasn't going to happen.

I walked into my apartment and immediately slammed the security door behind me. Made of heavy metal mesh, it allowed us to see each other, but we were separated by an impassable barrier. Bryan let out a little moan of surprise and dismay.

I turned around and faced him. He was looking at me with desperation in his eyes. He couldn't believe I had led him this far and now wouldn't let him touch me. I pulled down my shorts and ripped off my shirt. Completely naked once again, I resumed jerking off.

"You want me, man?" I asked, breathing heavily.

"Yes . . . ," he whispered.

"Yes, what?" He looked confused for a few seconds.

"Yes, *Sir*," he said finally.

"That's better . . ."

I kept jerking myself, licking my hand to slick it up. Bryan started rubbing his own crotch through his sweats, but I could tell he was nervous. Any of my neighbors could see him if they just looked out their windows.

He wasn't ready. If he had been, he wouldn't have been thinking about anything except how he could please me. My hand-job felt so good, I was tempted to let myself come. But I knew that that pleasure would be nothing compared with what I would feel when I completely owned this man.

"I want you, Sir . . . ," he said.

"What would you do for me?" I asked, increasing the speed of my strokes. My balls felt so full they might burst, and my cock was dying for release. But I wouldn't let it go. Not yet.

"Anything, Sir . . . ," he whispered, his eyes squeezed shut.

"Whimper for me, boy . . . ," I purred at him.

He started whining and crying like an animal. He took his hands away from his crotch and grabbed the door, pressing his face up against the screen.

"You've been thinking about my cock a lot, haven't you?"

"Yes, Sir . . ."

"You've been imagining it packed tight in my shorts, sweating as it gets hotter and hotter while I'm working out at the gym . . ."

"Yes, Sir . . ."

"You wish I'd let you clean it after I finish pumping, don't you, boy? You wish I'd pull down my shorts and let you wash my crotch clean, lick all the sweat away. You want this throbbing, dripping cock in your mouth . . ."

"Oh, yes, please, Sir!"

"Then press your cock against this door and *show* me how much you want it."

Instantly he moved up to the door and pressed his crotch against it. He started rubbing against the mesh. The erection beneath those shorts was so full and hard that I was surprised a hole didn't appear in it.

"Now look around and see if the coast is clear."

He glanced around.

"There's no one watching, Sir."

"Then show it to me," I said.

And there was Bryan's beautiful cock, almost completely smooth, with only a few veins popping out, and every bit as big as mine. His head rolled back as if the night air on his cock was making him swoon.

"Please, Sir . . . ," he whispered. "I'll do anything you want me to. Please let me serve you . . ."

"I don't believe you," I said. "You don't really mean it."

He gasped in dismay, then asked, "How can I prove it to you, Sir?"

"The night you follow me home and kneel outside my door naked with a collar around your neck — that's the night I'll believe you." I turned my back on him and walked into my apartment, shutting the inner door behind me.

The next night we were at the gym working out together again — never speaking, just staring at each other all night. He wanted me so badly, yet he could not do what I had asked. I was unreachable to him. He tried a thousand ways to seduce me, to get me on his terms, but I never let it happen. It was going to be my way or no way.

It went on and on. Every night he followed me home, and every night he begged and pleaded with me through the door to please let him in, to let him touch me, to take him and make him mine.

I never spoke to him, not once. I had said everything he needed to know. Jacking myself off just inside the door in his plain view every day, getting myself so close to coming and then stopping, pulling back so that the power between my legs grew stronger and stronger. It was driving us both mad, and my balls ached, but I would never give in.

Then he stopped coming to the gym. I didn't see him for days. I figured he must have given up and moved on somewhere else. Disappointed, I wondered what I should do with the tremendous amount of cum I'd saved up. I didn't want to waste it on some other boy. I had saved it for Bryan, and he was the boy I wanted to give it to — right before I claimed him as my slave for life.

Doing my workouts in a haze, ignoring the boys who were drawn by my scent and came sniffing like dogs, I thought only of Bryan. It seemed that he had captured me just as surely as I had hooked him on myself. As a rule, boys were mere toys, to be used and discarded — but not this one. Bryan was different. I wanted him in a way that I had never wanted anyone before, and the need to have him got stronger every day.

Then one night, there he was again. I almost shot my load right there when I saw him. He had a leather collar around his neck and was wearing just a pair of black shorts. He stared at me — waiting. His body was still, his boner plainly visible in his shorts.

I stared back. Even though I might be in love with him, I was still the one in charge — the Top, the Master. And it was time to claim my property.

I walked up to him, coming so close that I heard a tiny moan escape his lips. He wanted to hold me, to take me in his arms, to take my cock in his mouth, his ass, anywhere, everywhere. Yet he knew that disobeying my orders would rob him of ever touching me again. I put my lips to his ear.

"Do you have what it takes to wear that collar, boy?" I breathed. "Or are you just pretending?"

"I can do it, Sir," Bryan whispered. "Please let me try."

I walked out the door without another word. Like the twenty times before, he followed me back to my place. The familiar slam of the security door filled the night air. I turned around, dropped my bag on the floor, and looked at him through the steel mesh. I reached into my shorts and pulled out my cock, swollen with power from weeks of being denied release. It was hot and pulsing in my hand, and shimmering strands of precum trailed from the piss slit.

Bryan stepped forward until he was just a foot away from me, only the door separating us. And there he stood — my prize, my treasure, my man, now and forever — standing collared like a slave for the world to see. His cock was dribbling so much precum that it was staining his tiny shorts. He stared at me, his eyes filled with tension and frustration.

I felt invincible, suffused with power and strength. My cock glowed as my hot blood burned through its veins. I pumped it in my hand, and the friction of skin on skin filled every inch of me with ecstasy. Bryan had come to me; he had passed all barriers to join me on the other side. The time had come at last, and now I would claim him once and for all.

My fist stroked my cock back and forth, faster than the eye could follow. Being denied for so long, it was ready to shoot. The churning semen in my balls desperately tried to escape, previewing itself in more and more insistent dribbles of precum. And Bryan's eyes were filled with a desire bordering on insanity.

"Please, Sir," he begged. "Please let me be yours..."

"What will you do for me, boy?"

"Anything, Sir!"

"Are you ready to show me?"

"Yes, Sir!"

"Now?"

"Yes, Sir! Now, Sir!"

Bryan yanked off his shorts, ripping them, then flung them aside and dropped to his knees before me. The sight of him cowering naked at my feet with his head bowed and cock at full attention was what I'd been waiting for.

"Your collared boy is ready to serve you in whatever way you see fit, Sir! I await your orders, Sir!"

That was it. *The time is now*, I silently declared.

Incredible power surged through me, seeming to come from my groin and to rocket both up to my brain and out through the white-hot cock pulsing in my clenched hand. The orgasm rocked me so hard, I almost lost my balance. I threw my head back as cum splattered on the door, leaking through to the other side. Some spurts hit so hard that it actually flew through the tiny holes in the mesh and struck the naked, collared, kneeling slave.

"Use it, boy," I gasped. "Show me how much you want to be mine."

"Yes, Sir!" Bryan said as he scrabbled at my cum with his hands. Still in the throes of my own orgasm, I watched him greedily scoop up my jism and use it to lube his cock. He started flogging his meat, jerking it like a man possessed.

I squeeze-pumped my cock a few more times, coaxing the last milky drops to fall on the floor in front of me. The picture was complete. The man I had once imagined as a

Scent Slave

creature of mythology was kneeling in front of me, transported to another plane as if in a tribal ceremony. We had entered the realm of ecstasy together as mere men, and when we emerged we would be Master and slave.

"Come for me, boy . . . ," I whispered.

"Yes, Sir . . . ," he moaned.

"Come for your Master!" I shouted.

Bryan grunted like an animal and bent back on his heels, as if the power being released was forcing him to fold himself smaller. A geyser of cum shot out of his cock, curling in the air like water from a fountain. I could see it steam in the chilly night. Gasps of pleasure came from him as he continued jerking and more spurts of cum followed the first blast. Finally he let out a howl like a wolf baying at the moon and let go of his cock. He stared at his hand in shock, as if he didn't know his body was capable of such pleasure. Then he looked up at me.

"You've proven your worth to me, boy," I said. He was silent, anticipation in every inch of his body. "You are now my slave. You belong to me." The delight on his face was transcendent.

"Thank you, Sir," Bryan whispered. And I opened the door. ◉

Winner Takes All

I. Friday Night — Fucked by a Bruiser

How did I get into this? I asked myself as I struggled, bound hand and foot, inside a man-sized duffel bag in the back seat of the car of the guy who had won me for the weekend. That's right, won me for the weekend!

It all started a couple of hours earlier. My Master had taken me out to our city's leather bar, The Richter Scale, as he did every Friday night, dressed in tight shorts, no underwear, a sleeveless T-shirt, and black leather Army boots, with a light chain collar around my neck. He liked parading me around, showing me off to the other Masters, making them jealous that they didn't own such a fine piece of slavemeat as me — and making other slaves jealous that they weren't owned by such a fine-looking Master.

Well, this time it looked like he got more than he'd bargained for. The bruiser who approached us had caught my eye when we first walked in. A huge man, probably 6'6" or so, he wore a simple tank top, which showed off his hunky chest and arms, and bluejeans tucked into cowboy boots. Sitting by himself in the back of the bar, he was nursing a bottle of beer and watching the crowd. But as soon as we came in he did a double take, then looked at me with such lust and greed that I started to get hard.

He got up off his stool and headed our way. My Master saw him coming and tightened his grip on my leash, pulling me closer. The bruiser walked right up to him, and the two dominant leathermen looked at each other, not saying anything, like two big dogs scoping each other out.

Up close I could see he was a handsome man, probably

in his late 30s, with blond hair cut high and tight and a mustache just as blond. His bulging biceps sported intricate tribal-style tattoos, and ice-blue eyes burned in his stern face. *Ex-Marine?* I wondered. Unlike many other guys sporting that haircut, Max actually looked like he could have been a Marine. Besides muscles, he had the controlled stance, the darting eyes quickly evaluating a situation, and the contained potential for violence.

The man was so hot and masculine that my cock started pushing against my shorts. In fact, he reminded me a lot of my Master. I like men who know what they want and go for it, men who don't take shit from anyone. With them sizing each other up, it looked like a clash of titans was about to happen.

"Hot piece of meat you've got there," the bruiser said.

"Thanks," Master said. "He's the best."

"Master . . . ?" I started to ask.

"Shut up, boy!" he said as he jerked my leash. "Get on your knees and keep your mouth shut."

Silently, I obeyed, kneeling in place on the hard floor of the bar. I bowed my head respectfully, and my field of vision was filled by the pointed toes of the bruiser's boots. My cock got harder in my shorts: I wanted to lean over and lick his boots right then and there, worshipping them for everyone to see, but of course I didn't.

"Well behaved, I see." The bruiser was so tall that his voice sounded far away.

"Not always," Master said, "but his asshole makes up for it. . . . You're damn hot yourself. I'm Bill."

"Max," the bruiser said as I glanced up, and they shook hands.

"Mind if I check out your boy, Bill?"

"Sure, why not? His name is Josh, but call him anything you like."

And then the big man was hunkering down on one knee, trying to lower himself to my level. Even down there, he was still much taller than me. Around his thick neck was a delicate silver chain, so fine it was nearly invisible. Two small silver keys hung from it. As I learned later, that necklace remained around his neck at all times.

I was suddenly terrified by the attention. Having both of these men interested in me made me feel put on the spot, vulnerable. I was used to getting my ass plowed, doing my chores, eating out of my dog bowl, and otherwise staying out of Master's way until he wanted me. I never expected him to pay me much attention, even on these bar jaunts, and I was fine with that.

Now I had two incredibly hot men staring at me, taking in my every move. I must have let out a little whimper of discomfort, because Max chuckled and stroked my buzz-cut head.

"It's okay, boy," he said soothingly. And it was. "I just wanted to have a look at you. . . . You're one fine piece of slavemeat."

"Thank you, Sir," I whispered, embarrassed by my bulging cock, its shape clearly visible under my shorts. Suddenly Master stuck his boot between my legs and kicked my nuts. I yelped in pain and surprise.

"Speak up when you're talking to my friends, boy!" he said harshly.

"Yes, Sir!" I said loudly. "I'm sorry, Sir!"

"That's a good slave," he said, patting my head.

Max was touching my face then, running his hand along my skin. He found my mouth and stuck his index finger between my lips. I took it in and submissively caressed it with my tongue. The man frightened me, but I looked up into his eyes anyway.

His expression was the same as when he first saw me, a mix of lust and greed. Then he was pushing more fingers into me — two, three, then four — running them around the inside of my mouth, feeling the curves and contours of my gums, sliding along my teeth . . .

It was intoxicating to be entered that way, to feel the bruiser explore my mouth. I imagined what it would be like if he were to push those fingers into my asshole . . . . Suddenly he released me and stood up, and all I could see were his boots again. My head was spinning from his touching me, and I struggled to hear what he was saying to my Master.

"You ever arm wrestle?" he asked.

"Sure," Master Bill replied, "lots of times when I was in the Navy."

"Up for a match?"

"With you? Now? What're the stakes?"

The big man looked down at me and grinned, then back at my Master.

"If *I* lose," he said, "you get me as your slave for the rest of the weekend. If *you* lose, I get your slave for the rest of the weekend."

I was stunned, but with fear . . . or excitement?

"Mmmmm," Master considered. "Pretty hefty stakes." His hand shot out and gripped the bruiser's crotch, cupping the man's balls in his palm. "But I think it'd be worth it . . ."

Max grinned again, and before I knew it I was kneeling next to a low table, and Master and the bruiser were planting their elbows and locking fists.

"Either you're mine," Master said, "or he's yours."

His opponent nodded silently.

Instantly the match was on, each man grunting with surprise at the other's strength. I watched with my mouth hanging open as the tattoos on their arms writhed from the straining of the muscles beneath.

My Master glared into his opponent's eyes, and Max was gritting his teeth so hard I could practically hear them grinding. Sweat broke out on both their foreheads.

Other men in the bar caught sight of the match and gathered around, respectfully quiet. I was frightened by what was happening, and yet my cock was rock hard at the sight of these two giants battling it out — over me! I could hardly believe that part.

Can this bruiser really value me enough to risk having to

serve my Master for the weekend? And can my Master value me so little that he'd risk losing me on a casual bet? Apparently, I concluded silently, *because neither one is faking this.* The competition was for real, and it looked like the bruiser was winning.

Inch by inch, Max was forcing my Master's fist down toward the tabletop. Master snarled with anger and tried to get his hand back up, but it was no use. Max had the advantage and wasn't giving it up for anything.

Suddenly it was over. The bruiser slammed his fist down, pinning my Master's to the table beneath.

"Damn!" Master Bill roared, but his anger subsided quickly. "Good match," he said with a good-natured laugh, and he and his opponent shook hands again.

"You almost had me there for a while, Bill," Max said with a grin. He'd won, but he was sweating profusely, and his arm was quivering with fatigue. He turned his smile to me, and my insides felt hollow. *Are they really going through with this?*

"Stay, boy," Master said to me. "Max and I have to talk."

"Yes, Master."

I watched them walk away, out of the bar. *They probably need some fresh air,* I figured, but my mind was racing with excitement and fearful questions: *What's about to happen to me? Is Max really going to take me for the weekend? What will he do to me? And will he give me back at the end?*

Since Master Bill claimed me more than a year earlier, I'd never spent a night away from him, and it was frightening to think about. *But I've always been an adventurous boy,* I told myself, *and this* could *be the best adventure I'll ever have.*

In a few minutes they were back, carrying stuff they must have gotten from their cars.

"Stand up, slave!" Master Bill said loudly.

Everyone in the bar was watching again. He was carrying two small coils of rope, while Max hefted a large duffel bag, the kind camping tents come in.

I jumped to my feet, my cock tenting my shorts for all

to see. There was some pointing and laughing, and my ears burned with embarrassment.

Master Bill unhooked my leash and gave it to the bruiser, leaving my chain collar on. Tying my wrists together in front of me with one coil of rope, he wrapped the other around my booted feet. I whimpered in dismay, but Master reassured me.

"You'll be okay, boy," he said. "You can trust Max. He won't do anything to damage you. He'll bring you back here Sunday night, and I'll retrieve you then."

Glancing over at Max, Master Bill winked at him. *Now what does that mean?* I wondered. The bruiser stood with his arms folded, the big bag hanging from his grip, a dazzling grin on his face.

"Be good, boy," Master said.

"I will, Sir," I said, though I had never felt more helpless or desperate than at that moment.

"Obey Max. Understand, slave?"

"Yes, Master."

"Okay, then," he said and patted my head.

As he turned away, I felt like crying, but I had my orders. All I could do was follow them and try to make my Master proud. Then I felt new hands on me.

It was the bruiser, of course. As before, his touch made strange shivers course through me. He leaned in close and put his lips to my ear.

"I'm your Master now, Josh," he said. "I won you fair and square," — *but only for the weekend!* I protested silently — "and I'm taking you home with me now."

He shook the big sack open and then in one movement threw it over my head. It must have been huge, because it went all the way down to my ankles. Then I felt the bag, with me inside it, being lifted up and over his shoulder. He must have pulled the drawstrings tight, because I was in total darkness. I fought down my fear and the urge to struggle. It was my job to be obedient and not give my temporary Master any trouble.

The huge man rearranged the sack on his shoulder so that my weight was distributed better, and then he started walking. I heard appreciative murmurs from the crowd all around me as we moved through the bar. I have a bad sense of direction to begin with, and being carried upside down and traveling backwards got me completely disoriented. Then we were outside, but the only reason I knew that was by the sounds of traffic I suddenly heard through the heavy canvas of the bag.

We walked a little further, and I heard a car door open. I was lowered and shoved inside, laid across what must have been the back seat. The door slammed behind me, and I knew I'd crossed the point of no return. If there'd been some chance of escape before, there was none now.

I heard Max get in the front seat and start the vehicle. As engine roar filled my ears, I realized I was on my own — *Master Bill can't help me.*

Whimpering quietly, I curled up as much as I could inside the sack. Tears spilled down my cheeks. I was surprised that my cock was still as hard as it had been in the bar. As frightening as this adventure was, it was also exciting.

The car pulled out, and we were moving. I don't know how long we traveled, but finally the car slowed and then stopped. After Max got out of the car, he pulled me from the back seat, tossing the duffel bag over his shoulder again, and carried me a short way. When I felt the motion of an elevator, I knew he had an apartment, not a house. Eventually we reached his unit, a door opened, and he set me down on a hard floor. The door closed behind us.

I felt him untying the end of the sack, and he pulled it off me, spilling me out onto the floor. The sudden light hurt my eyes as I looked up at him. He was looking down at me with the same expression of greedy lust he'd had in the bar. That expression was burning into my brain — I was sure I'd see it in future wet dreams, if not nightmares.

"My slaveboy," Max said with satisfaction, as if he liked hearing his voice say those words. "My little fuck hole . . .

my whore boy for the weekend. . . . You have to do anything I say, boy. Your Master told you to obey me."

"Yes, Sir," I quickly agreed.

Looking around the entry area of the apartment, I tried to take in as many details of my surroundings as I could without losing sight of my abductor. An opening on the side led to the kitchen, and through an archway ahead of us I could see the living room, with a door at its far end that probably led to the bedroom and bathroom. The decor was sparse, functional, masculine, with framed sports photos and a Marine Corps poster the only "artwork" in sight.

Max scooped me up again and carried me over his shoulder into the kitchen. He laid me down on the floor, and I looked around again while he got something from a cabinet. My cock went soft the moment I saw the glittering blade of a knife, my imagination conjuring horrible scenes of castration and murder. I tensed up and tried to back away from him, but my wrists and ankles were still tied.

"Relax, boy," Max said as he knelt down and sliced expertly through the rope around my feet. The pieces slipped to the floor, and the big man started caressing my calves. Just as before, his touch electrified me, sending blood coursing down between my legs, hardening my cock again.

"Yeah, that's it," he growled softly at the sight of my fresh arousal. "That's a good slaveboy. . . . I had to untie your feet because you'll need to spread your legs."

While I puzzled that out, he took the knife and slid it between my shorts and flesh.

"You won't need *these* this weekend," he explained, "and I want maximum access to that butt hole of yours."

With quick strokes he sliced my shorts and T-shirt to shreds and pulled them off. Leaving my hands tied, he tossed the remains of my clothes into a trash can and put the knife down on the counter. Pulling me up to my feet, he steadied me when I staggered a little. Then he loosened his belt and pulled down his zipper, making his intentions crystal clear.

He pulled off his tank top, exposing a chiseled chest with big pecs and healthy brown nipples. The same blond hair as on his head and upper lip covered his chest, too, trailing down to his still-hidden pubes.

Yanking off his dusty cowboy boots, Max let his jeans fall to the floor. No underwear covered the nice, fat, uncut cock that hung between his legs from a nest of hair. Proportional to the rest of his huge body, it looked really big. Seeing him naked was awesome. One thought kept running through my mind: *This is the man who owns me for the next two days!*

My weekend Master grabbed a condom packet and a tube of lubricant out of a drawer. Tearing open the packet, he slid the latex sheath over his dripping tool, then slathered it with lube.

"Mmm, that feels good ...," he growled as his hand glided up and down the impressive length of his cock. Then he walked behind me and kicked my feet apart. When I yelped in surprise, he laughed. The bruiser planted his big, flat palm between my shoulder blades and pushed, hard.

"Lean over, slaveboy!" he said as he forced me to hang my upper body between my spread legs.

As if I didn't feel helpless enough before, now I was leaning over with my naked butt hole up in the air, my tied hands brushing the floor. But as scared as I was, I was also loving every second of it, my hard cock oozing precum onto my new owner's linoleum. Then Max was clutching my hips and positioning himself behind me.

"This is what I've wanted to do since the first second I saw you, boy." He stroked my back as he would a fine horse or show dog. "And now this sweet, tight hole is *mine*."

His monster cock pressed against that hole, probing and pushing like it had a mind of its own, and that mind was telling it to get inside me.

"Mmmm, yeah, open up, boy," the bruiser murmured above me. "Open up or I'll force my way in . . ."

Hanging down as I was, I could see his powerful legs pushing his hips into mine. Quivering in anticipation, I relaxed the tense muscles in my ass. Expecting a rape-like thrust, I was surprised by his slow, careful entry. But it was even more erotic that way, as if he knew I was his and couldn't fight him, that there was no reason to push hard, that he'd get into me sooner or later.

Though he had by far the largest cock that had ever fucked me (Master Bill's wasn't nearly as big), somehow I managed to take him all the way inside without whining or crying. That seemed to please Max, and he started fucking in slow, strong strokes. Having him inside me made my own cock even harder, as his intruding shaft teased and tickled my desperate prostate. The puddle of precum between my boots was getting bigger.

He started pushing harder and faster, and it was harder to hold my position. I'm strong, but I had nothing to match the force of the gorilla fucking me. Seeing my trouble, he grabbed my hips again and held me in place. This enabled him to push even further into me, and I moaned at the incredible sensations he was causing.

"Yeah, you like that, don't you slaveboy?"

"Yes, Sir!"

" 'Course you do, boy. I'm your new Master, at least for this weekend, and pleasing me is all you care about, isn't it?"

"Yes, Sir . . ."

"And giving me pleasure is what gives you pleasure . . ."

I pushed back, taking even more of him inside me, until I could feel his pubic bush against my ass. I wanted him to know how hot he was and how much I loved what he was doing.

Suddenly he was moving, pushing me forward.

"Move with me, boy," he said. "And you'd better hold onto my dick if you know what's good for you."

I struggled to obey, awkwardly shuffling on my tied hands and booted feet while the bruiser walked forward behind me, forcing his cock into my ass again with each step. It was very difficult, but obeying him was more important than anything else. It was what my Master expected me to do. Still, I couldn't stop some querulous yips from coming out of my mouth. We were heading right for a wall, but Max laughed and pushed faster.

"Don't worry, boy," he said. "Just go where I push you."

When my outstretched hands reached the wall, I bent my elbows back as much as I could. When my head reached it, Max grabbed me under the shoulders and pulled me upright. Then he slammed me against the wall, with my tied hands on top of my head and face turned to the side, and started *really* plowing my ass, fucking me even harder than before. He was raping me, pushing himself in and out in staccato movements that elicited squeals of pain.

I could feel his massive hairy chest against my back as he fucked me, our sweat mingling into a salty slime that I would have loved to lick off him. His assault was grinding my own hard cock against the wall, but my pain or pleasure wasn't important. All that mattered was serving him.

"Yeah, this is good," he murmured in my ear, his mustache tickling. "Good little slaveboy butt just for me . . ."

After what seemed like hours, Max pulled me away from the wall and folded me in half again, his cock never leaving my butt.

"Let's go boy," he said, and we were moving. I was a little better at the balancing act this time, managing to push back to keep him inside me while walking forward, my torso supported by my bound hands on the floor in front of me.

"I like fucking in different places, slaveboy," he said. "So think of this as a tour of your new home."

Laughing at his own joke, he guided me out of the kitchen, through a door on a different side from where we had come in, and into the living room. But we didn't stop there. He pushed me toward the door at its far side, then through it. We headed down a short hallway and through a door into his bedroom, where Max grabbed me and, still holding himself inside my ass, tossed my torso and arms up onto his bed. Now at least I wasn't dependent on my hands, which hurt from supporting me as well as from being bound so long.

Now that Max had me bent over the bed, he started pushing his cock in and pulling it out further and harder than before. He fucked me savagely, grunting and snarling like an animal.

"Yeah, you're a good little slaveboy," he said after some minutes of this pounding. "I'm real close to blowing my load . . . but there's something I want to do first. . . . I want to fuck you with your own cum . . ."

Gripping me tightly, Max managed to flip me over on my back without letting his cock slip out of my ass. This maneuver had me panting with exertion and moaning in ecstasy. He grinned down at me.

"This is what you're good for, boy," he said. "It's what you do best."

Then he was picking me up and pushing me forward at the same time. He followed me onto the bed, lifted my bound hands, and attached them to a hook at the top of his headboard. Now I couldn't move my arms, and my legs were spread with this huge ex-Marine between them.

He grabbed my cock and started pumping it. Lightning ran through my body as he stroked. The sensations of the moment — his cock screwing my ass, his hand gripping my cock, my hands tied helpless above me — joined with the memories of what had happened to me on that incredible night: being sighted by Max in the bar, being stuffed in a duffel bag and carried off like spoils of war, getting my clothes cut off and thrown away, getting plowed standing up, then against the wall, then on the bed . . . . *And I belong to this man for the next two days*, I reminded myself.

"Come on, slaveboy, pump out some jizz for me. Yeah, c'mon boy, c'mon baby . . ."

That low, husky voice of his sent me right over the edge, and I screamed as I came. My eyes were screwed shut, but I could feel the jets of cum hit my chest and face. The orgasm storming through my body made me strain at my bonds.

"Yeah, that's it, boy," Max said. "That's it . . ."

He kept jerking me off as more cum oozed out of my

throbbing cock, stroking and caressing it until he milked out the last drops of cream. I begged him to stop, to let me catch my breath. He did stop jerking me, but he didn't let me catch my breath. Swiftly and shockingly, he pulled himself out of my ass, gathered all of my cum with his hands, and slathered it over his rubbered cock. Then he plunged back in.

Master Bill would never let me come, if at all, until after he shot *his* load, and neither had other men who fucked me. This twisted fuck session with Max was painful, terrifying, and wonderful all at the same time. I moaned, cried, and whimpered.

"Oh, yeah!" Max shouted. "Yeah! I'm gonna come, slaveboy! Your sweet jizz on my dick as I fuck your ass . . . I'm gonna come *now!*"

His cock hardened inside me until it was stiff as a poker, and then it unloaded, shooting spurt after spurt of his hot mancum into the condom, its heat searing my insides with pleasure. The bruiser roared above me, his passion spilling out of his mouth and cock. Finally he pulled out and collapsed next to me, wrapping beefy arms around my torso.

"I was right . . . ," he said after a while, sounding sleepy. "You're one fine piece of slavemeat, boy . . ."

"Thank you, Sir," I whispered.

Max unhooked my arms from the headboard and untied them. He rubbed my wrists like he had my calves. It felt good, and I thanked him again, more clearly.

He smiled and kissed me with his tongue in my mouth. I wrapped my arms around him and hugged him tight. Too quickly, Max broke the hug and unpeeled the condom, plump with his hot jizz, from his cock, then tied it off and tossed it in a nearby wastebasket. With the rubber disposed of, he pushed my head down to clean his cum-slicked tool. Still reeling from the intensity of being fucked by this godlike stud, I serviced him as he wished, relishing the taste of his discharge — wishing it had been safe for him to shoot directly into my ass, but glad that he hadn't.

When he was satisfied, he got on his feet again. Taking a spare blanket from the closet and a pillow off the bed, he set these up on the floor next to it.

"There's your bed, boy," he said, then left the room.

Obediently, I crawled off his bed and onto mine. I assumed he'd want me to take off my boots and socks, so I did. After placing them neatly out of the way, I laid my head on the pillow and curled up in the blanket, wrapping myself tight like I used to do when I was a little kid.

I was almost asleep when Max came back, my leash in his hand. Crouching down, he looped one end around the nearest leg of his bed and fastened the other end to my collar. Glancing at my boots, he smiled.

"This is where you belong, Josh," he whispered as he stroked my hair, "tied to my bed."

"Yes, Sir . . . ," I said, but in my heart I didn't yet believe it. *I'm serving you only because my real Master ordered me to*, I insisted silently.

Max touched my face gently, as he had done in the bar, running his fingers along my jaw and slowly pushing them into my mouth. I caressed them dreamily with my tongue, suckling like a baby.

"Good boy," he told me. "Good slaveboy. Now go to sleep. You've got a busy weekend ahead of you."

I floated away on his voice like a piece of driftwood on the sea. I didn't doubt his words, though if I'd had any idea of the joys and terrors the next two days had in store, I might not have fallen asleep so easily.

But at that point it didn't matter. All that mattered was that I had been won for the weekend fair and square, as Max said, and that Master Bill's last order to me was to obey this man as if he were my owner. That was enough for me. I'd been well used, and that made me happy. My heart was full of love for both Master Bill and Master Max. With one hand clasping the collar around my neck, I fell into a dreamless sleep.

And no sleep is as deep as that of a well-used slave.

2. Saturday Afternoon — Domestic Torture

"**W**AKE UP, SLAVEBOY!" The voice was loud in my ears, startling me out of my deep sleep. *What's happening?* I wondered. *That's not my Master's voice.* . . . A bare foot nudged me in the stomach.

"I said, wake up!" the voice insisted.

My eyes flew open, and I saw the huge naked man standing over me, his body muscular and his face stern. The night before all came back to me suddenly, from being won for the weekend by this bruiser to being put to sleep on the floor, with some amazing sex in between. The clock on his bedside table said it was almost one in the afternoon. Even though he'd let me sleep in, there was plenty left of the weekend.

Max leaned over and unfastened my collar leash, then untied it from the leg of the bed. After attaching it again to my collar, he yanked on it, pulling me out of my comfortable nest on the floor.

"Come on, boy," he said as he dragged me into the adjoining bathroom. "Jump in the tub." I climbed in and crouched there on my hands and knees, wondering what to do about my full bladder. But he had that covered.

"If you have to piss," he said, "go ahead."

Relieved, I let the pee squirt out of my cock. As it ran down toward the drain, I felt a warm stream hitting my side. I looked up to see Max pissing on me from his huge cock.

"Mmmmm," he murmured in satisfaction as he sprayed it over my back, ass, and legs. "Feels good to let that go."

Master Bill had never pissed on me, nor had anyone else, so this was another new experience. I decided I liked it. Once my own bladder was empty, my dick hardened up in response. It was so primal, so hot to have this man piss on me like he was marking his property. And I *was* his, at least for the weekend.

"Thank you, Sir," I said and closed my eyes, savoring how his hot man-piss was cooling on my skin.

"Thanks for what, boy?"

"For the privilege of being allowed to piss, Sir, and for the pleasure of receiving your piss on me," I answered without hesitation, opening my brown eyes to look up into his big blue ones. Max laughed.

"You're well trained, aren't you?"

"Thank you, Sir. I try to make my Master proud."

"I'm sure you do, boy. I'm sure you do." Then he shook his cock, sending the last few drops flying at me. "Clean my dick, slave, get all the piss out."

I lunged for his cock, taking the enormous head into my mouth and caressing it with my tongue, slurping up whatever piss dribbled out. The salty, bitter taste spread throughout my mouth, making my own cock surge with blood.

"Good boy," Max said as he pulled himself out.

He reached for the shower controls, and suddenly cold water drenched me. I howled in shock and surprise, and my cock shriveled as the frigid water cascaded over my shivering body. I moved to climb out of the tub, but he blocked my way.

"Stay where you are, slave," he said in a menacing tone.

I'm not a pain pig, and never have been. I wasn't interested in finding out what punishment would be like at the hands of this Master, so I stayed underneath the chilling spray and whimpered in discomfort.

"That's a good boy," he said as he turned on the hot water until the temperature became more pleasant. "I wanted to make sure you'd be obedient even if it was uncomfortable." He unhooked the leash from my collar, then backed up and pulled the shower curtain closed, separating us with the sheet of plastic. "You'll have lots of chances to show me that later."

Oh, no, I thought. *What's he mean by that? More freezing showers? Probably worse*, I speculated glumly.

"Stand up and clean yourself off," Max was saying. "I don't want you stinking of piss all day. When you're done, report to the kitchen. And make it fast."

"Yes, Sir! Thank you, Sir!" I said as I rose to my feet and grabbed the soap.

I kind of liked the smell of his piss all over me, but orders were orders. Quickly, I lathered up and started washing myself, scrubbing until my skin was squeaky clean. Then I turned the water off, carefully stepped out of the shower, and dried myself with the towel he'd left for me.

When I walked out of the bedroom and through the living room, completely naked except for the chain around my neck, I could see Max working in the kitchen. And it smelled like he was making food. *Thank God*, I thought. I hadn't eaten since dinner the night before, more than 15 hours earlier.

Coming into the kitchen, I dropped to my knees respectfully before him. While I was in the shower he'd put on shorts and a fresh tank top.

"Reporting as ordered, Sir."

"Good boy. Here, have some lunch," he said as he picked up a dog dish from the counter and set it on the floor in front of me. "Your water bowl's in the corner."

"Thank you, Sir," I said and hunkered down to eat. My bowl was full of grilled chunks of vegetables and lean beef, apparently cooked on a skewer that he'd removed, along with cut-up fruit, all on a thick slice of multigrain bread. *Perfect!* I thought. I'd've eaten dog food if he'd wanted me to, but this was more nutritious as well as more palatable.

Max grinned at me and carried his own plate out to the living room. *No wonder he's in such fine shape*, I mused, *if he eats like this all the time.* He hadn't said that I couldn't use my hands, so I did, but sparingly. I was used to eating out of bowls on the floor and had no problem getting my fill, hurrying so I'd be finished when he came back or called me to join him.

I'd eaten everything in my dish, drunk some water, and was kneeling up, waiting patiently, when he returned. Leaving his own plate and utensils in the sink, he bent down to inspect my dish, then picked it up and put it on the counter.

"You ate it all, boy," he said, turning to me. "Did you enjoy it?"

"Very much, Sir. Thank you, Sir."

"Good. Now, slave, it's time for your chores."

Despite Max's ominous prediction in the bathroom, I was happy to serve him. Like any good Master, he'd taken care of my bodily needs before using me again for his pleasure. Since the kitchen was cluttered with debris from what had to be several meals, I expected to be told to clean it up. But he had other plans, at least for now.

"Come with me, boy," he said, then headed back to the living room.

Here we go, I thought as I obediently crawled after him. *Now I'm going to find out what he meant.* I heard his words again in my mind: "I wanted to make sure you'd be obedient even if it was uncomfortable" and "You'll have lots of chances to show me that later."

Max walked over to the couch and sat at one end. There was a coffee table in front of it and a big chest on the floor next to him. He reached over to raise the top of the chest, beckoning me closer.

"C'm'ere, boy," he said. "Gotta get you ready before you start working."

The bruiser motioned for me to kneel on the carpet at his bare feet. I stared at them and thought about sucking his toes. Despite my worry about what was going to happen, I got hard again. Hell, just the idea of his carrying me away and plowing my butt with his big pecker was almost enough to make me shoot a load.

Unlike Master Bill, this man was so unmistakably butch that "Master" and "slave" didn't seem like roles we chose to play because we got off on them — there was no other way we could relate to each other. In any situation, Max would be my superior. Even if my Master hadn't ordered me to, my natural role was to serve and obey him. And that's why I got off on it!

Apparently the chest held all sorts of gear — harnesses,

gags, ball stretchers, whips, rope, chastity devices, blindfolds.... Whether to aid his selection or to intimidate me, Max kept taking items out, holding them up for inspection, and putting them back. *Which will he use on me?* I wondered. Finally he selected a pair of alligator tit clamps and didn't put them back. Master Bill had assured me that my temporary owner wouldn't damage me, but it looked like he was going to enjoy giving me pain.

I'm no pain pig, as I said, but this weekend wasn't about what I wanted or even needed. It was about my serving this man however he saw fit. So I steeled my resolve: *Somehow I'll make it through this. Maybe it won't be as bad as I fear . . .*

It was worse. The clamps bit cruelly into my sensitive nipples, and I had to stifle a shriek as he applied each one. Taking deep breaths through gritted teeth, I was able to keep silent and even rear up to give him maximum access to my body. *I can handle this . . .*

"What do you say, slave?"

"Thank you, Sir," I said firmly.

Despite the pain, I was surprised to discover that my erection hadn't gone down. *The cold water in the shower made it collapse*, I recalled. *But cold does that, and this time I had warning. So I guess his power can turn me on even when he hurts me.*

Next, Max took small weights and hooked them onto the nipple clamps, which made the clamps hang down like ornaments on my chest. The pain was more intense, too, but after some initial groaning and shivering, I managed to regain composure.

The next thing my weekend Master pulled out of the chest was a long leather thong. He had me stand up, facing him, and used the thong to tie up my balls, cinching the wrap torturously tight. He also looped the thong around the base of my cock, trapping the blood so I'd stay erect no matter what.

"Thank you, Sir," I forced out as he inspected his handiwork. He slapped my bound balls — *hard* — and I gasped.

"You like that, boy?"
"No, Sir," I answered truthfully.
"But you're taking it anyway, aren't you, slave?"
"Yes, Sir."
"Good boy," he said with a smile, then slapped me again. It hurt so much I wished that I could retract my balls completely, bringing them up inside my body to safety. But they were stuck on the outside, hanging down between my legs, and well restrained so that he could torture them as much as he wished. Another slap, and I couldn't resist a small scream.

"Hang on, boy," Max said. "There's more to come." Then he reached into the chest and drew out a clear-plastic bag of wooden clothespins.

Oh, shit, I thought, as he emptied it on the couch beside him. I'd had clothespins used on me before and didn't enjoy the experience at all. But what I liked or didn't like was unimportant.

The bruiser who'd won me for the weekend took a pin and pinched it in his hand. The wooden mouth opened, ready to clamp onto my flesh like a hungry leech. He found a spot beneath my right nipple and, after bunching some skin together, let the clothespin grab it.

Thankfully, it didn't hurt as much as the tit clamps had earlier (and by now that had subsided to a dull ache), but I knew this was only a prelude. *The pain as these go on,* I told myself gloomily, *is nothing compared with what I'll feel when he takes them off. That'll really be something to scream about!* In the meantime, I had another duty: thanking Master Max for his attentions.

"Thank you, Sir," I said, not entirely hypocritically.
"You're welcome, slaveboy," he said with a wicked grin.

Then, one by one, he attached clothespins in a line from under my right nipple to my waist. I breathed deeply and thanked him for each one. After he did the same thing on the left side, I had two columns of those evil pins biting into the flesh of my chest and belly.

As he was attaching the pins, I watched his face. *He's very handsome*, I thought, but he was so intently focused on causing me pain that I tried to focus on his looks instead of the sharp pinches and growing dull ache in my skin and muscles. *His eyebrows and mustache just as blond as the hair on his head, the strong straight lines of his face, his squared-off chin with its sexy cleft...*

"Thank you, Sir," I said after he placed the last clothespin in the second line. Max leaned back on the couch and looked at me thoughtfully.

I hoped that he was finished "getting me ready" for my chores. *No more, please*, I thought, knowing better than to say it out loud. That would probably be the best way to get more. He grinned his greedy grin at me and reached into the chest again.

"One more thing, slave," he said as he lifted out a huge butt plug and held it up for me to see. "To keep you nice and filled, to remind you of my dick."

"Yes, Sir," I said helplessly, knowing there was nothing I could do to prevent that monster — far bigger than any I'd ever taken before — from going inside me.

"Turn around, and show that sweet butt to me," Max said as he pulled a lube dispenser from the chest.

Silently, I obeyed, facing away from him and bending over, my hands on the floor, to put my rear in easy reach. Max started playing with my ass, alternating between gentle and rough, first massaging it tenderly, then slapping it hard. He also smacked my stretched-out ballsac a few more times, bringing yelps of pain out of me.

Soon enough he was working his lubed fingers into my hole. It wasn't too bad, especially after I'd been reamed by his big cock the night before. But I knew the butt plug was wider than his cock, wider than his bunched fingers. *It may even be wider than his fist*, I speculated in horror.

When my weekend Master had me opened up to his liking, he lubed the butt plug and started working my asshole with it. Teasing and playing me, he'd start to push it in and then pull it back. After a few minutes, I was dying to be filled!

"Please, Sir," I moaned. My asshole was so desperate for the plug that I barely noticed the ongoing pains from the tit clamps, the clothespins, and my tied balls.

"What do you need, slave?" Max asked.

"I need your butt plug inside me, Sir."

I can't believe I said that! Only minutes before I'd been worrying about its size. But now, after he'd worked over my asshole so thoroughly, I *needed* the damned thing in me — maybe so it would keep my mind off my other pains.

"You *need* it, slave?"

"Yes, Sir."

"Beg for it, boy."

"Please, Sir! Please fill me up with your butt plug! Please fill me and remind me of your cock! *Please, Sir!*"

Max started to shove it in, and I was immediately sorry for what I'd said. The plug felt even larger than it looked! I screamed as it pushed past my sphincters. I felt as if my liver and other organs were being moved aside to make room for it.

"Oh, please, Sir . . ."

"What, boy? This is what you asked for. This is what you said you needed."

I could hear the smirk in his voice without even seeing his face. *He can't be serious*, I thought desperately. *He can't mean to leave this thing inside me. It's too big, I can't hold it . . .*

The pain was so intense, I was gasping. I took several deep breaths, trying to get myself under control.

"I can't hold it, Sir, I can't hold it, Sir . . ."

"Don't say the word 'can't' to me, slave. You can do whatever I ask you to. I won't order you to do anything you can't do. You are mine for the weekend, and you're going to do your chores the way I want you to: in pain."

I whined like a dog who just can't understand what its owner wants from it.

"Every minute you're in pain today," Max said, "you'll realize what a privilege it is to *not* be in pain. You'll remember that I am your Master now. You'll do whatever I ask of you, with no back talk. *Is that clear?*"

"Yes, Sir," I mumbled. He smacked the end of the plug, jolting more of it past my ass ring and sending another wave of pain crashing through me.

"What'd you say, slaveboy?"

"Yes, Sir!" I said loudly, fighting back tears.

"That's better," he said and stood up. "Come with me."

He headed for the kitchen at a fast pace. I followed on my hands and knees, struggling to keep up. Every movement caused pain somewhere in my body. It felt like my brain was going to overload with it. It reminded me of times I'd been sunburned all over and my slightest move had hurt. This was like that, only worse.

As I crawled, the weights hanging from my nipples swung back and forth. They dragged the tit clamps with them, making their sharp little teeth cut deeper into my tender nips and yank them up and down. The leather thong wrapped around my cock and balls, cinched tighter than I'd ever experienced before, made those hurt, too. My hard and horny cock, pointed in the direction I crawled, was desperate for release, but there was no hope of it anytime soon.

The rows of clothespins weren't too bad, but I knew they'd hurt like hell when they were pulled off. And the worst pain of all was from the huge butt plug, which felt as if it had invaded and conquered everything from my asshole to my belly button, shifting in my guts with every step. *This must be what being pregnant is like,* I noted sourly to myself.

Max is so tall that it was hard to keep pace with him on hands and knees under the best circumstances, let alone when each step had me whimpering in pain. But I did my best and eventually joined him in the kitchen, where he ordered me to my feet.

"Clean up this mess," he said, gesturing around the room. Every flat surface was covered with dirty dishes and pans, food containers, used utensils and knives, seasonings, and so forth. *How am I going to manage all this when I'm in such pain?* I worried. *At least he has a dishwasher.*

"And do it fast," Max said, then slapped my butt and walked out of the room.

Obediently, I stood up and moved to the nearest counter to pick up some dirty glasses. As brighter pain flashed through me, I understood the sadist's plan: I couldn't do the work without jostling some of the clothespins, each one a potential source of agony. And that was *besides* the other gear he had on me to make every moment miserable.

Moving as carefully as I could, I cleaned the kitchen — putting leftover food away, loading and running the dishwasher, manually scrubbing what wouldn't go in, tying off the full trash bag and putting a fresh one in the can, wiping the counters, and more. I soon realized that there was no way to avoid all surges of fresh pain and did my best to take them in stride.

Would my cock still be hard if it wasn't tied off? Strangely, I told myself, *I think it would be. Max has me totally in his intoxicating power, and no amount of pain seems able to diminish that.*

When I finished, I dropped to my knees and gratefully slurped from my water dish in the corner, then cleaned that, too. Finally, I went looking for my weekend Master, who was on the couch in the living room, reading a magazine with his feet up on the coffee table.

"All done? Good boy," he said. "Now pick up this room. Make it neater."

"Yes, Sir," I said, sighing inside. I'd hoped he would take the gear off me after I finished the kitchen, but I should've known there'd be much more to do first.

Luckily, this room wasn't too messy. I picked up the books and magazines on the floor and put them in the bookcase, then neatly stacked the porn DVDs next to the player. I rubbed wood polish into the table until it gleamed.

Somehow I carried out these tasks despite the intense pain I was in. I don't know how I did it. It must have been my devotion and obedience to the two men who had put me in this situation: my Master Bill and Max, my weekend Master.

After a while the pain dulled into a constant ache. But then something would happen — I would accidentally jam a clothespin against a hard surface, or Max would slap my clamped nipples — and the pain would return in full force.

It was torture. There's no other word for it.

When Max was happy with the living room, I did the bedroom. Making the bed was the hardest task so far because of all the leaning and stretching. I picked up his dirty clothes and put them in the laundry sack on the back of the door. I counted myself fortunate that his place wasn't in any worse shape. Thanks to my torturous outfitting, it took me a long time to finish, though not nearly as long as it would have if the whole apartment had been as bad as the kitchen.

But then came the bathroom. Making the bed was nothing compared with what I had to do there after I finished tidying. Max had come to the door to check my progress.

"Be sure to clean the toilet, boy," he said. I looked around for cleaning supplies but didn't see any.

"What do you wish me to use, Sir?" He reached inside the little room to slap my balls hard, and I bit my tongue so as not to scream.

"Use your mouth, slave, what else? Don't come out until that toilet is clean," he said as he backed out and closed the door.

So that's *what he meant,* I thought, *when he said he wanted to see if I'd obey even if it was uncomfortable. "Uncomfortable"? That's hardly adequate to describe my condition! At least this is the last room, though who knows what else he may have in mind?*

I got down on my hands and knees. As carefully as possible, I leaned forward to lick the porcelain bowl. The bathroom was so small and cramped, there was barely enough space for me to maneuver around the toilet, and there was no way to do it without causing myself a lot of pain.

Clothespins jammed against the wall or the toilet itself, the weights banged on my thighs and dragged my nipples along, and all the time my balls and cock were wrapped too tight and the huge butt plug was rearranging my insides. I followed orders as well as I could, licking the toilet inside and out and making it shine. The pain was so harsh that I didn't dwell on how repulsive this chore was.

Instead, I thought long and hard about what my weekend Master had said: "Every minute you're in pain today, you'll realize what a privilege it is to *not* be in pain. You'll remember that I am your Master now. You'll do whatever I ask you, with no back talk." The butt plug reminded me of his cock, and of how much better it had felt, despite its size, than the rubber monster inside me. The constant pain made me grateful for the times I'd been free of agony, and I hoped my obedience would earn me more periods like that.

My haze of pain blurred the passage of time, although I did notice the sky out the tiny bathroom window getting darker. When I stopped to think about it, I figured it must be almost evening. *I've been working under this torture since mid-afternoon. How much longer will it go on?*

I couldn't manage the pain anymore. Even when I held still, it refused to grow dull as it had earlier. It was getting worse and worse as each new onslaught hit my tired body. Finally, I decided that the toilet was as clean as it was going to get.

Exhausted, I pushed open the bathroom door with one hand and crawled out into the bedroom, then to the living room. From there, I could see Max in the kitchen, but I didn't think I could make it that far. Luckily, he heard my groans as I collapsed on the floor in front of the coffee table and came over to check.

"Toilet all clean?" he asked, crouching down near me.

"Yes, Sir," I croaked out.

"Wait here," he said and walked back toward the bathroom. Grateful for the chance to rest, I lay there on my back and closed my eyes. A few minutes later, I opened them when Max returned and stroked my hair. After a day of torture, the affectionate gesture brought tears to my eyes.

"Looks good, Josh," he said. "You did a fine job."

"Thank you, Sir," I said quietly, loving the touch of his hand on my head. But it left me when he backed up and sat on the couch.

"Come over here," he said.

I forced my weary, aching body to obey, suddenly fearful of what was coming next. All day I had longed for the pain to end, yet now I was nervous and frightened since I knew that the pain would have to get worse before it could stop. I didn't think I was ready. Fortunately, it didn't matter what I was "ready" for. Max was ready — he'd already opened the chest again — and that was what mattered. I knelt in front of him and bowed my head submissively.

"Time to get this gear off you," the big man said, and his hands were at my nipples, expertly unhooking the extra weights from the clamps. They fell to the floor, and the lightness I felt was amazing. But that pleasure was annihilated a second later when he released the clamps themselves, both at once. Blood surged back into the indentations it had been kept out of all day. Exhausted nerves reacted to the sudden pressure, sending pain signals of the highest urgency to my brain. Unlike the constant, throbbing torment I had been experiencing for hours, this was like fire burning me, like being sliced with razor-sharp shards of crystal.

I screamed in shock, my eyes imploring my weekend Master: *Please, no more, please, wait, please....* But his hands were between my legs next, untying the knotted leather cord that had kept me erect. Easing the tension felt good at first, but once the thong had some slack, he started pulling it — yanking it, really. It felt like it was slicing my skin and leaving a trail of blood as it unraveled. It was such a horrible pain that I dared to beg him aloud to stop it.

"Please, Sir . . . ," I began, but Max covered my mouth with one hand, shaking his head slightly as he stared into my tear-filled eyes.

Although I could see there was no blood on my balls, I kept yelling *Stop pulling it!* in my head as the thong unwound. *Stop pulling it, Sir, please stop!* Finally, it was over.

But not for long: Max started batting at my torso with his hands, slapping my pecs and abdomen, knocking the clothespins off. It was agonizing when he carefully removed the tit clamps by pinching them open, and removing the pins by brute force was far worse. Unable to hold in my distress any longer, I screamed at the top of my lungs, howling my torment into the air. Max didn't seem to care but just kept swatting clothespins off me, one after another.

Soon enough, they were all off, and blood was rushing back into the trails of marks that led from my nipples to my waist. It was as if the razor-sharp fire in my nips had spread and was burning its way through my torso.

Still screaming, I collapsed forward against the couch. I thought I was dying. This was the worst pain I'd felt in my entire life. *Master Bill never punished me so severely!* I wailed silently. Then, through eyes swimming with tears, I saw Max flex his fists and reach down toward my butt. Without further warning, he grasped the base of the plug and wrenched it out of me all at once.

Now I was beyond screaming — I was shrieking. The pain was so much worse than before that I couldn't believe it was happening to me. And the sudden absence of the butt plug was shocking, as if a gigantic hole had opened inside me. At least I was sure things couldn't get any worse. There was only one direction they *could* go . . .

And so they did. Max slicked up his hand, reached under me, and gently took hold of my cock. Incredibly, despite my agony, it responded to him, getting harder and harder in his grip as he began jerking me off.

As if levitating, I lifted my head off the couch and folded my body backward, opening my front side to Max's touch. After a minute or so of his stroking, a wave of pleasure started in the head of my cock, then flowed down its length and into every cell of my body, everywhere transforming pain

Winner Takes All

to pleasure. In seconds, my nervous system was overloading and I was screaming again, this time in absolute ecstasy as the pent-up frustrations of the day were released. Max was still holding my cock when I came, shooting volley after volley of white boy cream all over my chest.

"Thank you, Sir," I moaned. "Thank you, Sir!"

"You're a good boy," he said. "You did good work today. I'm very pleased with you."

"Thank you, Sir," I said, barely able to speak for the intensity of the pleasure. Then it was over. Max released my cock and let me lie there in front of him, smiling down at his totally spent piece of slavemeat.

After a while, he got off the couch, crouched down, and gathered me in his arms. He rose to his feet, cradling me gently. Kissing my forehead, he whispered to me — "Good boy . . . good Josh . . . good slave . . ." — as he carried me from the living room to the kitchen and set me down on the countertop. I rested my head on the pillow he'd put there for me, not even wondering why he had.

Max filled an enema bag with water from the sink and lubed the hose nozzle. Hanging the bag on a hook on the wall with one hand, he gently inserted the nozzle into my ass with the other. As if eager to cure the emptiness I'd felt since the butt plug came out, my ass let the hose slide in easily as far as it could go. When Max released the guard, warm water flowed in, filling me up.

"That's it . . . ," he breathed when the bag was empty. "I want you nice and clean for your workout tonight."

My workout? I thought dimly. *What's he talking about? This isn't over?* I had hoped he'd feed me again and then let me go back to bed, but it looked like that wasn't in my weekend Master's plans. I had my orders: obey this man as I would my own Master. So I had no choice — not as long as I was a slave.

"Hold that in until I come back," Max said as he pulled out the hose and left it and the empty bag in the sink. "It won't be too long, slaveboy."

"Yes, Sir," I said and settled back onto the pillow, lying there on the counter like meat to be cooked for dinner.

What's going to happen to me tonight? I wondered. *More of the same? Or some new ordeal? Will he really give me back to my Master tomorrow night? He seems so happy and pleased with me — maybe he won't want to give me up.*

Since it could do me no good, I gave up wondering. All I could do was lie there, clenching my butt, holding a gallon of water inside me. After a few minutes, I was able to calm down, secure in the knowledge of my utter submission, my total slavery. Only one thing was certain: my adventure was far from over.

3. Saturday Night — Serial Rape

DESPITE THE STUPENDOUS orgasm that capped the day, the afternoon of torture at my weekend Master's hands had left me with a lingering soreness all over. And now I was wracked with cramps from the enema he'd given me, which I was struggling to hold in.

I knew there'd be a price to pay if I let dirty water from my ass soak Max's kitchen counter. Having been tortured just for his enjoyment, I was in no hurry to risk punishment for actual disobedience. It was early on Saturday evening, and I still had that night and Sunday to get through.

Clenching my ass cheeks together so no water leaked out, I was surprised I hadn't lost any of it already. All that day the humongous butt plug had stretched me, and the night before Max had fucked the shit out of me with his big cock. I worried that my ass was in no condition for this new ordeal.

But just when I thought I would burst, Max came back into the kitchen and smiled down at me. This hulking blond stud, his chiseled body plainly visible through his flimsy shorts and tank top, made my heart pound and my cock stiffen, and the desire to serve him and submit to him was overwhelming. No one else had ever stirred such feelings in me, not even Master Bill.

"Time to empty you out," he said cheerfully, sliding his hands under my body to help me down from the countertop. I don't know how I managed to walk with all that water in me, but somehow I made it to the bathroom without any leaks. Planting myself directly on the toilet bowl (I had been trained not to use the seat), I released my bowels with a huge sigh of relief. I didn't even care that my weekend Master was standing in the doorway, watching me. As my ass muscles finally relaxed, I closed my eyes. When I opened them again, he was still there.

"Okay, let's see how you did, slaveboy," he said with an amused grin. He took my hand and pulled me up off the toilet. While I wiped myself, he looked into the bowl, then flushed it and said, "I think just one more enema will do the job."

He led me back to the kitchen and repeated the process. After the liquid drained out of me this time, there was hardly any smell, so I sat there for a few minutes, breathing deeply and enjoying not having to endure any more pain for a while. When the bruiser came in to check on me, he looked into the bowl and pronounced the water clear.

"Good boy," he said. "Now you're nice and clean on the inside."

"Yes, Sir. Thank you, Sir."

"I want you clean on the outside, too. Take a shower and report back to me in the kitchen — you have ten minutes."

I showered quickly, washing away the sweat and grime from the day's work. It felt great to stand under the warm spray with the fresh, masculine scent of Max's bath soap in my nostrils, but I couldn't linger. After drying off, I went to the kitchen. Max was fixing food again, and it smelled delicious. *Hope we eat soon*, I thought as I knelt respectfully in the doorway.

"Reporting as ordered, Sir," I said aloud.

The bruiser looked up and gave me a big smile. *I love how his mustache stretches when he smiles*, I said to myself.

"There's my boy," he said. "Hungry?"

"Yes, Sir!"

"Figured you would be. I'm just finishing up our dinner."

"Thank you, Sir," I said as he filled his plate and my dog dish. Assuming I'd eat in the kitchen, I started moving toward where he'd fed me before.

"No, boy," Max said. "You're eating in the living room with me."

Wonderful! I let out a yelp of happiness, and my weekend Master laughed.

"Thought you'd like that," he said as he put the dishes and stuff on a tray and headed out to the living room. I followed him on my hands and knees, watching as he set the tray on the coffee table. He put my dog dish on the floor with a napkin under it, sat on the couch, twisted open a bottle of beer, and turned on the TV with the remote.

Dinner was brown rice with steamed chicken and vegetables, cut into bite-size pieces and tossed with soy sauce and sesame seeds, fruit on the side as before. The delicious smells made my mouth water, and it tasted great, too.

It was pure joy to sprawl there on the floor at that hot stud's feet, eating my dinner without hands from a dog bowl while he ate his with knife and fork from a plate and watched the TV news. When I finished, I curled up next to his big bare feet. I had pretty much forgotten what he'd hinted earlier about his plans and almost thought this was all that was going to happen — simply a Master and his slave sharing a quiet night. I should've known better.

Just as I was dozing off, Max snapped off the TV and clapped his hands smartly. Instantly I was awake and up on all fours.

"Boy!" he said.

"Yes, Sir!" *Hope I haven't done anything wrong.* He hadn't had to discipline me so far, and I'd challenged myself to get through the whole weekend without being punished.

"My buddies'll be here soon," he said. "We've got to get ready before they arrive."

I froze in shock, thinking furiously. *His buddies? When did other people get involved in this wager? But maybe I won't be "involved" with them. Maybe I'll just be bound up, put out of the way, and ignored while they're here? Or put on display like a living sculpture? Or maybe he'll have me serve drinks and snacks while they play cards or . . . ?*

Or maybe he'll let them all torture and fuck me.

It doesn't matter what a slave wants, does it? I wasn't consulted on any of the weekend's other activities. I'm a piece of property. What I think and feel isn't important. All that matters is that my permanent Master told me to obey Max as if he owned me. And I guess that means even if he does things my real owner wouldn't do, *like letting other men use me sexually. . . . Except Master Bill did* exactly that *when he lost me in a wager with Max! If he hadn't, I wouldn't* be *in this scary situation . . .*

"Hey, boy, Josh, you with me? Snap out of it!"

"Yes, Sir!" I said, coming back from my confused reverie. "Sorry, Sir!"

The bruiser looked at me intently, then got up from the couch and snapped his fingers.

"Heel," he said, and I trotted alongside him on hands and knees as he walked to his bedroom. "Up on the bed, slave," he said when we came through the door.

"Yes, Sir," I said, jumping up and kneeling on the bed. "Thank you, Sir."

"Stay there, on your back in the center, while I get some gear."

"Yes, Sir," I said as he left the room. I obeyed his order, plus spreading my arms and legs apart to make myself more vulnerable.

While I waited for him, my thoughts raced. *What are the odds I'll get to sleep in bed* with *him? Never mind. Sleep is hours away, and I need to concentrate on the here and now to avoid being disciplined. And I don't want to disappoint this man . . .*

Everything he's done to me — bagging me, fucking me, tor-

turing me, kissing me, cleaning out my ass, rubbing my hair, smacking my balls, pissing on me, feeding me from a dog dish — only makes him hotter! Just being in the same room with him stiffens my slave cock. I want to serve and please him, whatever it takes . . .

"Move closer to the top of the bed," Max said as he came back through the door and dumped a small pile of gear at the other end. After adjusting my position until he was satisfied, he took my left arm and fitted a padded leather wrist restraint. Once it was snug, he pulled a chain from underneath the bed, fastened it to the wrist cuff, and anchored the other end to the bed frame so my arm was stretched out to the side. Then he did the same to my right arm.

"Test 'em, boy," he said. "Try to get loose."

Are you nuts? I thought. But I made a show of pulling on the restraints as if to struggle out of them. It was ludicrous. The chains, far too strong to be broken, were anchored out of reach, and the wrist cuffs were too snug and strong to get out of without more leverage than I had. I was trapped.

"Guess you're not going anywhere, slaveboy," my weekend Master said.

"No, Sir," I agreed sadly, and we both laughed.

"But wait, there's more," he said with a mischievous grin. Taking a rubber bit gag from the pile of gear, he stuck it between my teeth and fastened it tight around my head. Now I couldn't speak, at least not clearly, *or* move my arms. *What's next?* I wondered. *My legs?*

Not yet, I soon found out. The bruiser hooked a chain from the headboard to either side of my collar. Now my entire upper body was bound in place, with just enough slack for me to be fairly comfortable — for a while anyway. *And now for my legs . . .*

Max secured my ankles with another set of cuffs like the ones on my wrists, only larger, attached to another pair of strong chains he pulled out from under the bed. I thought he would finish with me in a semi-spreadeagle position, but I was wrong.

Pulling on the chain attached to the left ankle cuff, he raised my leg into the air and out to the side, finally locking the chain to the same anchor underneath the bed as my left arm chain. My thigh muscles were stretched to their limits, but I didn't have to exert myself to hold the position — the taut chain did that. Still, I knew it would become extremely painful before long.

He can't be serious, I told myself desperately. But he was, because he did the same with the other leg, which left my asshole totally exposed. If I thought I was vulnerable before, it was nothing compared with this. I was bound, gagged, and spread wide open for the whole world to see. I had never felt so exposed and helpless.

And incredibly horny! Bondage always arouses me, and being chained up ready for sex by a steaming stud like Max was fucking unbelievable. My hard cock was beginning to drip precum onto my belly.

My weekend Master got a bottle of lube, a fistful of condoms, and a hand towel out of his bedside drawer and put them on the bed next to me. Then he spread a bath towel below me, pushing one edge under my butt.

A moan of fear and uncertainty must have come out of me, because he smiled and patted my chest. He stroked my pectoral muscles as he would pet a frightened dog or horse, soothing me with his gentle touch.

"You'll be okay, Josh. Your Master wouldn't have given you to me if he didn't trust me. You'll be all right. You're strong, and you can hold that position till I let you down."

I lay there while Max got himself ready for the evening, which meant putting on a fresh tank top, draping a black leather bar vest over it, changing to leather shorts, and pulling on a pair of tall engineer boots. *I wish he was keeping me with him,* I lamented silently. *How can anyone look at someone else when he's around?*

Before leaving, he turned off all the lights in the room except a small one on the night table. He left the window blinds open — on his high floor, there was no way anyone could peek in — and I saw that it was black outside. The bedside clock told me it was past 8:00 p.m.

Framed in the open door, Max turned back to catch my eyes again, grinned, then said in a serious tone: "I expect you to be on your best behavior with my guests, slaveboy. And no matter what happens, *you'd better not come,* or there'll be hell to pay."

With that, the bruiser walked out and closed the door, leaving me alone in the dark, bound but free to wonder about what he said. Nothing like this had ever happened to me before, which filled me with excitement and terror in roughly equal amounts.

"Be on your best behavior"? Trussed up like this, what kind of "behavior" is even possible? "You'd better not come"? Does that mean I get a choice? I'll be at the mercy of his "guests," his "buddies," who'll probably each fuck me and "stimulate" me in some way, with pain or pleasure, to make sure I break that rule . . .

It was *very* quiet, and sound carried pretty far within the apartment — I hoped it didn't carry *beyond* Max's walls into his neighbors' homes. With him wearing those jumbo boots, I could hear his footsteps around the living room, just the other side of the wall at my left. A few minutes later, when the front door chime sounded, I heard him walk toward it. Straining my ears, I could hear him open the door and greet one of his friends. Talking loudly, they went into the kitchen. I guessed they were getting drinks, and the sound of bottles clinking back in the living room confirmed it.

Twice more the door chimed, and soon it sounded like three guys in the living room besides my weekend Master, talking and laughing loudly as they watched something on TV. From the exaggerated breathing and grunting noises I could hear, I assumed it was a porn video. But my back and legs were already starting to ache, pulling my attention away from sounds in the other room.

Max is right, I said to myself, *that I'm strong enough to hold this position, but it isn't going to be easy — or pleasant — to lie here chained in place until I can "be on my best behavior"* with his friends. Judging from the position, I figure that means I'm to give them each a good fuck. And I'd better not come, or my record of perfect obedience will be broken.

The men had been watching the video for almost half an hour when I heard footsteps, lighter than Max's, coming toward me. The door to the bedroom suddenly opened and bright light from the hallway spilled in, making me squint. Someone was walking into the room! He closed the door behind him and the dimness returned, so I couldn't see much. As he walked closer, he seemed almost as tall as Max, but slimmer, not as bulked out. I thought he was wearing jeans and a T-shirt, but I couldn't be sure yet.

"What have we here?" he said in a deep, sultry voice. "Looks like Max has got himself one hell of a slave for the weekend." He put a hand on my upturned exposed calf and stroked it, letting out a little whistle. "Yes, Sir, a *fine* piece of slavemeat." He startled me then by talking directly to me. "I'm Jake, boy, and you don't have to be afraid of me."

Grateful to be spoken to, I nodded my head to show him that I wasn't afraid, even though it was a lie. Jake got up onto the bed, and it sagged under his weight. My eyes had readjusted to the low light by then, and I was able to make out some of his features. I felt my soft cock fill with blood as I looked at him.

He's fucking gorgeous! While Max was super-hot in his hyper-masculine way, Jake was beautiful — not like a woman, but in a sleek manly way all his own. Clean shaven, with short blond hair and flashing blue eyes that I was sure had broken many hearts, he grinned as he saw me taking in his stunning looks.

"You're pretty hot yourself, boy," he said, as if reading my mind. "You'll do fine, just fine."

Kneeling between my legs, Jake unbuttoned his jeans and let his cock flop out. It was nice and long — and getting full and hard at the sight of me bound with my legs spread, ready to be plowed.

"That video got me all hot and bothered," Jake said as he

jacked his cock in his fist. "Max told us he had a slaveboy chained up in the bedroom who could relieve my tension."

"Yes, Sir," I said, but it was muffled by the gag. As scary and new and different as the situation was, the man's beauty and sexual heat made me *want* him to fuck me. I hoped my hardening cock made that obvious.

"What's that, boy?"

"Please fuck me, Sir," I tried to say through the gag.

"I can't understand you, boy."

"Please fuck me, Sir!" I said again, louder this time.

"What?"

"PLEASE FUCK ME, SIR!" I yelled, willing him to hear and understand.

"I understood you that time, slaveboy!" Jake said with a laugh, and scooted forward so that his cock head landed right on my puckering asshole. Still jacking his cock with one hand, he used the other to reach around me and grab a condom. He opened the packet and unrolled the rubber onto his boner, then picked up the lube bottle and squeezed some of the thick, creamy liquid onto his engorged tool.

"Mmmmm . . . ," Jake murmured as the lube made his cock slide in his hand. "That feels good. . . ." Then he was pressing it against my asshole, and I swear that thing was sniffing me like a fucking dog!

As Jake shoved himself inside me in one hard thrust, I howled from surprise and pain. Through my squinting eyes I could see him smiling, his bright white teeth flashing in the dark.

"Aaaahhhh . . . ," he said, as if completely unaware of my suffering. *But why should he notice it?* I reminded myself. *I'm here to serve and be used. Why should he care if he's hurting me? All that matters is making* him *feel good.*

I wouldn't have matched Jake's laid-back good looks with the savage way he made love. Like an animal, he fucked me long and hard, reaming my hole with his hot cock, grunting and snarling like a wolf, his beautiful face contorted by passion. It was an all-out assault, but even if I'd tried to escape, it would've been impossible. This man was using me like his property, and there was nothing I could do about it, because the man who *really* owned me had lent me to Max, who lent me to Jake. And because I *like* being owned and used, my cock was so hard it felt as if it could burst at any moment.

Sweat rolled down my forehead and chest while Jake fucked me for what seemed like hours but was probably less than one. I knew that if he grabbed my cock I would shoot, but I didn't have to worry about disobeying Max's order in this case — Jake wasn't interested in anyone's orgasm but his own. I never thought I'd be so glad that a top was ignoring my needs.

Finally he slowed his pace and, after a few final thrusts, gave a groan of ecstasy and yanked his cock out of me — leaving me with a hole as empty as a long dark tunnel. Stripping the condom off his boner, he dropped it on the bed next to me, and with one jack of his fist, the stud beat himself to paradise, splattering the proof of it all over me.

After Jake's victory shout, we were both still for a time, our labored breathing the only sounds in the room. The noise of the other guys and the video they were watching slowly came back to our awareness as we returned from our private world. Jake got off the bed and wiped himself with the hand towel. Then he buttoned up his jeans and patted me on the head.

"Good boy," he said. "Too bad Max can't keep you. I'd like to have another crack at that ass sometime." With a smile and a flash of those bright eyes, he was out the door, and I was alone again.

I might have dozed off, but it seemed like only a minute went by before the door was opened by my next "guest." As before, the combination of the dim room and the sudden bright light from the door made it hard at first to see details. All I could tell for sure was that he was shorter than Max and Jake, the 6-foot-plus giants who'd already fucked me, more like 5'8" or 5'9".

Though his musculature couldn't compare with Max's,

this man was stockier, more solidly built than Jake. As my eyes adjusted and he got closer, it became clear that he was also older than them by at least five to seven years — he looked to be in his late 30s to early 40s. His handsome beard and mustache were dark brown, like his hair and eyes. And he didn't waste any time, getting up on the bed right away.

"Too bad Jake got first dibs, slavemeat," he said, "but sloppy seconds don't bother me when they're laid out like you are." He reached between my legs and grabbed my nipples, twisting them painfully. I yelped like a puppy, which just made him twist harder. My breathing quickened as I tried to process the pain.

As before, it was useless to try to escape. But soon my nips were in such agony that I started twisting my torso, desperately trying to break the man's hold. When I finally succeeded, he growled in anger, slapping my face hard.

"Don't you try and get away from me, slavemeat," he said in a low, angry voice. "You're here to serve me, and you're damned well going to do it."

"Yes, Sir," I mumbled through the gag, collapsing onto the bed.

"Looks like you're not a good enough piece of meat to appreciate a real man," he said.

The disappointment in his voice was unmistakable, and my blood went cold. *What if he tells Max I didn't deliver the goods?* I didn't want to think about what the bruiser might do to me. *No*, I told myself. *I've gotten this far without disobeying, and I'm not about to stop now. There's still a chance. I have to redeem myself somehow with this Daddy-man.* He was turning to leave...

"Please, Sir!" I shouted into the gag. It came out garbled, but he turned around.

"You say something, slave?" He didn't look very interested in my answer.

"PLEASE USE ME, SIR!" I yelled as loudly and clearly as I could.

"Please use you? Is that what you said?" he asked, looking me in the eyes, still frowning.

"Yes, Sir!" I cried through the gag. "PLEASE USE ME!"

"Use you, eh?" he said, scratching his beard in an exaggerated "thinking about it" gesture. "Well...." A trace of a grin appeared on his face. "That's what I like to hear!"

The Daddy-man pounced back onto the bed, kneeling right between my legs facing my asshole, still hungry and empty after losing Jake's cock. He unbuckled his belt and unzipped his pants, letting his cock flop out. While it wasn't as big or long as Max's or Jake's, it was firm and stocky, like Daddy-man himself.

He reached past me and searched through the condom packets Max had left out, as if one of them was somehow better than the others. I think he just wanted me to make me wait and worry. Finally, he chose one and sheathed himself up.

But then he unhooked something from his belt that I hadn't noticed earlier: a wicked-looking flogger, with too many black leather tails for me to count. Daddy-man leaned forward, letting his cock fall across my hole. Having me at his mercy clearly turned him on, because it started to harden before my eyes, growing and filling out like a balloon being inflated.

He dragged the flogger across my chest, letting the tails slide over my sensitive nipples. I whimpered and moaned, hoping that dragging it across my skin was all he planned on doing. No such luck! Without warning, Daddy-man reared upright, threw back his arm, and snapped the flogger tails against my chest. I howled in pain and surprise, arching my back off the bed.

"Yeah," he growled. "*That's* what I like, slave, *that's* what I like."

He did it again, this time hitting one of my nips dead on. I'd thought it hurt when he'd been twisting them, but now . . . ! He got himself into a rhythm, flogging me with what felt like all of his strength.

I was so caught up in the pain that it took me by surprise when he lowered himself, shuffled forward, and slid his cock into my ass. Compared with what he was still doing to my chest, being fucked by him felt great.

My cock got hard again as I lay there looking up at this tough, bearded Daddy-man going at me with his flogger. His strokes were shorter now, so they didn't hit as hard, or as often, but they still hurt. I blocked out the pain and concentrated on the pleasure of his fucking.

Sweat from his forehead dripped down on me as he thrust himself into and out of my hole. I didn't have to worry about coming against orders. Every so often, Daddy-man would lash at my groin. The sting and shock of those tails hitting my cock and balls made sure that I never stayed hard long enough even to get close.

It was so intense, I was afraid I would pass out. Daddy-man was feeling the strain, too, panting like a racehorse as he screwed me good. Just when I was sure I couldn't take it anymore, he dropped the flogger and threw his head back. Daddy-man yelled when he came, a low-pitched, snarling roar like a bear's. I knew his spunk was unloading into the condom, filling it up as his passion spent itself.

I relaxed as much as I could, sagging back into the bed. My arms and legs ached miserably from being stretched out for what seemed like hours. But my job was to serve, not complain. Without another word to me, my second guest-fuck pulled out, threw the condom in the trash, zipped up his pants, and hooked his flogger back to his belt. Then he got off the bed and walked out of the room, closing the door behind him.

I breathed deeply, trying to regain control of my body, and closed my eyes. *At least I have some peace . . .*

But not for long, because suddenly light was spilling in on me again. I had figured there'd be at least one more guy. *Hope he's the last,* I said to myself as he entered.

There was nothing distinctive in his size or shape, but something about the way he moved was familiar. *Who is it?*

I wondered. *What about him reminds me of someone I know?* He closed the door and walked toward the bed. There was a self-confidence, even a cockiness in the way he moved that infused everything he did with a macho magnetism. I knew I'd seen it somewhere before.

Now he was standing right in front of me at the foot of the bed, framed by my painfully strained legs. I looked at his auburn hair, his bright brown eyes, his firm, muscular body in T-shirt and gym shorts, obviously shaped and honed by many hours spent there . . .

Then it hit me: *I know this guy! He goes to my gym. I see him almost every day!*

"My buddies told me you were hot, boy," he said, "but I wasn't expecting *this* . . ."

The voice was unmistakable. I'd overheard him talking to friends at the gym a hundred times. It was him.

"ADAM!" I yelled through the gag.

Looking unsurprised to hear his name, he hopped up on the bed with the ease of a panther.

I said it again, "Adam . . ."

"Yeah, it's me, boy." He put his hands on my chest and stroked sensuously down to my groin. "And I know it's you. I recognized you as soon as I came in."

One hand gently grasped my tortured cock, which felt so fucking good I could hardly stand it.

"I've wanted you for a long time, slaveboy," he said, "and now I have you."

The bulge in his shorts was huge, and a second later I saw why. With the hand that wasn't gripping my cock, Adam reached down and yanked his own free. It popped out like a big hard sausage, dripping and ready.

"The video got me primed," he said, "and now I'm going to let you have it."

The gym jock let go of me long enough to grab a packet from the bed, unroll the condom onto his protruding cock, and quickly coat it with lube. Then he was hunkering down between my legs, getting ready to invade me like the others.

I had seen and wanted this man so many times before. So many times I had imagined what it would be like if he threw me down and plowed me. Now it was happening, and I could barely believe it!

My hole, left empty and hungry by the other men's impersonal use, accepted Adam gratefully as he shoved himself in. His fucking was different from theirs, slow and intense — and maddening for just that reason. The guy knew I'd been daydreaming about him for months, and he was taking full advantage of it. He leered down at me like a demon of sex, screwing me as I lay, utterly helpless, beneath him.

I wanted to speak to him, to tell him . . . what? What could I possibly say to this man whom I'd worshipped for so long in my dreams, regardless of my loyalty to my Master? There was nothing *to* say — all the communication that could happen *was* happening. I'm a slave, and he was fucking me, using me, just like Bill, Max, Jake, and Daddy-man.

There was nothing else. I was nothing else, just a boy who's fucked by men. That's all I could ever hope to be, too. *How did this happen?* I pondered. *Could this be what Master Bill had in mind when he agreed to the arm-wrestling match with Max? Is it a lesson I'm supposed to learn?*

But my mental wheel-spinning was challenged by the unfolding drama between my ass and Adam's cock. *A fantastically hot man is fucking me, and all I can really do for him in return is to* be here now. *Being present in the moment is the only choice left to me — everything else has been taken away.*

I could choose to mentally remove myself from what was happening, or I could choose to be there. And because this was the most astonishingly real thing that had ever happened to me, I chose to be there — really *there,* much more than I had been with the other men who used me that night, even more than when Max fucked me.

My eyes searched frantically for Adam's as my thoughts raced again: *I have to lock eyes with him, I have to look into his soul. There's something there I have to discover . . . a connection that has to be made.*

The sparking, blooming jolts of ecstasy his cock was giving me were building and building toward an unbelievable, explosive climax — one that I realized at the last moment must *not* happen! *Max ordered me not to come*, I remembered.

Just then Adam's eyes met mine, and it was magic, as if the other men less than 20 feet away were not there and never had been, as if we were the only men on the *planet*. It was just the two of us: Top and bottom, Dominant and submissive, Master and slave, predator and prey . . .

"I'm gonna come, boy!" Adam yelled suddenly as he grabbed my cock again and started jerking it. I could feel myself sliding over the edge, the point of no return approaching faster and faster, the pleasure of being used by him sending me crashing into the forbidden place . . .

"No!" I screamed. "Adam! *PLEASE, NO!*"

It was too late. As the gym stud rammed his cock into me as far as it would go, roaring with passion and release, my long-delayed orgasm rocked my body. White-hot spunk shot out of my cock, splashing both of us.

I didn't care, then, because I was lost in the incredible bliss that flooded every cell of my tormented body. The blasts of cum went on and on, and above it all I could see Adam's face, still grinning at me, still smiling — as if he knew *exactly* what he'd done.

Max's last words rang through my mind: "No matter what happens, *you'd better not come*, or there'll be hell to pay." And then there was nothing as my body rebelled and shut down, unconsciousness taking me like a kidnapper in the night. I was falling into a blackness sweeter than midnight, sweeter than passion, sweeter than love . . . because it was the blackness of forgetting, the blessed curse that let me deny, at least for a moment, what would be waiting for me when I woke . . .

4. Sunday Morning — Discipline for Disobedience

MY DREAMS WERE TROUBLED — hot and sexy, but troubled. There was something wrong, something I was avoiding looking at, something I didn't want to see there in the murk of my well-earned slumber.

I had had an incredible night and was understandably exhausted. *What time is it now?* I wondered. *Must be Sunday morning.* Something about that bothered me. *Why? What am I afraid to see?* Like a loose tooth that I couldn't stop wiggling, the question of what I was avoiding kept popping up as I emerged from sleep to wakefulness. *Something about last night. What the hell is it?*

I remembered that early in the evening Max bound me to his bed with my arms and legs spread out ready for fucking, telling me to "be on your best behavior with my guests." Of course, that had meant being the best damn slaveboy I knew how to be, working my ass to give them the sweetest rides they'd had in a long while.

But wasn't there something else? I asked myself. *Something I'm missing? Something I've forgotten?*

I banished the thought, relishing the memories of the three quasi-rapes I'd surrendered to. Three different men, three different fucking styles, three different experiences: Jake the cover man, with beauty so devastating it could stop traffic, who had fucked me so easily, so assuredly, so completely; the bearded Daddy-man, who'd enjoyed flogging my chest and crotch as much as fucking my ass with his club-like dick; and Adam, the handsome, cocky jock I knew from the gym, a guy I'd fantasized about for months, who had finally nailed me with a passion scorching in its intensity . . .

There's something about Adam's fuck, something I didn't like. With mounting fear, I realized that whatever it was, *that's* what I was afraid of! The thing I'd been trying not to recall was just around the corner and about to flatten me . . .

Winner Takes All

At the end of his fuck Adam jerked me off and made me come, too. I remember how the explosion of ecstasy buried my qualms. . . . And suddenly I remembered the words of my weekend Master, the words that had followed his instruction to be on my best behavior for his guests. Clear as a bell, they sounded in my head as if he was actually saying them again: "No matter what happens, *you'd better not come*, or there'll be hell to pay."

Oh, no! I felt blood running out of my face and could picture the shade of white my cheeks were turning. In my head, I babbled scatologically: *I'm up shit creek without a paddle, I'm shit out of luck, I'm in deep kaka* . . . . After a day of perfect obedience, I'd disobeyed a clear order. Max's torture on Saturday afternoon had been bad enough — I was sure his discipline would be even worse. *He was torturing me then for his amusement, not punishing me for any wrongdoing. Now I'm really in for it* . . .

But maybe I can reason with him, I thought desperately, *show him it wasn't my fault, convince him that I couldn't help it. Adam jerked me off, and there was no way I could avoid coming, especially not after being fucked so long and so well by his buddies* . . . . *My arms hurt*, I realized suddenly, glad to think about something else, *and I'm hungry.*

I tried to bring my arms together and found they were still bound, but above my head rather than stretched out to the sides. I tried to move my legs and found them free, breathing a silent thanks for that mercy. *If Max had left my legs stretched apart from last night to this morning*, I realized, *I wouldn't be able to walk for days.* . . . *But that's likely to happen anyway, now that I'm tied to the tracks with the freight train of discipline hurtling toward me.* I knew that nothing I said or did could avoid it. I'd been given simple instructions and failed to follow them.

Cracking my eyes open, I was surprised to see bright sunlight peeking around the window shades. Neither a blindfold nor gag encumbered me. My cock was also unbound — and totally limp. And I was covered with dried cum.

The clock on the bedside table said it was a little after 10:00, and by the light it had to be morning. *That's why I'm so hungry*, I thought, glad of even a moment's distraction. *Max agreed to return me to my rightful Master on Sunday evening. That's hours and hours from now. He still has the rest of the day as my weekend Master. Plenty of time to make me wish I'd never been born!*

Just then his giant shape filled the doorway, again clad in a tank top and shorts, his feet bare and his heavily muscled body pumped up like he'd just worked out. As always, seeing his towering frame and bulging crotch made my knees weak and my mouth water. *Where'd he sleep?* I wondered, *and why didn't he move me off the bed to the floor?*

His expression as he looked at me was blank, unreadable, but I inferred the worst. The dog dish in his hands was full to the brim with . . . something. *I hope he lets me eat before punishing me. Or maybe he won't punish me after all? . . . Dream on,* I scolded myself.

Without a word, Max went into the adjoining bathroom, where I could see him dump the dish's contents into the tub. A little mumble of surprise must have escaped me, because he glanced back sharply. Leaving the empty dish in the sink, he walked back into the bedroom.

"Was that you, slavemeat?" he asked. "Did you make a noise just now when you saw me dump out your food?"

"Yes, Sir. I'm sorry, Sir."

"I didn't ask for an apology, did I, shithead?"

"No, Sir." *God, I'm already screwing up, and we've been talking less than 30 seconds!*

"Do you know why I did that, boy?"

"No, Sir," I lied, hoping against hope that there was still some way out of this, that I wouldn't have to suffer my weekend Master's wrath.

"I dumped your food in the bathtub because only good slaves get to eat out of bowls. Bad slaves like you have to get into the bathtub and eat there. When you're bad, you're dirty, and you don't deserve to eat like a good boy."

"Yes, Sir."

I was resigned to my fate. Now it was only a question of how he would punish me, how much it would hurt, and how long it would last, not whether he would do it.

Max untied my wrists from the headboard. I eased them down, my shoulders in agony after being frozen in place for so long. Now I was totally unrestrained — a naked dirty bad disobedient slaveboy on my weekend Master's bed, with the dried residue of my crime still on my chest.

He didn't even look at me when he spoke next.

"You'll eat and shower and report to me in ten minutes. Is that clear, slavemeat?"

"Yes, Sir!" I answered quickly.

"And not for one second will you stand on your hind legs. Crawling on your hands and knees is all you're good for. You got that?"

"Yes, Sir!"

As he turned and left the room, I painfully got off the bed, dropped to my knees on the floor, and crawled over to the bathroom. I climbed into the tub, where more than one unpleasant surprise was waiting for me. My weekend Master hadn't let my food fall in one place, where it could be eaten without moving around. That would've been too easy. No, the food was spread all over the bottom of the empty tub, so there was nowhere I could kneel without getting it on me. It would be difficult, to put it mildly, to eat this way.

And the food wasn't the delicious cut-up fruit, vegetables, and meat he'd given me the previous day. It was dog food, and not a very good brand either. It coated the bottom of the tub like red slime, chunky stinking pieces of gunk that looked more like shit than food. But slaves don't get to be picky. I had less than ten minutes to complete my assignments, and I had to do them right so all I'd get punished for would be last night's error.

I lowered my face to the bottom of the tub and started eating the dog food, fighting the impulse to gag and hack it right back out. It was disgusting, tasting even worse than it looked and smelled. I was getting just as much on my face, hands, and knees as in my mouth, and even though I was still hungry, after a few minutes I decided breakfast was over.

Time to shower. I reared up on my knees, remembering that I'd been forbidden to stand on my hind legs, closed the shower curtain, and started the water. Yow! It was cold! I quickly turned the dial to a warmer setting and basked in the spray for a few minutes as it sluiced sweat, cum, and dog food from my body. After soaping myself to remove the greasy residue, I rinsed off and made sure that the last bits of "food" disappeared down the drain.

When the tub was clean, I climbed out and dried off, still on my hands and knees. It wasn't easy, but it wasn't supposed to be. Praying that I was within the time limit, I crawled back into the bedroom, through the doorway, down the hall, and into the living room.

"Reporting as ordered, Sir!" I was finally able to say as I knelt in his sight a few feet from the couch. Master Max was working on something at the coffee table and didn't even look up. Disappointing him weighed heavily on my heart, and I wished there was something I could do to make up for my disobedience.

There's still hope, I thought. *He hasn't banished me from his presence or sent me back early to Master Bill. Or is that what I want? No, Master Max won me for the weekend, and I want to serve him and please him and take care of him exactly how he wants for the whole time he and Master Bill agreed.*

That's not to say I was looking forward to getting punished. Far from it! Like Daffy Duck, "I can't stand pain. It hurts me."

"You disobeyed me last night, slavemeat," Max said without looking my way, and my attention was instantly riveted on him.

"Yes, Sir. I'm sorry, Sir."

"I didn't ask for an apology, boy. It was just a statement of fact."

"Yes, Sir." I resolved to keep my mouth shut and my ears open.

He glanced at me out of the corner of his eye. *God, he's so fucking hot, this big blond god with muscles to spare . . .*

"I gave you simple instructions last night," he went on. "I told you to take good care of my buddies, and not to come. That's not hard to understand, is it?"

"No, Sir."

I was dying to say that it wasn't my fault, that Adam had jerked me until I came, that I couldn't stop him, or my response to his manipulation. After being fucked by three different men, I was so horny I was bursting. There was no way I could've avoided coming!

But none of that mattered. My weekend Master had given me a clear instruction, and I disobeyed. It was as simple as that — slaves don't get excuses.

"What do you think happens to disobedient slaveboys?" he asked.

"I don't know, Sir." I was hoping against hope for some answer other than *discipline* or *punishment*.

"I think you do know," he said calmly.

I paused and sighed deeply. *Here goes . . .*

"They're taught a lesson, Sir. They're punished."

"Good boy. You want to personalize that sentence?"

At least now he's looking me in the face, I told myself as I accepted defeat.

"I need to be punished, Sir."

"That's a good boy," Max said, standing up and coming over to where I was kneeling. "Your punishment will be less because you said that. Now, it's time to teach you a lesson in obedience, slavemeat."

"Yes, Sir," I said, cowering under him. "Thank you, Sir. . . . What are you going to do with me, Sir?" As soon as I said it I knew it was a mistake, but it slipped out.

"It's not your place to ask questions, shithead. It's your place to follow orders. Do you understand?"

"Yes, Sir," I said in a small voice.

"Crawl over to the couch and pick up that towel in the corner with your mouth."

I hurried to obey, scuffling so fast over the carpet that I gave my knees rug burns. I grabbed the rolled-up towel in my teeth and waited for further orders.

"Now spread it out over there, with your mouth," he said, pointing at the open space in front of the coffee table and glaring at me. "I don't want you making a mess."

Oh, great, I thought. *What is he planning?* I squelched my fear and did as he commanded. It wasn't easy without hands, but I knew better than to hesitate.

"Lie on your back on the towel, slavemeat, spreadeagle."

I did as ordered and stared at the ceiling, hoping the coming punishment wouldn't be too bad. But from my experience with my weekend Master so far, particularly the torture he'd inflicted on me Saturday afternoon, I wasn't counting on it. *This time there's a purpose, so it's likely to be ten times worse!*

As my mind spun, the bruiser got something from the kitchen. *That's odd,* I thought. I expected him to pull whatever fiendish device he needed to punish me out of the "toy chest" in the living room that held everything else he'd used. And next he went to the bedroom! *What's he planning?* He came back and knelt between my legs.

"I hope this is the only time I have to do this, boy," he said with audible regret.

"Me too, Sir."

He grinned humorlessly and reached between my legs. Feeling his hand on my crotch galvanized my cock, hardening it almost instantly. My eyes closed and my thoughts swam. *If this is punishment, bring it on!* But the thought was premature, because seconds later he opened a tiny bottle and turned it upside down over my hard-on.

I had time to register two facts: One, that Master Max was squeezing the head of my cock so that whatever dripped from the bottle would fall right into my piss slit, and two, that the bottle's label read, "TABASCO SAUCE." I was still trying to draw out the implications of those two facts when the pain hit.

"Mmmmpphhh!" I blurted as the fiery drops of Tabasco trickled down inside my cock. I'd never felt anything like it before. The pain was terrifying. This was no external hurt that could be brushed away or fixed with a bandage. It was internal, burning and stinging me from the inside out.

It hurt like hell, and I stifled a shriek of pain.

"Please, Sir . . . ," I mumbled. But what was there to say?

"What, boy?" Max asked. "Is there something you want to tell me?"

"I'm sorry, Sir!" I said desperately. "I won't ever disobey you again!"

"I'm glad to hear it. Now shut up and take your punishment like a good slave."

"Yes, Sir," I whispered, struggling to control myself. My instinct was to grab my dick, to cover the piss slit, to prevent him from dripping any more Tabasco into me. I twitched and quivered, dying to move my arms and legs, to protect myself . . .

"Don't you dare move a muscle, slavemeat," my weekend Master said. "I don't feel like tying you up right now, so you are going to be held there by my authority and my orders alone. Do you understand?"

"I don't know, Sir . . . ," I said truthfully.

"I haven't tied you up, but as of now you are immobile, because I say you are. You *will* hold yourself in place as if you were bound." He put the cap back on the bottle and stared me in the eye.

"You will not move your arms or legs," he said, speaking slowly and emphasizing almost every word. "If you do, your punishment will be doubled. Do you understand?"

"Yes, Sir!" I said loudly. "Please, Sir!"

Somehow, incredibly, my erection maintained itself despite the pain in my cock. It was as if just being in the man's power was arousing regardless of what he was actually doing to me.

I was grateful he was finished adding Tabasco sauce, at least for the time being. *But what is he doing now?* I heard latex being stretched. I lifted my head a bit and saw him put on gloves, open a small jar, and scoop white stuff out of it.

Then he grabbed my erect cock with one hand and my balls with the other. He started massaging me, and I could feel sticky warmth as whatever was on his hands rubbed off the latex and into my skin. The warmth from the cream was almost pleasant, and I wondered what kind of punishment this was. *Maybe it's something to counteract the Tabasco sauce, a post-punishment soother?*

Master Max finished his massage, and my entire crotch area was covered with the warm cream. I let out a little sigh of pleasure. The pain of the Tabasco sauce was much less with the pleasant sensation bathing my groin.

Is it my imagination, I asked myself shortly, *or is it getting warmer down there?* It seemed like the heat of the cream had increased, changing from a pleasant, soothing warmth to a more tingling feeling. *It has to be my imagination.*

My weekend Master peeled off his gloves and stood up. I caught a glimpse of the jar the cream had come out of and could read the bright red lettering: "BENGAY."

Oh, my God. It wasn't my imagination! It is getting hotter! Hotter every second, and more and more painful!

"It's burning me, Sir!" I cried out. "Please!"

"It's supposed to, slavemeat," he said calmly. "It's not damaging you — just hurting you."

A side effect of the increasing heat of the BenGay was to make the Tabasco sauce feel horrible again. It was as if my entire crotch was on fire, and the need to touch myself was urgent. *I have to stop the burning!* I screamed in my head. *But he ordered me not to move! . . . My cock and balls are in flames! . . . But he'll kill me if I touch them!*

The pain was so intense I couldn't think straight. I went back and forth, torn between my desire to stay obediently still and my instinct to "do something" about the pain. The stinging, itching, and burning were hideously painful, and

I knew the pain wouldn't die down for a long time. Equally, I knew it was ridiculous to think about touching myself, even if it hadn't been contrary to my orders.

What could I accomplish? I asked myself in a moment of lucidity. *I can't just rub the cream off; by now it's seeped into my skin. And I can't squeeze the Tabasco sauce out of my cock; it's deep down the urethra. There's no way I can be free of the pain except by waiting it out.*

This was my punishment, and I had to live with it.

Above me, the bruiser was stripping off his clothes. Even amidst the pain, his naked body was arresting in its beauty and power. His big cock was hard and dripping. *Looks like disciplining me has made him horny. But what will he do now?*

"Turn over on your stomach, slavemeat!" he barked. "And be sure you stay on the towel."

Somehow, despite the pain, I managed to turn myself over. Unfortunately, sandwiching my burning cock and balls between my belly and the rough towel made them hurt even more than before.

I spread my arms and legs again, hoping that my weekend Master would notice I did so without being told. But a second later I scolded myself: *What am I trying to do? Looking for mercy? This hard-ass doesn't have any. Yesterday proved that!*

And even if he decided to be merciful, it was too late. The insidious liquid and cream he used to punish me could no longer be removed. Their active ingredients were now a part of me, and would be until my body metabolized them. I tried to push the pain from my consciousness, or at least out of the forefront of my mind. Coping with it was taking too much energy. *How do I get it under control?*

I didn't think I could handle one more intense sensation. My body and brain were on overload already. But I was a slave being punished, a piece of property. What I thought, felt, or wanted could never outweigh my Master's intentions.

"Get up on your knees, boy. I want to see that butt in the air."

Whimpering pitifully, I raised the lower half of my body,

lifting my ass and supporting the weight on my knees and elbows, which I pulled in close to my shoulders.

"That's good," Master Max said. "That's a good boy."

If I'm a good boy, would you please stop punishing me? I thought anxiously. But I was smart enough not to *say* it — I was in enough trouble not to make it worse by back talk.

The bruiser got on his knees beside me. He let me see him pull a condom package out of his shorts pocket, open it, and put the rubber on. After spitting into his hand and wiping it onto his wrapped cock, he moved behind me and fingered my ass crack. I tensed at the imminent intrusion, because if there was one thing I was *sure* I couldn't handle right then, it was getting fucked — especially with nothing but spit for lube.

He shoved himself into me right to the hilt! On top of the torment I was already enduring, my ass hurt like a son of a bitch. His huge cock was plowing me so hard I thought he'd split me in two. Suddenly, with an animal grunt, he plunged forward, dropping down onto my back. I screamed and collapsed under him.

"You ever going to disobey me again, boy?" he asked, lying there on top of me, crushing me.

"Sir, no, Sir!" I yelled like a Marine answering a drill sergeant. "Never, Sir!"

"Good boy," he said. "Good slave..."

Then he started pistoning up and down, and in every respect it was the most painful fuck I'd ever experienced. None of those the night before could touch it. With every thrust of his cock into me, my tortured junk was rubbed against the towel, and practically every ounce of the man's weight was crushing my genitals into the floor.

I never knew a man could endure so much torment, especially a man like me, who's not a masochist. I closed my eyes, clenching them shut as he raped me. Tears squeezed out from under my lids, dripping onto the towel. I didn't know which pain was worst — the Tabasco inside my cock, the BenGay on my cock and balls, or the assault on my ass.

Crying openly now, as much in shame and humiliation as physical agony, I endured my punishment with reserves of strength I didn't know I had. Every second that passed seemed to last longer than the one before. Above me, Master Max seemed to be reveling in my distress, grunting and laughing, delighting in my torture.

How much longer can this go on? I asked myself frantically. I felt my awareness slipping away, as if my body was on the verge of shut-down. *I can't take much more of this. Something has to give. Something has to stop!*

But I wouldn't beg. That at least I could avoid. I'd dishonored my weekend Master by disobeying him in the first place, and I wasn't going to compound the error by begging for relief. I'd earned my punishment, and I'd take it like a good slave. I had to please him, and this was the only way left. I might cry, but I wouldn't beg. Not anymore.

And suddenly Max was grabbing me, wrapping his huge muscled arms around my torso, clutching me to him, crushing me against his wide chest. He exhaled loudly into my ear, and I felt him dump his Masterful jizz into the condom deep inside me. I sighed, hoping that at least the rape part of the ordeal was over. He kept his cock in me even as it softened in his afterglow.

After he pulled out, he stood up and got rid of the full condom, then knelt down again in front of me, presenting his half-hard, cum-streaked cock for service.

"Clean me up, shitface, and get it hard again quick, because it's going right back inside you."

What's he up to? I wondered as I dutifully licked and sucked his beautiful, dangerous organ once again. *What possible torment is left to put me through?*

The answer came a minute or so later when he pulled his newly hard cock out of my mouth and plugged it back in my ass. I immediately felt a warm flow inside me and realized that he was giving me a load of his piss.

"Keep it inside you, slavemeat," he ordered. "Hold it."

"Yes, Sir," I said through my tears, my humiliation complete. The acid piss stung as it bathed tissues that had been so recently pummeled by his punishment fuck. Only after he'd completely voided himself did Master Max pull out and stand over me.

"Get up on all fours," he ordered, and somehow I obeyed, crouching like an animal as I'd done earlier. "Take the towel to the bathroom with your mouth," he continued. "Put it in the laundry bag. Then lie down in the tub."

My groin and ass screamed for relief as I crawled, but none was to be had. There was nothing, in fact, in my whole world except the pain and my need to please my weekend Master. *I have to please him*, I thought. *I did so well in the first part of the weekend — there must be some way to redeem myself.*

Once in the bathroom, I disposed of the towel, then sat down in the tub. The burning from the Tabasco sauce and BenGay combined with the soreness of my raped asshole, still clenched to hold the stinging piss inside me, in a crescendo of pain. I was amazed that I could bear it without going mad.

"Let the piss out now," Master Max said from the doorway. "You should piss, too, if you can. That'll wash out the remaining Tabasco."

"Thank you, Sir," I said and released both of my sphincters. Rank-smelling urine poured out of my ass and cock into the tub and down the drain. The piss from my cock had a reddish tinge, and the pain inside immediately diminished, though it didn't vanish completely.

Now there's just ass soreness and burning on the outside of my cock and balls to deal with, I thought. *But how? Water won't wash away the cream, not by itself, but maybe cool flowing water will ease the pain?* I was reaching for the knob but jerked my hand back when Master Max spoke again. I'd almost forgotten he was still standing there, watching me.

"This is the last time I'm going to ask, boy. Are you *ever* going to disobey me again?"

"No, Sir!" I cried, looking up at him as more tears flowed down my cheeks. I felt guilty. Broken. My soul was as naked to him as my body, waiting on his pleasure. If he wanted to destroy me altogether, he could have done it with a word. But he wasn't finished yet.

"Lie down on your back," he said, "and wait for my call. While you're waiting, think about the cost of disobedience."

"Yes, Sir."

Master Max was turning to go when he stopped and said over his shoulder, "And boy . . ."

"Yes, Sir?" I said, tentatively reaching again for the cold-water knob.

"Don't turn on the water until I tell you." My heart sank.

"Yes, Sir," I replied, and he went out the door. I dropped my hand and lay on my back. My abused ass still throbbed, and the burning on my balls was almost as painful as when my punishment was at its height. *Now I'm truly broken*, I thought, *because I can't even imagine disobeying him . . .*

5. Sunday Afternoon — Winner Takes All

LYING IN THE TUB staring at the bathroom ceiling, I tried to think of something, *anything* besides the pain in my ass and groin, or how uncomfortable it was to lie on the bare porcelain without any water — just a puddle of Max's piss from my ass mixed with my own. Most of it had gone down the drain, but what remained stank.

Time plodded. I could hear the bruiser moving around in the bedroom and beyond, apparently in no hurry to let me turn the water on. Barred from that potential relief, I did the only thing I *could* do — suffer like a man, without complaint. There was no way I could sleep in that situation, but I closed my eyes anyway. I tried to separate myself from the pain by focusing on my whole experience as Master Max's weekend slaveboy and how it differed from my life with Master Bill.

Max is bold, demanding, like a force of nature — a true leath-

er Master. Now that I thought about it, though, I realized that he'd worn hardly any leather since I'd first seen him on Friday night at the bar. *He doesn't need to. The man is a walking porn image, every slaveboy's wet dream.*

Master Bill owned a lot of leather clothes and wore them often. *He's a strong, handsome man, too, but he dresses the part of a Master so that anywhere he goes other gay men will know he is one. Master Max doesn't need any special packaging. He exudes dominance as if it's his birthright to own and use other men, who are in turn happy to serve him. Master Bill waits for boys to seek him out. Master Max hunts. If he sees a boy he wants, he goes after him, like he did with me at The Richter Scale.*

Despite the agony he'd put me through — and still was! — I found myself feeling gratitude, sudden loyalty, even love for Master Max. *I'm Master Bill's slaveboy,* I told myself, *but does he* want *me in the same way Master Max does?*

When I first introduced myself to Master Bill at a leather function 14 months before that weekend, he said he was looking for a slaveboy and seemed interested in me. Two weeks later I moved in with him.

We've had a good run, I realized, *but there's been nothing like the intensity, the passion, the* commitment to the moment *I've experienced with Max. Master Bill was content to take me on as his slaveboy. But Master Max saw me, wanted me, and figured out a way to have me, if only temporarily. And there's nothing I want more than to be desired, to be taken . . .*

"Thinkin' deep thoughts, boy?"

My eyes flew open. Max was standing in the bathroom door, wearing his shorts and tank top again, grinning down at me in the tub. I hadn't heard him approach.

"No, Sir," I said. "I mean, yes, Sir . . ."

He raised his eyebrows at me.

"I don't know *what* I'm thinking, Sir."

" 'Course you don't," the bruiser said, stepping over to the tub and reaching down to the faucets. "No doubt that BenGay and Tabasco fried your brain as well as your dick and balls."

He turned the "Cold" knob, and wonderful, blessed cool water began to fill the tub. I sighed in relief as my burning balls and aching ass were bathed in it.

"Wash your junk with this, boy," he said as he handed me a bottle of mild dish detergent from the floor next to the tub. I hadn't noticed it when I came in. *He must have put it there before he fucked me.*

"That's how you get the BenGay off," he went on. "You can use hot water, too, when you're ready."

"Thank you, Sir," I breathed. "Oh, thank you, Sir."

"Learned your lesson, Josh? See what happens when you disobey me?"

"Oh, yes, Sir." The water was high enough to submerge my cock. "It feels better already!" I exclaimed, and Master Max laughed.

"Don't forget the dish soap," he reminded me.

"I've learned my lesson, Sir," I assured him again. "Whatever order you give me, I won't forget it."

"Good," he said with a smile. "Relax for a while, rinse and dry off, then join me in the kitchen. You have 15 minutes."

"Yes, Sir. Thank you, Sir."

Once he left the bathroom, I turned on the hot water, too, and poured in some of the dish soap. When the water in the tub was lukewarm, I rubbed the suds around my groin. The heat from the cream started to fade, and by then the inside of my cock felt completely normal. I lay there soaking for a while, then opened the drain and rinsed myself and the tub. Turning off the water, I climbed out and gently dried myself with a towel from the rack.

After making sure the bathroom was tidy again, I crawled to the kitchen, where Master Max was leaning on the counter reading the Sunday paper. He smiled down at me, and I was struck again by his rugged good looks, which drew me to him like bright flowers draw worker bees. He put the paper down and clapped his hands once, fast.

"On your feet, boy!"

Surprised but obedient, I jumped to my feet. My surprise

intensified when he wrapped his muscled guns around me, pulling me into his broad chest. I reached behind him to return the hug, nuzzling my face between his massive pecs. I loved this sudden, unexpected tenderness.

He rested his chin on top of my head and held us together for a few long minutes. It felt good — more, it felt *right* — to be naked in his arms. Then he lifted my chin so I was looking up at him — and kissed me.

I closed my eyes in delight as I felt his mustache, soft against my upper lip. He was a gentle kisser, caressing my lips with his own. Our mouths opened wider, and his big, hot tongue pushed into me, insistently exploring my mouth. This was so arousing that my knees were shaking.

Master Bill never kissed me like this, I thought. *He hardly kissed me at all.* Then Max moved his mouth to my ear.

"Josh . . . ," he said softly. The tone of longing and regret was completely unlike anything that I'd heard from him all weekend.

I squeezed the big man tight, all the time marveling at what strange behavior this was for a Master and a slave. *Or is it just strange to me because I haven't experienced anything like it with my own Master?*

Max broke the embrace and picked something off the counter I hadn't noticed before, something made of a shiny black fabric, maybe spandex. He let it unfurl until one end was pooled on the floor by my feet, the other in his hand.

"Get in the sack, boy," he said, handing it to me.

A sleepsack! I'd never been in one but had always wanted to try it.

"Yes, Sir," I said, pulling down the back zipper and stepping into the bottom part of the sack. Master Max took over then and snugged the rest of it up around me. It covered my ass, my waist, my chest, all the way up to my neck. Once he zipped it up, only my head was exposed, the spandex fitting snugly to every line and curve of my body.

I tried to move my arms, but the sack held them tight at my sides. I was bound as surely as if I were tied up, but in the softest, gentlest way possible. It was like being tightly hugged everywhere at once. The crotch area felt a little different, as if there was a second layer of fabric covering it.

"How's it feel, boy?" he asked, grinning at me.

"Great, Sir! It's amazing." Stupidly, I took a step forward and started to fall.

"Ally-oop!" Max said, laughing, as he caught me, picked me up, and tossed me over one shoulder. With his left hand holding me in place, he used his right hand to open the refrigerator and get a beer. He carried me out of the kitchen and into the living room.

Immobilized from neck to toe, I was swooning from the combination of snug bondage and being carried. I loved being there in the sack, over Max's shoulder, even more than his kissing me or anything else nice that had happened during the weekend.

Suddenly I knew that this was where I was meant to be, where I wanted to be — where I needed to be. With Master Max, *not* Master Bill.

The trip to the living room was far too short. Max sat on the couch and laid me out on the cushion next to him. I giggled at my predicament, flopping around like a fish out of water, unable to use my arms or legs. I tried to wiggle closer to him, but he grabbed me and positioned me how he wanted. I ended up lying on my back with my head on his lap. Looking around, I saw his bottle of beer on the coffee table in front of the couch.

"Josh?" he said, and I turned my face back to him.

"Yes, Sir?"

"You've had a pretty intense time since I brought you here, so I figure I'll go easy on you the rest of the day."

"Thank you, Sir," I said with relief.

"We're just gonna chill."

Picking up the TV remote, he put his big feet up on the coffee table, and we proceeded to spend the afternoon there, drinking beer and watching football. At least he watched it — I spent more time watching him.

I was, as they say, happy as a pig in shit. Or, better, happy as a slaveboy in a sleepsack, because I couldn't imagine any pig being happier than I was that afternoon — though it bothered me not being able to fetch more beer for him when he finished the first bottle.

As Max watched the game, he petted me, stroking my head like a favorite dog's. He also gave me some of his beer, dribbled from his mouth to mine. But mostly he watched the game, whooping and hollering at the TV like my Dad and brothers did when I was growing up — in fact, they still do when we all get together a couple of times a year.

Despite the noise, I was so comfortable that I drifted off a few times. *What could be more appropriate*, I thought, *than falling asleep in a sleepsack with my head on Master's lap? . . . Better make that "Master Max's lap,"* I chided myself. *I still belong to Master Bill . . .*

There was a strange feeling in my stomach, almost like dread of what was coming. Time, which had slowed to an agonizing crawl during parts of the weekend, now seemed to be racing.

It must be late Sunday afternoon, I estimated. *My time as Master Max's slaveboy is nearing its end. But that's good, isn't it? Since Friday night at The Richter Scale, my life has been painful and harrowing . . . . Yes, but also exhilarating, mind-altering, and full of amazing joy.*

Regardless of how I felt about it, Max had to fulfill his part of the bargain and return me to Master Bill, my rightful owner. *Don't my feelings matter at all? Has anyone even* asked *me about it?*

In jerk-off fiction slaves have no rights, no opinions, no decision-making power, and no feelings. Master Bill sure operated that way, and in the time he owned me, he had me believing it, too. *Master Max seems different,* I thought. *If I really need to talk to him, need him to* listen *to me, he would . . . wouldn't he?*

It doesn't matter, I told myself. *This whole thing is going to be over in a few hours, so I'd better stop thinking of Max as my*

Master and remember who's my real owner. I tried to relax and savor what was left of my time with Max, but it was difficult. Trying to distract myself, I glanced again and again at a wooden box on the far side of the coffee table.

"Master?" I asked finally.

"Yeah, boy?"

"What's in that box on the table?"

"My most prized possession."

The unspoken question hung in the air.

"Do you want to see it, Josh?"

"Please, Sir," I said quietly.

With my head still in his lap, Max reached for the box with one hand and pulled it close. It was locked. With the other hand he pulled his silver necklace from under his shirt. Without removing the long necklace, he leaned forward, lifted the box, and used one of the keys hanging from the necklace to unlock it. Seeing the big brute take such care with these delicate objects made me yearn for him even more.

He opened the box and let me see what was inside: a leather slave collar resting on a red velvet cushion. This was no cheap costume collar to be worn once on Halloween or Gay Pride Day. It was a serious collar for a treasured slave.

Made of thick black leather two inches wide, it had three rows of silvery studs and a D-ring at the front to attach a leash or chain. On either side, the studding was interrupted by engraved silver plates; one said "MAX's" and the other "BOY." Opposite the D-ring was a buckle that could be secured with a padlock. Whoever held the key would decide when this collar went on or came off, not its wearer.

It was the most beautiful slave collar I'd ever seen, and I was getting hard just looking at it. I wanted to wear it. More, I wanted to be worthy of it.

Too soon, Max closed and locked the box. I had hoped to touch the collar, but that clearly wasn't going to happen. Even he hadn't touched it. I settled back against him and looked up. His eyes were back on the TV, but he wasn't paying attention to the game.

"It's a beautiful collar, Master," I ventured.

"It's never been worn," he said in a tight voice.

"Why not, Sir?"

Now he looked at me.

"Because the morning my father left and never came back, he hugged me tight and said, 'Max, promise me one thing. When you finish school and go out on your own, do what makes you happy. And do it as soon as you can, because it may be your last chance. I don't know what the future will be, but don't think it's your friend. To the future, our lives are just a game. If you let it force your moves, you'll always lose. Don't let that happen. Play to win. The only way you can win is to do what makes you happy. Winner takes all. You understand, boy?'

" 'Yes, Dad,' I said. Then he threw his duffel bag over his shoulder, got in his car, and my Mom and I never saw him again . . .

"I thought long and hard about what he said. As I got older I learned that what would make me truly happy was different from what most other men wanted. Tons of money, fast cars, sleek boats, badass motorcycles, beautiful women, gambling and winning, tickets to the Super Bowl every season . . . none of that was gonna make me happy. So after college and a tour in the Marines, I started looking for what *would* make me happy."

"And what is that, Sir?"

"A slaveboy. . . ." He paused, his eyes locked on mine. I felt like a rodent paralyzed by a serpent's gaze, but I wasn't afraid. If I was a mouse, I *wanted* to be eaten.

"A true slaveboy I could call my own," Max continued. "Not a snot-nosed gay punk with an entitlement complex who wants to do 'scenes' and have 'safewords,' to pretend to be a slave all weekend and then on Monday go back to his safe vanilla life and his bitchy, queeny friends."

I was hanging on his every word. Even if I hadn't been confined in the sleepsack, his intensity would have rooted me to the spot.

"I want a boy who *needs* to be owned," he went on, "one who *needs* to be another man's property. A boy who'll pledge allegiance to his country, and then to his Master. A boy who'll do exactly what I want him to do, when I want it and how I want it. A boy who'll say, 'I belong to you, Master. I'm yours.' A boy worthy of the collar sitting in that box."

He paused, and I realized I'd been holding my breath. I let it out in a long sigh, then asked, "You haven't found the right boy yet, Sir?"

"No. Not yet," he confirmed. After another long pause, he seemed to shake off the somber mood. He looked at me, resting comfortably, and pretended to be outraged.

"What's this? My borrowed slaveboy lazing around *on a couch?* Have you forgotten why I won you for the weekend, boy? To serve me, damn it!"

I looked down at my body, encased and helpless in its shiny black prison.

"I can't do much stuffed in this sack, Sir," I said, wiggling helplessly.

"You can do plenty!" Max said, unbuckling his belt. He flipped me onto my stomach and placed my head between his legs, then unzipped his shorts and pulled out his cock.

"Get your mouth on this."

I gladly took his soft but still sizable uncut shaft between my lips.

"Mmmm," he moaned, "that feels good."

Max's cock hardened in my mouth, getting even bigger. The foreskin rolled back as I sucked it, giving him as much pleasure I could. He put one hand on top of my bobbing head, holding it there possessively. It felt so good to be in his power, bound up in his sleepsack and servicing his big Master-cock.

Precum oozed out of the head, and I licked it off. Master Max rumbled above me like a volcano building to eruption. I sucked as much of his cock into my mouth as I could, but it was so big at this point I didn't think I could get it all. I tried to pull off so I could lick up and down the outside of the shaft, but his hand tightened on my head and kept me in place. *Okay, big guy. I'll do my best!* I vowed silently.

My own cock strained between my legs, held tightly together by the sack, as I moved up and down on his, taking in more of it each time, until it finally slid down my throat. Then it just took breath control to get my lips all the way to his pubes. I could feel his hairy balls tightening up against my chin, getting ready to blow. Soon he let out a snarl and blew his first load right into my gullet. Grunting, he shot again and again as I pulled back, and I gulped it all down as fast as it came. When he finally finished, in my mouth, I licked him clean, every drop.

He gently pulled me off him and set my head down in his lap. I was glad to lie there for a few minutes, catching my breath from the world-class blowjob I'd just delivered.

"Mmmm . . . ," the bruiser finally said. "You do good work, Josh-boy."

"Thank you, Sir."

"After a performance like that, you deserve a reward."

He grabbed me under the armpits and flipped me over again onto my back. Then he pulled my head, arms, and torso to one side so that my ass was in his lap, which put my groin right in front of him and my legs on the other side.

It was an effort to lift my head from the couch to see what he was doing, so I laid back and let my other senses report. I felt his hands on my cock and balls through the part of the sack where the fabric was different. I heard a zipper pulled open, and then my pent-up cock was sprung from its spandex prison! When Max grabbed it in a meaty paw, I yelped at the unexpected attention, so different from when he'd handled me there to cause pain.

"You've wanted to be a good boy, wanted to please me, haven't you, Josh?"

"Y-yes, S-sir."

"Well, you have. You've been a great slaveboy, obedient and dutiful. And when you disobeyed, you took your punishment like a man."

I panted as he pumped my cock.

"S-Sir?" I forced out.

"Yeah, boy?"

"I don't know h-how much l-longer I can hold out . . ."

He chuckled. "Then let it fly, slaveboy. Let it fly. You've earned it."

I gave in to the waves of pleasure I'd been trying to hold back. As they crashed over me, it felt so incredibly good that I howled with joy. It was so right, so perfect, to be bound close to my weekend Master as he rewarded me with a fabulous orgasm. My cum splattered on the sleepsack over my stomach and chest.

"Thar he blows," Max joked and continued to stroke me even after I finished spurting. I had to beg him to stop before it became painful. He let me lie there, enjoying the afterglow, until my breathing returned to normal.

"Well," he said finally, patting my belly, "we'd better get you cleaned up. It's almost time to take you back to that Master of yours."

He rolled me off him, unzipped the sleepsack, and helped me out of it. I would have liked to stay in bondage longer, but Max was right — he had to return me. He got up and headed for the bedroom, leaving me naked on the floor beside the couch. As far as he knew, I was eager to get going!

I used the short period of privacy to try to sort out my feelings and desires: *How can I admit that I would rather stay here and be Max's slaveboy than go back to Master Bill? It would be a betrayal of him, behavior unbecoming a respectful slave. Bill trusted Max and me to carry out the agreement they made, that I would belong to Max for the weekend and then be returned. But if I'm so valuable, why did Master Bill risk ownership of me in the first place, even for a few days, as stakes in a casual competition? Wasn't that a betrayal of me and the commitment I'd made to be his slaveboy?*

I was very confused, but there was no more time to analyze things. Max came back from the bedroom wearing a fresh tank top, jeans, his bar vest, and short laced boots. He gave me a T-shirt, a pair of shorts, and my Army boots. *He must keep extra boy-sized clothes around*, I thought snarkily, *for when he turns slaves loose after destroying their own stuff!*

"Hop to it, boy!" the bruiser said. "Get dressed — we've gotta get going."

"Yes, Sir," I said, slipping into the clothes. It felt unnatural to be clothed in this place, in his presence.

"Wait at the front door," he said. "I'll be there soon."

Numbly, I walked to the door, and in a few minutes we took the elevator down to the building's garage. I noticed him carrying a small leather satchel but wasn't going to ask about it — or speculate.

Max's car, which I hadn't been able to see before, was a vintage black Mustang, direct and masculine in its lack of adornment, much like its owner. I stood there dumbly, half expecting the bruiser to throw the big canvas bag over my head and toss me in the back seat like when he'd brought me home Friday night. But he just got in on the driver's side and told me to get in on the other.

We hardly spoke during the drive. I was so strangled with contradictory feelings that I couldn't have talked anyway. What was happening felt *wrong*. But I didn't know what to do about it. *This is between Masters*, I told myself.

The Richter Scale's lot was packed, so we parked on the street a couple of blocks away. Max carried the satchel, and we walked in silence to the entrance. He put one hand on my shoulder as we entered the smoky bar. I thrilled at his touch even though I knew he was just making sure no one messed with me while he delivered me to my Master. I might have been a piece of lost luggage returned to its owner by an airline employee.

As the bruiser looked for Master Bill, I fought the urge to turn around and beg him to throw me over his shoulder, carry me back to his home, and take me as his slaveboy for the rest of my life. I thought I spotted Bill, and my heart sank as my mind raced.

What was I expecting? That he wouldn't be here? And what

would I do if he wasn't? Confess my sudden shift of allegiance to Max and ask him to take ownership of me after a mere weekend together? He'd never take me without Bill's release. It wouldn't be honorable.

And if Bill is here, what happens if I say I don't want to belong to him anymore? He can't keep me against my will, but that doesn't mean Max will take me. I just don't know enough to be sure how either of them would react. I could get badly hurt. Maybe neither would want to be my Master! Max showed me the collar he had made for his future boy, but he gave no indication that I'm a candidate. Most likely, Bill will take me back, and my dream of belonging to Max will be over. It's a done deal... or is it?

Master Bill was leaning against the wall looking very pleased with himself. With both his jacket and shirt off, he was wearing an elaborate leather harness that accented his stocky chest, black leather armbands around his biceps, and snug black leather pants tucked into shiny, expensive-looking tall boots. He couldn't have been any more different from Max, who wore his bar vest and boots like mere clothes, not fetish gear. But it wasn't what Master Bill was wearing that riveted my gaze.

On the floor to his left was a very familiar-looking duffel bag, and two very pretty and nearly naked young men were kneeling at his feet, their necks encircled with locked chain collars exactly like the one I wore. Bill petted them like dogs, pouring beer into the gaping hungry mouth of one while grabbing the other between his legs and squeezing his junk. The boys grunted and whined like bitches in heat. In my mind I instantly named them Ignorance and Want, after the feral demon-children who cower at the feet of the Ghost of Christmas Present in *A Christmas Carol*.

"Bill!" Max called, loud enough to get his attention.

Master Bill looked up from his conquests while Ignorance and Want bared their teeth and growled low in their throats at the sight of us.

"Max, right?" Bill said, avoiding my eyes.

"Yeah," the bruiser said. "I'm here to return your boy."

"Return him? Was he disobedient?"
"No," Max said.
"Disrespectful?"
"No."
"Was the experience unsatisfactory in any way?"
"No, Bill!"
"Then keep him, for God's sake!"

My heart leapt and my jaw dropped at the same time.

"Don't you get it?" Bill went on, as if explaining something to a very young, very dim child. "Our wager was the perfect way to unload his dead weight without having to actually dump him."

I gasped in disbelief. *Master Bill wanted to get rid of me? And he used Max's interest to engineer a situation where he would "lose" me? Yes,* I realized, *that way he wouldn't have to confront me like a man and just say he didn't want me anymore.* I was forgetting my own reluctance to confront Bill directly, but hey, I'm just a slave. No one would expect me to take a stand for myself. There was still something I didn't understand, but it was Max who asked Bill about it.

"If you didn't want Josh back, why'd you come here tonight at all?"

"To meet my new slaveboys," Bill replied, grinning at the feral boys, "and to give Josh's stuff back to him." He grunted at Ignorance and Want, and the one on his right grabbed the duffel bag and shoved it toward me.

It *was* my bag, the one that had held all I took with me when Master Bill brought me to his home. I knelt and opened it. *All my stuff*, I marveled: my clothes, my leathers, my shoes and extra boots, a few books, some photos, my cellphone, my toothbrush, my music player . . .

I didn't know what to feel. I'd been moved out of what I'd thought of as home without being asked, or even told what was happening. Bill was dumping me in the most unceremonial, painful way possible — very public and humiliating. I felt as if the floor beneath me had disappeared, and I had to grab onto something or plunge to a lonely death.

I was a slaveboy without a Master. Tears formed in my eyes as I comprehended the enormity of what had happened. But then a strong hand took my arm and pulled me gently upward until I was standing in front of him.

Max's mustache tickled my ear as he leaned in and whispered, "Do you trust me?"

"Yes, Sir," I answered softly.

"Then keep quiet. Only speak when spoken to. Got it?"

"Yes, Sir!" Suddenly hope took root in me, but it would need light and nourishment to bloom.

Master Max moved me to one side and took a step closer to Master Bill. The feral boys growled, but a stern look from the bruiser silenced them. They cowered behind Bill's boots.

"Master Bill," Max said, loudly and clearly, "do you release slaveboy Josh from your ownership and service?"

Bill didn't even spare a glance at me.

"Yeah," he said. "Sure. Why not? I'm tired of him. He thinks too much. And two're better than one anyway."

"Then get out the key for this lock," Master Max said in a stern voice as he touched my chain collar, "unlock it, take the collar off, and tell Josh to his face what you just told me."

Master Bill shrugged, removed his key ring, and pulled off a small brass key. Then he disentangled himself from Ignorance and Want, ordering them to stay where they were. Still not meeting my eyes, he stepped over to me, reached around my neck, and unlocked the collar he'd put on me more than a year earlier. He removed the chain from my neck and stepped back.

I felt naked, exposed. If Bill had met my eyes he'd have seen the tears that were about to fall despite the hope growing inside me. Finally, he looked at me and said, "I release you, Josh. You are no longer my slaveboy." And just like that I was cast aside. The tears overflowed and spilled down my cheeks.

Struggling for composure, I crouched down to close up my duffel bag. The glimmering of a plan led me to put the cellphone in my pocket. *I still have friends*, I thought. *I'll call*

Rick and ask if I can crash with him tonight. Then when I wake up tomorrow morning, I can start over. But before I could act on this plan, I felt a familiar strong hand on my shoulder.

"Turn around, Josh," Max said, "and kneel before me."

Obeying automatically, I found myself facing his boots, just as when we'd met two days before. But these were simple 8-inch work boots, nothing special at all. Still, my lips were suddenly dry, and I licked them . . .

"Look at me, Josh," he said.

I looked up, way up, to see the bruiser smiling down at me. One hand was behind his back, hiding something. His sparkling blue eyes held my damp brown ones. There was the same lust and greed in his look as the first time, but also something more — affection.

The crowded bar suddenly disappeared. All the people around us, all the noise, even Bill and the feral boys . . . all were gone. There was only Max and me.

"I *want* you, Josh," he said. "I want to be your Master and have you as my slaveboy for as long as we both feel good about it. What d' you say? Wanna be mine?"

Torn between between exhilaration and disbelief, I managed somehow to respond:

"Yes, Sir! Yes, please, Master Max. I want to be yours! I want to belong to *you*, Sir."

His hands moved down toward me, and I saw what he'd been concealing. The "MAX's BOY" leather collar felt wonderful as it encircled my neck, and even better after he locked it in place.

"You're mine now, Josh," Master Max said. "I claim you as my property. Your constant goal will be to serve me to the best of your ability."

"Thank you, Master," I said, kissing his boots, washing them with my happy tears.

"Let's get the hell out of here," he said. "On your feet, slaveboy."

Instantly I leaped up, feeling lighter than air, my heart soaring, my joy palpable. I was so happy to be "MAX's BOY" that I fairly danced around my Master. Wearing his collar made me feel like a kid who'd just gotten a new puppy — or, better, like a puppy that's just been given to a kid.

Master Max laughed at my exuberance, all sternness abandoned. His eyes were shining, and he was grinning ear to ear. "Okay, boy, settle down," he said as he pulled me to him with one muscular arm.

Bending down at the waist, he threw me over his shoulder, anchoring my legs with his left arm, then grabbed my duffel bag with his right hand. And with me over one shoulder and my duffel bag over the other, my new permanent Master carried me out of The Richter Scale and into a new life, the kind of life I'd always wanted but had only dreamed of before.

"Where are we going, Master?" I asked.

"We're going home, slaveboy. We're going home." ◉

About the Author

CHRISTOPHER PIERCE has been active in the gay leather–Master/slave–BDSM community since 1992. He met the man who would become his Master in 1994 and has been in a relationship of discipline and respect with him ever since. Like the narrators of some of his stories, Christopher is a devoted slave who also enjoys topping when he gets the chance.

Besides serving his Master, Christopher's favorite thing is movies, especially classic animation, and for several years he worked in a Hollywood studio. "People think it's incongruous," he said in an interview, "that I'm a leatherman and yet so into animation. The connection for me is that in animation, everything is exaggerated. It's a more passionate way to live. I found the same thing in the leather scene. . . . [With my Master,] I'm living the kind of life that I imagined, the life that I hoped for, that I played at with other people. Now the life has become real."

Christopher's first erotic story, "Headlights," was published by the groundbreaking and fondly remembered magazine *Cuir* in 1993. Since then his stories have appeared in numerous gay magazines, including *International Leatherman*, *Bound & Gagged*, *Honcho*, and *Mandate*. They've also been selected for anthologies, including Simon Sheppard's *Leathermen* and the 2005 through 2008 issues of Alyson's annual *Ultimate Gay Erotica*, edited by Jesse Grant.

He is the author of two novels in a planned four-book sequence from STARbooks Press, *Rogue:Slave* and *Rogue:Hunted*, and besides *Winner Takes All*, his short stories have been collected in *Kidnapped by a Sex Maniac: The Erotic Fiction of Christopher Pierce* (also STARbooks).

He has edited six anthologies: *Men on the Edge*, *Taken by*

Force, SexTime, I Like to Watch, Biker Boys, and *Men at Noon, Monsters at Midnight*. With Rachel Kramer Bussel he co-edited the three volumes in Alyson Books' Fetish Chest trilogy: *Ultimate Undies, Sexiest Soles,* and *Secret Slaves.*

    Christopher loves hearing from readers. You can e-mail him, chris@christopherpierceerotica.com, or visit his world online, christopherpierceerotica.com, for news, shopping, custom stories, and more. ◉

Also from Perfectbound Press
www.perfectboundpress.com

THE SLAVE JOURNALS and Other Tales of the Old Guard
Thom Magister

A novella and 17 short stories by Thom Magister, author of "One Among Many," the often-cited essay on the 1950s in the *Leatherfolk* anthology edited by Mark Thompson (Alyson). 5½ x 8½ inches, 325 pages, including eight full-page artworks by the author, $15.95.

Order your copy from Amazon.com or BN.com, or ask at better leather shops and bookstores.

7 x 10 inches, 239 pages, $19.95

Order your copy from Amazon.com or BN.com, or ask at better leather shops and bookstores.

Ask the Man Who Owns Him
The real lives of gay Masters and slaves

How do they make it work?
Ask the Man Who Owns Him is the first book to present, in their own words, the *real* lives of long-term gay Master/slave couples and families. Sixteen slaveowners and their properties around the U.S. and in Canada welcomed the authors into their homes and spoke candidly about how each relationship started, how it evolved to meet the challenges of living in conventional society, and how it works today. All of these bonds have lasted for at least three years — some for well over a dozen.

These relationships are different from the Master/slave stereotypes of erotic fiction. They're also different from what you may find in how-to books and Internet postings on the subject. Instead of reading what a single writer says this lifestyle "should" be, discover what gay Masters and slaves are actually doing.

Most striking is how different their relationships are from each other. Tradeoffs are made, deals struck, and power exchanged in ways that work for these unique individuals pursuing their respective dreams.

Who should read this book?
Anyone who's wondered if being a Master or slave is right for him, or who wishes to understand this lifestyle better. If you've read the fantasies and felt something was missing, or tried the experts' prescriptions and found them wanting, this book is for you. *Ask the Man Who Owns Him* describes real-life strategies and tactics for success as a Master or a slave.

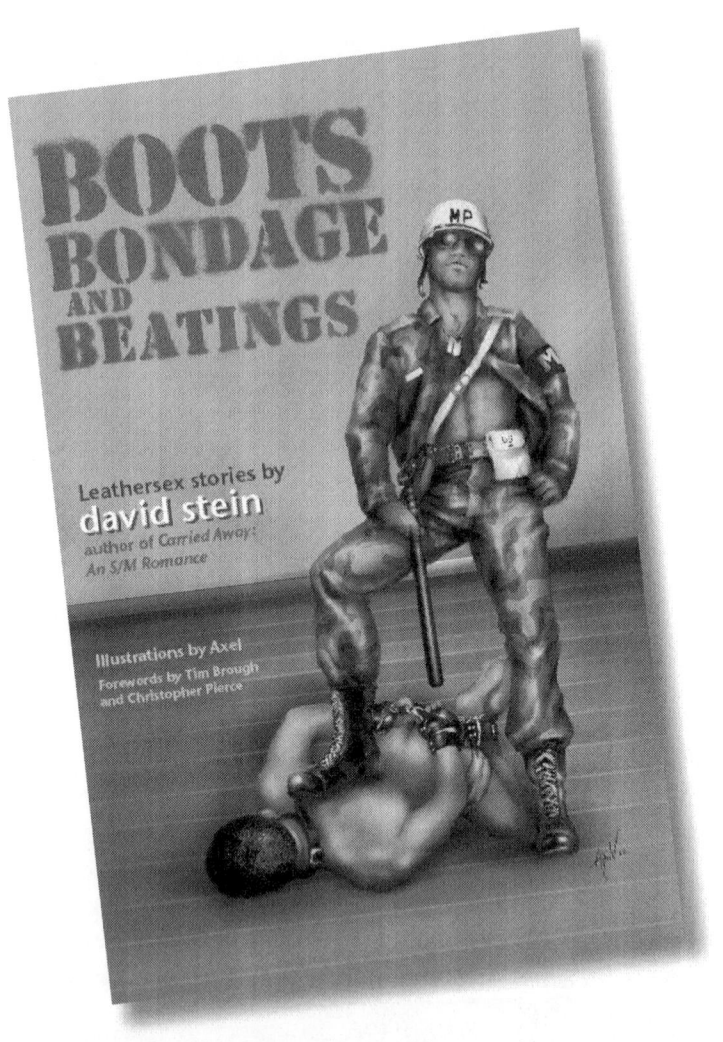

Masters and slaves, tops and bottoms revel in boot worship, erotic bondage, and dick-stiffening beatings with fist, belt, or whip in these stories by David Stein, author of the acclaimed novel *Carried Away: An S/M Romance*. 6 x 9 inches, 186 pages, including eight full-page illustrations by cover artist Axel, $17.95.

Order your copy from Amazon.com or BN.com, or ask at better leather shops and bookstores.

Made in the USA
Lexington, KY
27 January 2013